*The Theatre Student*

*GILBERT AND SULLIVAN PRODUCTION*

 THE THEATRE STUDENT SERIES

# The Theatre Student

## GILBERT AND SULLIVAN PRODUCTION

*Peter Kline*

PUBLISHED BY
RICHARDS ROSEN PRESS, INC.
NEW YORK, N.Y. 10010

*Standard Book Number:* 8239–0252–8
*Library of Congress Catalog Card Number:* 74–170281
*Dewey Decimal Classification:* 792

Published in 1972 by Richards Rosen Press, Inc.
29 East 21st Street, New York City, N.Y. 10010

First Edition

*Manufactured in the United States of America*

# DEDICATION

To my parents

who for many years listened to more Gilbert and Sullivan than flesh should have to
bear, in order that I might indulge my whims to the fullest, and who supported me
in those whims for many, many years

and

to C. R. Boyd,

one of the most ardent G&S fans in the whole wide world.

# ABOUT THE AUTHOR

PETER KLINE has been intimately associated with all aspects of Gilbert and Sullivan production since he founded the Lyric Theatre Company in 1951. Between that time and the present he has directed, produced, and acted in all fourteen Gilbert and Sullivan operas, and claims to be the only person in the world who has done *Thespis* four times and played three roles in it. In association with various companies he has performed at the Watergate, the Library of Congress, the Cherry Blossom Festival, and the Washington Monument. His efforts have been about equally divided between community theatre and college and high-school productions, and he has worked extensively with performers of all ages. At some time or other his efforts have included every aspect of production except the musical direction of performances. He has been head of the English department at the Maret and Sandy Spring Friends Schools, drama director for Dunbarton College, and director of the Valerie Warde Drama School; he is currently teaching at the Sidwell Friends School. His publications include three other books in this series as well as stories and articles in *The Kenyon Review, The Grecourt Review, The Savoyard, The Jack Point Press, The Independent School Bulletin,* and *The Friends Journal.*

Mr. Kline believes that it is in the staging that Gilbert and Sullivan productions are usually weakest, and so he has concentrated most heavily on that aspect of production in this book, which includes detailed analyses of all fourteen operas. It is hoped that this book will prove useful to professional as well as amateur producers of Gilbert and Sullivan, and will help to stimulate a greater and more widespread appreciation of these too-little-understood classics of music drama.

# CONTENTS

One rainy afternoon in the early winter of 1952 I stood at the stage door of Washington's Sam S. Shubert Theatre waiting for Martyn Green, who was then touring with the S. M. Chartock Gilbert and Sullivan company. I clutched in my hand a letter requesting him to write out for me all the "official" information on how to stage *The Sorcerer.*

I was at that time a senior in high school, and I had banded together with a number of my fellow seniors to produce Gilbert and Sullivan operas. Naturally we had dreams of rivaling the D'Oyly Carte Opera Company, which originated all these operas, but we didn't see how we could do so unless we knew all the traditional business. As D'Oyly Carte had not produced *The Sorcerer* within my lifetime, Martyn Green seemed to be the only link between me and the fulfillment of my ambitions.

Green is a very nice man indeed, as you will find if you ever engage him in conversation, and he wrote me some weeks later a kind and friendly letter. But alas! he was too busy to sit down and write out all the information I wanted, and so the mysteries remained within the inner sanctum.

But we high-school students went about our business anyway, and after fifteen years had passed we had produced not only *The Sorcerer* but all the other little-known works as well. Meanwhile, Green produced a book of libretti with marginal notes that revealed many of the secrets I had longed to have.

Looking back on the innocence of those early years, I have often thought how much I would have been helped by having easy access to all the information that had to be come by more or less by trial and error. Not knowing, for example, that the D'Oyly Carte Opera Company is most happy to rent out its orchestra parts, even to Americans, had cost the following expenditures of energy on the part of me and my cohorts: When a *Grand Duke* orchestration was needed, we hired a musician to do the job and payed him $100 in advance. He then skipped town with the money, so we intensified our efforts to find one already in ex-

istence. We finally found out that John Thoms had made one for the Philadelphia Savoy Company many years earlier, and we borrowed that, but had to go to the expense of reproducing it. Meanwhile we hired another musician to orchestrate *The Mountebanks,* which he dutifully did at some great expense before we realized that copying out the parts for individual players would be prohibitively expensive and time-consuming. It was only then that we became aware that D'Oyly Carte would rent us their originals at very reasonable rates.

Many other bits of information accumulated over the years and have been scattered through this book, but I think that I worked hardest to find and put into use information about the staging. Inasmuch as Gilbert staged all the operas himself, and sometimes wrote them with particular effects in mind, the question of tradition is probably of more concern in the staging of these works than is the case with anything else in the theatre prior to the twentieth century. But although the producer of a modern musical comedy can always get a complete staging guide that allows him to make almost a carbon copy of the original, the producer of Gilbert and Sullivan has had to rely on what he has heard and what he can observe for himself. If he is a genius, of course, he will work out his own new approach and receive commendation for it. But all too often he is just trying to get the job done and is told after it is done that he has left out all sorts of things that are usually put in.

Possibly someday complete information about Gilbert's original staging will be available as a result of scholarly research. At present, however, tradition is largely a matter of whatever the D'Oyly Carte Opera Company is currently doing, plus whatever scattered memories are recorded in books and the minds of older performers and theatregoers. I must classify myself among the latter, as I first saw the D'Oyly Carte company when they came to Baltimore in 1950, and have seized every opportunity to visit their productions since. I have also faithfully attended productions over the years by other professional companies, such as the American Savoyards, as well as amateur productions of unusual interest or quality. Out of all these memories I have tried to distill staging concepts that could be used in my own productions. With some operas the memories are quite specific. For example, when Martyn Green staged the television production of *Trial by Jury* for "Omnibus," I wrote down in my vocal score everything that was done. When later I visited D'Oyly Carte productions I was able to check and amplify those notes. On the other hand, there are certain operas that I have never had the opportunity to see in D'Oyly Carte productions, and with those I have had to rely on hearsay and whatever has been published on the subject.

But my notes on staging cannot be regarded as a record of what professional companies do, as a number of other factors have entered in as well. Since I have been continuously concerned with staging the operas from 1953 right up to the present time, I have also continuously elaborated the staging ideas of the professionals with my own ideas. Furthermore, although my own work is largely oriented toward tradition, I have from time to time been influenced by people who are extremely untraditional in their orientation. Finally, one finds that in working with amateurs, particularly high-school students, one cannot do quite the same things as one does with professionals. Certain kinds of subtlety are too elusive for them, and one must substitute other, more obvious devices in order to avoid dullness.

My notes on staging must therefore be regarded as a synthesis of several influences. No attempt has been made to make them consistent either in source or level of sophistication. The purpose is to give the reader a number of ideas which he may reject or modify according to the needs of his own production. It may be that his reading of my notes will serve merely to stimulate his own imagination, so that he will develop a staging quite different from what is suggested here. The main purpose is to help prevent what I have seen all too much of in the past: a production in which everyone simply stands around and sings. Such performances tend to discourage people from going to Gilbert and Sullivan productions at all.

In writing this book I have largely avoided comments on musical interpretation, as those are very adequately treated in two books by the late choral director of the D'Oyly Carte Opera Company, William Cox-Ife. These books, which are listed in the Bibliography, should be purchased and studied by anyone planning to conduct a Gilbert and Sullivan opera. One reason for their value is that Cox-Ife puts the emphasis on the relation between words and music, a relation that is too often overlooked by the conductor trained primarily in music.

In Part Two of this book I have tried to deal with those problems specific to Gilbert and Sullivan production, and have assumed that the reader will consult other, more general books for matters that such production has in common with theatre production in general.

This book has been slanted toward the completely inexperienced producer of Gilbert and Sullivan opera.

Having been frequently consulted by such people over the years, I have tried my best to answer all their questions here, realizing that problems vary greatly from one situation to another and that any given producer will therefore find many things here that do not apply to his situations.

In writing this book I have been reminded on every page of my vast indebtedness to the many people who have worked with and influenced me over the years, as well as the publications that have been most helpful. I have tried to cover the latter in the Bibliography, but one of them must be mentioned here. Reginald Allen's *First Night Gilbert and Sullivan* is extraordinarily valuable but, unfortunately, difficult to obtain. Its author claims that he himself is unable to get additional copies. It is to be hoped that his book will be republished soon and made easily available to the thousands of people who would enjoy it and benefit from it.

As to the friends and co-workers to whom I am indebted, I could not possibly do them justice without extending this introduction to book length. I must briefly describe only a few of them and then resort to the unfair tactic of listing the others in alphabetical order. At that, I will have inevitably left out a number of people who should be near the top of the list.

John Landis is among the finest living authorities on the music of the operas. He has examined the scores of all the extant works with Gilbert extremely carefully, virtually committing many of them to memory. He has prepared corrected editions of all of them. His edition of the vocal score of *Princess Ida* will, when published by G. Schirmer, set a new standard for accuracy and scholarly thoroughness. It was a privilege for me to work with Landis on several productions, as he greatly increased my insight into the musical integrity with which one must approach Sullivan. I also wish to thank him for his helpful comments on the manuscript of this book.

Barry Morley, during his high-school days in Greenwich, Connecticut, founded an operetta company that is still in existence. He went on to perform Gilbert and Sullivan at Harvard University, and subsequently to produce the operas with high-school students at Sandy Spring Friends School. Morley is untraditional in his approach, and has done a better job than any other I have seen in adapting the staging so that it is effective for the amateur group. His ideas are extremely imaginative, and though I have made no attempt to suggest what his productions are like *in toto,* I have drawn heavily on his staging ideas for *The Pirates of Penzance, Iolanthe, Princess Ida, Ruddigore, The Yeomen of the Guard,* and *The Gondoliers.*

David Austern worked with me closely during the years of the Lyric Theatre Company, and actually produced several of its shows. His cool-headed practical approach to the problems that arose greatly influenced my thinking on production in general, and many other things as well. His successful career in the law confirms the fine qualities demonstrated in his younger days as a Gilbert and Sullivan producer.

Michael Greenebaum broke all laws of probability when, as conductor of the Bach Society Orchestra at Harvard, he received a letter from me asking him to come to Washington for the summer and conduct *Princess Ida.* He answered by saying that he wasn't planning to come to Washington, and didn't particularly like *Princess Ida,* but would do so anyway. His participation in that production greatly elevated the stature of the Lyric Theatre Company, and probably assured its later success more than any other single factor. Greenebaum's combination of musical genius with an unusual capacity to deal effectively with people set high standards for all the rest of us. As mentioned elsewhere in this book, he later rescued a production in distress in the most dramatic possible manner.

Barbara Kline, the chorister *par excellence,* in addition to helping to keep my head out of the clouds over the years, gave me an awareness of, and sensitivity to, the problems of being a chorister and handling the chorus that I could not have achieved in any other way. Her comments on the manuscript proved very helpful also.

John Hoke, Lyric's public relations man, held productions together in the most amazing ways, often held me together, made everyone think of human problems as a complement to production problems, recorded the early productions, and kept a photographic record of everything that went on. In short, he would have been our Pooh-Bah if he had known how to sneer.

Albert A. Truelove of the D'Oyly Carte Opera Company is a living example of the graciousness and concern for excellence that pervade that company. He was extremely helpful in making orchestrations available for many productions, as well as making pictures available for this book.

Finally, I should like to thank my editor, Paul Kozelka, for his many helpful comments on the manuscript of this and my other books in this series.

Each of the following people should have a chapter devoted to him. Some of them are liberally, if anonymously, represented in this book, and all have provided me with some kind of service or inspiration for which I am extremely indebted. They are, of course, in no way to be held responsible for the faults and limitations of what appears here.

John P. Ansell, Mary Alyce Bennett, Daniel Berg, Robert Brandzell, Ken Chafin, Robert Cumming, Dexter Davison, Linda Ellinwood, L. Carl Gardner, Roger Golde, Anne Hancock, Douglas Huebner, Eloise Humpel, Harold Isen, Hibbard G. James, Dennis Jelalian, Keith Johnson, Thomas O. Jones, Stephen King, Liz Kramer, Mary Jeanne Kreek, Fred Levy, Herman Levy, Philip Levy, Eugene Lipkowitz, Joel Mandelbaum, Carroll Mattoon, Ivan Menzies, Manuel Milan, Elinor Miller, Hon. Morris Miller, Kay Moran, William Murray, Dora Odarenko, Omar B. Pancoast, Thomas Rasmussen, Frederick S. Roffman, Michael Sahl, Howard and Joan Silber, David Steinman, Jonathan Strong, Jr., William Struhs, John Craig Toy, Frank Viera, Arthur Waldstein, Joseph P. Weeks, J. Kirkwood White, Greg Wise.

Peter Kline

# PART I: THE OPERAS

## Chapter I

# A BRIEF HISTORY OF GILBERT AND SULLIVAN OPERA

The history of Gilbert and Sullivan opera actually begins in 1728 with the production of *The Beggar's Opera* by John Gay. For many years the English musical scene had been dominated by Italian operas written for English audiences by imported composers. The popularity of Italian opera was brought to an abrupt end with the advent of Gay's musical satire, which became the smash hit of its time and has remained popular ever since.

*The Beggar's Opera* told a story of love and intrigue among prostitutes, highwaymen, and receivers of stolen goods. Just as its characters were the reverse of the kings and queens who populated the operatic stage, so its moral sentiments were the reverse of the noble reflections that formed the substance of most of the arias in the operas. In attacking the pomposity of grand opera, *The Beggar's Opera* introduced a new dramatic form having several characteristics that paved the way for Gilbert and Sullivan opera. They included the following:

(1) The spoken and sung words were as important as the music. Whereas in all forms of grand opera right up to the present the text merely provides a vehicle for the music, in *The Beggar's Opera* the music tended to be an adornment to the text. Yet the music was important and memorable too, since Gay had selected the most popular songs of his time and written new words to them. Inasmuch as the play contained sixty-nine songs, music was an extremely important part of it.

(2) The work commented satirically on the foibles of institutions and political leaders contemporary with the time when it was written. Italian opera, on the other hand, was for the most part devoid of social comment, and usually dealt with characters and events associated with the distant past.

(3) The characters were types rather than fully developed human beings. They existed only to contribute to the satire, and they were allowed to say and do anything that would underline the absurdity of the situation. As a result, the text contained many lines that could be quoted out of context and remain humorous and effective.

(4) The work derived much of its literary quality from parody of other dramatic works. Most important was its mocking of the sentimental comedy of its time. Many of the situations that were common in sentimental comedy were handled in a way that made fun of them.

Clearly though *The Beggar's Opera* established a new dramatic form, 148 years went by before a further development of that form took place. Gay's second play, *Polly*, was never produced, thanks to the censor; and perhaps for that reason later playwrights were discouraged from attempting to repeat the success of his masterpiece. Meanwhile, the form diminished into what came to be called the ballad opera, and later the burlesque.

It was on the burlesque that W. S. Gilbert began to cut his teeth, dramatically speaking. His first play, *Dulcamara, or The Little Duck and the Great Quack*, was a burlesque, or parody, of the Italian opera *The Elixir of Love*. It is a play with a few songs set to music from the opera. In the process of writing words for already existing Italian and French music, Gilbert mastered the great variety of verse forms that were later to characterize his operas.

Many paradoxes are associated with Gilbert

and Sullivan opera. Not the least of them is that both the librettist and the composer regarded themselves primarily as serious artists and looked upon their comic efforts as relatively inferior work. Time and again Gilbert attempted serious drama, always without success, since his plays were sentimental and pretentious. Only when he wrote whimsy did he achieve success. Sullivan, on the other hand, was quite successful in his own time as a composer of serious music. Beginning as a choir boy who wrote hymn tunes by the bushel, and winning early fame as the composer of music for Shakespeare's *Tempest*, he went on to write oratorios, a symphony, and a grand opera, and to win knighthood from Queen Victoria for being the first English composer in two hundred years to write highly regarded serious music. Yet today nearly all of Sullivan's serious music is forgotten. One sentimental song, one hymn, and perhaps the *Tempest* music and the *Di Ballo* overture are all that continue to win public favor. The fact is that as a serious artist Sullivan was as sentimental and pretentious as Gilbert.

Gilbert and Sullivan shared two things that made them able to work together to produce the most successful partnership in the history of theatre. One was their high degree of professionalism, as both were extremely well trained in their fields, and both were perfectionists who consistently brought a high degree of polish to all of their work. The second quality that they shared was a sense of the absurd. They were able to laugh at their own pretentiousness and at that of everyone else as well. Gilbert's words, which poke immortal fun at the foibles of institutions and of character types, are echoed in Sullivan's music, which pokes the same kind of fun at musical foibles and at the same time reinforces the humor of the words without smothering it in beauty as a greater composer might have done.

While Gilbert was writing his early burlesques, Sullivan was writing short operettas often designed for unpretentious occasions. One of them, the one-act farce *Cox and Box,* is still successful. The first Gilbert and Sullivan opera was actually an historical accident. The composer and librettist worked with each other just as they might have worked with any other partner. Gilbert wrote a burlesque, hardly one of his best efforts, and Sullivan was selected to compose the music. The result, *Thespis,* was produced during the Christmas season and ran for two months. Rehearsal conditions were far from ideal, and the work never in any respect achieved the polish of later Gilbert and Sullivan collaborations. Although it was successful for the purposes for which it was intended, it was regarded as so unimportant that no attempt was made to publish the music.

*Thespis* was produced in 1871, and it was not until 1875 that Gilbert and Sullivan began to work together in real earnest. Credit for that must go to Richard D'Oyly Carte, who is as important in the history of the operas as either the composer or the librettist, since it was he who recognized their genius, who held them together through many quarrels, and who provided them with a theatre and a company of actors selected especially for their works. Carte was producing a French operetta and needed a curtain raiser for it, so he commissioned from Gilbert a one-act operetta, the music of which was to be by Sullivan. Gilbert expanded a short dramatic piece he had published earlier and read it apologetically to Sullivan, who found it deliriously funny and was delighted to set it to music. The half-hour *Trial by Jury* was so successful that it had to be moved from the opening of the evening to the close, and audiences flocked to see it rather than the major work on the program.

Carte then decided to form an English opera company, and he leased a theatre especially for the purpose. Gilbert and Sullivan were to provide all the works for the company to perform. They were also to set a new standard of respectability for the theatre. No woman would ever appear in a man's part (a practice quite common in burlesques) nor would any woman appear on the stage in a costume she would be embarrassed to wear to a fancy dress ball. Furthermore, the productions were to be rehearsed much more carefully than was customary at the time, and no limit was to be put on the expense of providing beautiful scenery and costumes.

Gilbert was as skilled a theatrical director as he was an author, and under his leadership the D'Oyly Carte Opera Company set many new standards for the theatre. Whereas it was customary at the time to have actors simply walk onstage and speak their parts with little physical movement, Gilbert worked out elaborate blocking and choreography for his productions and thus modernized theatrical staging. Before he appeared at the first rehearsal he would have worked out on a model stage with model actors all the movements that were to be performed. In the theatre he could be an absolute dictator, giving the actors every gesture and often the inflection of words almost by rote, though leading actors who had proved their skill were allowed more freedom. One actress complaining of the practice observed that she was not a member of the chorus. "No," replied Gilbert. "Your voice isn't strong enough, or you would be."

It is important to understand how Gilbert worked as a director, since the operettas were conceived with particular staging practices in mind, and even today some of the performances of the D'Oyly Carte Opera Company are closely modeled on Gilbert's original productions. An article in *Fortune* magazine once observed that if photographs were taken of the same production at the same time on two successive evenings, they might be superimposed on each other without producing much deviation.

When D'Oyly Carte conceived his English opera company, he built up a troupe of actors, some of whom were to remain together through many successive productions. Thus it came about that the operas were written with certain performers in mind, and the performers themselves determined to some extent the form that the operas would have. Even today certain roles are associated with the performers who created them. Most notable of those performers were George Grossmith, a comedian with little skill as an opera singer but a great deal of personality and the ability to dance well; Rutland Barrington, a large, dignified man with a big voice who had trouble singing on key; Jessie Bond, a coquettish young lady with an attractive personality who preferred that her roles be not too large; Richard Temple, a man with a gift for the macabre and a fine singer; and Rosina Brandram, a beautiful and dignified actress with a fine contralto voice who was condemned to play unattractive older women and somehow made them appealing. Each operetta has an important role for one of those performers. In addition there were the romantic leads, usually for tenor and soprano; but possibly because Gilbert disliked tenors more than most other performers, or possibly because youth is a prerequisite for such parts, the turnover was rather frequent among them.

The first opera written especially for the new company was *The Sorcerer*. Compared to everything of its kind that preceded it except *Trial by Jury*, *The Sorcerer* is a masterpiece, but it fades by comparison with the operas that came later. At any rate, it was a moderate success and ran for 175 performances. It was followed by a dis-

mal failure that nearly put an end to the D'Oyly Carte Opera Company. *H.M.S. Pinafore,* which opened in 1878, aroused little public interest. It had in common with *The Beggar's Opera* the fact that it satirized a noted public official, but otherwise it seemed inconsequential. Shortly after it opened there was a heat wave in London, and people stopped coming. *Pinafore* was nearly ready to close when Sullivan had the idea of including some selections from it in a pops concert he was conducting, and suddenly the music caught on. All over London people were whistling "I'm called Little Buttercup" and "He polished up the handle on the big front door," and *Pinafore* suddenly became a national craze. It was almost necessary to enact legislation to prevent people from saying "What, never?—Well, hardly ever." D'Oyly Carte expanded his company to include a troupe of children who performed a children's version of *Pinafore*.

Then began the piracies. All over America *Pinafore* was being performed to full houses. Several companies played it simultaneously in New York. Yet, as there was no international copyright law, Gilbert and Sullivan received not one penny in royalties. In fact, no American company has ever paid royalties on the performance of any Gilbert and Sullivan opera. D'Oyly Carte decided to capitalize on the American interest and to attempt to secure an American copyright by taking his company to America. The official version of *Pinafore* opened in America and was a smash hit. Then followed the next Gilbert and Sullivan opera, *The Pirates of Penzance*, written especially for American production. It, too, was a popular success, although in its original run it was no rival for *Pinafore*, as it ran in London only 363 performances, compared to *Pinafore's* 700. Nevertheless, Gilbert and Sullivan opera had now firmly established itself as an institution as English as the Union Jack, and the theatre, which had for a hundred years been hardly the place for a respectable young lady to go, once again became fashionable. Indeed, Gilbert took such a personal interest in its respectability that when a young pleasure-seeker invited a chorus girl whom he had not previously met out for the evening following a performance, he had an angry Gilbert to contend with at the stage door.

During the 1880's there was a fad in Britain that somewhat resembles a more recent development. A small group of young men took to growing their hair long, dressing in an unusual manner, and parading about carrying flowers in their hands. These young men called themselves Pre-Raphaelites because they consisted largely of artists who wanted to purify art by deriving their aesthetic principles from works that were in vogue before the time of Raphael. Among the leaders of the movement were William Morris and Algernon Swinburne. Finding that Pre-Raphaelites were extremely popular with young ladies and extremely unpopular with elderly gentlemen, Gilbert and Sullivan decided to base their next opera on the Pre-Raphaelite movement. Caricatures of Swinburne and Morris were the central figures in the opera, which also included lovesick maidens and their rebuffed dragoons. When *Patience* opened in London, the Irish writer Oscar Wilde was neither particularly wealthy nor particularly well known. He was, however, extremely intelligent and a master of wit. He was an ideal person in the lecture hall, since he could hold an audience spellbound for hours. D'Oyly Carte wished to send *Patience* to America, but he knew that the opera's satire would be lost on American audiences, who had never heard of the Pre-Raphaelites, so he arranged for a lecture tour of America for Oscar Wilde, complete with long hair, unorthodox dress, and lily in his lapel. The tour made the fame and fortune of Oscar Wilde, and Oscar Wilde made the fame and fortune of *Patience,* which followed in his footsteps all over America.

Gilbert and Sullivan opera had become so successful that the time had come to build a theatre for it. D'Oyly Carte did so, making it the most modern theatre of its day. On October 10, 1881, the Savoy Theatre opened, introducing two modern conveniences. It was the first theatre that required its audience to queue up for tickets, and it was the first theatre anywhere in the world to be lighted internally with electricity. To understand the value of this second innovation you must understand that in a theatre lit with gas it was rather difficult to see what was happening onstage, there could be no change in the lighting, and the audience suffered from the overheating and lack of oxygen caused by gaslight. The opening of *Patience* in the Savoy Theatre may truly be said to be one of the most important milestones in the development of the modern theatre.

*Patience* was very popular, and was followed by the only slightly less popular *Iolanthe,* the greatest of Gilbert's political satires. The whole House of Peers dances off to fairyland at the end of *Iolanthe,* having discovered that they are of no possible use down here. It was pri-marily for that reason that Gilbert had to wait until after Queen Victoria's death for his well-deserved knighthood.

Gilbert's laziness caught up with him after *Iolanthe. Princess Ida,* which followed, was simply a reworking of an earlier play that was, in turn, a dramatization of a long and rather bad narrative poem by Tennyson. It is an attack on education for women, an attack that was already outmoded when Tennyson first thought of it. It is the only Gilbert and Sullivan opera in three acts, and the only one to use blank verse (and rather bad blank verse at that) for its dialogue. Nevertheless it contains some of Sullivan's finest music and two or three of Gilbert's best lyrics. Rutland Barrington, who created the role of King Hildebrand, modestly attributed the comparative lack of success of *Princess Ida* to the fact that his part in it was so small.

Both the collaborators were disappointed by the fact that *Princess Ida* ran only 246 performances, and when it closed they had nothing new. Sullivan declared he was played out and could do nothing further in the way of operetta music. Gilbert offered him a "lozenge" plot that Sullivan thought too similar to *The Sorcerer,* and that he was to refuse to set several times, until Gilbert finally collaborated with another composer on it. *The Sorcerer* was revived in order to keep the company in business, and for that revival additional words and music were added at the beginning of its second act. Thus the second-act opening of *The Sorcerer* contains some of Gilbert and Sullivan's finest and most mature work.

It is said that *The Mikado* began to be written when Gilbert was disturbed in his study by a Japanese sword falling off the wall. There was in London at the time a fad for Japanese things, a fad that had already been referred to in *Patience.* As Gilbert set to work on *The Mikado,* he gave it all the external trappings of Japan, including some Japanese lyrics, but made it in essence the most British of all his works. Sullivan handled the music in the same way. Once the veneer of Japanese atmosphere had been established, Sullivan rose to his greatest heights, time and again harking back to the best in the traditions of British music.

The brilliance and complexity of *The Mikado* transcend the fact that it is probably the most popular work for the stage ever written. (Whole decades may have passed when not a single day went by without somebody somewhere performing *The Mikado,* and as you read these words it is most probable that it is being performed somewhere in the world.) Not only is it thoroughly British as well as being superficially so Japanese that the Japanese like to perform it themselves, but it also blends a whimsically telling perception of civilized man with an uncanny feeling for primitive ritual.

It is difficult to imagine today the first-night tension that the performers of *The Mikado* experienced. Gilbert and Sullivan were both most unsure of its success and made changes right up to the last minute. On opening night the Mikado's song, "My object all sublime," would have been cut had not the entire chorus pleaded with Gilbert to leave it in. The opening performance was unusually rough, but despite that fact *The Mikado* was an immediate and spectacular success.

Gilbert's professionalism was nowhere better demonstrated than in his preparation of this work. He rewrote the plot many times before he began to write the dialogue and lyrics. In the staging of it he paid the greatest attention to detail, and he hired a Japanese person to make certain that the behavior of all members of the company was suitably Japanese. His efforts were rewarded: There is scarcely a dull moment anywhere in *The Mikado*. During a recent New York run of the work, one critic marveled that Gilbert and Sullivan could toss off such a hit song as "A wandering minstrel I" less than five minutes after the curtain goes up. The high quality of both libretto and music is consistently sustained throughout the entire evening, and there is scarcely a song in the whole opera that is not a classic of its kind.

The great success of *The Mikado* did not have a salutary effect on Gilbert and Sullivan. Their next collaboration, although brilliant in its own way, did not achieve the high degree of polish of its predecessors. For the inspiration of *Ruddigore*, Gilbert turned again to an early opera of his, *Ages Ago*, in which a picture gallery of ancestors had come to life. The idea was a great one, and there are moments in *Ruddigore* that are as brilliantly theatrical as any Gilbert and Sullivan have produced. But there were many signs of hasty writing in the libretto as well, although all of the music is among Sullivan's finest.

The premiere of *Ruddigore* was probably the unhappiest of all the premieres. The trouble began with the title, which was originally *Ruddygore*. Englishmen who were highly sensitive to the word "bloody" saw an unpleasant pun, which Gilbert had never intended. Then there was the "poor Parley-voo" song, which made such fun of the French that it created severe diplomatic tension and even talk of war between the two countries. Finally, in the original libretto of *Ruddigore,* Gilbert had had an entire picture gallery of dead ancestors come back to life at the end. This was offensive to some people, and *Ruddigore* was the first Gilbert and Sullivan opera to be greeted with "boo's" at its opening.

Perhaps realizing that *Ruddigore* was not his best effort, Gilbert harbored the intention of rewriting it up to the time of his death, but he never did so. Because of its unspectacular first run it was written off as a failure for many years and was consequently not revived until 1920. Since then it has found increasing favor with audiences, and is now among the more popular of the operas.

The next work, *The Yeoman of the Guard,* is unique among the operas, for it is the one serious work the librettist and composer attempted together. Although *Yeomen* has its moments of fun, it is dominated by sentiment and it rises to tragedy at its conclusion. For the story Gilbert turned to the England of Henry VIII and the atmosphere of tragedy and death that surrounded the Tower of London. The central character, Jack Point, was a buffoon with whom Gilbert could identify many of his own feelings as a humorist. The attempt to make Point a character whose romantic feelings run far deeper than his futile stabs at humor thinly disguised Gilbert's own frustrations at his inability to write serious drama. Sullivan rose to the occasion and provided some music that was genuinely serious and moving. It was in *Yeomen* that Gilbert and Sullivan came closest to grand opera, and indeed *Yeomen* is a better opera than some that hold the stage at the Metropolitan today.

That is not to say that wit and absurdity were lacking, for *Yeomen* contains many moments of the purest fun, and the complexity of its plot brilliantly reflects Gilbert's essentially topsy-turvy view of life. But it is in *Yeomen* that Gilbert and Sullivan most nearly express genuine human feeling, and the role of Jack Point is usually a favorite with actors.

It may be that *Yeomen* sowed the seeds of the end of the Gilbert and Sullivan partnership, as it increased Sullivan's longing to write grand opera, and it was not long afterward that he was working on a setting of *Ivanhoe*, which D'Oyly Carte would produce with disastrous consequences. Meanwhile, however, *The Gon-*

*doliers* was in the offing. Bernard Shaw referred to this opera as "machine-made" and in a sense it is, as all the absurdity and topsy-turvydom of the previous operas is concentrated in it without any essentially new ground being opened up. Satirically it has little to offer except a glancing attack on communism—("When every one is somebodee, then no one's anybody!")—but it is fine entertainment that sparkles throughout. Gilbert's dictatorial impulses affected the work in a peculiar way. He did not wish anyone in his company to feel that he was the "star," so he deliberately constructed a libretto in which the major romantic leads were doubled and always performed together, frequently sang duets, and were given exactly the same number of solos. To make matters more complicated, there was a third pair of romantic leads, Luiz and Casilda, who had the important love scene in the first act and then little else of consequence.

*The Gondoliers* gave rise to the famous carpet quarrel, a trivial issue that caused Gilbert and Sullivan to refuse to work together for several years. During that time each collaborated with someone else, always with limited success. Whereas previous to *The Gondoliers* there had been a new Gilbert and Sullivan opera almost every year, four years went by before the next opera was produced. During that time Gilbert's creativity decreased considerably, and it is therefore with *The Gondoliers* that the history of his great success comes to an end. That was unfortunate, since Sullivan's genius as a composer continued to develop right up to the time of his death, and in the last two Gilbert and Sullivan operas we find him exploring many new avenues of rhythm, melody, harmony, and orchestration.

*Utopia, Ltd.* should have been among the greatest of the Gilbert and Sullivan operas. It offered Gilbert the finest opportunities for political satire of any of his librettos, since he undertook nothing less than a parody of all of English life. The South Pacific island of Utopia decides to "anglicize" itself, and imports from England a group of "Flowers of Progress" to do the job. They do it so well that all strife is eliminated from the country, and as a result nearly everyone is thrown out of work. What is to be done? Evidently something has been omitted. Introduce Government by Party, "that great and glorious element—at once the bulwark and foundation of England's greatness—and all will be well! No political measures will endure, because one Party will assuredly undo all that the other Party has done; inexperienced civilians will govern your Army and your Navy; no social reforms will be attempted, because out of vice, squalor, and drunkenness no political capital is to be made; and while grouse is to be shot, and foxes worried to death, the legislative action of the country will be at a standstill. Then there will be sickness in plenty, endless lawsuits, crowded jails, interminable confusion in the Army and the Navy, and, in short, general and unexampled prosperity!"

Never was Gilbert's social comment more penetrating, and yet he failed to develop it with the imagination and skill he had lavished on *The Mikado*. *Utopia* was given the most beautiful and expensive production of any of the operas, and its opening was one of the greatest occasions in the history of the English theatre. But although its libretto is thoroughly polished, it drags in many places, and the work lasted only 245 performances. The fault was certainly not Sullivan's, because that most exemplary of music critics, Bernard Shaw, wrote "I enjoyed the score of *Utopia* more than that of any of the previous Savoy operas." More than one critic of our own time has agreed with that sentiment.

"In justice to Sullivan's memory as well as Gilbert's, it is to be hoped that it will never be heard again," wrote Thomas F. Dunhill of *The Grand Duke* in 1928; but such was hardly the feeling of the first-night critics. There was a sense of excitement and expectancy at the opening that was not entirely disappointed, and though the consensus was that the work was certainly not another *Mikado,* the critic Justin McCarthy, after giving the opera seven months' consideration, concluded that "it may claim to stand in the front rank of comic operas." Gilbert's tiredness as a craftsman is felt all too often in the work, and it is distinguished from all the other operas by containing genuine lapses of good taste. Nevertheless, it seems to open up new territory, and had it been accorded more care it might have become the first of a new line of Gilbert and Sullivan operas. There is much in it that reminds one of modern musical comedy. In *The Grand Duke,* Gilbert carried topsy-turvydom further than in any of his previous works, and many of its scenes are uproariously funny. It is almost totally lacking in satire, but it contains a kind of whimsy that can be found nowhere else, and had Gilbert's dramatic instinct been surer of itself at that time in his life, he would most certainly have created a classic of a different order. Sullivan's music responded to the growing interest in Continental operetta, and the score contains many suggestions of Johann Strauss, Jr. As it was, *The Grand Duke* was a failure, running only 123 performances, and with it the collaboration came to a final end. On the opening night, Gilbert and Sullivan bowed from opposite sides of the stage, and then they parted, seldom to see or to speak to each other again.

After the close of *The Grand Duke,* D'Oyly Carte's opera company produced a number of revivals of earlier Gilbert and Sullivan collaborations and then tried to develop successors to Gilbert and Sullivan. English operetta continued to flourish for a few more years and then gradually developed into musical comedy. During the early years of the present century, the success of the D'Oyly Carte Opera Company was only intermittent, but then in the early twenties it again became firmly established, and, except for a short intermission during the war, has continued to produce Gilbert and Sullivan operas ever since. Richard D'Oyly Carte's son, Rupert, took over the company when his father died, and it subsequently passed into the hands of Rupert's daughter, Bridget. Until 1961, Gilbert and Sullivan opera was protected by copyright throughout the British Empire, and remained under the exclusive control of the D'Oyly Carte management. There was considerable anticipation that after the lapse of the copyright, D'Oyly Carte would be unable to survive, but those fears have so far proved groundless. Meanwhile, good productions have appeared elsewhere, notably at Sadler's Wells, at the New York City Center, and in the series of recordings conducted by Sir Malcolm Sargent with the Glyndebourne Festival Opera Company. The effect of those productions has been to give Sullivan's music all the careful attention it deserves and to raise the musical standards of productions everywhere. Meanwhile, D'Oyly Carte has continued to keep the operas alive and has permanently preserved the performance traditions that developed under Gilbert's direction. Through photographs, recordings, and films it is possible to study productions and performers dating as far back as the early 1920's, and many who worked under Gilbert and learned their style of acting from him can still be heard on recordings today. They include Sir Henry A. Lytton, who was in the original cast of *Princess Ida,* and who dominated the Grossmith roles throughout the 1920's and 1930's, and Leo Sheffield and Sydney Granville, who flourished in the Rutland Barrington roles at about the same time. Although most of the members of the D'Oyly Carte Opera Company have remained largely unknown outside of Gilbert and Sullivan circles, a few have made outstanding reputations as a result of their work with D'Oyly Carte. Most notable of those is Martyn Green, Lytton's successor, who has become synonymous in many people's minds with Gilbert and Sullivan.

But the operas are not vehicles for star actors, since they depend for their effectiveness on good ensemble work. Most of the leading performers of today began in the chorus and worked their way up through understudy parts. They have thus absorbed the tradition gradually, and have evolved a feeling for working with one another that brings a high degree of polish to their work. For that reason many D'Oyly Carte productions have been among the most carefully polished work that the theatre has to offer. In the next chapter we shall consider the particular style that characterizes those productions.

# Chapter II

# STYLE OF PRODUCTION DEVELOPED BY W. S. GILBERT

In order to understand the traditional style in which the Gilbert and Sullivan operas are usually acted, we must understand something of theatrical practice in Victorian England. Classics, such as the plays of Shakespeare, were performed by actor-managers who traveled around the country, often picking up supporting actors in whatever province they happened to be playing. Those actors usually acted the same roles in much the same way throughout their lifetimes. Realistic acting as we know it today was not characteristic of them. Rather, style of declamation and beauty of gesture distinguished the great actor from the insignificant. About that time, however, realism of setting began to be introduced, and historical accuracy of stage design turned into something of a fetish.

The modern drama of the time had just outgrown the melodrama that typified the first half of the century and discovered the well-made play, the drama in three or five carefully constructed acts taking place in a realistic box set, often a living room, and concerning the lives of people contemporary with the time of its writing. The acting of those plays was realistic compared with the acting of the classics, but would seem quite stilted to us today.

The third, and probably most common, type of theatre was the burlesque, with its quickly thrown together productions which depended for their effectiveness more on the personalities of the performers than anything else. It was in that theatre that Gilbert did his apprentice work, and it was into it that he introduced some of the values of the other two types.

From the classic actors he learned a respect for refinement in acting style and declamation as well as a respect for absolute realism in settings and costumes. From the modern drama of the time he learned a respect for careful craftsmanship. The style of production he evolved was based first on the personalities of given actors (he wrote with their particular styles in mind), second on realism of detail, third on a sense of careful theatrical craftsmanship, and fourth on precision of declamation and gesture. It is important to remember that he did not impose a style on his leading actors, but rather used their style as his inspiration. Once the work was completed, however, he molded his company as rigidly and dictatorially as a drill sergeant in the army. Every word had to be clearly heard in all parts of the theatre. Every gesture was determined in advance and was most precise. The interplay between the styles of the leading actors provided the variety of the piece. The chorus sang, danced, and acted completely as a unit. The instinctive British love of pageantry found an ideal place on Gilbert's stage.

If the modern director wishes to recapture the spirit of the original, he must remember the conditions under which Gilbert worked, and that he wrote his operas with particular staging techniques in mind, often conceiving the stage business while writing the actual dialogue. A deviation from his approach to staging must be regarded as cautiously as a deviation from his written text would be. Deviations are, of course, possible, and we shall consider them in the next chapter. They should be approached, however, out of an understanding of Gilbert's personal concept of the staging.

A good example of the approach that Gilbert

took to the chorus may be found in the opening chorus of *The Mikado*. The curtain rises to reveal a group of Japanese gentlemen grouped in various characteristic Japanese attitudes. They do not simply stand in a semicircle as many amateur directors are inclined to place them. They stand, sit, or kneel in small groups. At various points in the music they shift their positions, some of the kneeling ones standing, and vice versa. At specified times they open, close, or wave their fans, sometimes all together, sometimes in counterpoint to one another. Occasionally one of them will leave his group and join another group, as if shifting from one conversation to another. He will do so in a way that is stylized, without being stiff. All of the movements are carefully planned in advance so that the scene becomes increasingly interesting. They are executed so perfectly that they look exactly the same from one performance to the next. Thus is created the effect of figurines rather than actual people. And this is how the words that they sing ask us to see them:

> We figure in lively paint:
> Our attitude's queer and quaint—
> You're wrong if you think it ain't . . .

The point is that they are not to give the impression of real people. Every gesture, every move of the fan, every fold in the draperies of the costume should create the impression of something more quaint than actual people.

Again, the opening chorus of *Pinafore* finds the sailors in characteristic attitudes about the ship, some of them coiling rope, some repairing fishing nets, some polishing the brass, some washing the floor. Everything that they do reminds us of real sailors, but the total effect is that of people who are not people, who are a little too quaint, too jolly, too perfect in their joyous love of what they are doing to be real people. They live in a world that never existed, a world confined to the theatre, and extremely conscious of itself as theatre. Any attempt to make us believe in their reality as human beings violates a basic premise of that world; the dominant aesthetic effect that Gilbert sought to attain was an ironic contrast between the realism of the setting and the never-never-land idealism of the people. Continual variations on that contrast provide one of the main sources of his humor. If the courtroom in *Trial by Jury* does not appear to be a real courtroom, then half of the absurdity of what is happening in it is lost. If the fairies in *Iolanthe* do not dance

about in a recognizably English countryside or in front of what appear to be actual Houses of Parliament, then their presence onstage is not nearly as topsy-turvy as would otherwise be the case.

The aim when working with the chorus is not only to drill them so carefully that if they were all doing exactly the same thing they would all look exactly alike, but also to divide them into groups most of the time and have the groups doing different things that relate to one another and are consistent with their characters and visually interesting. They should never become so unreal as to make us abandon the possibility that they are human nor so real as to make them appear to be real people rather than types. The precision that is required to create that effect demands a great many hours of rehearsal, and the members of the chorus should know their actions so well that they can do everything perfectly without thinking about it.

In working with the leading actors, Gilbert allowed considerably more freedom, but there were definite boundaries that could not be crossed. It was possible for an actor to originate a piece of business, but it could never be used unless it had been cleared with him in advance. The fact that the audience might laugh was irrelevant; Gilbert knew from experience that audiences will laugh at many things that are not funny. Everything that happened had to be in good taste and in keeping with the style of the production as a whole. Furthermore, if the production was not carefully designed so that it became funnier as it progressed, it would seem to get less funny. Therefore it was necessary to ration one's inventiveness and not get too many laughs too soon. You will find if you examine the text of a Gilbert and Sullivan opera that the first two or three scenes contain relatively little humor and that the funniest scenes nearly always occur in the second half of the second act, although not immediately preceding the finale.

Because Gilbert and Sullivan opera depends so heavily on ensemble acting, it is necessary that the actors be familiar with one another's styles and avoid duplication. Each should add his own distinctive contribution, and this should be so carefully designed that the audience knows approximately what to expect from each actor after he has been onstage for a few moments. There is no room in Gilbert and Sullivan opera for the introspective gropings of a Hamlet—everything about character must be clearly stated and must remain largely unvaried. Variety should exist between the characterizations, not within them.

Singing, acting, and dancing are all extremely important in the production, and they must all be done in a way appropriate to it. Although it is desirable to have singing voices that are as good as possible, it is not desirable to have singers who subordinate everything else to the music. Personality must always shine through the singing. Every word must be distinct, and it must be expressive of character. If the same performer were to sing different parts in the same opera, he would have to change his style of singing for each of them, as the manner of singing is one of the primary means by which the role is acted. But the singing must always be singing, and the habit of declaiming the words without reference to the music that characterizes some popular performers is certainly to be discouraged. Many people have the impression that Gilbert and Sullivan opera does not require good singers because they identify the Grossmith parts with people who have weak voices. As a number of recent recordings have demonstrated, Sullivan's music always benefits from good singing, providing the verbal nuances are not lost. Although more ample statements will follow as we deal with each of the operas in turn, it might help to identify each of the typical roles with an adjective that describes the manner in which it should be sung. In general, the Grossmith roles are drily comic, the Barrington roles pompous, the Temple roles deliciously macabre. The soprano is either blithe or precious, the tenor moderately heroic, the contralto menacing or motherly, the light baritone charming and happy, and the mezzo-soprano flirtatious or lovelorn. One should always be able to tell from the manner in which a particular song is sung what character is supposed to be singing it.

As to the acting, it must be restrained. Humor is not increased by doing more of something or saying it louder or making it more ridiculous. Humor is achieved by underplaying and by effective timing. Furthermore, the audience must never feel that the actor is laughing at the character. Acting comedy is a serious business. The actor must identify with the role sufficiently so that while he is onstage he believes the character's peculiar form of eccentricity to be valid. Dorothy Raedler, one of the most outstanding American directors of Gilbert and Sullivan, believes that the Stanislavsky Method of acting is not inappropriate in the preparation of Gilbert and Sullivan, though it must be that side of the Method that emphasizes the behavior of the body as well as the spirit. The actor should have assurance that what he is doing is funny, but he must avoid overdoing it, and he must always use good taste, preserving the style of the production as a whole. Gilbert and Sullivan is never a matter of pie throwing, excessive mugging, or irrelevant claptrap. Yet the finest moments in a production can come when an actor invents pieces of business or pantomime that are appropriate to the occasion. For example, when Ko-Ko says, "I mean to begin with a guinea pig, and work my way through the animal kingdom till I come to a Second Trombone," he uses his fan as an executioner's knife and pretends to behead several animals lined up in a row. At the end of the row he comes to the neck of Nanki-Poo obligingly extended for the purpose on Nanki-Poo's previous line, "Very well, then —behead me." He is about to chop away at that too when he realizes what he is doing, gives a little scream, and jumps away. Gilbert and Sullivan is full of that kind of thing, appropriate to the situation, and carefully timed with the lines. Sometimes the stage business even has the effect of punning. When Nanki-Poo says, "Very well, if you can draw the line, so can I," he pulls out of his belt the rope that he is going to use to hang himself. If the stage business is timed exactly right, the audience will catch the pun; otherwise, it will not.

The dancing, also, must be unpretentious. The chorus dancing must be attractive, varied, and serviceable without drawing too much attention to itself. Nevertheless, the chorus should dance much of the time that they are onstage, and their dancing should form interesting patterns and be executed with precision and grace. Several of the leading actors are also required to dance, and this dancing may provide some of the best moments in the performance. Ko-Ko's shenanigans during the trio "Here's a how-de-do" are legendary, as are those of the Lord Chancellor in a similar trio. The gavotte scene in *The Gondoliers* offers the Duke opportunity for some excellent comic dancing. Jack Point's dancing at the end of *Yeomen* before he falls senseless offers an opportunity for the kind of pathos associated with some of the work of Marcel Marceau. Then there are the show-piece dances when the performance gives way for a few moments entirely to dancing. These include the country dance in *The Sorcerer,* the hornpipe and the gavotte in *Ruddigore,* and the tarantella in *Utopia, Ltd*. For such moments as these a choreographer should be used and the dances executed with great precision. Too often such dance scenes come across in amateur productions as embarrassing afterthoughts.

Finally, we should observe that nothing is more English than Gilbert and Sullivan opera, and that too obviously American accents can be most obtrusive. That does not mean that an American company must all learn Oxonian English, but a certain elegance of speech among the actors is essential to the stylistic integrity of the occasion.

# Chapter III

# VARIATIONS IN PRODUCTION STYLE

Gilbert and Sullivan opera is a unique phenomenon. It has been performed almost without interruption in one way or another for nearly a hundred years, and although speculations about its mortality have been common since its beginning, there is no indication that its production will diminish during the next hundred years.

Two major questions are raised, however, by anything that is performed as frequently as the most popular of the operas. One concerns its relevance for modern audiences, and the second concerns possible means of rejuvenating productions held in a straitjacket by a rigidly observed tradition.

Spectators at a recent production of *Patience* at M.I.T. must have felt that history repeats itself, since the production was in contemporary dress—the aesthetes and lovesick maidens became hippies and their girl friends. The dragoon costumes, of course, remained unchanged. In order to bring the libretto up-to-date it was necessary to change only one word—Bunthorne's "I do *not* care for dirty greens by any means" became "dirty jeans." It is said that the first weekend audience knew what they were seeing and enjoyed it immensely, whereas the second weekend audience thought they were seeing the latest English import and enjoyed it even more.

Such an example makes credible the possibility that Gilbert and Sullivan opera has more meaning during the 1960's and 1970's than it did during the 1930's and 1940's. History has finally caught up with Gilbert's sense of fun, and the world recognizes its own topsy-turvy characteristics. Once again people are dressing like the Victorians, and much that was passé only a few years ago is again in vogue. The new age is sure to discover in the operas much of its own *Weltanschauung*. Furthermore there is something in Gilbert and Sullivan for everybody. The angry young radical can find in it many of the same dramatic impulses of the avant-garde theatre. He can view it as a mirror of the absurdities of the Establishment. His corporation executive grandfather can turn to it for the nostalgia and reassurance of the old days. Five-year-old children can enjoy the lilting tunes of the music and the fantasy of the acting, teen-agers can learn to appreciate Bach and Mozart by training their ears on Sullivan's music, and can gain a respect for good theatrical and poetic craftsmanship from Gilbert's libretti. Professors of literature and music can write dissertations on the relationship between Gilbert and Aristophanes or Sullivan and Mendelssohn, and can develop new concepts about the aesthetics of comedy. Therefore, if there is any one thing these days that has a chance of bringing the whole family together, it is a performance of *The Mikado*.

Granted that Gilbert and Sullivan has a lot to offer and that only the superficial observer will conclude that it is nothing but marching songs and nursery rhymes (as detractors here and there are likely to tell you), what possibilities exist for doing something original with the operas?

One must remember that they are already parodies, and therefore to parody them is perhaps too much of a good thing. Nevertheless, if one is not too much of a purist, there is considerable fun in Anna Russell's "How to Write Your Own Gilbert and Sullivan Opera" and Danny Kaye's renditions, complete with original words by his wife. The possibilities of updating have been explored previously with such versions as *The Hot Mikado* and *The Swing Mikado*. Why not a *Rock Mikado*? Gilbert and

Sullivan, if it is to be tampered with, lends itself more readily to the psychedelic techniques of modern musical and theatrical experimentation than it does to the more conservative popular music of the past. A Mikado carried through the audience on a litter while a light show is in full progress onstage and the chorus is grooving to electronic sounds would certainly have its effect. There is no reason to take offense at such an approach. One can see it and return to more traditional performances feeling refreshed. Even the same company might undertake both techniques of production.

The theatrical techniques associated with the words and music are so much a part of the total effect that tampering with the basic staging concepts is akin to tampering with the text. If one is going to stage the operas in an original manner one need hardly have scruples about rewriting them here and there when it seems appropriate to do so. Indeed, occasional minor rewriting seems appropriate to the text as originally conceived. When Ko-Ko is asked where Nanki-Poo has fled, he replies, "Knightsbridge." This appealed to the original audience, who knew that Koko was referring to the part of London where Japanese people lived. If there is a place in your city associated with the Japanese, that is the place Ko-Ko should refer to. If not, he should make some other topical reference at that point. In Washington, D.C., at a time when the whole city had been suffering for a year over the building of a Dupont Circle underpass, Poop-Bah reported the following: "The Mikado approaches, and is just entering the Dupont Circle underpass." It was the best moment of the evening, and entirely in line with Gilbert's original intentions. We get some idea of Gilbert's love of the topical reference when we remember that the head of the London fire brigade was one Captain Shaw. Gilbert knew exactly where he would be sitting at the opening performance of *Iolanthe,* and he made good use of his knowledge. During the second act the Fairy Queen is singing about how it is necessary to extinguish the fire of one's passion with the "hose of common sense." At this point she moves toward the audience, arms outstretched toward the seat in which the fire chief sits, and sings,

> Oh, Captain Shaw!
> Type of true love kept under!
> Could thy Brigade
> With cold cascade
> Quench my great love, I wonder!

Making changes in the texts has always been regarded by some people as anathema, and by others as a temptation. Indeed, in this regard, certain details of tradition seem to be almost an extension of the text. Gilbert himself was not exempt from the trials and tribulations that beset anyone who would sully the sacredness of tradition. The following story related by Rutland Barrington exemplifies the problem. During the 1908 revival of *The Mikado,* Barrington was again playing the role of Pooh-Bah, which he had created, and Gilbert was again acting as stage director.

> In one situation where Pitti-Sing, now played by that delightful little artist Jessie Rose, puts herself forward in place of Yum-Yum, Gilbert did not like the "business," and when told by the stage manager that it was the original way of doing it, appealed to me for confirmation, which I was able to give, whereupon he remarked, "Oh, it's classic, is it? Well, we must not interfere with the classics."

The *Pinafore* revival of the same year produced the following reminiscence, again from Barrington about the opening night:

> It was almost as great a night as the *Mikado* revival, and I have an impression that it is "new" to many more people than is the Japanese piece.
> That it was not new to some of the "galleryites," and most particularly to one man amongst them, I had ample and personal experience on the first and second nights.
> Gilbert had introduced a line into my part which might be, and was, construed into a reference to the present "strained relations" existing between certain well-known and deservedly popular naval officers of high position, and the line was received with mingled laughter and "booing," some few cries of "Author! Author!" and from one stentorian voice the remark, "Stick to the book!"
> It is manifestly unfair to visit the sins (?) of the author on the actor, and might have been somewhat distressing to an artist with a less phlegmatic temperament than Captain Corcoran; but, of course, it is quite possible that if a reproof was intended it was meant for the author, in which case I for one still less can understand the justice of it, for surely the man who wrote the piece has the right to alter or add to his work if he wishes!

This argument, however, would not seem to hold good with these Savoy classics, and Gilbert himself, when giving me the line, said something to the effect that "the Press will very likely object to it, Barrington."

Gilbert's response upon reading the above passage was: "I find myself in the Gilbertian situation of being the only man alive who is not permitted to gag these libretti!"

So, if the spirit moves you, by all means experiment. Experimentation begins with the occasional ad-lib line and ends with the unrecognizable. Somewhere along the line characters are reinterpreted, and staging is experimented with. The Savoy Theatre was the most traditional kind of proscenium stage, but there is no reason other kinds of stages may not be used. If the operas are performed in the round, it is a good idea to have several levels to the stage so that the leading actors do not get lost among the chorus. Platforms built out from a proscenium stage may greatly increase the possibility for grouping the chorus in interesting ways, and may also make it possible to increase the size of the chorus. If one wishes to use a large chorus, it is common to divide them into groups, having some do the first act and others the second act. When an act includes various groups of people, such as pirates and policemen, further subdivisions become possible. During the time that a group is not onstage it may sit in front of the stage and sing, forming what is called a pit chorus.

As the production opens up into the auditorium, it becomes interesting to have performers enter up the central aisle, singing as they come. The March of the Peers in *Iolanthe* is particularly impressive done that way. In a production of *The Gondoliers,* when the Duke of Plaza-Toro and his retinue made their way down the aisle in a gondola, matters were somewhat complicated when the gondola had a flat tire. One can bring the Mikado in on a litter, Sir Joseph Porter and his sisters, cousins, and aunts in a rowboat, King Gama on a hobby horse, and so on. In general, it is a better idea to enter though the audience than to exit through it.

It is possible to open the production up vertically as well. The storming of the castle in *Princess Ida* is particularly effective with girls up on the battlements pushing the invading men off their ladders. *Pinafore* provides an opportunity for the sailors to climb ropes, *Pirates* for the girls to come in over the rocky mountains, *Iolanthe* for Iolanthe to come up from in front of the stage, where she has gone to live among the frogs.

A staging technique, or rather a scenic technique, that is worth investigating for possibly adding a further dimension to the experience is the use of slide projections and film material in place of scenery. It is possible to project slides onto a scrim behind which the actors move so that the scenery appears to be in front of the actors. Additional slides can be projected onto a screen behind the actors so that several levels of imagery are possible at the same time. Furthermore, more than one projector can be focused on each screen so that several slides can be joined to form a particular setting, and these can be constantly varied in order to produce a constant shifting of the scenery. Some of the more romantic scenes in the operas, such as the opening of *Iolanthe* or the end of the first act of *The Gondoliers,* might be greatly enhanced through the use of such techniques. Or imagine a Ghost Scene in *Ruddigore* done impressionistically so as to include all the images referred to in Sir Roderick's song. Again, an Incantation Scene in *The Sorcerer* in which the sprites of earth and air flit across the screen in breathtaking shapes should be unforgettable.

Although the use of projections in the manner indicated above is enticing, some caution should nevertheless be exercised. Inasmuch as there is no opera in which they can be used with equal effectiveness throughout (except possibly *Thespis*), the transition from scenes in which they are used extensively to others in which they simply provide an unchanging background can be jolting. That is particularly true if they are used early in the performance and not later (as might be the case with *Iolanthe* or *The Sorcerer*). The director will need to consider carefully, therefore, if he is going to use projections, how he intends to avoid scenic anticlimax.

As the satirical value of Gilbert's libretti weakens with age, the value of fantasy and absurdity in them may increase. If one does not wish to attempt a realistic setting, one may go a long way in the other direction. A courtroom all in red with hearts and flowers all about it for *Trial by Jury* is certainly not as funny, but it might be more delightful than a realistic courtroom. The current D'Oyly Carte production of *Princess Ida* has acknowledged the fact that satire may go out-of-date and that fantasy may be the answer when that happens.

Once that concept has been accepted, the designer may have a field day.

There are two approaches to rewriting the operas. One is to make in a less successful opera changes of the very kind that Gilbert and Sullivan might have made had they done additional revision. Examples are attempts to liven up the second-act finale of *The Sorcerer* and the third-act finale of *Princess Ida*. Even D'Oyly Carte has indulged in such rewriting, providing *Ruddigore* with a new overture and drastically changing its second-act finale. Minor changes in the orchestrations have also crept into the official productions over the years, as have a few changes in the dialogue and songs. If one wishes to do any rewriting, the less successful the opera was originally, the better. In an amateur production of *The Sorcerer* a second-act solo for Mrs. Partlet right before the quartet made her part seem more important and provided one of the hit songs of the evening. A conscientious attempt had been made to keep that song in the style of the rest of the evening. The only two operas, however, that really provide fair game for frustrated playwrights and composers are *Thespis* and *The Grand Duke*. We shall have more to say on the subject when we consider those operas. We shall also consider the problems involved in changing the orchestration in the chapter on that subject.

Any major rewriting of the other operas would involve the creation of an essentially new work, and would relate to the opera in question as *Carmen Jones* does to *Carmen,* or *West Side Story* to *Romeo and Juliet*. There is also the question of trying to create another Gilbert and Sullivan opera. Imitations have come and gone, but the most successful to date has been an adaptation of Gilbert's best play, *Engaged,* so that it contains songs from many of Sullivan's lesser-known works. The result was produced in New York by the Village Light Opera Company and received excellent reviews. The score of *Engaged* has been published by Chappell, so it may easily be produced.

Regardless of what changes are made, however, the question of taste should never be ignored. For example, in a production of *Pinafore* the Captain appeared in full dress uniform except that he was wearing no trousers. The effect was to keep the audience laughing throughout his opening song with the result that none of it was heard. Unfortunately the laughter was in no way relevant to anything that *Pinafore* is or might be about; it was the product of a cheap and tasteless device that communicated nothing except the total lack of imagination of the director. The moral is that one should stick to traditional methods of presenting Gilbert and Sullivan unless one is sufficiently imaginative to devise an approach that will enhance rather than destroy the theatrical experience.

In the chapters that follow, we shall generally assume that anyone interested in producing Gilbert and Sullivan in ways other than the traditional will have his own ideas and little need for this book. We shall consider most of the operas primarily as they are usually produced today by the D'Oyly Carte Opera Company, as well as by the leading nonprofessional companies that adhere to traditional staging and musical concepts.

# Chapter IV

# THESPIS, OR THE GODS GROWN OLD

## PRODUCTION NOTES

*Thespis* is the Gilbert and Sullivan work that offers the most opportunity for the producer who is interested in doing something innovative. Because all but two of the musical settings have been lost,* it is necessary either to compose a new score or to arrange one from existing music of some sort. Numerous composers have attempted to set the words more or less in the Sullivan style, and there has even been an arrangement of music from Sullivan's less popular operas. It was put together by Dr. Terence Rees and Garth Morton and was produced at the University of London in 1962 and introduced into America in 1967 by the Comic Opera Company of Baltimore.

Furthermore, there is some evidence that the libretto we have is not the libretto used in the original production, but an earlier version published before Gilbert had finished revising and developing it. Apparently there was even an additional character, Venus. Thus there is some justification for filling out the libretto with additional topical jokes, and perhaps even songs. Some of the situations in the second act are not as fully developed as one might expect, and there is plenty of opportunity here for additional material. Since *The Grand Duke* is rarely performed and is also about a company of actors, some of its songs can be appropriated for *Thespis* with great effect. Ernest's song in Act One, "Were I a king in very truth," can be given to Thespis. The duet for Julia and Ludwig in Act Two, "Now Julia, come," neatly fits into the scene between Thespis and Daphne in Act Two of *Thespis* with the change of a single phrase:

* See pages 263–267.

A sweet Calliope,
Undeniably
   Innocent ingenoo!

Rudolph's song in Act One of *The Grand Duke* might well be used by Thespis in Act Two when he hears of the petitions. There is also a wonderful song in the second act of *Utopia, Ltd.,* which, with new words, fits neatly into Act Two of *Thespis.* "Society has quite forsaken all her wicked courses" can become, "Olympus has entirely reorganized the planet." Anyone who is clever at comic verses should have a field day with this situation.

Also, there is little reason for not bringing the libretto up-to-date. For example, Jupiter's line to the effect that the sacrifices have positively dwindled down to preserved Australian beef might refer instead to frozen TV dinners. In that vein, a capable satirist should find much opportunity in *Thespis* for comment on current situations.

The general belief that *Thespis* was a failure is simply not accurate. It was written to be performed during the Christmas season, and like all such productions was designed for a run of about two months, which was exactly what it got. The opening performance was completely sold out and was attended by more people than any other Gilbert and Sullivan opening night. Because of inadequate rehearsal, the opening performance was not a smooth one and dampened the enthusiasm of the audience. Nevertheless the reviews were generally favorable and found the work imaginative and appealing. When it is produced today it usually surprises audiences with its unpretentious charm and fantasy.

*Thespis* may be produced on any scale that

one prefers. It may be changed into a play simply by paraphrasing the songs or reciting them as clever verses. In that form it can be handled by a small company of actors working on a very limited budget. If you are trying to organize a company of your own, *Thespis* is a good place to start. You can begin to build up production facilities without having to face all the complexities of a musical production the first time.

If there is a composer in the group, it may be possible to produce *Thespis* as an opera without even writing down the music. The composer may set the tunes and then tape-record them. The actors can learn their music by listening to the recording. The chorus can be taught their music by rote. *Thespis* was twice produced in this manner at the Maret School in Washington, D.C. with music by Dexter Davison. Five songs were added to the second act, including one for Cupid. At the beginning of the second-act finale he entered followed by lovesick maidens all of whom had been the victims of his arrows. Another song was an adaptation to be sung by the gods of Gilbert's *Bab Ballad*, "Roll On, Oh Shallow World." The show proved ideal for a school that wished to include children of all ages in its production, as there was the opening chorus of stars sung and danced by little children, and the chorus of lovesick maidens for sixth and seventh graders, in addition to the many opportunities for high-school students. Gilbert's dialogue and lyrics proved able to hold the attention of easily distracted audiences much better than many operettas specifically designed for such audiences.

If one wishes to mount a semiprofessional production, one may either use Sullivan music or have the work scored by a professional composer. There is no limit to the elaborateness that the production can be given, as there are many hints in the libretto of possible spectacle. One example is the Transformation Scene that occurs shortly after the opening chorus when Jupiter tells the fog to be off. One may have someone perched on the stage with a sign on him that says "fog," one may lift a scrim with fog painted on it, or one may, as was probably done in the original production, change the entire set before the audience's eyes. The technical staff can have good fun with Jupiter's thunderbolts. The manner in which the actors take over the symbols of office of the various gods during the Act One finale may be as simple or elaborate as one likes.

## CRITICAL DISCUSSION

*Thespis* is stylistically on a different level from the other Gilbert and Sullivan operas because it was written under different conditions. It is low rather than high comedy for the most part, though the lyrics are usually imaginative and sophisticated. The pseudo-dignity of the gods is contrasted with the almost vulgar horse-play of the actors, so that contrasting styles of acting are required for the two sets of characters. The opening scene must be dry, crisp, and businesslike, whereas the picnic scene must be full of rough-and-tumble knockabout. Highly effective comedy is possible when Thespis and the gods first meet and their two styles are contrasted. Although the gods attempt to intimidate Thespis, he quickly brings them down to his level. Much of the early part of Act Two depends on flirtatiousness and sexual intrigue not to be found in any of the other operas. The interplay between gods and mortals at the end of Act Two is much more slapstick than the similar situation at the end of *The Mikado*, but if the gods are made sufficiently ominous, something of the same effect can be achieved, and the ending of *Thespis* can attain a pseudo-tragic quality that is far more effective than mere farce. It is often true in the operas that if one can manage things so that the audience is not really sure whether to laugh or cry, the comedy is greatly heightened.

Although *Thespis* as we have it is rather hastily written and poorly developed, its basic idea is an excellent one and provides many of the comic concepts that were to be better handled in later operas. Gilbert was throughout his dramatic career interested in role-playing and the switching of roles. One example of such switching is the end of *Pinafore*, when it turns out that Ralph is really the Captain and the Captain is Ralph. Frederic, in *Pirates*, changes his behavior in exact accordance with his legal commitments because of an overdeveloped sense of duty. In *The Mikado* the idea of the victim becoming the executioner and then the victim again is extraordinarily well handled. Nearly every opera contains some variation on this theme, and some of them handle it in several ways. The theme is far more potent for us with our modern concern for identity and the hypocrisy implicit in role-playing than it was for a Victorian audience largely unconscious of the psychological ironies involved. In *Thespis*, of course, the entire cast is involved in the switching of roles, and the action is a symbolic movement from the sublime to the ridiculous. The classic concept that history is a retreat from a hypothetical golden age rather than a progression toward greatness is implied in the comedy of *Thespis*. Today, when every high-school student thinks he knows more about how the country should be run than the President of the United States, the experiences of the actors attempting to be gods must give us pause for thought. Gilbert lampoons both sets of characters. The gods, for all their experience, have become stale and irrelevant. The mortals, for all their imagination, are completely impractical. Only Mercury, the messenger of the gods, the drudge who does all the work, seems to understand how things should really work, but Mercury is seldom consulted and is too clever to volunteer advice. In Gilbert's topsy-turvy world it is the trivial that is taken seriously. One example of the mischief caused by the actors' inept ruling of the world is the fact that since Bacchus is played by a teetotaler, the grapes give nothing but ginger beer. This is reminiscent of the Fairy Queen's vengeance upon the Peers in *Iolanthe*:

> You shall sit, if he sees reason,
> Through the grouse and salmon season.

Confusion between the serious and the trivial is entirely consistent with Gilbert's main theme of role-playing, for it is when one becomes least human and most concerned with one's assigned role that one tends to be most trivial. Thus, much of the action in Gilbert's libretti is symbolic of what actually happens in society. The disorganization among the members of Thespis' company, who provide everything for the lobster salad except lobster and everything for the claret cup except claret, foreshadows the disorganization with which they will later rule the world. When Thespis attempts to get to the bottom of the reasons for the disorganization, he runs up against the old bugbear, role-playing. Tipseion has neglected to bring wine for the claret cup because of Thespis' earlier insistence that he take the Pledge. Thespis is the victim of the consistent carrying-out of his own commands. How often in later operas will that sort of literal response to a command form the whole basis of the plot structure! Before Thespis can do anything to remedy the situation, he is distracted by more role-playing: Preposteros, the villain, has picked a meaningless fight with Stupidas. The situation is too much for Thespis, who engages in one of those soon-to-be-interrupted mock soliloquies that tormented Gilbertian characters indulge in. His philosophical question is treated by the other actors as a conundrum. Thespis is thus the first of those Gilbertian comic figures who are autobiographical in that they long to be taken seriously and can be successful only when funny. The underlying importance of Gilbert's concept is that in assuming roles we limit ourselves until finally we can no longer break free of the roles, and have become the very caricatures with which the satirist peoples his stage.

What could be more basically Gilbertian than a conflict between actors and gods? The actors, who specialize in roles, but whose personalities may be eventually absorbed in the roles they play, represent human behavior. The gods, with their antique irrelevance, represent human ideals, which are always behind the times. In later operettas the part symbolized by the gods will be taken over by institutions—the law in *Trial by Jury*, the Royal Navy in *Pinafore*, and so on. The actors will play other roles, derived either from society or from literary stereotype. Gilbert wrote better than he knew in *Thespis*, and it is a pity that he never returned to this work to develop it further.

## CHARACTER SKETCHES

### Thespis

Created by the famous comedian J. L. Toole, this role has often been considered unworthy of his efforts. Perhaps that is because Thespis' dominant character trait is negative: He is simply ineffectual. He combines his ineffectualness with a naive blindness to his own inadequacies. Although he has his hands full attempting to keep peace among his own company of actors, he sees no difficulty in ruling the world for a year in the absence of the gods.

But although Thespis' lines are not usually very funny, there is no reason to assume that he cannot become a memorable character. The naive innocent lost in a world that he does not quite understand can be unforgettably portrayed. Almost never does Thespis speak in anger. He is charming and helpless, and the combination is enough to win the trust of the gods. There is in him just a touch of the tragic, as he feels the irony of his role, feels estranged from his company by it, and yet does not attempt to eschew it. If the actor can suggest the mask of sorrow behind the consistent smile (and it is only a mask, not a complete reality), he may be able to create a comedy that runs deep into pathos. If at the end we can take the curse of the gods with just a touch of sympathy for Thespis, the actor's achievement will be a significant one.

The actor who played the role in the University of London production gave Thespis, in contrast to the rest of his company, a cockney accent and a bluster reminiscent of Stanley Holloway. It did much to help create the effect suggested above, as well as underline the absurdity of Thespis' snobbery.

## Mercury

Originally created by Nellie Farren, and (aside from Sparkeion) the only male role in the operas meant to be played by a female, Mercury is a descendant of Shakespeare's Puck and Ariel. He is the only character in the opera who understands the situations the other characters are trying to deal with. He is capable of solving all problems, and yet he is kept in his place—the celestial drudge. Mercury has a little of Pooh-Bah in him in that he combines all roles into one, yet he has none of Pooh-Bah's snobbery. He stands back and watches with feelings of irony as the others bungle. If asked for advice he will always give it, but he knows better than to give it when it has not been asked for. In the end, of course, Mercury is the triumphant one, since he has the satisfaction of seeing that he was right all along about everyone. As his reading of the petitions reveals the clumsy mess Thespis has made of things, the mortals grow more humble and the gods more angry, but Mercury merely enjoys the joke, sharing the perspective of the audience. Strangely enough, Mercury may be the one character in all of the operas who is totally charming, since Gilbert was so busy making him the perceiver of irony in others that he put no irony into Mercury. We laugh with him, never at him. Therefore, Mercury should never try to be funny, he should simply sparkle. His part, for all its clear perception of the difficulties of others, is pure and delightful fantasy. Although he says he is overburdened with all the work the others give him to do, he is the only god who has not grown old, the only one still full of youthful bounce and energy. The actress should never attempt more than the most superficial suggestion of Mercury's supposed weariness. Playing Mercury should be fun from start to finish, and the audience should share in the fun.

## Sparkeion

A tradition in English pantomime (to which *Thespis* is closely related) holds that the male romantic lead should be played by a female, who was called the Principal Boy. Therefore, the original Sparkeion was played by a woman. There is no reason other than historical accuracy to have the role played that way today, but it is a handy thing to know if one has more actresses than actors to work with.

Sparkeion and Nicemis have a love scene before the entrance of the other actors, including a charming duet. Sparkeion could hardly be called aggressive by modern standards, but he is a little too fast for the prudish Nicemis, and this provides the conflict for the scene. Because Sparkeion is so lacking in any genuine emotion, it is well to play his role as pure fantasy, emphasizing his delight at the beauty of the scenery, his ethereal thoughts about Nicemis, and the ease with which he asserts that if Nicemis will have nothing to do with him, Daphne will. In the second act when the two "goddesses" fight about who is married to him, Sparkeion enjoys the situation thoroughly. He has an oportunity to sing the charming song, "Little Maid of Arcadee." He should be elegant, effervescent, and always smiling. He should not attempt to give the part any dramatic depth; it has none.

## Nicemis

Here is the first of Gilbert's unbearable romantic leads. Nicemis is a prude, she is vain, and she is conniving. All of those qualities are quite clear, and yet we are supposed to look adoringly at her whenever she is onstage. The actress must be charming, beautiful, and apparently ingenuous without a hint of the qualities that so obviously permeate her lines. One of Gilbert's most delicious ironies is that he can have an insufferable female say preposterous things without ever destroying our love for her. When Nicemis argues with Sparkeion about Daphne, or contests with Daphne over Sparkeion, her anger, like the rest of her character, goes only skin-deep.

## Daphne

Daphne can afford to be more sultry than Nicemis, since we are not supposed to identify with her in the same way. She is the "other woman" trying to break up the romance, taking advantage first of a lover's quarrel and then of *Lemprière's Classical Dictionary*. In quarreling with Nicemis she is the more vixenish of the two. Her flirtatiousness and pique in dealing with Thespis in the second act contrasts with the much milder flirtatiousness of Nicemis and Pretteia in their scene with Sillimon. She is much more obviously moody than Nicemis, much more openly flirtatious, much more clearly and successfully manipulating situations and people to her advantage. Remember that when she attempts to flirt with Thespis in the first act, Nicemis is unsuccessful. By contrast, Daphne is overpowering.

### Pretteia

This lady's character is pretty well summed up in her name. She is given a single scene and a single plight. She prefers a pseudo-marriage to her father to one to her grandfather. She thus sets the scene for the intrigue about connubial relationships that will dominate the next few scenes. She should be very flirtatious, winning Sillimon over to her point of view by her tone of voice and her physical behavior rather than by her logic.

### Sillimon

This is a minor part, but one in which it is possible to make a major impression. His opening of the second act can provide an excellent foil to Thespis, since as Olympian stage manager it is he who must keep order. He is efficient where Thespis is moody; but he gets no more done, as he is easily distracted. Thespis is obviously not a ladies' man, taking his duties far too seriously; but Sillimon is, and thoroughly enjoys being surrounded by adoring females hoping to get favors from him. He has none of Thespis' tragic awareness of responsibility; he is simply trying to do his duty in a conscientious and workmanlike manner. The role should be taken by an actor with a crisp delivery who can keep his scene moving along at a swift pace. The second-act opening should be fun, and should certainly not drag. It is the mortals' only opportunity to show that side of being gods that they enjoy.

### Tipseion

This is another minor character with a major opportunity. He is the company's low comedian, and he is a reformed drunkard. He should be big and rowdy, still having the manners of an alcoholic, and superimpose upon that a mildness of manner that he breaks through as he ludicrously cries out to Thespis, "Embrace me!" He is a fanatic about having taken the Pledge, and there is a fiendishly happy glow in his eye. During his two short scenes the stage belongs entirely to him, and he should make the most of one of the most truly delicious of all minor parts.

### Preposteros

The company's heavy villain, always picking fights for no reason, Preposteros has all the emotional restraint of an infant. He wears a handlebar mustache, which he twirls. He speaks in a deep, moody voice, and lurks about the corner of the stage, hiding in his costume. He should caricature all the clichés of the melodramatic villain. His function in the picnic scene is a rather interesting one, as he is the only one who is not enjoying himself except Thespis and Nicemis, both of whom are rather bland characters. He functions like a dark cloud in a clear blue sky, casting a gloom over an otherwise pallid scene even when he is not speaking. If he is interesting enough he adds a whole additional dimension to the scene, since he can make the audience feel a little uneasy all through the trivialities that make up the bulk of the scene. He is the time-bomb everyone is waiting for to go off.

### Stupidas

Stupidas' sole purpose is to be picked on by Preposteros. He should therefore contrast with the latter as much as possible. He should be small, thin, pitiful, and emaciated, since the sadder a figure he is, the more brutish Preposteros can seem.

### Timidon

This character has just a few lines and a single solo. He should appear as his name implies, but he should also appear lazy. As he must make an impression in a very short time, it might help to give him a nervous laugh and an obvious case of the jitters.

### Cymon

Giving the role of Father Time to a little boy is typical of Thespis' casting techniques. The actor should be as little and young-looking as can be managed, but also aggressive and sure of himself. He knows what he is about and is very proud of what he has acomplished. His pomposity thoroughly irritates the gods.

## Jupiter

In Gilbert's words, "An extremely old man, very decrepit, with very thin straggling white beard, he wears a long braided dressing-gown, handsomely trimmed, and a silk night-cap on his head." It would be dangerous to take that too literally, for Jupiter's curse in Act Two should be delivered with commanding authority. Thus, Jupiter must have the power to grow from a wizened, somewhat helpless old man to an angry potentate. The actor should be a large, powerful man with the capacity to appear bumbling in the first act, particularly in his scene with Thespis, but also to suggest the powers that Jupiter once had as Father of the Gods and that he will exercise again upon his return to Olympus.

Jupiter, in common with the other gods, should have an elegance of acting style that sets him apart from the Thespians. His accent should be Oxonian, and his manner that of a fine old English gentleman. He should attempt to preserve high comedy throughout and avoid slapstick.

## Apollo

In Gilbert's words, "He is an elderly 'buck' with an air of assumed juvenility, and is dressed in a dressing gown and smoking cap." Apollo has a languidity, almost a depravity that helps us understand why the gods are no longer respected: They simply are not doing their work. Apollo, the man of leisure and pleasure, won't go out today, but will send the Londoners their usual fog instead. His relaxed approach to things presents a foil to Jupiter's driving concern.

## Mars

This character has only a couple of lines that set him apart from the other gods. Other than that he appears with Jupiter and Mercury and echoes what they do. He should therefore be chosen for physical appearance and look as much as possible like a decayed warrior.

## Diana

Although it is not a major part, this role is large enough to be given to the actress who would ordinarily sing the contralto lead in one of the operas. She is an elegant, aged lady who specializes in complaining and reprimanding. Any attempt to rewrite the text should develop her part, particularly in the second act, in which she is no more than a member of the chorus. She should have a forceful personality, and perhaps relate to Jupiter as Katisha relates to the Mikado, i.e., as the virago that makes him as potent as he is. There is little justification for it in the lines, but it is something that can be played visually with considerable effect.

## NOTES ON STAGING

Four basic moods must be captured in the various scenes: fantasy, spectacle, high comedy, and low comedy. The opening chorus belongs to the choreographer, and should be as beautiful to look at as possible, since it has no humor of its own and no connection with the plot. If the company is large enough, it might be sung by a pit chorus while a ballet dances onstage. In the scenes that follow with the gods, good crisp high comedy should dominate. Mercury's excellent solo (the first of Gilbert's autobiographical songs) needs little apart from the personality of the performer to carry it, but the quartet that follows should be elaborately staged. The "Goodness gracious" refrain needs an appropriate dance step so that the four characters work together, but it should be varied each time so that the focus is on a different character. It might help this number if it is assumed that the actors are approaching Olympus from the front, rather than the rear of the stage, so that the gods can peer out into the auditorium rather than run up toward the back of the stage.

With the entrace of Sparkeion and Nicemis, the mood shifts again toward fantasy. The young lovers are exhilarated with the beauty of the scenery and the presence of each other. There is no possibility of humor in the lines, but the scene can be delightful if the actors seem delighted with it. The staging of the duet can be very simple, with the lovers either standing together and walking occasionally so that they eventually occupy about four basic positions, or standing and sitting in combination, depending on which is singing at the moment. The chorus, "Climbing over rocky mountain,"

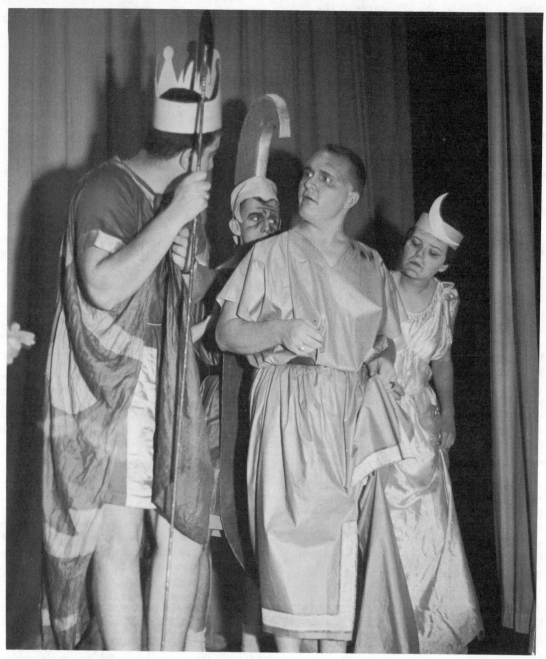

*Jupiter, Apollo, Thespis, and Diana in* Thespis. *Jupiter: "So that's arranged—you take my place, my boy."*                    (*Lyric Theatre production*)

for which the *Pirates* music should definitely be used, requires elaborate choreography. One or two actors should skip on during the opening measures and then summon the others, so that by the time they are ready to sing, all of the chorus are onstage. The problem the song presents is that whereas when it occurs in *Pirates* it is sung by people all of whom are dressed the same, here it is sung by a collection of people who appear quite different from one another. The problem can be solved by having groups of characters that are somewhat similar occupy different basic stage areas. There can be a few simple dance steps that all do throughout the song, while groups take turns moving to the center of the stage and engaging in more complex choreography. Because they are a troupe of actors, their dances can be quite varied and interesting. It is plausible that their number should contain dancers of various sorts (ballet, tap, etc.), and various groups of comedians. Thus, the number may become a collection of vaudeville "acts." The director should not get so carried away, however, that he loses touch with the lilting, carefree quality of the music.

In the dialogue that follows, the director can have a field day. Here is an opportunity for low comedy, and all sorts of business can be invented. It is perfectly all right for the dialogue to come to a standstill while the "business" proceeds. For example, when Tipseion announces a hard-boiled egg for the lobster salad, another character might take the egg from Tipseion, bounce it on the floor and catch it again, then hand it back to Tipseion with a look of disgust. Or, in the old pie-throwing tradition, he might break the egg, finding that it is not boiled at all, so that he gets it all over his hands. He can then scrunch the egg in Tipseion's face. Tipseion, having suffered this calmly, can wipe the egg off his face and onto the other actor's costume, and so on, until they are both covered with egg. Almost every line in the scene offers some opportunity for this kind of thing, though the number of such bits used should not exceed five or six throughout the whole scene.

Thespis' song about the railroad engine offers the chorus an opportunity to sing a refrain (if the composer provides it) in which they do various imitations of railroad engines. It is a song that should have an encore of one or two verses if it has been effectively performed.

When the three gods enter they should be so placed that they are above the other actors, and their appearance should thus be quite awesome. Here, for a moment, the director's attention should be on spectacle. If the entire company cowers effectively enough, and if the gods are impressive enough, Thespis' blissful unawareness of them will be much funnier. The humor of the scene lies in its reversal of the expected and the gradual acceptance by the gods of the fact that Thespis, ridiculous as he is, has something to offer them. Anything that detracts from their dignity will make the scene less funny.

An important stage direction is lacking from the text. Evidently the entire company of Thespians clear the stage just before Jupiter's line, "There! Now we are alone." There is not enough time for the company to drift off gradually, as a moment before they have all kneeled to the gods. It is possible to have the gods threaten them again so that they all run off screaming, or it is possible to drop some sort of curtain so that as if by magic Thespis appears to have been whisked away to some other part of heaven. The curtain could then rise again following Mercury's "Here come your people!"

The finale of Act One emphasizes spectacle. During each of the solos a mortal takes upon himself the symbols associated with one of the gods. The more elaborate the symbols, the better. Best of all would be the appearance of four chariots, from each of which a god would descend in order to give way to the appropriate mortal. The chariot can then circle the stage during the choral refrain that follows the solo. Simpler to arrange than chariots would be four sedan chairs. If chariots are used, they can be drawn by people in the costumes of horses. Sedan chairs can be carried by muscular men stripped to the waist and wearing chains.

The last part of the finale offers the costume designer opportunity for a real display as all the old gods come onstage to bid the mortals good-bye. It is desirable for this scene to have as many stage levels as possible, so that we can see people arranged vertically as well as horizontally. The curtain should fall on a beautiful tableau.

The opening of Act Two should be a sight gag. The effect should be of a dissolute Roman banquet, and the chorus should be grouped in positions reminding one of a painting of such a banquet. Bunches of grapes, great hunks of meat, and silver and golden goblets should be much in evidence. The curtain should rise several measures of music before the chorus begins to sing. It would be effective to have everyone frozen in position, perhaps bringing the lights up gradually, until the singing begins. Then, in slow motion, the dissipation can begin. A good deal of it can involve people feeding one another in comical ways.

Sillimon's scene should move rapidly and with dry humor. Although susceptible to flattery, he is rather crotchety and businesslike, and he does not really understand the flirtatious advances of the girls. They are therefore forced to overdo it, with considerable fun.

Sparkeion's delightful song, "Little maid of Arcadee," * should be sung to Sillimon, who is seated with his back to the audience. It offers some opportunity for pantomime, but little stage action is needed in it. Mercury's song that follows is very funny and will be funnier if Mercury consistently pantomimes the action described in it.

In the scene between Mercury and Thespis we enjoy primarily the change in Thespis from pompous certainty that he is doing everything right to growing suspicion that everything is all wrong. The more pompous he is at the beginning, the funnier he will be by the end. Mercury plays the scene rather quietly, with tongue in cheek.

The two scenes that follow call for righteous indignation from Daphne and Nicemis, and growing concern from Thespis. Sparkeion is quietly amused by the whole thing. The staging of the quartet is easily suggested by the words. The two girls struggle to capture Sparkeion or angrily confront each other. Thespis stands by helplessly watching until his solo in the second half of the song. The refrain, "Please will someone," is addressed to the audience and should be accompanied by a humorous dance step suggesting the confusion of the four singers.

Now the mood changes drastically. The lights dim down, the three gods enter wearing masks and cloaks, and we have a melodramatic version of Greek tragedy. Thunder and lightning should accompany the scene both in actual fact and in the manner of the gods. Poor Mercury is the victim of most of this, as Thespis is too blasé really to understand what is happening. The

---

\* For the original music to this song, see pages 263–267.

more frightening the scene, the funnier Thespis' unawareness will appear.

The last dialogue scene comprises a meeting and a series of humorous interviews. The effect of the scene depends primarily on the effect of the three minor characters who dominate it. For the rest, crowd reactions to what is happening are most important and should be carefully rehearsed. This is the sort of thing that tends to be put off until the last minute and consequently is sloppy in performance.

The finale offers a wonderful opportunity for the choreographer. The first part of it involves moving large groups of people about the stage in stylized ways. Then there is the exchange between Thespians and gods, which offers an opportunity for genuine ballet. Following is Jupiter's curse, which should be delivered from the highest point on the stage and should be extremely frightening. Finally, there is Thespis' solo, which gives the entire company another opportunity to join together imitating railroad engines, a suitably irrelevant ending for a delightfully absurd entertainment.

## COSTUMES AND SCENERY

The fact that the costumes are basically Greek robes should not be allowed to hamper the costumer and prevent him from recognizing character differences. The text is full of anachronisms, and these should be reflected in the costuming. Time and again the basic Greek robe can be adapted into something with more modern connotations. Preposteros can wear a black robe and a top hat. Apollo's dressing gown and smoking cap over his robe offer a clue to the dressing of the other gods. Perhaps only Mercury should look exactly like the mythological figure.

The scenery is fully described in the printed text, and little need be added here. Bear in mind that Gilbert was thinking in terms of realism, whereas a production of *Thespis* today should concentrate on fantasy. If the budget allows, three-dimensional mountains and columns will enable the stage director to move his actors about vertically in interesting ways. If the budget is limited, *Thespis* can be effective with a simple backdrop or simply with a well-lighted cyclorama or blue curtain.

Chapter V

# TRIAL BY JURY

## PRODUCTION NOTES

Of all the Gilbert and Sullivan operas, *Trial by Jury* is certainly the easiest to produce—not only because of its length, but also because it has a small cast and simple setting and costumes. Furthermore, it is bound to be successful with audiences, as it is a perfect one-act operetta.

It is frequently produced on the same bill with one of the shorter two-act operas, such as *Pinafore* or *The Pirates of Penzance*. On the other hand, it may be produced along with a one-act play by a company of modest resources, perhaps having its first experience with a musical play.

Although twelve jurors are required by English law, many small productions get away with only six or seven. It is also possible to eliminate the Public from the chorus, and to have the Bridesmaids sit on one side of the stage from the beginning rather than make their entrance later. Thus, the entire cast might be made up of fifteen people. In a larger production, the cast might run as high as fifty people.

If one has an auditorium available, it is possible to produce *Trial by Jury* with almost no expense. The jury box and the judge's bench are the only essential pieces of scenery aside from chairs, and can be put together quite simply either with cardboard and lumber, or with the tops of large folding tables. The Bridesmaids may wear formal dresses, the Jury ordinary business suits with lapels and collars adapted to look Victorian, and the legal officials can wear choir robes. Wigs can be made from cotton. If each member of the group pays for his own music, there should be no expense at all.

## CRITICAL DISCUSSION

It is sometimes possible to reveal through humor a reality that would be unbearably frightening if taken seriously. Trial by jury is regarded as a basic constitutional right and one of the chief guarantees of justice in our society. We like to ignore the inequities of the system and to think of the occasional miscarriages of justice that come to our attention as anomalies. But the system depends on the human beings that make it up, and the influences to which those human beings are susceptible are brilliantly satirized in this opera.

The opening chorus sets the stage for what is thought of more as an entertainment than as a legal process: "Hearts with anxious fears are bounding." The Usher gets things started by telling the Jury to lay prejudice aside and to condole with the Plaintiff and condemn the Defendant. Small wonder, then, that the appearance of the Defendant is greeted with cries of "Monster." The Defendant quite properly points out that the Jury as yet has no basis on which to judge him. He then relates an experience that everyone has had—that of tiring of one lover and falling in love with someone else instead. The Jury, in chorus, admit that they have all behaved in the same way, but that having reformed themselves, they condemn this sort of behavior in others.

In the action so far recounted we find an interesting, and indeed profound, moral statement. Both the Usher and the Jury have admitted inconsistencies in their behavior and committed themselves to hypocrisy. Only the Defendant has acted honestly and spoken of the events in his life exactly as they have occurred. Yet it is the Defendant who is on trial, and the

*Richard Walker as the Usher quiets the Jury in* Trial by Jury. *Jury: "Monster, dread our damages, we're the jury, dread our fury!"*                    (*D'Oyly Carte production*)

others who set themselves up as standards against which he should be measured. The topsy-turvydom of the opera has a topsy-turvy morality. Yet, when we consider the hypocrisies of Victorian society, and to a lesser extent our own, we recognize that this topsy-turvy morality is in fact the one according to which we often operate.

If we examine the music that accompanies this opening scene, we find that Sullivan has brilliantly reinforced the moral impressions noted above. The opening chorus, with its suggestion of a crowd scurrying into the courtroom, and its rhythmic accentuation that suggests the ticking of a clock, also manages to set the scene for a festive occasion, rather than a serious one. This might be a crowd at a circus or a theatre. The Usher's music is both pompous and devious. The use of musical phrases to interrupt the flow of the words contrasts with the ongoing drive of the opening chorus and suggests that the Usher is carefully calculating his words. His "Silence in Court!" sung over the chorus refrain of his own words indicates the importance he really attaches to those words.

The music that introduces the Defendant is dramatic and exciting, the first suggestion we have had that something important and serious is about to happen. The contrast in the Defendant's recitative between his romantic vocal line and the chorus' ominous one is one of the most brilliant examples of Sullivan's clever use of recitative for subtle characterization. The Defendant's song is an obviously sentimental melody, suitable for a love song, and beautifully contrasts the chorus' judgment of him as a character with the composer's. The chorus of Jurymen that follows has all the stealth and suggestion of guilt that we have been led to expect in the Defendant. Note that in the first section of this chorus the predominantly descending vocal line suggests stealth, whereas in the second, though the music is almost the same, there is a shift to the major and an upward leap in pitch at about the middle of each line that suggests respectability. And yet the close relationship musically between the two sections indicates just how thin the veneer of respectability is. The degree of responsibility felt by the chorus is indicated by the gay little tune with which they return to their Jury box, and by the adaptation of "tra-la-la" into "trial-la-law," one of Gilbert's finest puns.

When the Judge enters, we suddenly have a ceremonial occasion. We are given ceremonial music to match: "All hail great Judge!" is pure

Handel, and the sort of music Handel composed for State occasions. Simple enough thus far, but the same music flows effortlessly into the Judge's request for the court's attention and the court's refusal to give him that attention, they are so busy shutting each other up—surely among the funniest musical effects ever achieved.

The Judge's autobiographical song might be seriously studied as the key to success for any aspiring young lawyer. Certainly his ethic is close to that of the average lawyer:

> All thieves who could my fees afford
>   Relied on my orations,
> And many a burglar I've restored
>   To his friends and his relations.

The entrance of the Bridesmaids brings into the courtroom the pure romance so often found in the early scenes of Italian opera, but the effect of such music in this setting is humorous indeed. Although the Bridesmaids attempt to cheer up the Plaintiff, she indicates all too clearly that she doesn't need cheering up, and for sound philosophical reasons. One gets tired of too much beauty and enjoyment in life. A little tragedy is necessary to keep things interesting. Thus Gilbert has compounded the ludicrousness of the scene, as we have the triple effect of the romantic music, the stern courtroom setting, and philosophical sentiments that we doubt could ever issue from the mouth of any disappointed young bride-to-be.

In the following interplay between Judge, Jury, and Plaintiff, the music becomes as flirtatious as the words and actions, and it is immediately clear that the Plaintiff will have no trouble finding another man from among those present. It is an excellent foil for the Counsel's song with its melodramatic words and music, painting the tragedy of disappointed love in grotesque and then ludicrously inappropriate literary terms.

The reaction that follows is expressed in sorrowful vocal lines mocked by an accompaniment as sprightly and flirtatious as anything that has preceded. The chorus rise in fury against the Defendant, and once again we have a moment of truth. To music of the greatest unconcern, he explains that it is quite natural to vary in one's taste with the passage of time. He offers a compromise: He will marry the Plaintiff if he is also allowed to marry her successor in his affections. The Judge thinks this an excellent suggestion, but the Counsel, who is somewhat better acquainted with the law, sings, to a tune appropriate for a national anthem, of the criminal implications of such an action.

In the number that follows the entire cast sing, to music that reminds one of the ensemble "D'un pensiero," from *La Sonnambula,* of the dilemma in which they now find themselves. It is a beautiful irony that the one moment of serious and indeed tragic concern in the entire score arises from an actual confrontation with the law. It seems that the law is a somewhat unwelcome guest in this courtroom.

To the Plaintiff's plea of disappointed love, the Defendant replies with stern realism that he will surely thrash and kick her under the influence of liquor. The wild energy of this music rises toward a climax after the mock seriousness of what has preceded it. Everyone except the Judge is shocked by Edwin's truthfulness about himself, but the Judge, being a practical man, wishes to put the matter to a test. When everyone objects, he brings the affair to an abrupt conclusion by offering to marry the Plaintiff himself. Surely the Defendant's proposal of marriage was not more headstrong or hasty than this, and we can smile with him as he wonders how the marriage will work out. We learn, however, that the Judge may not be much at the law, but that he is an excellent judge of beauty, which is, after all, what really counts in the world.

## CHARACTER SKETCHES

### The Learned Judge

This is the most demanding singing role in the opera, and it is extremely effective when, as rarely happens, the performer sings the music exactly as written. The voice should be an attractive high baritone with the capacity to express humor and to project words clearly. As an actor, the Judge needs two qualities. One is dignity (he is not as pompous as the Usher, nor as dramatic as the Counsel, but he does set the tone of the proceedings). The other is flirtatiousness. Much of his pantomime involves flirting with the First Bridesmaid, and then with the Plaintiff. He is very calm and even dry as the situation unfolds, until finally his temper is aroused, and in a single outburst he throws his books and papers about. Since he spends his entire time until the finale sitting at his bench, he must act primarily with his face and hands. During the finale he skips about among

the various soloists, which is simple enough to require no special dancing ability. A great deal of the effectiveness of the Judge will depend on the way he is made up. If his face conveys a combination of aged dignity and puckish humor, half of the acting is already accomplished.

### The Plaintiff

It is quite possible to be an effective Angelina with no acting ability whatever, provided one is beautiful and can sing well. All that is required is to flirt outrageously with every male character except the Defendant and to sob effectively on any breast that is handy. The drama of "I love him" is accomplished simply by tugging the Defendant across the stage. That is not to say that acting will be wasted on this part, as there is opportunity for graceful gesture and melodramatic emotion. One should, however, consider singing ability first in casting the role.

### The Defendant

In some respects this is the most difficult acting role in the opera, as one must convey a good-humored ironic understanding of the situation. He must simultaneously seem hateful to the Jury and likable to the audience. He must be attractive, debonair, and carefree, capable of melting the hearts of the Bridesmaids. It is an advantage to him to be able to dance well, though this is not necessary. He should have a pleasing tenor voice, though only limited demands are made on his vocal range. In general, he should be able to contrast his own performance with those of all the other actors without unduly drawing attention to himself.

### Counsel for the Plaintiff

The Counsel is authoritative and emotional without being as pompous as the Usher, nor as dignified as the Judge. He is the intellectual in the group, understanding, as he does, both the law and the means to sway an audience. He should spend considerable time with his law books, in consultation with the Associate. Of all the characters, he is the most serious and commanding. He should have a good baritone voice, capable of emotion, and more lyric than that of the Judge. Although his solo is very musical, he can project it enough with strong acting so that the audience will not notice if his voice is somewhat unmusical.

### Usher

This is a bass-baritone part with a relatively wide range. He should be a large, pompous, commanding personality, somewhat lower class in appearance than the other characters. He is completely humorless in his constant attempts to keep order in the court. He is one of those people who are so class-conscious that they are always either subservient or domineering. When the Judge gives him an order, he rushes to carry it out, but he orders the Jury about with a pompous lack of reserve.

### Foreman of the Jury

The Jury have many important pieces of comic business, and the foreman takes the lead in them. Thus, though he has only a few solo lines, he can make quite an impression in the part. He thoroughly enjoys everything that he has to do, from excessive flirtation with the Plaintiff to vigorous denunciation of the Defendant. He will determine, to a large extent, the success of the rest of the Jury, as he will be most easily seen by the audience and the Jury alike, and much of their more subtle comic business will develop as a result of watching him.

### Associate

Gilbert considered this role important enough to play it himself. The Associate is seated directly beneath the Judge's bench, and can thus have an important part in the action, although he has nothing to sing. He may be constantly referring to the law books piled up on his desk, and may advise the Counsel in a manner that suggests that he is the brains behind what the Counsel does.

### First Bridesmaid

She is simply a member of the chorus. She should be attractive enough to capture the fancy of the Judge, and able to express in pantomime her discontent when she is asked to return the note the Usher has given her from the Judge.

### The Jury

These are all smartly dressed young men who take pride in their moral superiority to the De-fendant. They are charming and somewhat disorganized. All their action is performed with gusto. This makes it difficult for the Usher to keep them under control, and much comic business results from his attempts to do so.

### The Bridesmaids

Six or more beautiful maidens who react to the Defendant much as the Jury react to the Plaintiff. They have less to do than the Jury, and decorum prevents them from being quite as demonstrative in their actions, but they should keep their attention on the action and react to it consistently.

### The Public

This group may be omitted if the Bridesmaids are present at the rise of the curtain. Or they may be of any size desired. No specific action is required of them, so they must simply be alert to what is going on. They provide an opportunity for interesting variety of costume, although if too much attention is drawn to them they will distract from more important characters. They should be rehearsed carefully enough so that they function as a unit rather than as individuals who distract from one another and from the central action.

### Notes on Staging

*Trial by Jury* can be staged in relatively few rehearsals if the entire company is cooperative and the director efficient. There is little movement of groups, and most of the staging is confined to moments of business that underline the comic effect of the words. In the discussion that follows, we shall describe virtually all the business that might be used in a particular production, with the understanding that each individual director will wish to vary it according to his tastes. It is particularly important that the business be smoothly handled and not draw the audience's attention away from the words and music. Also, one should avoid using so many bits of business that they tend to cancel out one another's effectiveness.

The curtain rises on an empty stage. The Usher enters, pulls out his watch, crosses the stage, pulls out a key, and lets in the public. Then he crosses to the jury box and brings down his staff in such a manner that the entire Jury rise up out of their box (in which they have been concealed) just in time to sing the

*Joseph Riordan as the Defendant in* Trial by Jury: *"Tink-a-tank."*

(*D'Oyly Carte production*)

first note of the opening chorus. A few gestures may be used during the chorus to pantomime the words, but this is not necessary as the chorus is effective without any action at all. On the last two chords the Usher motions for the Jury to sit, which they do by going up on tiptoe and sittting down exactly together. The Usher then moves to the center of the stage, waddling in time to his music. He sings his first verse at the center, rushing first toward the Public and then toward the Jury on his "Silence in Court!" The second and third verses begin as asides to the Jury, but on "From bias free" the Usher rushes back to the center again, waving his arms as if arousing the crowd to excitement. At the end of his solo, he waddles backwards in time to the music, so that he is standing between the witness stand and the Public. This allows the Defendant to rush in on the faster music that follows.

The Defendant runs in, carrying a guitar. He addresses the Jury, who nod in unison as they sing. His next line may, for the sake of clarity, be changed to "Be firm, my heart resplendent." He stands in the center of the stage gesturing outward and up. The Jury lean forward on "Who are you?" and the Defendant turns again toward them. They rise, shaking their fists at him. On "permit me to remark," he snaps his fingers under the nose of the Foreman and then crosses the stage.

It is useful to introduce another character into the cast, who may be called the Other Woman. If she is present, the Defendant greets her at this point and remains with her while the Jurymen skip out of the jury box and line up across the front of the stage. The Defendant then tunes his guitar and strums it as he sings the verse of his song. At the end of the verse, he hands the guitar to one of the Jurymen, who continues to strum it while he waltzes in front of the Jurymen with the Other Woman. The other Jurymen do a simple dance step in pairs, facing one another. At the end of his song, the Defendant sits among the Public with the Other Woman, and the Jurymen sing their chorus. They remain lined up across the front of the stage. Each line has a gesture appropriate to it. They may do these in perfect unison. It is amusing if there is one Juryman who is constantly getting things wrong, a little fellow at the end of the line. At the end, when they all point to the Defendant, this Juryman finds his face covered by the arm of the person next to him and flings the arm down in anger.

Beginning with "He shall treat us with awe," the Jurymen raise alternate hands above their heads and snap their fingers in rhythm, smiling broadly. They just have time during the music that follows to skip back in to the jury box and sit on the last chord. At the Usher's command to "bend," he himself bends. Everyone else stands together facing the Judge's bench, arms extended toward it, pointing with the full palm. The arrangement of the arms should be uniform. The Judge enters unceremoniously during the second verse of the chorus and arranges the books and papers on his desk before beginning to sing. At the conclusion of the chorus, they all sit together, and the Usher unbends.

The Judge looks gracious at first, but as he is interrupted he becomes more and more distressed until finally he puts his hands over his ears and his head down, where it remains until he begins his song. The chorus all nod to one another during "He'll tell us how," as if discussing the matter among themselves.

The Judge's song requires a few simple gestures that the chorus may imitate on their refrain. During the chords that introduce each new stanza, the Jurymen in the front row lean forward, placing their elbows on the box and their chins on their elbows. They switch arms once in rhythm, so that they are first looking toward the Judge and then toward the audience at the beginning of each stanza, then they sit back while the Judge sings.

After "The rich attorney my character high tried vainly to disparage," the entire chorus lean forward and say in unison, "No!" to which the Judge replies "Yes," and they then lean back to their normal positions.

When the Counsel enters, he stands next to the table that is directly beneath the Judge's bench. The Associate is seated at that table. It is possible to have the Associate enter preceding him. It is also possible to have the Associate enter preceding the Judge. A third possibility is to have the Associate enter at the very beginning, yawn, and fall asleep. The Counsel can then awaken him when he enters. The Counsel sits following his opening line and confers with the Associate or studies the law books.

During the music that precedes the Usher's solo, he directs the Jury with his hands. They rise slowly, in time to the music, coming to a full standing position on the penultimate note, and then kneel so that they all disappear into the jury box. When they begin to sing, they raise their hands, and only their arms can be seen extending above the jury box. The Usher is dissatisfied with the positions of their arms, and uses his staff to straighten them. On their last note they all rise and sit together, except for the little fellow at the end of the line, who remains standing. The Usher whispers to him grumpily, "Sit down!"

The Counsel stands and commands the Usher to call the Plaintiff. The Usher crosses down in front of the jury box and sings "Angelina" out toward the audience. The Defendant is now inconspicuously placed at the back of the stage with his back to the audience, and he sings the echo. Everyone looks everywhere to see where the echo is coming from. The Usher takes a different position, calls "Angelina" again, and again the echo answers. This time, however, the echo cannot reach the lowest note, and the Usher points to the Defendant and sings it for him. Everyone is delighted to discover the source of the echo.

It will be easy enough to find a simple step for the Bridesmaids to enter on. They carry bouquets of flowers, which might be joined with ribbon, so that as they form a semicircle they are all joined together. Simple gestures and very little movement are adequate for this chorus, as the main interest during it is the affair between the Judge and the First Bridesmaid. Immediately upon her entrance he discovers her, waves to her, and writes her a note. This he gives to the Usher, who attaches it to the end of his staff, creeps around behind the Bridesmaids, and offers it to her. She reads it, waves ecstatically to the Judge, kisses it, and places it in her bosom. About that time the Plaintiff enters. The Judge discovers her and waves to her. Then he instructs the Usher, using obvious gestures, to retrieve the note from the First Bridesmaid and give it to Angelina. The First Bridesmaid does not part with the note easily. She pretends at first not to understand. Then she throws the note on the floor. As the Usher attempts to pick it up, she stamps on his fingers. Finally he gets it to the Plaintiff, who responds to it exactly as the First Bridesmaid did.

At the end of the chorus, the Bridesmaids seat themselves in front of the Public. Gilbert's original stage directions called for Angelina to collect the flowers and distribute them among the Jury, who would then wear them. He assumed, however, that the chorus would be repeated, and as it is not, there is no time for that action.

During the following short scene, Angelina is busy making the acquaintance of the Jury. "Ah, sly dog!" calls for the shaking of forefingers from everyone who sings it. All members of the Jury extend both arms to Angelina as they sing, "We love you fondly." They rise, shaking their fists on "Monster," and have to be silenced by the Usher. Angelina remains downstage of the jury box. The Defendant is with the Other Woman, and both of them enjoy the Jury's anger immensely.

The Counsel bows to the Judge and the Jury. As he sings his song, he gradually draws the Plaintiff into it, and her melodramatic gestures reinforce the pathos of his words and gestures. At the end of the song, she is sobbing on his breast. He comforts her, as does the Usher also, so that she is alternately sobbing on their two breasts. The Counsel leads her to the witness box. She stands there looking as if she is going to faint. When the Foreman offers comfort, she runs across the stage to him. When the Judge offers his help, she rushes up to join him on his bench. When the Counsel calls for perfumed water, the Usher decides he means a glass of tap water, and rushes out to get it. The chorus rise again in anger, but the Defendant calmly gestures to them to sit down.

During the Defendant's song, all but the Bridesmaids pull out newspapers and proceed to read them. The Judge and Plaintiff share a newspaper. Halfway through the first verse, the Usher rushes in with the glass of water, which he hands to the Judge. The Judge tastes it, finds it not very good, empties it on the Associate, hands the glass back to the Usher, and returns to the newspaper. The Usher exits with the empty glass and then returns to the courtroom, where he peers at one of the Jurymen's newspapers. During the refrain, the Bridesmaids all kneel center stage, gesturing to the Jury, who put down their newspapers. The Judge, too, tries to enjoy the Bridesmaids, but the Plaintiff pulls him back behind the newspaper.

During the music that introduces the Judge's recitative, the Plaintiff climbs down off the Judge's bench. The Counsel responds to the Judge's suggestion by hastily going through several books, along with the Associate, until the Associate points out the passage he is looking for. He reads from the book and then hands the book to the Judge, who looks perplexed. When the Counsel finishes "that we can settle it," the Judge, who has been following his words with great interest, allows the book to slip from his hands, so that it falls on the Associate's head. There is no stage action whatever during the "nice dilemma" ensemble. Following it, the Defendant leaves the witness box and crosses the

*Jennifer Toye as the Plaintiff and John Reed as the Judge in* Trial by Jury. *Judge:
"Though homeward as you trudge you declare my law is fudge, yet of beauty I'm a
judge."* (D'Oyly Carte production)

stage toward the Other Woman, but the Plaintiff catches him halfway and drags him about. At the beginning of his verse, he flings her on the floor, and on the words "perhaps I should kick her," pretends to do so. When his verse is finished, the Plaintiff rises, and the two of them struggle, center stage, until the number is over.

The score contains three notes preceding the Judge's next recitative. At this point he should pound his gavel. If a piano accompaniment is used, these notes should not be played. On the successive objections, each person rises, in turn until the whole chorus rises together. Now the Judge stands up at his bench and throws his books and papers around. There should be a shower of papers in the air all the time he is singing this section. On the chorus "ah!" the Judge comes down off the bench and embraces the Plaintiff, center stage. From this point on the entire chorus is standing. The Usher is in front of the jury box and the Counsel next to him. The Judge is center, with the Plaintiff next to him. Next to her (but not too close) is the Defendant. During the chorus and repeat, "Oh joy unbounded," the Judge takes the corners of his robe in his hands, extends his arms, and skips merrily around, weaving in and out among the soloists, arriving back at his proper position in time for his solo.

Gilbert's original stage directions for the end run as follows: "Judge and Plaintiff dance back, hornpipe step, and get on to the Bench—the Bridesmaids take the eight garlands of roses from behind Judge's desk and draw them across floor of Court, so that they radiate from the desk. Two plaster Cupids in bar wigs descend from flies. Red fire. Five pans each side. One in each entrance—to be lighted when gong sounds."

These staging ideas are almost invariably omitted from modern productions, but they are well worth considering. If, on the first embrace of the Judge and Plaintiff, two Cupids suddenly drop into place in midair, the effect is very funny and likely to draw applause from the audience. The air of fantasy that would result from following all of Gilbert's ideas at the end would add a real flourish to the finale and make an exciting final curtain.

## COSTUMES AND SCENERY

Costuming *Trial by Jury* is simple. If one wishes to be completely authentic, one uses standard Victorian clothing for the Public and the Jury, and the appropriate robes, wigs, and collars for the Judge, Counsel, and Associate. The Usher wears robe and collar, but no wig. He carries a staff of about his own height.

If we view left and right from the audience point of view, the scenery is arranged as follows. The jury box is left, the Judge's bench upstage center, with the table for the Associate and Counsel directly in front of it. Right of the Judge's bench, and slightly forward from it, is the witness box. On the right is a box for the Public, similar to the jury box. In front of this, there are chairs for the Bridesmaids. The Defendant and the Other Woman may also sit in this area. If the set is realistic, there is little decoration except paneling. Above the Judge's bench is a coat of arms. The quill pens on the Judge's bench and the Associate's desk add a note of elegance. The courtroom may or may not contain windows. It usually does not contain a clock, despite the fact that as the opera opens the clock is striking ten.

# Chapter VI

# THE SORCERER

PRODUCTION NOTES

Both dramatically and musically, *The Sorcerer,* being an early collaboration of its authors, is relatively easy to produce. The greatest challenge is offered by the scenery and the lighting effects, which can be spectacular. Spectacle is not essential, however, as *The Sorceror* can be pleasantly entertaining in a simple production.

The key scenes from the production standpoint are the Incantation Scene and the disappearance of Mr. Wells at the end of Act Two. The Incantation Scene benefits from eerie lighting with occasional flashes of brightness, and from the use of ballet as the sprites of earth and air make their appearance. Gilbert's intention was that the love philter should be brewed in a teapot, and if Mr. Wells is characterized successfully enough as a cockney tradesman, the contrast between his appearance with the teapot in his hand and the weird effects taking place around him can be amusing. If the contrast is not to be played fully, it may be that the philter should be brewed in a more spectacular way. A punch bowl placed on a stump with light coming through its bottom, and containing liquid that changes color as various chemicals are poured into it, together with dry ice to make it pour forth "smoke," can add greatly to the fantasy of the scene.

Mr. Wells's final exit should be made through a trapdoor in the center of the stage. If the stage has no trapdoor, some alternative must be found. Mr. Wells may simply walk offstage during a brief blackout, perhaps with accompanying thunderclaps, smoke bombs, and the like. It is also possible to cut a hole in the backdrop and have a door open through it with red light behind and blackout in front. Other more elaborate devices may occur to the enterprising technical director.

For the rest, the production requires a Victorian atmosphere with good, though relatively simple, character acting. Both musically and dramatically, the work of the chorus is probably easier than that demanded by any of the other full-length operas. They have an excellent scene near the beginning of the second act in which they must act and dance effectively. The rest of the time that they are onstage the interest centers on the principal characters.

Care must be taken in the acting to distinguish between upper- and lower-class characters. The chorus are villagers, but most of the major characters pride themselves on their elegance compared to their surroundings. A good deal of the fun of the second act stems from placing dignified characters in undignified situations.

CRITICAL DISCUSSION

*The Sorcerer* is weaker in musical and dramatic satire than most of the other operas, perhaps because the magical element in the plot requires so much attention for its own sake. Although the love-philter plot is rather common in comic operas of the time, we do not find Gilbert parodying the traditional form so much as merely exemplifying it. The two major sources of satire in the piece are Dr. Daly, the vicar who seems to derive more distinction from his worldly loves than his godly ones, and Alexis, the fanatic who believes that all the world should share his particular brand of happiness. Mr. Wells, by contrast, is a comic rather than satirical figure. The love affair of Sir Marmaduke and Lady Sangazure is a splendid mixture of the sublime and the ridiculous. For the rest, we have primarily sentiment in the first act and situation comedy in the second act.

The music is almost entirely English in its effect, drawing little upon the European models that Sullivan so often used in other operas. Much of it is pleasant and fresh without being comical. There are, however, brilliant comic touches, mainly in the duet for Lady Sangazure and Sir Marmaduke, the song for Mr. Wells, and the Incantation Scene. Sullivan also uses counterpoint rather effectively in a number of places. Many of the songs are fine examples of the sentimental songs popular at the time, and are good enough to merit repeated hearings. Occasionally, however, Sullivan descends to the banal, as in Alexis' first-act solo, which should be omitted unless the singer who performs it is truly outstanding.

## CHARACTER SKETCHES

### Sir Marmaduke Pointdextre

This paragon of dignity and ancestral snobbery ("but where is the family, other than my own, in which there is no flaw?") is nevertheless capable of passion. He sets the tone of the whole opera, since if his dignity is compromised, much of the absurdity of the havoc wrought by Alexis is also lost. He should be an imposing, heavy man with a heavy bass-baritone voice that communicates character as well as tunefulness. Snobbery is second nature to him, and he thoroughly enjoys the sense of superiority he derives from it. This accounts for the gusto of which he is capable in his drinking song, and the ease with which he welcomes all the villagers to his mansion, certain that they look upon him as the source of all good in their village.

Sir Marmaduke is concerned that Alexis is too open in his expression of passion. Nevertheless, he is not prudish; he is concerned with decorum, with the manner in which passion is expressed, not the passion itself. Style is a great delight to him—he likes to do things exactly as they ought to be done, and that motivates the demonstration of proper lovemaking that is his duet with Lady Sangazure. In the second act when, under the influence of the potion, he is in love with Mrs. Partlet, there is the same love of style, all the more ridiculous now that it is contrasted with Mrs. Partlet's total lack of style. But there is an added warmth that suggests the potion may have made Sir Marmaduke just a touch more human.

### Alexis

This is in some respects the most difficult part in the opera. Vocally it is not terribly demanding, and a good strong A is the highest note needed. But the part requires an actor capable of giving charm to a basically unsympathetic character whose lines can be tedious if they are not well handled.

Alexis is a fanatic. He parodies the ardor of the Bolshevik or the social reformer so common in the serious drama of the late nineteenth century. He believes that true love experienced by everyone would break down all the artificial barriers in the world. He is narrow-minded and completely blind to the consequences of his logic. Nor does he accept responsibility for what he brings about, since when, at his insistence, Aline drinks the potion and falls in love with Dr. Daly, he blames her as if she had been willingly unfaithful.

It is ironic that Alexis, who is so convinced of the perfection of the love he shares with Aline that he wishes all others to share that same love, should find their love in need of improvement from the elixir. Like many fanatics, he places his principles above the reality of the situation and allows himself to be destroyed by his unwillingness to compromise. It is through Alexis that this opera rises to the level of social commentary, as the elixir of love becomes a symbol for any panacea that is offered as a cure for social ills, and the comic mishaps that result from its use parallel the serious social ills that invariably follow too rigid an application of any particular doctrine of reform.

Alexis should be capable of a passion that can be taken seriously and still, through its superficiality, contrast with the more genuine love that Aline expresses. He should characterize the rashness of youth as it casts off the intellectual shackles of the older generation and forges its own shackles. He should contrast with each of the other characters with whom he has a scene, for in a different way he attempts to dominate each; with each of them, except Mr. Wells, who is in his employ, he finds some kind of fault.

### Dr. Daly

The vicar is genuinely lovable. He has two beautiful songs, the music of which cannot fail to win us over. His confused love for Aline in the second act makes him something of a tragic figure as he confronts the vengeful Alexis. In the first act we feel Constance's love for him and his pathetic failure to see it because he believes he is too much of an old fogey for her. There is genuine nostalgia as he contemplates the great love he inspired in others in days gone by and reflects by implication that those days are no more. Yet he takes great pleasure in contemplating the happiness of others. The only quality he has that is less than admirable is his circuitousness of thought. His blessing of Alexis' coming happiness is a delightful collection of clerical clichés. All of these qualities combine to make his confusion, when the whole village approaches him in a body and asks him to marry them, something whimsically delightful to contemplate without being the least cutting in its humor.

The part requires a warm, light baritone voice with a strong high F-sharp. The most attractive music in the opera is his, and the quality of his singing will tend to set the musical tone of the whole production.

*Notary*

A small but delightful part. His bit with Constance in the second act is one of the highlights of the show. He must be capable of a low E-flat that can be clearly heard in order to make this scene effective. He has no spoken lines, and his part in the first act does little to develop his character, since he merely supervises the signing of the marriage contract.

*John Wellington Wells*

This is the first of the George Grossmith roles, and it can therefore be played by a comedian whose acting is superior to his singing, though the music is rewarding for anyone who has a good voice. The incongruity of a sorcerer who has a middle-class cockney businesslike manner and attire is one of the chief sources of humor in the opera. If he is a very good comedian with a quick, light delivery and a keen sense of timing, he will find it easy to play to play Wells as a typical shopman. If not, he may find it easier to concentrate on the more melodramatic aspects of his role and attempt to project an imposing, almost Mephistophelian figure.

Mr. Well's first song needs excellent diction and comic dance ability. The Incantation Scene requires more interpretive dancing and a feeling for improvisation. The scene with Lady Sangazure in the second act requires him to shift rapidly from one mood to another. The descent into Hell at the end of the opera should be handled with a combination of comedy and pathos that requires truly sensitive acting.

Mr. Wells takes great pride in his profession, and he is highly efficient. His shop is able to provide anything that may be required, but like most tradesmen he is well aware that some items sell better than others. He is proud of his business ethics ("We are not in the habit of puffing our goods"). His approach to the supernatural is extremely matter-of-fact. He knows exactly how everything will work, and it all works just as he plans it. Finally, his sense of fair play is tremendous. He does not wish to die because "it would not be fair on the Company." But when Aline points out that if Alexis dies she will be left without a lover, he cheerfully yields to the force of that argument.

*Mr. Wells's Page*

This character has three lines, two of which are "Yes, sir." If he is a cheerful young boy in a fancy costume who lisps, he should be able to get a laugh. In any case, his appearance should accord with the high standards of J. W. Wells and Company.

*Lady Sangazure*

This is the first of the aging contraltos that are so often objected to by critics of Gilbert's libretti. Lady Sangazure is a woman of dignity and passion. She has no spoken lines, two duets, and one recitative. Her recitative can be performed with enough feeling to suggest a tragic figure. The duet with Sir Marmaduke is brilliant in its alternation of passion and dignity, with the emphasis entirely on the dignity. The duet with Mr. Wells in the second act offers the opportunity for a good actress to make an outstanding impression. It should be a parody of operatic acting in the grandest style. It should, however, be parody that is approached seriously, so that it never descends to slapstick. If the audience is uncertain whether to laugh or cry, the effect will be intensified. Lady Sangazure should be capable of the broadest comedy without a hint of vulgarity. All the better if she happens to be larger than Mr. Wells. The fact that she is acting under the influence of a love potion will account for the extreme manner of her acting, which must not, however, be so intense as to violate the overall tone of the production.

*Aline*

Aline is perhaps the most sympathetic of all Gilbert's heroines. She is, throughout, the victim of Alexis' narrow-mindedness, yet she never complains or wavers in her love for him, strong as her misgivings are. It is important that she have a good voice, as her opening solo, her love duet with Alexis, and the song during which she drinks the love potion provide excellent opportunities for beautiful singing. Since she has no opportunities for comedy, little is required of her in the way of acting, and almost any pretty girl with a fine voice can do the part adequately. She is perhaps the only character in the opera who maintains the audience's unqualified sympathy throughout, and her second-act duet with Dr. Daly has enough pathos to make it a serious criticism of Alexis' fanaticism.

*Mrs. Partlet*

This role is confined to one scene in each act, but Mrs. Partlet is the focal point of interest much of the time she is onstage, and a good actress can make a strong impression in the part. Like Lady Sangazure, she is an aging woman, but she should contrast with her as much as possible in style and manners, as she is lower class and should appear incongruous as a lover for Sir Marmaduke. She is warm and loving, and in her attempts to marry off her daughter she reminds one a little of one of Jane Austen's characters. There should be a suggestion of cockney in her speech.

*Constance*

She, like Aline, has little opportunity for genuine acting, though there is some good comic business in the second act with the Notary, and consequently she should be the better actress of the two. Her two songs are good but less vocally demanding than Aline's. She is young, pretty, and lovesick. Her melancholy shyness contrasts strongly with Mrs. Partlet's down-to-earth aggressiveness, and one feels that she is completely dependent on her mother.

*The Chorus*

Although men and women sing separately at times, there is no particular distinction between them. They are simple villagers whose manners contrast with those of the more elegant characters. Their best scene is near the beginning of the second act when they awaken and discover the effects of the love potion. Here they lapse into a cockney accent, and their rustic quality (perhaps under the influence of the potion) is much stronger than during the rest of the opera. Their Country Dance can be one of the high points of the show if it is well handled. Since they are not fully themselves during it, the dance should be parody and accentuate their rusticity. The rest of the time they are observers of the action, looking up to and admiring the main characters or joining with them in the festivities.

NOTES ON STAGING

*The Sorcerer* makes fewer demands on the imagination of the stage director than any of the other operas because it is so simple. Almost every number is either obvious in its melodramatic qualities or perfectly straightforward. The director who wishes to be highly creative should probably avoid *The Sorcerer,* as its many ballads would only be less effective if handled in other than an obvious way. In the discussion that follows we shall hit only the high points, assuming that such numbers as "Time was when love and I" and "When he is here" do not require discussion. In Part II in the chapter on singing and acting, the general philosophy of how such numbers should be handled will be discussed.

The curtain rises on "the end of a large marquee, open, and showing portion of table covered with white cloth, on which are joints of meat, teapots, cups, bread and butter, jam, etc." Several of the women should be grouped around this table, putting the finishing touches on the banquet. Other women stand apart watching and talking to the men, all of whom are watching. For added effect extras dressed in livery might enter carrying elaborate dishes of food. Much of the business around the table should take place before the chorus begins to sing, however, since the chorus should direct their attention primarily to the ringing of the bells while they are singing. Variety of staging can be achieved by having various small groups walk across the stage half talking to one another, half directing their attention out toward the audience. The stage directions call for the men to exit into Sir Marmaduke's mansion; however, there is no particular dramatic reason for this, and crowding the men all through one exit will slow the exit down considerably. Since no exit music is given the men, they should leave as unobtrusively as possible during the entrance of Mrs. Partlet and Constance. A few of the women might wave good-bye with their handkerchiefs, but the scene should quickly settle down to attention on Mrs. Partlet. At the end of her recitative, she motions for the women to exit, and they should also do so unobtrusively, stepping offstage by the nearest exit.

During the dialogue that follows Constance's song, Mrs. Partlet and her daughter should be on one side of the stage, leaving most of the stage area for Dr. Daly, who enters slowly, musing. The long idyllic introduction to his recitative offers an excellent opportunity for comedy. If one or two birds on wires are flown across the stage, Dr. Daly can watch them and sigh deeply, feeling his apartness from spring and what it represents. Otherwise, he may merely cup his hand to his ear, listening to the music in the air and making a slight attempt to trace its source. Here is his opportunity to display the passionate side of his nature before he lapses into the melancholy that must accompany his singing.

In the dialogue following the song, Mrs. Partlet should have a determination that contrasts with her daughter's shyness as she accosts Dr. Daly. He consistently misinterprets her emotionalism and remains aloof, not out of disdain, but out of self-diminution. This gives particular humor to the scheming tone in which Mrs. Partlet utters her second "we will try again."

Sir Marmaduke and Alexis enter from the mansion. The recitative and minuet that follow parody the formal speech that is so different in style from that of Mrs. Partlet's class. Exaggerated gestures suitable to the pulpit might be used here, together with bowing and dignified walking. To attempt a dance during the minuet, however, would be going too far.

In the scene between Sir Marmaduke and Alexis the contrast between the former's down-to-earth practicality and the latter's romanticism should be sufficient to produce a laugh when Alexis says, "Oh rapture!" and Sir Marmaduke replies drily, "Yes." This scene needs an equal amount of energy from both characters, as Sir Marmaduke's pomposity is extremely energetic. The section beginning "Oh, my adored one!" is intended to be sung to music that is found on page 128 of the Cramer score, but should be transposed a fourth or a fifth down.

The chorus of girls that precedes Aline's entrance is one of those that so easily fall into the trap of the deadly semicircle. It is difficult to avoid this, as there is no action implied, nor is there any satirical point to the chorus. Furthermore, the idea is simply to greet the entrance of Aline. I would be quite natural for the girls to be interested in Alexis, however, and during the relatively long introduction two or three can run on, see him as he is leaving, and motion others to follow, so that they enter in clusters from various parts of the stage.

Remember that the attitude of the chorus toward Aline is one of awe because of her superior social class. Thus, when she enters they will not cluster too closely around her, but they may come up to her and curtsey. They will naturally be interested in her dress and the flowers she carries. As she walks slowly among them, they can look respectfully at her until she is past and then rush up behind her, attempting to feel the material of her dress. Perhaps only one is bold enough to do so, and the others attempt to prevent her. That would allow for some comedy, and would also make it possible to establish in pantomime Aline's forgiving nature, since when she discovers the attempt, she can perhaps draw the interested girl over to her, allow her to feel the material of her dress, and let her hold the flowers she carries. The others can then clamor around begging to hold them also. During the staccato section near the end of the chorus, the girls may have forgotten their fear and may have come quite close to Aline. Then, during the closing phrases of "Heaven bless our Aline," they can remember their manners and fade back into groups, curtseying as they go, and leave the center of the stage for Aline.

Aline's solo is quite straightforward, but one must not neglect the possibilities for pathos in the beautiful recitative that follows. Lady Sangazure enters slowly and draws Aline aside to a front corner of the stage. A change in the lighting to highlight this brief moment of melancholy will help to prevent the monotony of too much youthful rapture all at once. The recitative is a brilliant but unfortunately short means of suggesting the contrast between youth and age, which lends a tinge of irony to the proceedings. The director should make certain that its effect is not lost.

Alexis, for reasons that have more to do with operatic tradition than with the plot, is a member of the Grenadier Guards. The men's entrance will best contrast with the women's if they maintain strict military formation in honor of his uniform. Perhaps they could enter carrying picks and shovels. They could then form a double line facing one another and, holding these implements up at angles, form a bridge through which Alexis can make his entrance.

At the end of the chorus Lady Sangazure remains in her corner of the stage. Sir Marmaduke enters at the other corner. They gesture passionately toward each other, but then turn aside, concealing their passion. When this has been completed, Alexis and Aline should rush into each other's arms singing their recitative. The music for this is not in the Cramer score at this point, and must again be drawn from page 128, along with the musical accompaniment this time. The accompaniment ends with the single chord following "joy." The music must be transposed from the key of B-natural to B-flat.

Sir Marmaduke and Lady Sangazure meet center stage. He kisses her hand, bowing gracefully as he does so, on the trill preceding his solo. On "wild with adoration" he steps forward, facing the audience, and gestures passionately. Rutland Barrington, who created the role, had previously been known as an actor of melodrama, and one may be sure that his gestures were completely unrestrained at this point. According to theatrical convention, anything said or done during an "aside" represents what is passing through the character's mind and is not actually happening in a physical sense. The duet continues with the characters alternating between gracefully facing each other and expressing their passion aside to the audience. This number probably should receive an encore beginning with Lady Sangazure's solo. No attempt need be made to vary the staging for the encore, as it is the idea of the duet and not how it is handled that is most important. However, if the minuet is danced during the counterpoint section, with the characters alternately dancing and turning aside, it is possible to vary the dance step for the encore.

In the original libretto a distinction is made between a Counsel in the first act and a Notary in the second act, so it is possible that Gilbert originally had in mind two separate characters. At any rate, there is no opportunity during the signing of the marriage contract for the Notary to display any of the humorous characteristics he has later. The scene should be dignified pageantry and no more. Its function is to contrast a world of realistic legality with the spirit world of the Incantation Scene, in which an-

other kind of preparation is made, also having a bearing on the affections of Alexis and Aline.

The scene that follows is probably the weakest part of the libretto. We have as yet had very little action, and the time is ripe for the entrance of Mr. Wells. Instead, we are treated to an uninteresting ballad by Alexis and a good deal more talk than is necessary about love. Although there are a few amusing lines in this scene, anything that can be done to reduce its length will be helpful. For example, Aline's joke about the filter seems labored and pointless. Once Mr. Wells is onstage, all is well for the rest of the act. Martyn Green played the role with a furled umbrella not called for in the libretto, and found it made an excellent conjuring stick. With umbrella and top hat, Mr. Wells can engage, during his solo, in some entertaining dancing of the soft-shoe variety. In his dialogue with the two lovers that follows the song, he brings things rapidly down to earth with his businesslike tone, a tone that Alexis is quick to reflect in his own speeches.

During the Incantation Scene, Alexis and Aline need do very little. They simply stand together and react fearfully to the entrance of the sprites. Alexis attempts to comfort Aline, but he is frightened, too, as is evident when he joins her in the repetition of her aria. Mr. Wells, however, can dance wildly about with the sprites, carrying the teapot with him. There is a pan of flash powder on each side of the stage and one at the back of the stage. At the indication "flash" Mr. Wells holds the teapot over one of these pans and empties a phial into the tea as the stage manager ignites the flash. During the ballet work, Mr. Wells should always be the focal point, the sprites following him about, recognizing him as their master. His matter-of-factness even in dancing contrasts with their spookiness. At the end of the number they fade gradually offstage so that they are completely gone by the time the lights come up.

If the size of the company is limited, it may be necessary to have the chorus sing offstage while a few dancers perform the sprites. It is even possible to have the sprites immobile, popping up from behind walls and bushes with flashlights of various colors held under their chins. If this is done, the scene will require little rehearsal, as it becomes virtually a solo number for Mr. Wells.

At the beginning of the finale there is plenty of music during which the company may enter. Mr. Wells beckons the villagers, who come skipping in and gather round the table. Mrs.

Partlet and two or three others serve the food referred to in the song. By the time they begin to sing, the chorus are gathered in groups about the stage. Two or three folk dancers perform in the center of the stage while Mr. Wells and Mrs. Partlet distribute teacups. When the chorus is finished, there is enough music so that the entire company can execute a few steps of folk dancing before Sir Marmaduke takes the center of the stage. Beginning "Come, pass the cup round," Mr. Wells and Dr. Daly begin pouring tea for the villagers. This process is completed in time for Mr. Wells to join Alexis and Aline at the corner of the stage for "See—see—they drink." They should have a spotlight on them for this section, and the rest of the lighting should be dimmed. Then Dr. Daly takes the center of the stage, and the chorus, during their music, wave their cups in the air joyfully. Again the lighting dims, and a spot is on Alexis and Aline for their duet. They should remain absolutely stationary for this song, as any movement would spoil it. By the end of the song, the chorus no longer have their teacups, though we have not been permitted to see how they got rid of them.

For "Oh, marvellous illusion!" the spotlight dims down and the lights come up a little, but not full. The chorus begin to stagger around, rubbing their eyes and groping. Their movement is rather chaotic except that Mr. Wells, Aline, and Alexis are clearly set apart from them as they comment on the action. When the chorus begin their sixteenth notes they are once again stationary, and a beautiful tableau has been achieved. This is one of those ensemble numbers when we should simply listen to the music. At the end of the finale all except Alexis, Aline, and Mr. Wells fall insensible upon the stage.

In the original version of *The Sorcerer,* the second act opened with a sprightly chorus. This chorus is reprinted in the Appendix. The revised second-act opening is greatly superior, however. It is possible to combine the two versions by appending the chorus "Happy are we" at the end of the Country Dance, but it may be found that this gives the chorus too much to do all at once and provides a letdown in the dramatic tension of the opera.

Mr. Wells, Alexis, and Aline enter, stepping over the sleeping bodies. Mr. Wells carries a dim lantern. Alexis and Aline look about for people they know, so that they are some distance to either side of Mr. Wells when they ask him about their parents. The three are

*Martyn Green as John Wellington Wells in* The Sorcerer: *"He can raise you hosts of ghosts."*
(*D'Oyly Carte production*)

*John Dean as Alexis and Martyn Green as Mr. Wells in* The Sorcerer: *Mr. Wells: "Yes, sir, we practice necromancy in all its branches."* (D'Oyly Carte production)

together again during their ensemble, "And shown more delicate appreciation." Following this, a few villagers stir and stretch. Aline, Alexis, and Mr. Wells move backward upstage, preparing to tiptoe off as more of the villagers awaken.

The villagers are so arranged on the stage that each of them will discover a partner during the chords leading into the part they sing. It would be in keeping with Mr. Well's rather strict moral sense if the men and women awakened on opposite sides of the stage. During their two-measure musical interlude the more aggressive ones cross the stage to their partners, so that they are together in pairs for "Eh, what a nose." The lighting should gradually brighten during this part. The opening of the chorus, "If you'll marry me" is mimed. Folk dancing can begin on "All this will I du" as an introduction for the dance that follows.

The Country Dance should take into account the situation. All of the dancers have just fallen deeply and perplexedly in love. They are ill-matched pairs, but they don't allow that to bother them. They combine ecstasy with consideration for one another. During the early part of the dance they are still shy and unused to one another. As the dance continues they become bolder and more ecstatic. By the end their dancing should border on frenzy. Everything should contribute to make the scene happy so as to accentuate the sorrow of Constance's solo that follows.

The scene for Constance and the Notary should be humorous. She expresses passion in the manner of grand opera with wild gestures that differ markedly from her restraint in her first-act solo. The Notary staggers after her carrying an ear trumpet, trying desperately to hear her and every now and then catching a phrase that pleases him. His facial expressions are important in this scene. The chorus should stand and watch the action, reacting to it with face and gesture, always keeping the focus on the main characters.

When Alexis and Aline enter at the back, it is effective if they can be on a higher level than the other characters. This serves to project their voices better, and to symbolize their relationship to the rest of the action. On the "Oh, bitter joy!" ensemble a simple dance step may be executed by everyone except Aline and Alexis. This should be designed to keep all of the characters more or less in one place, as the words suggest a tableau effect rather than a further development of the action. At the end of the number all the characters dance offstage.

The scene for Alexis and Aline that follows is the most serious in the opera. The dialogue should be paced rapidly, and Alexis should be so overbearing and uncompromising in his demand that Aline drink the potion that she will have our entire sympathy when she finally does. Alexis's ballad expresses the passion not of love but of domination, and should be sung powerfully and almost angrily.

In the scene preceding the quintet we see the beginning of Alexis' undoing. The more charming and sentimental this scene, the better it will counteract the mood established in the preceding one. Although we can see the ridiculousness of the union between Sir Marmaduke and Mrs. Partlet, we should, for the moment, believe in their happiness. The singers position themselves for the quintet during the dialogue so that it is not necessary to move at all while they are singing, except to turn slightly to acknowledge each solo in turn. The soloist, of course, will use expressive gestures,

but should not walk about the stage other than to step forward a little if he prefers. The static staging for this number is appropriate to its character as an English part-song, and also helps to increase our delight in the extremely stagy number that follows.

During the original rehearsals of the "family vault" duet, Sullivan told the principals to imagine themselves singers of opera in the grand style with appropriately flamboyant gestures. The effect of the potion on Lady Sangazure is sufficient to justify intense and passionate gestures, so long as they are done seriously and without violation of her dignity. Mr. Wells reacts to her with the shocked concern appropriate in Victorian melodrama. So long as the actors do not suggest that they are making fun of the characters, they should ham things up as much as possible. It is not necessary to go into detail on the staging of this number, as the words and the music are so explicit. Suffice it to say that the two characters should frequently be on opposite sides of the stage, that there should be some attempt on Mr. Wells's part to sneak off while Lady Sangazure is not looking, that for his asides Mr. Wells should lean over the footlights and address the audience confidentially, that no dancing is needed except possibly at the very end, and that at the end Lady Sangazure chases Mr. Wells off the stage after gesturing menacingly at him.

For Aline's drinking of the philter a cup has been left onstage previously by Alexis during the scene in which he asked her to drink it. Perhaps this cup can be specially lighted or have smoke pouring out of it. As she enters, Aline appears transfixed by the cup, toward which she slowly moves. This is more dramatic than having her enter with it. As she drinks the philter, the stage should become dim, and there should be a spotlight on her. This dim lighting is maintained until the next entrance of the chorus.

Gilbert's directions call for Aline to "meet Dr. Daly." She should not actually meet him, as he must not see her until the end of his solo. But as he sings she should express in gesture her growing passion for him. She must be careful to do so in a way that makes the point without distracting from his solo. The only problem with Dr. Daly's song is that he should play the flageolet solo himself if he can. He should end the solo at the corner of the stage most distant from where Aline is standing, so that they can rush into each other's arms center stage. They

The Sorcerer: *Finale of Act Two. Mr. Wells is about to yield up his life to Ahrimanes in order to break the spell of the love potion.* (*D'Oyly Carte production*)

should be together for their duet until the last few phrases, at which time they should separate enough so that Alexis on his entrance can fail to take note of Dr. Daly's presence. If during the duet they walk about the stage arm in arm and turn toward each other, gesturing passionately, it is quite credible that their passion can carry them apart momentarily. Thus, Aline is center stage and Dr. Daly to one side as Alexis enters at the other side. She recoils from Alexis and then, on the words, "I lov'd the very first I saw!" returns to Dr. Daly's arms. On his denunciation of Aline, Alexis is center stage, but he rushes upstage to call the chorus in on both sides. The entire company enter, but should be kept as far upstage as possible, so that the focus can remain on the three central characters. It is possible to bring people forward during the dialogue section that precedes the finale.

We come now to the problem of Mr. Wells's descent into Hell. We have already discussed alternatives to the descent through the trapdoor. In the D'Oyly Carte production, Mr. Wells took off his hat, pulled out a handkerchief, and wiped his brow and hatband. He then listened to his watch and wound it. He took off his shoes and arranged them neatly on the stage. As he descended through the trap he tossed up behind him a few calling cards and then carefully pulled on his white kid gloves. Sir Henry Lytton, at the end of his farewell performance, did not appear for a curtain call, but instead held up above the flames a sign that read, "Come down and see me sometime!"

The end of the second act can be handled much as the same material is handled at the end of the first act. Unfortunately the last two bars of chorus music do not make a very effective ending, and Edmond Rickett provided with his orchestration (rented by Schirmer) a few bars to replace them. The words for this new ending were, "the eggs and the ham and the strawberry jam, the strawberry, strawberry jam!" The last two "straw's" and "jam" were on sustained high notes, which gave the finale a flourish at the end much more in character with Sullivan's other second-act finales. If the orchestration in question is not used, it should be easy enough for anyone with musical training to supply a similar one.

## COSTUMES AND SCENERY

The visual demands of *The Sorcerer* are moderate. The setting is contemporary with the first production in 1877. Sir Marmaduke, Lady Sangazure, and Aline must all wear clothing fashionable with the upper classes at the time. Alexis wears the costume of the Grenadier Guards, easily obtainable from any costumier, and rather difficult to make. Dr. Daly wears clergyman's garb, and this can be simulated with a black coat and trousers, a black vest worn backward, and a stiff white collar worn backward. The hat is a top hat. More accurate costuming, if it is desired, should be rented. Dr. Daly also carries a cane. The Notary should be costumed exactly as the Counsel in *Trial by Jury*. Mr. Wells is dressed as a fashionable shopkeeper of the time. He wears a Prince Albert coat, dark trousers, a vest with a watch chain hung across it, a flamboyant tie, and a turned-up collar. He too, wears a top hat. Mrs. Partlet wears a full brown or black dress, a shawl, and a bonnet. Constance wears a simple dress with a white apron that covers her bust and a white cap. Elbow-length gloves are also possible for her. Aline is dressed as a bride. The chorus wear the type of villager or peasant costumes so often found in light opera. If possible, they should all be dressed somewhat differently.

Although the stage directions call for the exterior of Sir Marmaduke's mansion, there is little in the text that suggests this. The action might equally well take place in almost any part of the village, and the scene designer has a free hand to represent whatever part of the English countryside most appeals to him.

# Chapter VII

# H. M. S. PINAFORE, OR THE LASS
# THAT LOVED A SAILOR

## PRODUCTION NOTES

*Pinafore* is certainly among the simplest of the full-length operas to produce. Not only is it the shortest of them, but also the musical and dramatic demands it makes on the cast are minimal. The most complicated feature of the production is the setting, which, for best effect, should be as close to an authentic ship of the period as possible. It contains a cabin with a poop deck above it, on which the Captain can make his entrance, and a hatchway, through which Josephine can enter from below, just in time to prevent her lover's suicide. Those elements need not be regarded as essential, however, as many a *Pinafore* has been successfully launched on a stage containing almost no scenery. Sailors' costumes are easily obtained, and the ladies can be dressed in whatever fashionable wear is available and appropriate. All in all, the production can be done with little expense, and if it is rehearsed carefully enough to keep it moving at a rapid pace it should make a successful entertainment.

## CRITICAL DISCUSSION

The libretto of *Pinafore* raises a question central to democracy, the question of equality in a situation in which some must give orders and others obey them. The hypocrisy of Sir Joseph Porter who, having risen from the lower classes to become a man of the highest rank, believes that a British sailor is any man's equal excepting his, focuses on the central paradox of democratic government in a society that abolishes social privilege only to restore it in other guises.

The desire of Ralph Rackstraw to marry his captain's daughter produces the situation within the framework of which the problem of social inequality can be worked out. The situation is common to melodramas of the Victorian period, and anyone who really wishes to understand *H.M.S. Pinafore* should read *Black Eye'd Susan* written in 1829 by Douglas Jerrold. The latter is a serious play that has most of the quaintness that *Pinafore* parodies. The sailor talks in nautical terms, the villain is all bad, good lower-class characters use language that belies their social station, and class conflicts are treated as if they were whimsical accidents easily rectified by appropriate plot devices. It is perhaps ironic that Gilbert has crowded into *Pinafore* more genuine realism and awareness of actual social issues than is ever to be found in the serious works that he parodies. Sir Joseph is a radical suffering from many of the delusions about life that trouble rich radicals of the time. Josephine has an almost Dickensian awareness of the possible liabilities of marriage beneath her station. Dick Deadeye transcends mere villainy and betrays a touch of psychological realism. The Captain is as weak in the very areas in which he believes himself strongest as any officer who is at the same time loved and feared by his men. There is in *Pinafore* enough suggestion of humanity to keep the whimsy from being purely nonsensical, yet the overall effect is one of delightful nonsense.

Gilbert is as much a critic of language as he is of human folly. The stilted character of the dialogue derives from the melodrama of the time, yet is manipulated in such a way that it slyly betrays the dramatist's awareness of the absurdity of the belief that people actually talk as they do in *Pinafore*. The extreme complexity of Ralph's language, which Josephine refers to as "simple eloquence," is one example of this. The constant use of asides is another. The happiest absurdity in the dialogue, however, is the bureaucratic utterance that characterizes Sir Joseph and is sometimes picked up by the other characters; for example, Sir Joseph's line, "Captain Corcoran, it is one of the happiest characteristics of this glorious country that official utterances are invariably regarded as unanswerable."

It is in the lyrics that Gilbert's command of language reaches its zenith. Many of them have the same sort of universal appeal that characterizes nursery rhymes. These combine rhythm, sound effect, childlikeness, and enigma. Others incisively reveal character and provide the motivations for the actions to follow. Still others manage to forward the action while retaining a high degree of verbal appeal in their own right. Then there is the mockery and affirmation of the spirit of a nation: the Englishman's love of being English.

Gilbert's plot structuring has something in common with Shakespeare's in that it parodies the very devices it uses. One feels the tongue firmly planted in the cheek during the closing moments of *As You Like It* when everything is untangled far too neatly. The same effect is to be found at the end of *Pinafore* when it just happens that the Captain is Ralph and Ralph is the Captain. On cue, the two men step forward, having exchanged costumes. The only logic here is that of the dramatist who wants to work things out, and Gilbert is poking fun at that logic exactly as Shakespeare did. But there is an irony, too. In Gilbert's *Bab Ballad* "General John" (one of the sources of Pinafore), General John and Private James exchange ranks as soon as the latter points out that they were probably exchanged at birth. The casualness with which such a reality is accepted highlights the absurdity of the whole concept of social classes, a concept that entirely eliminates from consideration any sort of individual human achievement. In his plot structuring Gilbert thus suggests that the whim of the dramatist and the whims of society are equally absurd, and he makes his poor bumboat woman an instrument of fate just as surely as are the Witches in *Macbeth*.

Another Shakespearean characteristic of Gilbert's writing is his liberal use of phrases that can be quoted out of context. That tend-ency is encouraged by the fact that many of the phrases were already epigrams before being incorporated into *Pinafore's* libretto. The duet for the Captain and Buttercup is a collection of such refashioned epigrams.

For all its ingenuity and popularity, *Pinafore* is far from being Gilbert's finest achievement. Its characterizations are relatively superficial, and the complexity of its plot is by no means equal to that of many later operas. Much of the appeal of *Pinafore* lies in its subject. English and Americans alike are fascinated by the combination of the freedom of roving the seas and the discipline of life in the Navy. Nautical stories are often more successful than equally good stories on more arcane subjects.

The music, too, is more distinguished for its tunefulness than for its craftsmanship. There is little in the score that does not appeal at first hearing, but careful examination of the orchestrations reveals them to be thin and often rather uninspired. For the most part the music is thoroughly English in its character, and we must wait until later operas for the mixture of styles that characterizes Sullivan at his best. Furthermore, both acts are somewhat slow in starting, and much of the success of the opera depends on the combination of spectacle and zest that dominates the second half of each act.

## CHARACTER SKETCHES

### Sir Joseph

There has been considerable controversy as to whether and to what extent Gilbert based Sir Joseph on the character of W. H. Smith, who was at the time First Lord of the Admiralty, and a man who had risen from the lower classes and had never been to sea. It matters little, since Sir Joseph is the finest characterization in the opera, and contains within his character much that typifies all bureaucrats. The official tone in which he speaks is completely inappropriate to the sentimental purpose for which he has come to see the Captain. He is as lacking in a sense of humor as he is in human feeling, and yet he attempts both. Furthermore, he fancies himself a composer, and he has written a song extolling his radical principles. Sir Joseph makes a first impression by being surrounded by two things, both of which seem incongruous when he is taken at face value. The first is the pomp and ceremony that greets his entrance. He is an unimposing little man with a sense of dignity that is easy to see through and that makes little impression on Josephine. The other is the bevy of beautiful sisters, cousins, and aunts that make up his retinue. He does not seem the type to attract beautiful maidens.

Sir Joseph's façade of dignity makes it possible to say and do many things that would render a less dignified person ridiculous. He confesses his queasiness when on board ship, a trait that contrasts with the Captain's hardly ever being sick at sea. He explains the somewhat questionable means by which he obtained his present post. He establishes immediate rapport with the sailors and attempts to get them to speak ill of their captain (which they are unwilling to do). He insists on the supreme importance of good manners. He is, in all ways, a person with whom it is delightfully impossible to deal on any terms other than his own.

The reaction of the other characters to him is interesting indeed. Although Josephine is disgusted by him, she never openly betrays an awareness of his absurdity. But there is a great difference between the awe of the Captain and the easygoing attitude of the sailors in his presence. One feels that they are taking him on the basis of his principles rather than his actual behavior. As soon as he is on deck, Pinafore becomes a sort of never-never land in which such principles really do operate merely because Sir Joseph says he believes in them —at least until belief in them becomes inconvenient for him.

The role requires a first-rate comic actor with excellent diction. The demand for a good singing voice is limited, as there is almost no part-singing, very little real melody, and no demands on the upper register. The dominating impression should be one of total, imperturbable dignity.

### Captain Corcoran

The Captain is a genuinely attractive man who loves his daughter, respects his crew, and admires his superiors. He is deeply concerned with naval etiquette. His one limitation is inflexibility; he cannot handle situations that would not be difficult for the other characters. We learn this from his response in the first act to Sir Joseph's reminder that he should use the expression "if you please." This confuses him as to the sources of authority, and his attempts to hold his temper under control are very amus-

ing. In the second act his anger at Ralph causes him to use bad language, and this is his downfall.

Perhaps the most touching thing about the Captain is his affection for Little Buttercup. He is distressed that his rank does not permit him to express this affection openly, but when he is with her he is able to relax, and his humanity shines through. He is a man of easy dignity, not stiff, like Sir Joseph, and his warmth is never completely stifled. He should have an attractive light baritone voice capable of rising to the A at the end of his second-act solo.

### Ralph Rackstraw

Ralph, pronounced "Rafe," is a common sailor, simple and unassuming in his manner. He has none of the snobbery or sense of mission that characterizes so many G&S tenors. He is motivated by his love for Josephine and his desire to be a good sailor. He loves and respects his Captain quite without irony. The big words that he uses in his scene with Josephine will be funny only if their delivery is completely sincere. Yet Ralph has pride in his dignity as a sailor and as an Englishman, and he is not afraid to stand up to his Captain to the point of mutiny when he is apprehended while eloping with Josephine.

As a singer Ralph must have beauty and passion. His opening madrigal is one of Sullivan's sweetest and gentlest numbers. Sometimes Ralph sings out with dramatic fire, but more often he is the melancholy disappointed lover, the very sound of whose voice must evoke sympathy in the audience.

### Dick Deadeye

This is one of Gilbert's finest creations. Dick has some of the same dimensionality that is found in Shylock. Cast as the villain of the piece, Dick nevertheless gives us enough insight into his own feelings so that we are not completely against him. One of his eyes is covered with gauze so that it appears to be lacking a pupil. He has a hunchback, which causes him always to be bent over. One of his arms is withered and useless. It is his appearance that causes everything he says to sound like "the black utterances of a depraved imagination." Yet he is the one character who consistently speaks the truth, cynical though it may be. His single crime is that he reveals to the Captain the fact that his daughter plans to steal off and marry Rackstraw. For the rest, his utterances consist of reflections on his own misfortune, realistic appraisals of the sailor's lot, or warnings. He has suffered too much to be sentimental, and the other characters' treatment of him reminds us that their rosy outlook on life is something of a veneer.

Vocally, Dick must have a voice that can suggest dark qualities without ever going very low. The part lies in a baritone register, but would be more effectively handled by a bass with a deep voice who can sing the notes and who can act the villain with his singing. The words should be spit out rather than merely enunciated. The voice should suggest at once beauty of tone and ugliness of character. No one has ever better captured those qualities than Darrell Fancourt, who recorded the role twice.

### Bill Bobstay

A good, hearty, attractive baritone is needed for this part. He should be able to make "He is an Englishman" sound like a national anthem. For the rest, he is a rough-and-ready sailor, always friendly, always certain of what should be done and how to do it. He supervises the activities of the rest of the crew. He should always give an impression of competence.

### Bob Becket

He is essentially a member of the chorus, except that he sings a part in the glee "A British tar." Sullivan has humorously differentiated between him and the other two singers in the trio; although they alternate in their parts as if they could not sight-read very well, he carries the vocal line consistently, and is clearly the best musician of the three. His voice must therefore be strong, and he must be sure of himself musically. He should also be enough of a dancer to manage the hornpipe that goes with the trio.

### Midshipmite

During the opening chorus, the Midshipmite is supervising the work of the crew. He is played by a very small man, a boy, or a girl dressed as a sailor. He also appears at climactic moments during the opera as part of the official paraphernalia of the ship. He has no lines and need not sing at all.

### Josephine

Although repertory companies often have the same soprano do all the leading roles, they are not all equally suitable to the same person. Evidence of this is the fact that Blanche Roosevelt, who created the part of Mabel, was a poor Josephine. Mabel requires a coloratura soprano of a somewhat flighty character. Josephine is far more intense, perhaps the most intense of all Gilbert's heroines. She should be a combination of a lyric and dramatic soprano who can put real passion into her great aria in the second act. She is a genuinely noble woman torn between her duty to her father and her love for Ralph. We do not entirely condone her, since she obviously is motivated partly by snobbery, as the duet "Refrain, audacious tar" reveals, despite its asides. She is, throughout, a woman weighed down by the awful step she must take and mustering up the courage to elope with her lover. There is nothing saccharine about her, nor is she in any way passive, like Aline. She must be chosen primarily for her voice, but if she is also a good actress she has the opportunity to lift many of the moments in *Pinafore* beyond the level ordinarily associated with light opera.

### Cousin Hebe

This part was written for Jessie Bond, who wanted a small part with no dialogue. The recitative found in the original version at the beginning of the finale of the second act was written at her request.* It is today replaced with dialogue. Despite the small part, she is a strong character because she dominates Sir Joseph both at his first entrance and at the end. She is always in the thick of things and delights in the complications that arise. She should be played by an actress who can project personality and charm.

### Little Buttercup

Buttercup is one of the few middle-aged women in G&S opera who are treated sympathetically. She is well loved by all the crew and has an engaging personality. About her is also a sense of mystery drawn from the melodrama, since she knows the secret that will eventually unravel the plot. Thus there is motherly charm, but, too, by her own admission, something of the gypsy in her. The musical demands of the

---

* See pages 271–272.

part are not great, but if she is not a strong dramatic character much of the effectiveness of the production will be lost.

### Sailors

They are a "gallant crew" who are "very, very good." They are "sober men and true." They are, in short, a caricature of the idealized simple sailor who always does his duty, is always a gentleman, and who could not possibly exist. There should be an atmosphere of cleanliness and sprightliness about them. They are always smiling, they are always happy, they love whatever is happening. For them, tragedy cannot exist, as we see when they put their fingers in their ears as Ralph is about to shoot himself.

### Sisters, Cousins, and Aunts

They are pretty girls out for a holiday. They love to see the sailors, and although they accompany Sir Joseph, they have none of his pomposity, nor do they allow his presence to overawe them. Like the sailors, they should nearly always be smiling and thoroughly enjoying themselves.

### Notes on Staging

The sailors are discovered cleaning brasswork, splicing rope, and so on. The Boatswain is chief among them, but it is the Midshipmite who supervises. He wanders about the stage, watching each man in turn and calling him to task if he does not approve of his work. Central to the activity is the coiling up of a large rope, and this involves the activity of three or four men. Most of the men will remain in the same place, shifting their positions from time to time, but a few will have jobs that cause them to walk here and there about the stage, so that there is a greater impression of activity. All the sailors must be so placed that they fill the stage, do not block one another, and can be looking out toward the audience most of the time. There may be a few bits of stage business such as the following: Two sailors are eating an apple, passing it back and forth between them. The Midshipmite reprimands them, so they offer it to him. He looks at it, turns up his nose, and throws it overboard. One of the sailors takes out a fresh apple, polishes it, and hands it to the Midshipmite, who takes a bite. The sailor then takes out another apple, and he and his

partner share it. Angrily, the Midshipmite confiscates it, throws both apples overboard, and walks off in a huff.

Little Buttercup enters at the back and goes from group to group of the sailors during her song. At the end, all crowd around her buying various items. She is left with a peppermint stick, which she hands to the Midshipmite, who skips offstage sucking on it happily. The sailors' reactions to Little Buttercup are vocal as well as physical, and this same tendency to vocal reaction greets the entrance of Deadeye. Each of his comments about himself gets a strong reaction from the chorus to accompany Buttercup's reaction.

According to the libretto, Ralph is supposed to enter from the hatchway, but in fact he usually enters from down left. Even if the stage permits a trapdoor, it is better to save this for Josephine's dramatic entrance in the finale. Buttercup, on seeing Ralph, goes to the down right corner, acting mysteriously. She is recalling that he is one of the babies that she mixed up.

On the chorus "They sang 'Ah, well-a-day!'" the sailors gather around Ralph, but he pleads for solitude, and on the introduction to his ballad they withdraw to the corners of the ship. The Boatswain leads them back during the dialogue by clapping Ralph on the back and trying to cheer him up. When he speaks, Deadeye gets the same kind of reaction he did before.

The sailors should be distributed about the stage so that they can fall into a neatly arranged formation on the Captain's entrance. The salute of a British sailor is the same as that of an American soldier. The Captain enters on the poop deck, from which he sings his recitative. During the introduction to his solo he comes down the steps and crosses to the front of the stage, where he stands center, using appropriate gestures. On the second "What, *never?*" in each verse, the crew lean forward, extending the arms toward the Captain, and smiling knowingly. He looks rather embarrassed on "Hardly ever" and precedes these words with an apologetically spoken "Well." At the end of the song, the sailors might suggest a hornpipe on their exit.

The Captain crosses down right, wiping a tear from his eye. Buttercup enters up left and crosses down to center. The Captain crosses to her on his solo. Buttercup sees Josephine coming from the right and exits down left. As she goes, she emits an audible sigh. The Captain is

*Christene Palmer as Little Buttercup in H.M.S. Pinafore: "Hail, men-o'-war's men—safeguards of your nation."*                              *(D'Oyly Carte production)*

*Muriel Harding as Josephine, Peter Pratt as Sir Joseph, and Jeffrey Skitch as Captain Corcoran in* H.M.S. Pinafore. *Josephine: "He little thinks how eloquently he has pleaded his rival's cause."* (*D'Oyly Carte production*)

obviously much taken with her and smiles broadly before he exits.

Josephine's mood during her ballad is such that it is more appropriate for her to lean sadly against a railing or post than to stand stage center. She might move from this position into a more central one, however, as the ballad progresses. The stage directions call for her to twine some flowers that she carries in a small basket, and although this business is seldom performed, it is a good way of giving Josephine something appropriately sentimental to focus her attention on.

Captain Corcoran enters briskly, and the tone of his dialogue is one of brightness and efficiency. Out of respect for Sir Joseph, he raises his hat every time he mentions his name. When Josephine confesses her love for a common sailor, her father is shocked, and his "Oh fie!" is explosive. We must learn at this point that Captain Corcoran is a man whose temper is not easily controlled. He quickly gives in to his love for his daughter, however, and pats her comfortingly on the back, offering a picture of Sir Joseph as consolation. His sentimental tone quickly changes to one of the greatest enthusiasm when he spies the approach of Sir Joseph's barge. Josephine's last line offers several choices. She may show her love for her father, scarcely looking at the photograph. She may look at the photograph, react negatively, and say the line sarcastically. Or she may look at the photograph, start to react negatively, and then sigh and shake her head, realizing that her father is doing his best and showing that she loves him in spite of all. Perhaps the last reaction is most consistent with her character.

The barcarolle is sung by the ladies offstage. During it, the Captain ascends to the poop deck. The Midshipmite comes rushing on, sees the ladies, and gestures to the rest of the sailors, who come on one by one, looking back to call each other. They have changed into their dress uniforms. As they crowd around the side of the ship, they take the Midshipmite's space and he can no longer see. When his attempts to do so are noticed, he is hoisted on their backs, where he pulls out his telescope and then waves happily to the ladies.

As the sailors begin to sing, they come downstage, filling up around the sides, and work together in small groups to make certain that they look just right. Hats are adjusted, specks removed from jackets, and so on. The Midshipmite takes a position on the steps leading to the poop deck. The ladies enter and dance around the deck. This number should be choreographed so that the ladies eventually end up with particular sailors.

The Captain's "Now give three cheers" is delivered from the poop deck, and during the chorus response he comes down the steps and makes his way to a position down right center. Two marines with snare drums enter and take their positions at either side of the entrance at the back. The Midshipmite calls "Attention" and one of the Marines responds, "Pree-senn-'tumps!" They then give several rolls on the snare drums. At that point the musical vamp introducing Sir Joseph begins and continues over and over. We wait a few seconds before we see him. He appears up center with Cousin Hebe and slowly walks to the front of the stage. All this time everyone is saluting.

Sir Joseph is obviously not expecting to be interrupted by Cousin Hebe, and is slightly annoyed each time she sings. His annoyance, of course, grows. But we can see that she so dominates him that he must suffer in silence. There is relatively little moving about during either of his songs, but gestures symbolizing the action are important. Sir Joseph is stiff and dignified the whole time, so much so that one suspects he is incapable of bending over.

Following his song, Sir Joseph inspects the crew. His efforts quickly take him to the Mid-

shipmite, who is at the end of the line, and who is the object of his comment that a British sailor is a splendid fellow. When Captain Corcoran claims that he never bullies his sailors, those behind Sir Joseph's back gesture to remind him that there *have* been occasions. When Sir Joseph desires a sailor to step forward and Deadeye does so, we marvel at the admiral's *savoir-faire,* since, though the sight of Deadeye shakes him, he quickly recovers himself and dismisses Deadeye cordially. When Rackstraw is commanded to march forward, he begins to do so. But Sir Joseph's "If what?" interrupts the process and leaves him with one foot frozen in the air. When Ralph finally comes forward, he comes to attention next to Sir Joseph and facing the audience. He salutes and stamps his right foot. Sir Joseph taps him on the shoulder, indicating that he wishes him to face him. Ralph does so and again salutes and stamps his foot. On "Yes, your honour," Ralph repeats this business. Sir Joseph's interest in the foot-stamping has grown, and this time he returns Ralph's salute and brings his right heel down on his own left toe.

When Sir Joseph asks Ralph if he can dance a hornpipe, Ralph hesitates and turns to the others. They all break into a hornpipe. Ralph tries it and stumbles. He then says, "No, your honour." When Sir Joseph asks Ralph how his captain treats him, his back is to the Captain, so he does not see him make a threatening gesture to Ralph and indicate to the chorus that they should join in Ralph's endorsement of him.

When Ralph speaks the word "hum," he drops the "h." Sir Joseph echoes this, then catches himself with a cough, which also becomes the "h." The business at the end of the dialogue scene concerning the Captain's saying "If you *please*" gets the Captain worked up into a perfect frenzy and establishes a kind of rapport between Sir Joseph and the Boatswain, both of whom enjoy his discomfort. As the Captain stamps his foot he attempts to exit. Sir Joseph stops him with an extended arm, sings to him the solo part of the song, and immediately exits, ahead of the Captain. The exit for the girls at the end of this song is one of those that must be handled quickly. They should be standing near all of the exits and leave as if to explore the rest of the ship, so that there is no delay in proceeding with the next scene.

The sailors have waved good-bye to the girls and now gather together near the center of the stage with Ralph and the Boatswain in front of

*Donald Adams as Dick Deadeye in* H.M.S. Pinafore.     (*D'Oyly Carte production*)

them. The Boatswain gives the scene a vitality that contrasts with the formality of the dialogue that has preceded. As Deadeye speaks, the others fall away from him. In response to the Boatswain's answer to him, he retires upstage gloomily. Ralph quickly takes the center, picking up the Boatswain's enthusiasm. His gestures are expansive and reflect his words. When Deadeye is heard from again, several of the sailors rush to him and on the Boatswain's line, "What is to be done with this here hopeless chap?," they pick him up eager to throw him overboard. After a moment's pause, the Boatswain suggests that they sing to him instead. Deadeye is deposited on a barrel near the front of the stage where he can listen to the song. The sailors arrange themselves across the stage in two lines with the three soloists in front. They should be spread out enough so that each can comfortably do a hornpipe in place. During the solo part of the glee, the three who are singing struggle with the music and attempt crude but appropriate gestures. When the chorus picks up the refrain, the gestures are exactly together and go like clockwork. During the first hornpipe, the Boatswain and his companion attempt to teach Ralph to dance while the chorus dances perfectly. The second time, Ralph pushes them aside and executes his own crude dance while they watch admiringly. Again the chorus does the dance perfectly. This time the two lines split in the center, and the sailors hornpipe their way offstage, so that as the music stops Ralph is alone onstage. Immediately he becomes moody and crosses to the bulwark and leans against it.

Josephine enters from the cabin, looking again at the photograph of Sir Joseph and shaking her head at its ugliness. She addresses her words about him to the photograph, as if trying to puzzle out its enigmatic qualities. From the moment she sees Ralph the scene takes on a character that we have not seen before in this opera. Exaggerated gesture, energy, and tone of voice give the scene an operatic quality that will be funny provided the actors handle it with complete sincerity. If the lines are spoken more or less in a normal tone of voice, what we have is simply another love scene, and a dull one at that. If, on the other hand, there is Shakespearean gusto in the delivery, it can be the funniest scene in the opera. The actors must ham to the hilt, but they must never let on that they are conscious of hamming. Josephine's sudden changes of attitude from assumed aloofness to sincere love

should occur like lightning—the faster the funnier. Ralph's "I hope I make myself clear, lady?" is underplayed, but everything else in the scene is overplayed. At the end of the duet a tableau with Ralph kneeling near the brokenhearted Josephine, who is turned away from him and weeping, can be effective. On the closing music she turns to him; he rises hopefully, then she quickly turns away and exits.

Ralph's exaggerated manner continues through the recitative, which should be delivered at the front of the stage. Then he crosses to the back to call the sailors in. The entrance of the chorus is rapid, but they do not move far. The main movement is provided by Ralph's cross from the back to the front of the stage and the shifting focus of the chorus' attention on him as he moves.

Deadeye breaks through the chorus line at the rear for his short solo, then retreats behind it as it closes up again. When he next sings he appears on the side, downstage. The chorus line moves somewhat, to show everyone's revulsion from him and to focus attention on him while he sings. Then everyone looks out toward the audience, so that the chorus's music and Deadeye's counterpoint provide two separate focal points.

As Ralph threatens to kill himself, he crosses to a downstage corner in about the time that it takes to sing his solo. The chorus all turn their backs while the Boatswain loads the pistol. Deadeye watches the proceedings with considerable satisfaction. As all stop their ears, he is the only one who is watching, and he is grinning broadly.

Josephine's entrance will be most dramatic if she comes from below up the hatchway, though this is completely illogical. She may also appear on the poop deck. In any event, she should enter in such a manner that she immediately becomes the center of action. Ralph, who has the pistol in one ear and his finger in the other ear, does not know she is present until the chorus echo her opening statement. Slowly, disbelievingly, he withdraws the pistol. The two are united when the chorus sings, "Yes, yes—ah, yes." Cousin Hebe comes forward a little down right in order to join in the singing of the trio. Deadeye again becomes prominent down left. For his solo it is possible to use a spotlight on him and to dim the rest of the lighting. If that is done, the other characters should all freeze, so that what we have is a representation of Deadeye's thoughts rather than his actual spoken words. At the end of his solo, the stage directions call for him to exit. This is by no means necessary, as he is on again very shortly, and his second exit is more dramatic if he does not exit here.

For the quartet "This very night," the four soloists get into attitudes of walking stealthily. They take one step for each measure that is sung. When the chorus enter, they all assume attitudes of stealth with hands up. They can remain in the same position and appear to be creeping if they place one foot forward on the downbeat and draw it back into position half-way through the measure, then step forward on the next foot for the next downbeat. The soloists continue in the same direction until the beginning of the fast part for the sopranos, at which point they bunch tightly together and reverse direction. They continue reversing direction as necessary, but come to a full stop at the end of the chorus for the *a capella* part. During the fast music that follows the chorus, they continue their actions of stealth until Deadeye sings, at which point they freeze in exaggerated attitudes of creeping. Again the lights may dim and a spot may focus on Deadeye. On "Back, vermin, back," the chorus turn to Deadeye and use threatening gestures. He creeps offstage. During the hold that follows the music, the Boatswain hurls the revolver after Deadeye, and there is the sound of breaking glass. Everyone onstage laughs heartily. There follows a simple chorus dance step in which the entire company participates in unison. When the ladies sing "For a British tar," they come forward a step or two and use the same gestures the men used when they sang the song earlier. When the men sing, they come forward until they are a step or two in front of the ladies. When all join in together, the ladies move up so that they are again next to the men. The same gestures continue until the singing is completed, at which point a hornpipe may be executed for a few bars. The curtain falls during the last five measures, and by that time the entire company should be in a tableau, probably maintaining the same attitude with which they ended the singing.

Act Two opens with a darkened stage. Moonlight floods the stage and is focused on the Captain. The stage directions call for placing him on the poop deck, but it may be more effective to have him farther forward, particularly if there are acoustical problems. He has changed his costume and is now in full naval mess dress. Little Buttercup is so seated that she can be seen by the audience, but not by Captain Corcoran. If he is forward, she can be at the back and to the side. If he is on the poop deck, she should be down left, but dimly lit. As he sings, the Captain accompanies himself on a mandolin. There is no need for any other action.

The dialogue scene that follows should be played seriously. The sentimental mood of the Captain's song carries over and should not be spoiled. Furthermore, the love of these older people contrasts with the wilder passion of Ralph and Josephine. (We are expected to forget completely that Ralph and the Captain turn out to be the same age.) As Little Buttercup says that she can read destinies, she takes the Captain's hand and begins to read his palm. Her last two lines are spoken mysteriously.

During the first half of the duet, Buttercup plays in the down right area with the Captain standing somewhat behind her, looking puzzled. She is deliberately trying to confuse him, and her face betrays her joy in doing so. On the chord that follows the Captain's first remark he places his chin on his hand in an attitude of puzzlement. On the second equivalent chord he shrugs and at the same instant Buttercup turns suddenly toward him. Beginning "Drops the wind," she advances slowly toward him with sleuthlike steps. The Captain faces Buttercup for "Though to catch your drift," but on "Stern conviction's" they turn away and advance toward the audience, moving apart from each other. They turn toward each other again respectively on "Yes, I know" and "That is so." During his half of the duet, the Captain advances slowly toward Buttercup, using appropriate gestures. On her first emphatic chord she folds her arms decisively. On her second, she nods her head. If the stage is small, it may be more effective to have the Captain move behind Buttercup and around to her other side. On "Though to catch my drift," Little Buttercup again faces the audience so that the Captain is behind her. When the two sing together they advance toward each other so that Buttercup can take the Captain's hand on "That is so." They continue singing, he to her, and she to the audience while she continues to hold his palm like a gypsy, all the time looking as if she were about to turn her head to read it. On the last chord she does, and the two hold a tableau effect during the applause.

This number may be encored. If so, return to "Though to catch my drift he's striving," at which point Buttercup can move away from the Captain, and they can exactly repeat their previous business, although for variation doing it from opposite sides of the stage. As soon as the applause begins to die down, Buttercup moves mysteriously toward the exit, while the Captain looks confusedly after her. He need not wait until she is off to begin his line.

At the end of the dialogue scene, Captain Corcoran starts to exit. Sir Joseph haughtily exclaims, "Captain Corcoran!" After a moment the Captain realizes his mistake and steps back. Sir Joseph pulls a handkerchief out of his sleeve, touches it to his nose, and then exits with great dignity, haughtily swishing it as he goes. The Captain, amused, does an exaggerated imitation of this business.

Josephine's song requires nothing special in the way of staging, but should be sung with great passion and dramatic intensity. The trio that follows is the high point of the opera. In D'Oyly Carte productions it has received as many as seven encores, each of which is staged a little differently. During the introductory music, the three soloists do a simple dance, which might be of the step-kick variety, or as simple as an allemande left. While each soloist is singing alone, the other two do a step-halt walk upstage and back down again on each side of the stage. On "Ring the merry bells," the Captain and Sir Joseph do an imitation of pulling a bell rope, while Josephine steps aside. During the four solo lines that follow, each character steps into a new position, with Josephine on the outside and singing confidentially to the audience on "And a *tar* who ploughs the water." When the three are again singing together, the bell-ringing continues. If there are to be encores, the first time the song is done, the bell rope is adhered to exclusively. If no encores are to be taken, Sir Joseph may during the second and third verse introduce some of the encore ideas that follow. When the singing is completed, the three should do a sprightly comic dance that ends with Sir Joseph escorting Josephine to the cabin door.

Martyn Green introduced into this number various types of pantomimed bells that kept the encores coming in profusion. The bells he used were a carillon, a piano, a hurdy-gurdy, a triangle, a try-your-strength machine (which involves hitting a weight high enough so that it rings a bell) a telephone, and an electric doorbell. After he had had several encores he would lean exhaustedly against the ship's steering wheel, which sent the wheel spinning. Much of the comic effect derived from the fact that the other two soloists continued to do exactly what they had done previously, though somewhat taken aback by Sir Joseph's antics. The encore, incidentally, repeats only the third verse.

The dialogue that follows gives the Captain a good chance to contrast his adulation for Sir Joseph with his repulsed aloofness from Deadeye. The duet is not difficult to stage. All that is needed is a grotesque dance for Deadeye and a dignified dance for the Captain during the interlude music. Deadeye can prance in circles about the stage while the Captain remains in one place doing elegant footwork. Near the end of the duet, the Captain pulls out a cat-o'-nine-tails and lashes the bulwark during his last dance.

Deadeye and the Captain seclude themselves upstage, the Captain hidden in a cloak. Josephine and Little Buttercup enter from the cabin, Josephine carrying a bundle of necessaries. The crew enter at the two downstage entrances and upstage left. Everyone is bent forward, tiptoeing exaggeratedly. Josephine and Ralph meet center, with the Boatswain just behind. They begin a line that circles around the stage, moving toward the up left exit, the crew all following behind. On the loud chord, the Captain stamps and strikes Deadeye with the cat-o'-nine-tails. (Deadeye's costume is heavily padded.) The chorus all look horrified, but they are reassured and continue stealing forward. As Ralph and Josephine reach the up left exit, the Captain throws off his cloak and takes Josephine down center, breaking through the crowd, while Ralph follows. The chorus thump their chests with both fists on "thump any" and bow on "a lady like you." No movement is needed during the duet that follows, or the song "He is an Englishman," except that the Boatswain can swagger about the stage on his solo and the chorus all put their hats over their hearts, looking very patriotic. At the end of the song, Deadeye comes forward and stands not far from the Captain. He reacts to the Captain's swearing with great glee, while everyone else looks horrified. Sir Joseph enters the poop deck just as the Captain begins his solo, and the ladies enter at the three places the men have entered from. Sir Joseph comes down the steps from the poop deck as he sings and arrives next to the Captain just in time to show him the expression of his eyes. The Captain exits sadly, followed by Josephine. During the reprise of "He is an Englishman," some movement from the chorus in formal patterns would be appropriate. Ralph is hoisted onto the shoulders of some of the sailors and all wave their hats to him, honoring him. During the dialogue Ralph remains in this position, and Sir Joseph has to crane his neck to talk to him. This gives particular point to his line, "Your position as a topman is a very exalted one." On the line that follows, Ralph is lowered to the deck just in time for Josephine to rush into his arms. Sir Joseph is so horrified that he collapses into Buttercup's arms, and she has to revive him with her red handkerchief. Sir Joseph cries out, "You shall repent this outrage," and attempts to draw his sword. It will not come out of the scabbard, so he calls to the two Marines to seize Ralph. The ensemble that follows requires no staging, as everyone finds an appropriate attitude and remains in about the same position throughout. The concentration here is entirely on the music.

Sir Joseph again calls attention to the terrible expression of his eyes, and the chorus creeps forward, hoping to catch a glimpse of it, as he is looking directly at the audience. At Buttercup's "Hold!" all fall back fearfully. Sir Joseph's dignity is momentarily interrupted by his surprise at the sound of her voice. During the introduction to her solo, Buttercup mysteriously gestures for the chorus to crowd around her. This number is done with great pseudo-seriousness and much use of exaggerated gestures. The chorus, during their refrains, nod and gesture to one another in unison.

Buttercup, on her line, "That is the idea," salutes Sir Joseph. On his reply he is about to salute her back, but catches himself just in time. She snaps her hand back to her side and stamps her foot on "Aye! aye! yer 'onour." Sir Joseph's reaction to her in "Dear me!" should convey a double meaning.

Ralph and the Captain, having exchanged costumes, march in from opposite sides of the stage. The Captain salutes Ralph, who salutes back, gives the command "At ease," and both face the audience, looking very serious. The ladies are extremely taken with Ralph's new uniform and some of them crowd around him to examine it. Others react to the Captain, but with somewhat less enthusiasm. The Boatswain claps the Captain on the back and shakes his hand, welcoming him as a member of the crew. Sir Joseph, having realized that he cannot marry Josephine, responds to Hebe's proposal by first examining all of his other cousins until he comes face to face with Deadeye. This decides him to resign himself to a match with Hebe. The last portion of this dialogue may be sung if the original version, reprinted on pages 271–272, is adhered to.

There is little for the chorus to do other than sing during the finale. A few gestures and dance steps as they are appropriate are all that is needed. Each of the soloists relies more on personality than stage business to make his final verse effective. When they are finished singing, the entire company shout "Hooray!" three times and throw their hats in the air as the curtain falls.

## SCENERY AND COSTUMES

If one wishes to be authentic, little variation is possible in the settings for *Pinafore*. Gilbert based his scene design on the *H.M.S. Victory* and gave careful attention to detail. Although the D'Oyly Carte set has been changed since then, the most striking difference between the set in use in 1908 and that used now is that the *Victory* (which is seen in the background) has been turned around. Therefore, the most effective way to learn what is needed is to study a photograph of the D'Oyly Carte set and to work from there. It is certainly desirable to have a cabin and a poop deck that are practicable because of the amount of action that involves them. A practicable hatchway, however, is unnecessary. The ship should appear as clean and brightly polished as possible, in keeping with the spirit of the crew. If one wishes the set to be abstract, a ship that looks as if it has just stepped out of a nursery rhyme would be in keeping with the spirit of things.

Enough has already been said about the costumes, except to observe that Sir Joseph is not an Admiral but a cabinet officer, and his costume is unique. His coat with tails is heavily brocaded on the front, the tails, and the cuffs. He wears a wig reminiscent of George Washington, a monocle, white knee pants and stockings, and ballet slippers. His hat is a British naval officer's except that it has white ruffles throughout the top central portion. He wears a ceremonial sword. Deadeye, of course, has a patch over one eye. One of his arms is withered and useless.

In some productions the girls are costumed simply as Victorian maidens wth bonnets. The current D'Oyly Carte costumes are more inventive, making the girls look as sailorettes might look if they existed. Josephine is given a more dignified and conservative dress, more suggestive of romance than seamanship.

# Chapter VIII

# THE PIRATES OF PENZANCE, OR
# THE SLAVE OF DUTY

## PRODUCTION NOTES

*The Pirates of Penzance,* because of its great popularity and tunefulness, may lead one to believe that it is simpler to produce than it actually is. It differs from *Pinafore* in that it requires two complete sets and in that the music is, in general, more difficult to perform. The part of Mabel is certainly among the most difficult roles in the series and requires an extremely well-trained soprano who can touch an E-flat, has a firm high C, and is equally skilled at staccato and legato singing. The chorus is onstage a good percentage of the time. The men's chorus must be large enough to be divided into Pirates and Policemen in the second act, which means that it must contain a large tenor section. As most of the second act is sung, there is little chance for the performers to disguise musical insecurity with dramatic excellence.

An additional difficulty is that *Pirates* tends to appear visually rather drab. There are several reasons for this. Pirate costumes are usually simple and rather ragged. The Policemen add little in the way of spectacle, as they are dressed uniformly all in blue. The first-act set, a rocky seashore, is usually predominantly gray, brown, and blue. The second-act set, an ancestral ruin, can be more colorful, but must be dimly lit, as the second act takes place at night. Given all those factors, even a lavish production will appear drab if careful thought is not given to means for making it visually interesting. We shall consider some of them in the section on scenery and costumes.

Although talent and ingenuity are required for the production of *Pirates,* it may neverthe-less be done inexpensively. Both settings are easily suggested with relatively little expense. Nothing in the set necessarily has to be climbed on or walked across. Costumes, except for the constabulary uniforms (which can easily be borrowed), are not difficult to make. *Pirates* is therefore an excellent opportunity for a company with lots of talent and enthusiasm and not much money, which is perhaps one reason for its popularity with amateurs.

## CRITICAL DISCUSSION

In many ways *Pirates* represents an advance over *Pinafore,* both musically and dramatically. That is true despite some unevenness in the quality of both libretto and music. Sullivan wrote the score under greater pressure of time than he did any of the other operas, and in places (primarily in the first act) his haste is revealed in the ordinariness of the tunes or the thinness of the orchestration. In its total structure, however, *Pirates* is so well put together that its weaknesses are not easily noticed. Indeed, it was the consensus of the first-night critics that the score, though possibly not as tuneful, was musically more sophisticated than that of *Pinafore,* and the composer shared that view.

What is the secret of the structural success of *Pirates*? A large part of it lies in the fact that so much of the music is devoted to carrying forward the action. Indeed, the dialogue is used mainly for exposition, and is in itself rather stiff and undistinguished. Another factor in the success of *Pirates* is that each of the chorus groups plays a unique and distinctive role in the action. The conflict in the first act between the girls and the Pirates who wish to marry them is fully and clearly developed. This is followed in the second act by the Policemen, who are championed by the girls, but who fall at the hands of the Pirates. Indeed, as in perhaps no other operetta, the action of the chorus seems more important than that of the leading characters.

Further, as a literary concept, *Pirates* is much better developed than *Pinafore*. Although the libretto leads us to believe that Frederic is the slave of duty, we find on closer examination that *each* of the characters is actually a slave of duty. The Pirates, being orphans themselves, make it a self-imposed duty never to molest orphans. As word of this has got about, most of the ships they attack are manned entirely by orphans, and they are rapidly reaching the point at which piracy does not pay. The Policemen are compelled by their sense of duty to attack the Pirates, despite their failing courage.

The Major-General's daughters are moved by a sense of loyalty to him, and the Major-General, having told a lie, is plagued by his conscience for having brought disgrace on his ancestors-by-purchase, toward whom he has a fully developed sense of loyalty. Ruth, having mistakenly bound Frederic in apprenticeship to a pirate instead of a pilot, remains herself loyal to the contract anyway. Finally, Mabel promises that she will remain true to Frederic until 1940, when he reaches his twenty-first birthday and can marry her.

Absurd as all those loyalties are they seem scarcely less absurd than many of the loyalties that have actually motivated people and molded their lives throughout history. The Victorian sense of duty, loyalty, and propriety, which time and again came into conflict with the desires and often the necessities of life, is richly reflected in this operetta.

Sullivan has supplied music that works as much by the interrelationship between the melodies as by the melodies themselves. Most obvious in that respect is the brilliant counterpoint section sung by the girls and the Policemen. Then there is the juxtaposition of the chattering girls' chorus with the love duet of Frederic and Mabel. This duet in turn seems somewhat ironic when we contrast the simple, plaintive music of Frederic with the ornate coloratura of Mabel on her first entrance. How ill-matched this pair are made to seem from a musical point of view, yet how beautifully they sing together anyway.

Quite the opposite effect is achieved when we compare the music of the Pirates with that of the girls. There is enough restraint in the Pirates, enough jocularity and earthiness in the girls that when they sing the same music at the end of the first act it seems to suit both groups perfectly. Here, we are made to feel, are a large number of compatible couples. It hardly seems a surprise when we learn at the end that the Pirates are all noblemen gone wrong, and consequently excellent suitors for the hands of the daughters of a Major-General.

There is motion and character interplay throughout this opera, but there are also times when the action stops and we can contemplate the absurdity of the characters. The Major-General, who is knowledgeable about everything except his own profession, is given one of the finest of all patter songs. The Sergeant of Police speculates warmheartedly and at length on criminal psychology. And the Pirate King makes us aware that there is less difference between outlaws and the Establishment than the Establishment would have us believe.

For all its weaknesses, *The Pirates of Penzance* may well be the best structured of the Savoy operas.

## CHARACTER SKETCHES

### Major-General Stanley

More opportunity for singing, less for acting is offered in this role than in that of Sir Joseph, its predecessor. The opening patter song is very difficult and requires first-rate diction and avoidance of the temptation to speed it up beyond intelligibility. The sequence that follows shortly after, "I'm telling a terrible story," has the same characteristics. Much of the rest of the music is quite lyrical in style and should be sung with taste and musicianship.

On the other hand, the Major-General hasn't nearly the opportunity to appear humorously authoritative that Sir Joseph has, for the Pirate King keeps upstaging him. The humor of his lines stems from situation rather than character, and even the best actor can do little to make an impression with them.

The Major-General's real opportunity comes in the second act with the ballad "Sighing softly to the river." This can either be a dull interruption in the action or a show-stopper. If it is well sung it is musically beautiful, but during the musical introduction and the chorus, the actor has an opportunity to do a mock-ballet dance that can be excruciatingly funny.

The main problem the actor faces with

this role is its inconsistency. Although he must be rather stiff and crisp during his patter songs and because he is a Major-General, he must also be capable of sentiment. When he claims to be an orphan, and later, when his conscience is troubling him, he must reveal internal fires of passion.

The Major-General is traditionally thin to the point of lankiness, has white hair, and wears a monocle. Perhaps his appearance more than his acting must be relied on to contribute to the effectiveness of the production.

### The Pirate King

Discussing the sources of the operetta, S. J. Adair Fitz-Gerald writes, "But above all it is wildly reminiscent of the toy drama, which was always penny plain and two-pence colored. Those jolly cardboard characters that were manufactured by the Skeltons and the Webbs in the Grecian and City Road emporiums, which were such a joy to the boys of long ago." Much of the character of the Pirate King is suggested in that remark. He is a child's toy, a mixture of the blood and thunder of childhood dreams with their innocence and naiveté. He must be idealized as the hefty and handsome bearded hero the boy might imagine himself to be, not a villainous Long John Silver or Captain Hook. Vocal effectiveness is as important in the dialogue as in the singing, as the lines must have a sound that is something between a growl and an operatic recitative. The superlative delivery of Donald Adams in the recent D'Oyly Carte recording is worthy of study as a model.

The more imposing, heroic, and declamatory the Pirate King is in his delivery, the funnier will seem the naive aspects of his character: the sympathy for orphans, and the righteous indignation upon finding out that the Major-General is, indeed, *no* orphan! Although the character is fashioned from brightly colored cardboard, there is nevertheless in him a great deal of Gilbert's own personality, as the dramatist combined bloodthirstiness with sentimentality in much the proportions found in the Pirate King.

However, there is nothing stiff about the Pirate King. He contrasts with the Major-General by having an earthiness of which the Major-General is incapable. Since the opera centers around the conflict between these two characters, there must be as much contrast between them as possible. Whereas the Major-General muses and becomes introspective, devi-

ous, and conscience-stricken, the Pirate King reacts immediately and fully to each situation. The Major-General lacks a sense of humor, but the Pirate King, although pompous, has a well-developed sense of humor, macabre though it be, and thoroughly enjoys the paradox of the second act.

### Samuel

Samuel reinforces the effect of the Pirate King without being nearly as imposing. It is his job to lead the chorus during their entrances and to verbalize many of their sentiments. He has a somewhat quieter sense of humor than the Pirate King, but it is nonetheless there, and Samuel can easily make an impression as a strong character.

### Frederic

A chance for heroic acting as well as singing lies in this role. Frederic's position is absurd, but he must take it seriously and play the straight man to the other characters. He has grown up never having seen any woman except the aging Ruth and also with a strict sense of duty. When he meets Mabel he falls in love instantly and enjoys the luxury of uncontested happiness. However, in the second act the classic conflict between love and duty arises, and as both emotions are extremely strong in Frederic, he rises to a frenzy of excitement.

As much of the humor of *Pirates* stems from Frederic's seriousness as from the clowning of the other characters. It is through Frederic that we sense the social reality toward which the satire of the piece is directed. It is to some extent with him that we identify, realizing that we, too, have commitments that we take as seriously as he takes his.

The characterization of Frederic has consistency throughout the piece, and the music reinforces the heroic quality suggested in the words. It is lyric and dramatic at the same time, suggesting a soul with great reserves of passion that never fails to express itself decorously. Taken all in all, Frederic is perhaps the most satisfactory of all Gilbert and Sullivan tenor roles.

### Sergeant of Police

Although he is onstage only seventeen minutes, the Sergeant is truly unforgettable. That is perhaps because of the unified character of the impression he makes. He always marches in in the same way and stands facing the audience with an attitude that combines bravery and cowardice. The stance is one that has all the formally expressed characteristics of bravery, but that constantly seems about to collapse in fear. Through long experience the Sergeant has learned to accept his lot and is resigned, rather than self-pitying.

Ironically, though he is the most restricted of characters physically, the Sergeant has perhaps the most unrestricted philosophy. His chief torment is that the exigencies of the law do not take into account the full variety of human nature, and he is inclined to forgive the criminal in the very act of arresting him. Whether this is mere rationalization or the sensitivity of the timid, it causes him to lose the battle with the Pirates. We are not to believe, however, that that battle is not courageously fought.

In the character of the Sergeant it is suggested that though the Englishman may suffer many woes he is always in the end redeemed by his love for his country and his Queen. That is perhaps why the Sergeant never really gives in to his cowardice. In that respect he captures something essential to the character of the English people.

### Mabel

Mabel has little chance to establish her character in the spoken dialogue, and consequently must do most of it in the singing. Here she has an excellent opportunity, provided she has a voice that combines coloratura agility with dramatic bravado.

She provides something of a contrast to Frederic's simple, rustic character in her flashy, worldly-wise style of singing. Like many of Gilbert's females, she is the aggressor, and under a thin veneer of blushing modesty lurks a designing woman who knows what she wants and intends to get it. It is only under the hypnotic effect of Frederic's intense sense of duty that Mabel agrees to wait for him until 1940. Once he is gone, she immediately returns to her thoughts of exterminating the Pirates.

### Edith

Down-to-earth and somewhat hedonistic, this girl leads the others in specific plans for enjoyment. Her suggestion that the girls take off their shoes and stockings and paddle was a bit

on the naughty side in her own day. She has two short but important solos that should be well sung.

### Kate

Kate is more the romantic. She admires the countryside and idealizes it. She has only one short solo.

### Isabel

A lively damsel, both practical and romantic. As she has no solo singing, she should be that member of the chorus who is the best actress. By reacting strongly herself and leading the reactions of the chorus, she can do a great deal to add sparkle to the production.

### Ruth

Ruth is a somewhat difficult and thankless role. The low notes of her opening solo are difficult for some contraltos to manage with sufficient volume, and it may be that if only piano accompaniment is used the song should be transposed upward a little. The duet with Frederic requires strong operatic singing. The "Paradox" trio requires strong comic projection.

Although much is required of the actress, she has little opportunity to be appealing: Ruth is distressingly somber most of the time and almost solely concerned with her unrequited love for Frederic. The actress will have to work hard to avoid appearing colorless and unattractive in the role.

### Pirates

They are picture-book pirates, strong, handsome, energetic, and sentimental. They should do a great deal of swaggering and shouting without ever becoming unlovable. It is their very innocuousness that serves to make the Policemen's terror so funny. Throughout the opera they give the impression of thoroughly enjoying themselves, whether they are engaged with wine, women, song, or their own specialty of "burglaree." Their single moment of disappointment comes when the Major-General reveals that he is an orphan. But as they have encountered this difficulty many times before, they quickly recover and enjoy the situation for what it is.

*Policemen*

They are in every way the opposite of the Pirates, appearing stolid but cowardly, hardly daring to turn their heads, but rather looking to right and left out of the corners of their eyes. They are funniest if they are of widely assorted sizes and shapes and are dressed in uniforms that, although immaculate, are just slightly ill-fitting. It is unlikely that any of them has ever learned how to smile.

*Daughters*

Theoretically they ought to range in age from 15 to 35, but usually they all look exactly 18. They enjoy life much as the Pirates do, and are thus quite well suited to them as mates. Their reaction to being surprised by the Pirates has as much delight in it as fear, and one feels they can handle the situation quite effectively. They have a good sense of humor, playing a number of the scenes somewhat tongue in cheek, as for example the first meeting of Frederic and Mabel, and the mock heroism of their scene with the Police.

NOTES ON STAGING

Gilbert's direction reads, "As the curtain rises, groups of Pirates are discovered, some drinking, some playing cards. Samuel, the Pirate Lieutenant, is going from one group to another, filling the cups from a flask. Frederic is seated in a despondent attitude at the back of the scene. Ruth kneels at his feet." Much of the business of filling the cups can be accomplished immediately after the curtain rises and before the chorus starts to sing. At the rise, the Pirates cheer, growl, and make other piratical noises until they begin to sing. In general, they are involved with their own little groups until the singing begins, when they have evolved into positions facing the audience, giving the effect of a unified chorus without breaking up their groups. The gestures of swinging their cups in the air, drinking heftily, and wiping their mouths with the backs of their hands are obvious. Some fun can be had with the flask from which Samuel pours, one pirate grabbing it, drinking from it directly, and passing it on. Samuel can recapture it on the chorus following his solo.

Keeping Frederic at the back of the stage can have a humorous effect if it is handled properly, for his moping contrasts with the merriment of the song about him. It might work better, however, if Ruth tried to cheer Frederic up by bringing him forward on Samuel's solo, thus drawing attention to him and identifying him. During this some of the Pirates can make passes at her, which she rebuffs, indicating her love for Frederic.

Following the chorus, the Pirate King enters, comes straight to Frederic, and claps him on the back. His bluff bravado immediately contrasts with the cool reticence of Frederic's attitude. His manner boils over with an enthusiasm that even tops that of the opening chorus and is picked up by the chorus in their responses. A somewhat melodramatic effect in the reactions will set the stage for Ruth's revelation and lend more dramatic coloring to her rather uninteresting song.

The song can be varied slightly by taking a different position on stage for each of the three verses. There is little opportunity for interaction with the chorus, except on the words "I bound him to a pirate—you—" at which point Ruth can gesture toward some of the Pirates, who react defensively. The success of the song will depend on clear enough diction to get the story across and on the capacity of the performer to project her personality across the footlights.

In the dialogue that follows, Ruth is at first overcome by guilt and soon withdraws into a corner. The Pirates are much distressed to learn from Frederic that they are too tenderhearted, and for once he seems to have the upper hand over even the King. The somewhat somber opening of the scene quickly turns to merriment over the question of what to do with Ruth. The Pirates think it is an excellent joke to try to convince Frederic that Ruth is beautiful, and indulge in much glee behind his back.

For his song, the Pirate King waves a large Jolly Roger over his head during the introduction and chorus. For their exit, the Pirates maintain the jollifications of the song, laughing and slapping one another on the back as they leave.

The scene between Frederic and Ruth is much more serious in effect than anything that has preceded it. The youthful innocence of Frederic and the middle-aged infatuation of Ruth offer little chance for humor. The scene should be played as straightforwardly as possible, and a relatively rapid tempo maintained for it. There should be no attempt to make it funny, nor to make either Frederic or Ruth appear more unattractive in behavior than

*Christene Palmer as Ruth and Philip Potter as Frederic in* The Pirates of Penzance.
*Frederic: "Compared with other women, are you beautiful?"* (*D'Oyly Carte production*)

*The Major-General's Daughters in* The Pirates of Penzance: *"Let us gaily tread the measure."* (D'Oyly Carte production)

necessary. In the duet, Frederic's attitude should be one of unhappy disillusionment rather than anger. The duet should be staged much as dialogue would be, with the relationship between the characters as natural as possible. Only at the end are somewhat melodramatic gestures possible as Frederic renounces Ruth and she goes off in despair.

The naturalness of the scene carries over into the recitative, which should be as simple and straightforward as possible. Frederic is genuinely concerned about being seen by all the girls, whose beauty has much affected him.

During the long chorus for the entrance of the girls there is an opportunity for ingenious choreography. Emphasis should be on carefully designed groupings of people rather than complicated dance steps. Using the image of an eighteenth-century formal garden, try to create a series of positionings that are attractive, interesting, and varied. Try to avoid the semicircle as much as possible.

The dialogue scene following should be quickly paced, with the fragility of the girls contrasting with the robustiousness of the Pirates without any compromise of the atmosphere of enjoyment.

When Frederic sings "Oh, is there not one maiden breast," he appeals in turn to a number of individual girls, each of whom is tempted, but turns away. Frederic should be well over to the side of the stage at Mabel's entrance so that the center will be left entirely to her during her opening song. There is nothing intimate about the music, and the lovers should not be together until later. Operatic tradition demands that she sing directly to the audience and that nothing distract from her singing. Her character demands that she immediately establish herself as, in her own mind, superior to her sisters.

At the end of the song, Mabel joins Frederic at the side of the stage, and the scene is left to her sisters. The girls have been slightly annoyed by Mabel's display, and there is some cattiness in their behavior. As they sing about the lovers, they keep glancing at them, wondering what to do. Finally they all sit on the floor, singing about the weather. As Mabel and Frederic begin to sing, walking across the stage in front of them, the girls stop singing and cup their hands to their ears. As their solo music comes to an end each time, Mabel and Frederic notice that the girls are not singing and cast a quick glance at them, at which point the girls guiltily try to appear as if they had been singing all along. In order to achieve comic effect, the girls will have to act with great precision in this scene.

In the traditional staging of the entrance of the Pirates, they enter stealthily behind the girls and simply seize them by the wrists, a mild struggle ensuing. It is far more effective to have some of the Pirates pick up girls and carry them around on their shoulders, the girls meanwhile kicking and hammering with their fists. General mayhem on the stage at this point suits the music and avoids the stale Victorian stiffness into which Gilbert and Sullivan staging can easily fall. It is also much funnier to have the Major-General come upon a scene of general chaos and calmly sing his patter song.

During the patter song, the Major-General need do nothing except stand at attention and look soldierly. He may wish to march to the side of the stage and back to the center during the chorus. He breaks his stance slightly while searching for the rhyme at the end of the stanza. In order to make clear to the audience what he means by "*sat* a gee," he puts his sword between his legs and rides about on it as if it were a hobby horse. Incidentally, Gilbert originally wrote "gineral" for "general" throughout the song and consistently rhymed it that way, and that is how the word should be pronounced.

During the dialogue, the Major-General attempts to assert himself, but everyone else present asserts himself more forcefully. For example, the Pirate King advances toward the Major-General with his pistol, causing the latter to back away on the line "We object to major-generals as fathers-in-law." On, "We look over it," he actually waves the pistol above the Major-General's head.

At the beginning of the finale, the Major-General makes copious use of a handkerchief for his crocodile tears. He also uses it to prompt the girls to kneel when he refers to their kneeling. Finally, when all kneel on "Hail, poetry," the Major-General carefully places the handkerchief on the floor and kneels on it on one knee.

On "Oh, happy day, with joyous glee," all the characters join in a simple but joyful dance. The mood of the scene abruptly changes with Ruth's entrance. All should assume stern, tragic expressions, and the lights should be dimmed. The scene should be melodramatic without being excessively hard on Ruth. Finally, the girls retire up onto the rocks while the Pirates join

hands and dance in circles. The Pirate King and the Major-General, on opposite sides of the stage, wave flags appropriate to each.

For the opening number of Act Two, much depends on the stage picture created by the placement of the girls around the Major-General, who is sitting on a bench to one side of the stage, his head in his hands. They should be placed so that their gaze can focus on him while their singing voices are projected forward. They should also fill the stage, which means that some of them will have to be quite a distance away and still appear intimately concerned for his happiness. Mabel should be standing close to him, perhaps behind, with her hand on his shoulder. That way she can lean forward to caress him and whisper in his ear. Graceful motion with the arms is possible as the girls reach toward their father and then point toward the moon. (The stage director and the lighting man should coordinate their efforts here.) Other than that, there is no need for stage action.

As Frederic enters from the downstage side opposite the Major-General, Mabel moves to greet him, her happiness at seeing him tempered by her sorrow for her father. The scene should be as tragic as possible without a trace of melodrama, since the Major-General's concern for his ancestors becomes more humorous as it is made to seem more psychologically real.

The Major-General stands in a downstage corner, ready to review the Policemen as they march in. Their marching should be very stiff and contain a couple of right-angle turns, meticulously observed by each in turn before they are in place, lined up facing the audience. On their belts are bull's-eyes, or lanterns, lighted to guide their way in the night. The Sergeant is the last to enter, and he takes his place in front of them, center. All continue marking time during the song, the Policemen using their clubs as trumpets for the refrain. On the chorus of "Tarantara's" preceding Mabel's solo, the Policemen should move into a new position on one side of the stage so that they can be addressed by the girls who are gathered on the other. Mabel and Edith can then in turn take the center with appropriate heroic gestures. Finally, the General, brandishing his sword (which he has had some trouble removing), can move to the center for his lines encouraging their exit.

The recitative and trio that follow are easy to stage. Gilbert's directions clearly indicate how the King and Ruth are to threaten Fred-

*Donald Adams as the Pirate King and John Reed as the Major-General in* The Pirates of Penzance. *All: "Often—often—often."* (*D'Oyly Carte production*)

eric with their pistols. During the stanzas of the song Frederic remains center stage, while the one who is not singing sits. Not much in the way of gestures is required except the exaggerated attitude of laughter. The attitudes of all three should be relaxed and happy, as they all enjoy the joke together. Frederic, who does not yet understand its implications for him, is as delighted as the other two. In the following dialogue, however, the mood quickly changes to one of great urgency. This dialogue scene should be paced very rapidly, mounting in tension toward the trio that follows it. This trio should be threatening, the three characters close together, facing the audience and brandishing weapons. During the short solo lines, the two who are not singing may face the one who is,

but their bodies should be kept facing the audience. On the ensemble at the end a dance step may be used, but it should be from side to side so that the bodies continue to face forward, and should involve pronounced stamping of feet.

When Ruth and the King have left, Frederic throws himself down on the bench weeping. Mabel enters to announce the readiness of the Policemen but quickly rushes to Frederic to comfort him. He rises and grasps her in sincere agony. The scene between them should be played with absolute sincerity and tragic effect. No attempt to point out the ridiculousness of the situation should be made, and the audience should feel that what they are witnessing is as moving as the parting of Romeo and Juliet. At the end, Frederic's dramatic exit through a window of the ancestral ruins climaxes the dramatic tension of a beautiful love scene.

In Mabel's scene with the Policemen a contrast should be established between her heroism and vivacity and their stiffness and cowardice. It is not quite the same contrast as in the earlier, similar scene, as Mabel's romantic courage has now been tempered in the fire of experience, and she must force herself to face the crisis. The business of having the Policemen's lines chanted makes the scene almost ritualistic and greatly increases its humor.

For the Sergeant's song it is customary to use simple gestures that are echoed by the chorus and performed with extreme sobriety. When the Pirates are heard offstage, all the Policemen visibly shake and look as if they were facing a firing squad. Only when the Sergeant decides to hide do they break ranks and run for the side of the stage. They are all on one side, just off in the wings, so that they can stick out their heads whenever they have something to sing.

Although the Pirates enter on tiptoe in keeping with Gilbert's stage direction, as soon as they begin to sing they stamp their feet loudly on the chord following each phrase. They remain on the side of the stage opposite the Policemen, with Samuel, who carries a lantern in addition to the tools of "burglaree," leading the way. He roams more freely than the others, looking for the proper place to enter the General's house. Frederic, who is with the Pirates, has remained near the back of the stage where he will be able to see the imagined light offstage.

The Pirates hide as the General enters, taking positions symmetrical with those of the Policemen. The General carries a lighted candle and looks about the stage for some sign of life. During the shouted "ha! ha!" from the chorus he registers no reaction. Finally he sets down the candle near the center of the stage, and with his hands above his head, his fingers suggesting the rippling of the breeze, he dances on tiptoe across the front of the stage. The quality of these gestures is maintained while he sings. Then, as the chorus sings, he dances about the stage much as before, elaborating his dance enough to suggest some of the antics of a ballerina. This frolic in the breeze should be the comic highlight of the entire production.

When his daughters enter, the General quickly changes character back to the doddering old man and appears perplexed at all the questions they ask as they gather round him. All this should be managed enough upstage to leave room for the combat between Policemen and Pirates, which must occur in front of the girls. At the Pirate King's command several of the Pirates seize the General. A few moments later two Pirates have their pistols at Frederic's head, giving special force to his statement that he is unable to offer assistance. The General is then forced to his knees as the King confronts him.

As the Policemen spring up, the Sergeant twirls a ratchet noisemaker, a somewhat ineffective and prosaic call to arms to his men. The Policemen engage the Pirates in a combat of swords against clubs, the clubs being used as swords, and in a few chords all the Policemen are lying on the ground or kneeling. As the Sergeant charges the Pirates to yield, he pulls out a Union Jack. The Pirates, taken aback, politely kneel and allow the Policemen to stand triumphantly over them. The General, whose sword has been taken from him, retrieves it from the Pirate King. When the Pirates confess to loving their Queen, the Policemen pull out handkerchiefs and weep.

During the finale it is effective to have a simple dance step that can be performed in place. The General goes to each of his daughters (there are two to a Pirate) and bids her farewell. Meanwhile, the Sergeant has discovered Ruth, and after a quick flirtation during which she is suitably coy, offers her a rose, which she accepts. At this point the General reaches him and attempts to congratulate him. He, however, indicates his desire for a tip. The General, finding a few coins in his nightgown, tips him and then turns his attentions to Frederic and Mabel.

SCENERY AND COSTUMES

The major problem with the scenery is to provide appropriate colorfulness while at the same time making the sets appear reasonably natural. An interesting variety of blues can be used in the sea and sky, which form a major part of the first-act backdrop. A ship anchored offshore can add to the variety of the seascape. In addition, the coastline might jut out into the ocean a little distance away. On either side of the stage rocks jut out. These provide an opportunity for a raised area on one side, making entrances more dramatic and groupings more interesting. The set designer should work closely with the costume designer so that the costumes fill in the bright colors that cannot be included in the set, and these bright colors are distributed among the characters enough so that they are always present on the stage.

The ruins in the second act offer the opportunity for a moody, romantic setting, which can be both elaborate and beautiful. Here the dominant colors will be the green of the foliage, the gray of the ruins, and the dark blue of the sky. The ruins may be stylized, but they are extremely effective if they give the appearance of a nineteenth-century etching.

Of the original production Sullivan wrote, "I never saw such a beautiful combination of colour and form on any stage. All the girls dressed in the old-fashioned English style, every dress designed separately by Faustin, and some of the girls look as if they had stepped out of a Gainsborough picture." Probably never since the original production have the girls been given such elaborate and individual attention. It is in their costumes that most of the elaborateness of the production should be concentrated. For their first entrance they should have parasols designed to match their dresses. For the last part of the second act, however, they are all in white nightgowns and carry candles.

The Pirate costumes should convey sparkle rather than fierceness. Individual chorus members can have fun with variously styled beards and mustaches. Ruth should be dressed as a female Pirate. The Pirate King wears a large black hat with a skull and crossbones on it, a black coat with epaulets on the shoulders, and very large boots. The costumes of the Major-General and the Policemen are standard and should probably be rented. In the second act the Major-General wears a nightgown of either brown or red, a nightcap, socks, and slippers. If he also wears his sword, the effect can be quite amusing, assuming that the sword does not interfere with his dance. The Sergeant is, by tradition, a redhead.

# Chapter IX

# PATIENCE, OR BUNTHORNE'S BRIDE

## PRODUCTION NOTES

More than any of the other operas, *Patience* depends for its effect on a highly developed sense of style. Any crudeness in the acting, any lapse into low comedy, and much of the effectiveness of the total production is destroyed. Since the music is neither as effective nor as demanding as in most of the other operas, great emphasis must be placed on the acting. *Patience* will be either uproariously funny or terribly dull, as the satire depends not on particular moments, as in the other operas, but on the total effect, and if the total effect is marred, the audience will simply get tired of too many lovesick maidens and oddly dressed poets.

If you are considering a production of *Patience*, begin by finding outstanding scenery and costume designers. The Pre-Raphaelite satire of the production must be felt visually as clearly as in the words and music. Then steep yourself and your company in the art and poetry of William Morris, Sir Edward Burne Jones, James Whistler, Dante Gabriel Rossetti, Algernon Swinburne, and Oscar Wilde. Authentic aestheticism is more important to *Patience* than, say, authentic Japanese effects are to *The Mikado*, because *Patience* is so clearly *about* the aesthetic subtleties of a particular movement.

If matters of style have been properly attended to, there is nothing particularly difficult about *Patience*. The music makes no unusual demands on the chorus or any of the soloists. Aside from some comic numbers in Act Two, choreography is at a minimum. Furthermore, there is no absolutely essential reason that there be two settings, as is the case with many of the operas. Conceivably the exterior of Castle Bunthorne of Act One could be combined with the glade of Act Two.

## CRITICAL DISCUSSION

It is an indication of the excellence of Gilbert's achievement that although *Patience* was based on a subject that should have guaranteed its being ephemeral, it is nearly as effective and relevant today as it was when it was written. The Pre-Raphaelite aesthetic movement, which began in the 1860's and lasted thirty years or so, was based on a desire to break away from Victorian stodginess and hark back to the supposed artistic freedom of the period prior to Raphael. An interest in stained glass, lilies in the lapel, and poetry more effective in the lyricism of its sound than its sense were outstanding characteristics of the Pre-Raphaelites. Although the originators of the movement were genuine artists, they created a fad of art for art's sake that attracted people whose manners and conversation became absurdly affected.

In mocking the fadism of an artistic movement rather than the art itself, Gilbert achieved a satiric concept universal in its implications. The tendency of people to identify with movements whose implications they do not fully understand, but whose style they blindly ape, is found in all places and during all ages. Small wonder that we recognize the absurdities of our own time so fully reflected in *Patience* that history seems to have repeated itself.

The rivalry of Bunthorne and Grosvenor for the adulation of the twenty lovesick maidens whom as individuals they despise might easily have been repetitious, but Gilbert has carefully differentiated the two aesthetes, placing emphasis on Bunthorne's posing and his artistic abilities and on Grosvenor's physical beauty. The valiant attempts of the Dragoons to win back the love of their ladies by imitating the absurdities of the aesthetes provides a humorous subplot. The result is that to an unusual extent this opera concentrates on a single idea, continually ringing changes on its various implications.

Part of the secret of the opera's appeal lies in the fact that although its target is the poseur, its subject is love—not the intimate kind, but the sort that is felt at a distance for the unattainable. In Bunthorne and Grosvenor we see contrasting kinds of self-love. In the Maidens we see infatuation. In Lady Jane, suffocating loyalty. In the Dragoons, the frustration of losing a love that has been more or less taken for granted. Patience, who begins the opera free from the shackles of love, is the one character who seems to experience anything that we can take seriously. Her ballad, "Love is a plaintive song," rises, in its words, above the level of comic opera and becomes a genuine poem. Its apparently sentimental words achieve depth from the realization that the singer does not want to feel the love that moves her to such eloquence.

In almost all of his lyrics for *Patience*, Gilbert was at his best. Bunthorne's "If you're anxious for to shine" captures the torment of the poseur who must pretend to like the things he doesn't for the sake of his audience. Grosvenor's "Magnet and Churn" song offers a parable that combines the nursery-rhyme quality of his poetry with a dramatic statement of how the idolized can have everything except what he really wants, and concludes with a brilliant series of puns that thoroughly mix the seriousness of the song with its absurdities. The Colonel's "When I first put this uniform on" makes short work of the whole business of dressing in order to appeal to the opposite sex.

Sullivan, on the other hand, though he wrote some excellently tuneful comic numbers, took too many opportunities to write pseudo-serious music that is obvious and potentially banal. We easily tire of hearing from the Love-Sick Maidens. Several moments in the finale of Act One suggest that we are really in church, and the songs for Patience have little distinction. That is not to say that much of the music is not good. Only two moments, however, seem truly excellent. The first-act finale ends with an exciting ensemble, and the duet for Bunthorne and Lady Jane is one of Sullivan's best comic numbers.

## CHARACTER SKETCHES

### Colonel Calverley

The prototype of the British officer: stuffy, humorless, stiff, but large and powerful. He should be a good singer with a heavy, dark voice that lies in the high-baritone range. Diction is especially important, as his two songs require rapid delivery and clear enunciation. His commanding, masculine quality makes the more ridiculous the gyrations of his aesthetic rivals. He, more than the Duke or the Major, establishes the character of the Dragoons, and consequently he should be good at working along with the chorus.

Interestingly enough, he has a much more important part in the first act than the second, during which his role is largely limited to joining the Duke and the Major in imitating the aesthetes. This scene is one of the funniest in the opera, and in order to carry it off, the Colonel must be a good comic actor. He must mimic the superficial gestures of the aesthetes without ever really losing his stiffness or conveying an understanding of their internal mechanism.

### Major Murgatroyd

In D'Oyly Carte productions this role is always given to the man who understudies the Grossmith parts. Although it is quite small, it offers an opportunity for good character acting. The Major is portrayed as quite old, and one of his comic bits is that he gets a severe cramp in his leg while mimicking the aesthetes and puts his foot on a tree stump in order to slap the pain out of his leg.

### Lieut. the Duke of Dunstable

A soldier with some sense of humor and an income of £1,000 a day. The Duke has attempted to avoid the adulation that he suffered in excess while a Duke by joining the regiment. In that respect he is perhaps a foil to Grosvenor, who does not seem to have found such intelligent means of dealing with *his* idolators. Because he is a member of the aristocracy, the Duke combines the stiffness thereunto with that of a soldier, becoming the most unbending of the lot. The fact that Gilbert assigned this role to the tenor may have had something to do with his trials in trying to get any acting out of his Frederic in *Pirates*. In any event, this role can be played by a man with a good voice and relatively little acting ability who can simply manage to sound always as if he were sneering.

### Reginald Bunthorne

Bunthorne is one of Gilbert's finest creations, possibly because he has so many sources. Early in his genesis was the influence of the *Bab Ballad* "The Rival Curates," in which two curates compete for the love of the village maidens. There is, therefore, a trace of the ecclesiastic in Bunthorne. His real-life sources included William Morris and James Whistler, whom he is made up to resemble physically. Late in his development he achieved a considerable dose of Oscar Wilde, who was in the process of becoming a public figure while Gilbert was working on the libretto.

His motivations are at least as complicated as his genesis. Primary is his insane craving to figure largely in the daydreams of young ladies. Then there is his love for Patience, a love not so much for any flesh-and-blood maiden as for a poetic ideal, Patience being the archetypal milkmaid. His love is in no way compromised by his dignity, as he is quite willing to have Patience even though he knows she thinks he is unattractive.

Next, we must consider Bunthorne as a schemer. He has adopted the aesthetic style of behavior, even though he has no taste for it, simply because he knows it will make him popular. When Archibald arrives on the scene and becomes more popular than he is, it does not take him long to dream up a means (abortive though it may be) of robbing Archibald of his popularity.

Then, we have the specialist in dramatic effects. Bunthorne knows just how to make an entrance, just how to hide behind a book, just how to appear to be caught in the agonies of creation. Since his love life is a public affair, it seems quite reasonable that the tension as to its outcome should be heightened by arranging for a raffle. (Here is the ecclesiastic in Bunthorne: Raffles were often held to aid churches.) Finally, he is able to terrify Archibald by playing on his sentiments and then threatening a curse.

A deeply ironic streak is an element in Bunthorne's character. Although he is a sham who does not really care for lilies and the rest, he is left at the end of the opera with only a lily for companionship. He has so thoroughly identified himself with his role that there is nothing beyond it for him to fall back on. He is the victim of his own devices. He must be played, then, not merely as someone who puts on aestheticism when he is observed, but rather as a man with no private life, who desires that all his intimacies be on view. His exaggerated gestures are all that there is, and if we look at him too closely, we can see implicit the tragedy that ended Oscar Wilde's life and pervades the lives of many Hollywood actors: the inability to be anything except an actor. Fortunately, Gilbert has provided that we shall not look too closely.

### Archibald Grosvenor

Whereas Bunthorne schemes to achieve his success, Grosvenor merely stumbles into it. He is among those who are born great, and he finds his greatness a burden from which he would gladly escape except that he is addicted to it. He consequently regards himself as something of a public charity, refusing to deprive others of the opportunity to enjoy his beauty. The humor of this situation was intensified in Gilbert's mind by the fact that Grosvenor was intended to be rather stout. When he calls himself a Narcissus, the remark has perhaps more psychological implications than he realizes.

There is a great deal of the child in Grosvenor, a quality that Gilbert rather invented than based on any particular trend among the Pre-Raphaelites. The idea is a good one, since many public figures achieve fame rather accidentally because of some quality that appeals to audiences that they themselves do not understand. Such characters are often more like children than contrivers after fame. We meet him first as the little boy that Patience loved, merely grown older and stouter. We then see him writing poems about children. Throughout, we feel that he takes every situation at face value and is incapable of any thought beyond naive innocence. He should be played, therefore, with a gentleness that pervades even his cry of "Horror," and a pleasant, smiling manner that becomes rather cloying. For the most part he is given sweet melodies to sing that require a beautiful voice lying quite high in the baritone range.

## Mr. Bunthorne's Solicitor

A pantomime part that should be cast entirely for the way the man's looks convey a quietly humorous personality. Here is the typical Gilbertian joke of an official doing his job officially, even though the job is completely absurd. He is dressed formally and wears a top hat, which he uses to collect the lottery slips. His official manner is broken through when he quails at the Dragoons' curse, but he recovers quickly and goes about his business, supervising the lottery.

## Lady Angela

She is more dignified than delicate, and gives a certain official stamp to the sorrows of the lovesick Maidens. She makes it her business to instruct Patience in the inner mysteries of love. She also, to a certain extent, sets the standards of taste among her fellows, finding approval as she does for the aesthetic attempts of the officers. Her character is that of a leader of fashion in taste who in fact understands nothing of the elements of taste. She finds her counterpart today among certain leaders in artistic circles.

She has an important singing role, most of the music of a delicate legato nature. As the acting of her role is relatively easy, she should probably be chosen for her singing voice.

## Lady Saphir

She is the classical scholar who, though she has not the force of character to lead the fashions, has the skill to communicate the impression that she understands them by frequently using arcane expressions. She attends closely to Angela's thinking and consistently supports and elaborates her point of view. She is perhaps a little more spontaneous and scintillating than Angela because she is not quite so oppressed by the responsibility of aesthetic priesthood. Vocally, the part lies higher and is less demanding. Her voice should glitter.

## Lady Ella

Dramatically, there is little to set her apart from the other Maidens, but she should be an excellent musician with a strong and beautiful singing voice.

## Lady Jane

Although Gilbert's lyrics are unkind to Lady Jane, the role is nevertheless popular among actresses. She is a domineering but dignified personality who stands apart from the other Maidens by always having a slightly original slant on things. Her sense of humor includes the ability to laugh at herself. Her loyalty to Bunthorne after all the others desert him makes her, in some respects, the most lovable character in the opera.

Her opportunities as a singer are quite good. She must have a deep contralto voice that carries well and has personality. Her work with the cello at the opening of the second act is one of the high points in the opera, and provides a perfect blend of acting and musicianship.

The role offers temptations to low comedy that should be religiously avoided. Any compromise of Lady Jane's dignity would spoil the tone of the whole production. The one exception is in her duet with Bunthorne in which her massiveness can be contrasted with his slightness, to comic effect. Many a Lady Jane has carried Bunthorne off the stage during an encore to the duet.

## Patience

Patience is a somewhat un-Gilbertian heroine in the degree of modesty she possesses. She admits that Grosvenor is more beautiful than she and consequently feels it would be selfish to marry him. Her propensity for unselfishness is perhaps dictated by Lady Angela, but her modesty is real, and is part of the generally naive quality of her character. At the beginning of the opera she considers herself somewhat more fortunate than the Maidens because she has never loved. She too soon discovers, however, what love is, and acquires a more pensive manner.

Her naive puns delightfully confuse Bunthorne, and are, indeed, the only instrument that cuts through his façade. With Grosvenor she is more congenial. Her naïveté blends well with his, and she seems capable of providing all the admiration he secretly longs for.

She is not the milkmaid of reality, but that of the poet's imagination, descended, perhaps, from the Arcadian shepherdess of pastoral poetry and thus closely related to Phyllis in *Iolanthe*. Her garments, although simple, should be romanticized, and contain no suggestion of actual contact with farmyards.

*Lady Angela, Lady Saphir, and Lady Ella in* Patience. *Angela: "There is strange magic in this love of ours!"* (*D'Oyly Carte production*)

Vocally, the part is much simpler than corresponding parts in the earlier operas. She must sing attractively, but little in the way of vocal gymnastics is required of her. Indeed, too ripened a technique would hardly correspond with the simplicity of her nature.

NOTES ON STAGING

The impression as the curtain rises should be of a three-dimensional painting. The Maidens are grouped in poses that cause them to resemble Greek statuary. Some of them play on lutes and lyres. They remain frozen until they begin to sing, at which point they break into slow and graceful gestures in time to the music. In keeping with their woeful yet etherealized state, their faces are turned rapturously upward.

The staging remains static until the entrance of Lady Jane, who surprises the Maidens by coming in from behind, but quickly moves among them downstage so that she is in a corner from which she can address the audience for her aside.

If Patience can enter on a platform near the back of the stage and deliver her recitative from there, she will have the opportunity to skip lightly toward the front on the introduction to her solo. The song should have as much variety both in gesture and in placement on the stage as can be managed in order to accentuate the difference between Patience's carefree mood and the sorrows of the Maidens. It is a good idea to have her relate to them as individuals while she sings, particularly in the second verse, in which she seems almost to be chiding them. Each Maiden addressed turns away with disdainful amusement at her innocence.

During the following dialogue, it is well to have Jane and Patience some distance from each other to accentuate the lack of closeness between them in character. The ladies exit with the same formal poses and gestures they have used heretofore, while Patience watches open-mouthed after having remounted her platform, and then laughs heartily and skips off.

The entrance of the Dragoons requires an exaggeration of the pomp and ceremony characteristic of the British Army. They should march in across the stage at an angle, then fall into formation, marking time. When they are in place, the Major enters, flourishes a handkerchief, puts one foot up on a tree stump, dusts his boots, blows his nose, and takes a position waiting for the Colonel. This business should be in time to the music just as if it were part of the ceremony. The Colonel should make his entrance during the introduction to his song, so that he is rapidly striding in right up to the point when he sings. During the song he must maintain his military posture and movement. Although the song has much in common with the Major-General's in *Pirates*, the effect is quite different. The Colonel exudes robustious vigor rather than brittle stiffness, and he should indulge in the kind of mannerisms that reinforce that impression.

The brilliance of this scene lies in its total oppositeness from the languid quality of the song that has preceded it. The Chorus and the Colonel should have so established their vigor that the dialogue following does not suffer from the listlessness of the Duke, who takes over the scene in very droll fashion. Reactions from the Dragoons to the Duke's remarks are quite vocal and involve, at one point, a number of added lines, which, in the D'Oyly Carte production are as follows:

DUKE. Great Heavens, what is there to adulate in me!
CHO. Good Lord, nothing!
DUKE. Am I particularly intelligent?
CHO. No!
DUKE. Or remarkably studious?
CHO. I should say not!
DUKE. Or excruciatingly witty?
CHO. Heavens, no!
DUKE. Or unusually accomplished?
CHO. Definitely not!
DUKE. Or exceptionally virtuous?
CHO. Virtuous! Ha! Ha! Ha!

Furthermore, the Duke's reference to a second-class cavalry regiment draws an indignant, "What?" and drawing of sabers from the chorus.

At the entrance of Bunthorne followed by the Maidens, the Dragoons are in two lines on opposite sides of the stage so that the ladies pass between them without noticing them. Bunthorne is writing in a gold notebook with a gold pencil, and is obviously in the throes of creativity, as his physical contortions as he walks are elaborate. These contortions allow him to observe without seeming to do so that he is being followed by Maidens and watched by Dragoons. We surmise that his physical performance is more spectacular than his intellectual one.

The Dragoons have the opportunity for very funny reactions to the ladies, at first being glad to see them, then noticing their costumes, then noticing that they are being snubbed, reacting sorrowfully and finally indignantly. The ladies, meanwhile, wish to make it obvious that Dragoons, wearing their uniforms of primary colors, are utterly beneath their notice. They walk in a double line with arms extended ahead of them in a beseeching attitude.

During the following dialogue it will be necessary to keep the audience simultaneously aware of the Dragoons' good-natured contempt for Bunthorne, the Maidens' adoration of him, and Patience's noncommittal reaction to him. The Dragoons frighten Bunthorne with their loud "No!" when he offers to read his poem, and further remark, "Oh, no! Anything but that!" following Patience's "You can if you like." The exaggerated passion of Bunthorne's antics throughout the scene, especially while he is reading the poem, is of dominating importance. He expresses this passion largely through frequent angular contortions of his body.

After Bunthorne's exit, the Maidens seem to have the upper hand, reproving the Dragoons so thoroughly for their presumed inadequacies that the latter are quite taken aback. Their amusement and contempt fade into genuine concern. The Dragoons watch the Maidens off rather listlessly, and then attempt to reassure themselves with the bravado of the Colonel's song. During the chorus they can march into double-line formation across the middle of the stage. This will position them so that they can march straight off into the wings at the end of the song, a much more forceful exit than having to march out at an angle, or not in a line at all.

Bunthorne's next entrance reveals him in a totally different light. He rushes melodramatically across the stage as if looking for a hidden

*Peter Pratt as Bunthorne in Patience: "Oh, Hollow! Hollow! Hollow!"*
*(D'Oyly Carte production)*

*Marjorie Eyre as Angela, Martyn Green as Bunthorne, and Ivy Sanders as Saphir in*
Patience: *"Let the merry cymbals sound."*       (D'Oyly Carte production)

observer. The loud chords of the orchestra frighten him as if someone were sneaking up on him from behind. For the recitative, the gestures are sweeping and wildly exaggerated. He adopts several memorable poses, snapping into each of them in turn. By contrast, the song is almost nonchalant. He returns again to the pose of the aesthete, this time exaggerating it slightly in order to poke fun at it. The song should be sung at a brisk tempo, but not so fast that any of the words are lost. The ideas will be clearer and funnier if numerous gestures are used to illustrate the words. Bunthorne should, of course, demonstrate the walk with the lily. This should be mincing, with the toes pointed, a good deal of action in the hips, and the flower held in front of the nose with the nose slightly up and the wrist curved out.

In the following dialogue there should be as much contrast as possible between the simplicity of Patience and the studied artiness of Bunthorne. His attempts to bring himself down to her level only make him the more absurd. When he offers to show her his frolicsome side, she has such a sick expression on her face that he quickly postpones the opportunity. His artiness is expressed both in elaborate and flourishing gestures and in the tone of his voice, which paints with vocal color each of the moods he suggests. At the end of the scene he rises to a dramatic pitch suggesting suicide as he recites the poem.

Patience's curiosity about love reaches a point of vexation as a result of watching Bunthorne's antics, but Angela's authoritative manner quickly changes her whole attitude, and she longs to share the love that everyone else is experiencing. This scene has a genuineness that should not be played for comedy. Although Angela is meant to be a caricature, Patience's reactions to her are sincere and lead eventually to emotions that transcend those of the other characters. The simple joy with which Patience recalls the little boy that she once loved should lend the sparkle of childhood to her eyes and cheeks.

Both the duet with Angela and that with Grosvenor are sentimental in the best sense and should be so played that they cast a spell of tenderness in the theatre. Grosvenor's proposal and Patience's refusal of it are accomplished with gentility rather than emotionalism, though there is a hint of the renunciation to come as the two join their voices at the end of the song. The gestures for "Prithee, pretty maiden" should be stylized, formal and simple without any attempt at ingenuity. The situation and the words carry the song from a staging point of view.

Grosvenor's love for Patience is sincere, not showy like Bunthorne's. He also sincerely and with regret believes himself to be beautiful. Therefore, his tone should have an impassioned, sing-song quality entirely unlike the melodramatic, arty tone that Bunthorne used earlier. Here, not contrast but similarity should be suggested between the characters, Patience's simplicity being much like Grosvenor's. She also rises to the same impassioned level as she suddenly realizes the full joy of love. But she goes a step beyond: On discovering her joy, she realizes that she is being selfish and that she must renounce this love. This leads her to dramatic heights unequaled by Grosvenor, who quietly acquiesces in her decision. The end of the scene and the duet have brought the lovers to a resigned longing for each other. Thus these characters have run the full gamut of love's joys and sorrows in about three minutes.

The finale begins with the entrance of Angela and Saphir leading in Bunthorne by rose garlands, with which he is draped in addition to being crowned with roses. All the Maidens follow in a double line, looking quite happy and attempting a dance that they imagine to be Grecian. They are playing musical instruments. Lady Jane takes up the rear with very large cymbals, looking extremely imposing.

The Dragoons enter and march in a circle around the crowd of Maidens and Bunthorne, before they fall into place at the sides. Bunthorne is then half-mockingly addressed by the Duke and the Colonel, but he continues to take everything very seriously. He introduces his Solicitor, a man dressed in top hat and tails, who enters with a little table and bows solicitously to everyone, smiling and showing his teeth. The stage directions call for him to rush off in horror at the Dragoons' curse, but it is better to have him merely recoil and remain onstage in order to prepare for the raffle. While the Dragoons are imploring the Maidens (who regard their performance as exhibitionistic and tasteless), the Solicitor (at Bunthorne's instruction) takes from his coat a large white tablecloth, which he arranges on the little table he has brought. He then takes off his hat, places it on the table, and places in it some raffle tickets. Finally, he takes from his pockets some change and stacks it in little piles on the table. The whole performance should be brisk and businesslike, and contrast with the sentiment of the Dragoons.

The Maidens, who have given the cold shoulder to the Dragoons, are affected by their weeping, and this greatly irks Bunthorne. He becomes very impatient and gives the impression that he is breaking in with his "commercial" as soon as he can. The Maidens gradually recover their equanimity and line up in front of the table, Lady Jane last. While they are making their purchases, each in her own manner (some quickly, some fumbling for their money, some counting their change), the Dragoons are nonchalantly dancing around their side of the stage. They all pull out cigarettes to give themselves an air of indifference, but they never light them. When Lady Jane at last buys her ticket, Bunthorne tries to take it from the Solicitor, so that it will not be placed in the hat, but the Dragoons see this, and with gestures force him to put it back.

At the conclusion of the chorus sung by the Maidens, Patience enters and asks the Solicitor what is going on. She is thus fully informed in time for her interruption of the proceedings. Bunthorne grabs the hat from the Solicitor and rushes to Patience with it. She rejects it, and he sadly hands it back to the Solicitor. Patience then offers herself as Bunthorne's bride, to the great indignation of all the Maidens and Dragoons. She calms them, however, with her logical explanation of her conduct. At the end of this, Bunthorne superciliously takes her hand and leads her off, casting a glance at Jane that shows his relief at having escaped her clutches. The Maidens all join the Dragoons, while the Solicitor efficiently packs everything up and leaves.

When Grosvenor enters, he seems oblivious to the presence of anyone else onstage. As he walks toward the center, Angela, as if hypnotized, follows him. The word "aesthetic" causes the girls suddenly to break away from their lovers and lean forward as if hypnotized. On "Then, we love you!" they all fling themselves at his feet. Bunthorne enters, followed by Patience, who with difficulty restrains him from rushing at Grosvenor. To express his contempt, Bunthorne throws a daisy in Grosvenor's face. He now has to restrain Patience from rushing angrily at the Maidens. As he holds her back, he grimaces angrily at Grosvenor. The act ends with a tableau.

Act Two finds Lady Jane onstage listening to an offstage chorus of Maidens singing *a capella* "Turn, oh, turn in this direction." She is behind the stump with a cello, which rests on the stump. She is angry and indignant that the other Maidens have been so fickle. There is no self-pity, however, in her observations about her own aging. Both the musical setting and the action with the cello contradict the words in this respect. She is to be thought of as philosophizing in her robust way on the lot of the elderly woman. Her work with the cello should be carefully rehearsed, so that she can give the impression of actually playing the instrument. She throws herself into this task with all the unmusical enthusiasm of the amateur who loves music without being sensitive to it. If the production is done with piano accompaniment, it should be possible to find a cellist who can work with the piano on this number, as the cello is absolutely indispensable in the staging. The total effect of the number should be one of dignity and enthusiasm, rather than maudlin self-mockery.

The scene between Grosvenor and the Maidens is not difficult, as the Maidens simply enter following Grosvenor, who is reading. He then sits on the stump and talks to them, as they lie in a semicircle at his feet, leaning their chins on the backs of their folded hands. Both his recital of the poems and his song should be as simple and straightforward as possible, except that the enthusiasm with which he throws himself into the narrative should never flag. In his childlikeness, Grosvenor has only his energy to help him sustain interest, and the scene must not be allowed to become dull either because

it is paced too slowly, or because it so lacks the magic of stage presence as to make us wonder what on earth the Maidens can find in him to admire.

The following scene between Grosvenor and Patience is a good example of Gilbert's technique of following up a relatively serious scene with a later parallel scene that is comic. Here is none of the sentiment of Patience and Grosvenor's first scene together, but rather the broad comedy of Patience's quick changes of mood from pleading for love to rebuking Grosvenor's advances. Her changes should be decisive and not anticipated.

In the scene between Bunthorne, Lady Jane, and Patience, the trick is to have the proper comic interplay between Bunthorne and Lady Jane along with a clear indication that Bunthorne's love is not so much for Patience as for himself. The first two times that Bunthorne "crushes" Lady Jane, she reacts pitifully. But the third time, she refuses to be crushed. When, later, he says, "Oh, can't you, though!" he looks from Patience to Jane, who by this time is looming very large indeed. The implications of his remark hit him as he looks at Jane, and he shudders at the thought of what he has said. Later, flaunting his superior knowledge of love, Bunthorne crosses in front of Patience, following her last line, and snaps his fingers in her face. He then moves upstage as Jane performs this same business. Seeing Jane coming, he suddenly dashes offstage, and she hotly pursues him.

For her ballad, Patience must put aside any of the comic mannerisms she may have used earlier, and sing sincerely and with deep emotion. This ballad is the most serious moment in the production, and the more moved the audience is, the funnier will seem the scenes that immediately follow it. The staging of it should be based on the comments in the chapter on singing and acting.

In the scene between Bunthorne and Jane, we see Bunthorne gradually won over by Jane's desire to help him. All that has been on his mind so far is his peevishness at Grosvenor's success with the Maidens. He is therefore quite irritable and tries to keep his back to her until she offers to help him. Their duet is the high point of the production, and should be staged in such a manner that both words and personality are well projected by both characters. That means all of the action in it should occur well toward the front of the stage. Both characters should dance, but as Bunthorne must

*The Major, the Duke, and the Colonel in* Patience, *Act II: "It's clear that mediaeval art alone retains its zest."*                    (*D'Oyly Carte production*)

appear more agile than Jane, they cannot dance in the same way. Immediately on the introduction, Bunthorne should break into a rapid, comical dance suggestive of how he intends to confront Grosvenor. While Jane sings, his dance continues, but in a more reserved fashion, so as not to draw attention away from her words. When he sings, he addresses the imaginary Grosvenor with ridiculous contempt, facing the audience directly.

During the refrain, when both sing together, their steps must complement each other, reflecting the division of the voice parts. They might either face each other, alternately backing each other up, or face their bodies in the same direction and their faces directly to the audience, with exaggerated comic hand motions.

The duet presents a problem in that the second stanza requires Jane to dance as Bunthorne has danced in the first, and it is both impossible and undesirable for her to "top" the comedy of his dance. This problem is solved by placing Bunthorne center stage and allowing him to use exaggerated expressions while Jane moves behind him. Her interjections always take him by surprise. The second refrain must not repeat the action of the first, but must be an elaboration of it, which is even funnier.

In professional productions this number is usually encored, often many times. Martyn Green has described in detail the encores he used for it in his book *Martyn Green's Gilbert and Sullivan*.

The following trio, although difficult to sing,

*Martyn Green as Bunthorne and Leslie Rands as Grosvenor in* Patience. *Grosvenor: "I'm a Waterloo House young man."* (*D'Oyly Carte production*)

is rather easy to stage. The Colonel, Duke, and Major enter, carrying respectively a sunflower, an orchid, and a poppy. Their movements imitate those characteristic of Bunthorne (Grosvenor's are not nearly so exaggerated), but they never acquire the relaxed, languid flow that Bunthorne uses. Consequently they appear consistently stiff, like clockwork figures. The song will be funnier if stiffness rather than excessive exaggeration is its source of humor, since the idea of the Dragoons dressed as aesthetes is funny enough without being added to. If anything, their gestures should be less absurd than those of Bunthorne, so that they will appear more like soldiers who are earnestly trying without much success, rather than like ham actors.

In the dialogue scene the secret is for the three Dragoons to simulate the outward quality of aesthetes without ever giving up their military attitudes. Thus, when the Colonel gives a command, the three move elaborately and militarily into new poses one at a time, after the fashion of the parade ground. The Major has more difficulty with this than the other two, as he is old, and his left leg is bothering him.

The three Maidens are unstinting in their approval of the Dragoons' efforts, though they are not yet ready to commit themselves, since

Grosvenor is not yet committed. Thus, their attitude has more the quality of a potential business transaction than of romance.

The quintet requires good choreography, though there is no need to make it funny, as the two preceding numbers have been. It should sparkle with style and precision. On the introduction, the five may do a grand right and left that finally places the Duke with Saphir and the Colonel with Angela. After the Duke's part of each stanza, one character dances alone quite elaborately in the center of the stage, while the two couples dance on either side. The grand right and left should not be used to introduce the second and third stanzas, but rather a continuation of the dance used during the previous stanza, somewhat more elaborately done, as the characters do not have to sing. The couples become properly assorted again only as the Duke begins to sing. At the end of the number they are linked arm in arm across the front of the stage, and they dance off in that manner, continuing to face the audience until the last one has disappeared.

Grosvenor enters, looking at his reflection in a hand mirror. In the original stage directions, a lake was suggested, in which Grosvenor would see his reflection. He and Bunthorne were to recline on its bank until Bunthorne's "I will

*Peter Pratt as Bunthorne in* Patience: *"If you walk down Piccadilly with a poppy or a lily in your mediaeval hand."*                          (*D'Oyly Carte production*)

do so at once." Apparently the set designer made this action impossible, and it has never been used in D'Oyly Carte productions. If the designer can properly suggest a lake so that the audience can tell what Grosvenor is looking into, this action might be restored.

The humor of the scene rests on Grosvenor's ready acquiescence to Bunthorne's desires, up to the point that a sense of duty stands in his way. What has earlier been peevishness in Bunthorne now becomes much more threatening. Beginning with the line "Take care! When I am thwarted I am very terrible," Bunthorne

should, in looks and sound, become increasingly frightening. For the threatened curse, Bunthorne assumes a vampirelike pose.

The threatening atmosphere established in the dialogue gives way to the euphoria of a light patter duet in which the dancing should be as agile and delicate as the sound of the words. The feet of both characters should be moving constantly in this duet, though they alternate in taking the center of the stage, and while one sings the other watches him, while himself dancing unobtrusively. Their actions cannot, of course, be the same, as each is demonstrating a different characterization. This will certainly be the most difficult number in the production to choreograph, and work on it should start early in the rehearsal period. Bunthorne must, of course, be a good dancer, but if Grosvenor is not, it should be possible to invent steps that are easy to do and yet fit into the style of the character he is portraying. The point is that the number requires the precision of a great deal of rehearsal much more than the skill of elaborate dancing technique.

Another thing that will need plenty of rehearsal is the costume change for Grosvenor immediately following this duet. This should not be left until the last minute, as nothing could be worse than holding up the performance at its climax by the tardy reëntry of Grosvenor.

In the scene between Bunthorne and Patience, Bunthorne's aping of Grosvenor's manners should be very funny indeed. Superficially, he is no longer ill-natured, but his new style fits uncomfortably onto his old character, and his effects are forced.

Grosvenor reënters a transformed man, followed by a transformed group of Maidens, all dressed in the fashionable modern clothes. Not only Grosvenor's clothing has changed, but also his way of moving and talking. His actions are abrupt rather than graceful, and he speaks in a cockney accent. The denouement is accomplished quickly and with flourish, and Bunthorne is left in the center of the stage dancing seductively with a lily. As the others dance in place, he sinks onto the stage and gazes contemplatively as the flower while the curtain falls.

## SCENERY AND COSTUMES

We have already observed that a combination of imaginativeness and taste is required in the visual design of the production. The scenery should reflect the influence of the artists who were part of the aesthetic movement. In this respect, the nineteenth-century style of scene painting was perhaps more evocative than more recent designs have been. A Gothic setting combined with Grecian costumes for the ladies will help to make the effect of the opening chorus cast the spell that it must if the first act is not to seem too long. The costumes of the Dragoons are standard, and should be rented. The aesthetic costumes are made up of ballet slippers, knee socks, green velvet knee breeches, a tight-fitting, long-sleeved green velvet jacket with large gold buttons, a wide satin collar with a huge bow tie, and long hair. Four of the five who wear aesthetic costumes must have wigs, as at other times their hair is short. Bunthorne has a large white streak through the center of his hair. For the end of the second act the Maidens change into dresses that may either be contemporary with the original production (1881) or contemporary with the present time. Gay Nineties costumes might also be effective. Patience wears a dress and hat that would be suitable for a country girl of the period, except that they are a little too elaborate and immaculate.

# Chapter X

# IOLANTHE, OR THE PEER
# AND THE PERI

## PRODUCTION NOTES

*Iolanthe* is not as challenging to produce from a stylistic point of view as *Patience* is, as it is so thoroughly entertaining both in libretto and music that absolute genius in tastelessness would be required to make it dull. Both settings and costumes can be enormously simplified, as we shall demonstrate. Although two settings are necessary, they may be simpler to provide than would be a single setting for one of the other operas. Both acting and singing lie within the range of the capabilities of the average company, except that excellent diction is required in the role of the Lord Chancellor. It is the chorus that requires the greatest attention in this opera, since both Peers and Fairies have much difficult music to sing and must accompany it with expert stage action. The chorus parts are extremely rewarding, however, and if you are anxious both to show off and to satisfy a fine chorus, you should do *Iolanthe*.

If a modest production will leave *Iolanthe* unharmed, a painstaking one will enormously enhance it. Authenticity in the Peers and the Lord Chancellor and sparkle in the Fairies should be developed as far as possible. The second-act set should be almost a photographic reproduction of the House of Lords, with a guardhouse for Private Willis in the foreground. In the first act we should see a milieu so beautifully appropriate for the Fairies that the Peers' presence in it will be a continuing visual anomaly. Also possible in the first act are a bridge across which most entrances are made, and a trapdoor through which Iolanthe can make her first appearance, seeming to come from the bottom of a stream. Although a trapdoor in combination with real water were used in the original production, most modern productions are satisfied with an Iolanthe who comes from behind a bush near the bridge. Gone, too, is the band of Grenadier Guards, who in the original production preceded the Peers on their first entrance.

Choreography plays a major role in this opera. Not only are there a number of choral sections (beginning with the opening chorus), which must be danced as well as sung, there is also the necessity that the Fairies should be so trained in movement that they are never allowed to relax into mere mortals. Furthermore, the second-act trio for the Chancellor and two Earls requires excellent dancing.

To sum up, *Iolanthe* is an opera that will entertain in the most modest of productions, but that will reward all the affectionate, painstaking care that can be lavished upon it.

## CRITICAL DISCUSSION

Although *Iolanthe* may not be the best of the operas in overall structure, it is the most consistently delightful of them except possibly *The Mikado*. Every moment of both libretto and score is a reminder that its creators are masters of their trade in the highest sense.

This is the opera that concentrates most heavily and obviously on political satire. The problem of Parliamentary reform has been of frequent concern in recent British history, and was very much in the air in 1882, at the time of the original production. The Peers are represented as being persons of no intelligence whatsoever who are motivated entirely by custom and desire. The idea of having Strephon, backed by Fairy power, carrying reform measures through the House of Lords at a rapid rate is not only delightfully absurd, it is probably also the only kind of political reform measure that would really work. The reaction of the Peers to this state of affairs calls forth some memorable dialogue as well as a number of lyrics that in the stylish tradition of British pomposity make short work of British pomposity. Gilbert's satire has its cake and eats it too, as it provokes affection for the very thing it lampoons, and that is perhaps why Gilbert and Sullivan opera is as much a part of British heritage as the House of Peers itself. "When Britain really ruled the waves" sounds, both in words and in music so much like a national anthem that one easily overlooks the sense of the words and feels simple patriotism. Much the same is true of Private Willis' solo, "When all night long."

But if *Iolanthe* is satirical, it is also, interestingly enough, psychological. The competition between father and son for the hand of the same lady, as well as the confusion about whether Iolanthe is Strephon's mother or his mistress, provide interesting material for psychoanalytic speculation. After reading of the intensely hostile but ambivalent relationship between Gilbert and his mother in Hesketh Pearson's recent biography, one can easily see the mother figure divided between the odious lawgiver represented by the Fairy Queen (Gilbert's mother as he experienced her) and the beautiful, loving creature ready to sacrifice her life for her son, represented by Iolanthe (Gilbert's mother as he would have liked to experience her). Strephon's conflict of identity as the world of fairy idealism competes with the world of legalistic reality in his psyche might be taken to symbolize the conflict between mother and father images in the mind of the developing child.

Such speculations are probably supererogatory from a production point of view, but attention to the seriousness of this opera is not. *Iolanthe* has moments that come as close to tragic grand opera as Gilbert and Sullivan ever got (*The Yeomen of the Guard* notwithstanding). The whole opening of the opera up to the entrance of the Peers has more of the kind of fantasy that verges on the tragic than it does of comedy, particularly in the music, which suggests a fairyland far more human than the institutions of Great Britain. The love duet for Strephon and Phyllis is, both in words and music, a classic of its kind. Then there is the brilliant scene in the second act in which Iolanthe reveals herself to the Lord Chancellor. The haunting offstage wailing of the Fairies offsetting Iolanthe's impassioned determination is one of the rare instances of Sullivan's being successfully serious.

Thus *Iolanthe* presents a fascinating interplay between a world that is actual and contemporary and is yet made to seem absurd and fantastic, and a world purely of the imagination that is made to seem human, realistic, and dramatic. The question of whether reality lies in the everyday roles we play or the whisperings of our inner humanity is of the greatest importance, and though it is never allowed to surface in this opera, it always lies just beneath the surface and gives the action a kind of impact that pure fantasy or pure satire never could achieve alone.

We have earlier commented on the importance of role-playing in Gilbert and Sullivan. In this opera, the role-playing takes on a new dimension, as the roles are not so much assumed for inner and unexplained reasons (a characteristic of all the previous libretti) as they are products of the situation. Strephon's identity crisis is a product of his heritage. Iolanthe's need to conceal herself from the Lord Chancellor forces her to play a role that is determined entirely by the circumstance of fairy law. Phyllis' engagement to two Earls whom she doesn't like is determined by her misunderstanding of what she has observed. The Queen's determination to crush her love for Private Willis is a *tour de force* for purposes of demonstrating a principle, and is quickly and happily discarded. Even the Lord Chancellor, who comes closest of all the characters to being a mere façade, is caught in inner turmoil as a result of attempting to resolve the conflict between his personal desires and his professional conscientiousness. Many a governmental official since has probably had similar nightmares for similar reasons. The Nightmare Song, incidentally, goes by so fast that we have no time to reflect how perfectly it dramatizes the psychological plight of always being completely dominated by other people, a somewhat paradoxical plight for a Lord Chancellor to find himself in, unless we conclude that in embodying the law he has given up his prerogative to embody anything more human than the law. His resolution of his plight and everyone else's by changing the law through the insertion of a single word that releases everyone to go to Fairyland is probably of a type that characterizes the daydreams of many public men.

We might reflect at this point that Gilbert's particular delight in using amorous motives to resolve legal dilemmas may result from an interesting combination of his own early and unsuccessful career as a barrister and the type of unresolved conflict we pointed out earlier in Strephon. As a child he must have wished for a felicitous combination of lawgiving and loving in the relationship between his parents, and many of the situations in his libretti suggest an unconscious working out of this desire.

Although Gilbert offers a great deal in this libretto through the combination of psychological drama and political satire, he perhaps offered Sullivan the most through his instinct for poetic and musical traditions. Phyllis and Strephon, the Arcadian shepherd and shepherdess, are straight out of the Elizabethan pastoral tradition, and they give Sullivan several opportunities for effects that go at least as far back as Thomas Arne. Arne it was who wrote "Rule, Brittania," and who is consequently also the godfather of "When Britain really ruled the waves." We can find the inspiration of the quartet, "In friendship's name," about a century earlier in English musical history.

Then there are the several ballads, some of which are parodies, and some of which are the genuine article. These opportunities for musical expression surely satisfied Sullivan enough so that he was willing to subordinate music to words for the many patter sections. The accompaniment of the Nightmare Song is as ingenious a patter setting as any ever written, with its complete subordination of melody to words and its accumulation of musical effects to reinforce the nightmarish images. This is accomplished through gradual chromatic ascension in a minor key combined with occasional orchestral comments on the words. When the darkness is passed, the shift to a major key perfectly reflects the relief of awakening from such a dream without too rapidly releasing the tension.

Perhaps the only non-English element in the music is the influence of Mendelssohn, particularly in the music for the Fairies. Here, the music often takes on a symphonic quality that raises the tone of the opera beyond that of any of the previous collaborations. Incidentally, the overture was probably the first that Sullivan composed entirely by himself, and is possibly the best of all his overtures.

## CHARACTER SKETCHES

### The Lord Chancellor

The best clue to the portrayal of this character comes from Sullivan, who has provided a solemn fugue as a kind of *leitmotiv* for the Lord Chancellor. The actor should listen carefully to this music and try to walk and think as the music sounds: slow, meditative, methodical, always weighing the complexities of a situation. The Lord Chancellor manages at all times to seem as if he were about to deliver a verdict. Although he is a descendant of the Learned Judge in *Trial by Jury,* he has not the Judge's sly humor and obvious interest in female charms. His love for Phyllis troubles him, keeps him awake at night, and it is perhaps with relief that he is able to relinquish it and return to a much deeper love for Iolanthe.

Much attention should be paid to the Lord Chancellor's walk. He has gout, and so he walks with his toes a little off the ground, slowly and in rather short steps, a bit of a waddle, but nevertheless methodically. Once or twice he loses his temper and stamps on the ground, causing himself some pain. His head is carried slightly forward, and he peers at the world from under his wig and through his pince-nez. His hands are usually in front of his waist to keep them from being engulfed in the large sleeves of his robe. Being an aged man he sometimes has a little difficulty in telling what is going on, but he is always attentive, very attentive, as if following the intricacies of a difficult case. When he turns, he usually turns his whole body, which is much easier than trying to manipulate the wig.

If the Lord Chancellor has been perfectly consistent in maintaining his character from a physical point of view, by the time he gets to the trio in the second act he has an opportunity for one of the funniest comic moments to be found anywhere. After a bit of slow and workmanlike dancing for the first two verses, he suddenly launches into a scissors step performed so rapidly that his toes seem to twinkle. This unexpected vitality is the only real sign of life from the Chancellor in the entire opera.

His diction for the Nightmare Song must be impeccable, but it is not necessary to deliver the song at a tremendous speed. The audience should catch every word and follow the action easily. Martyn Green has pointed out that if one speeds up at the very end of a patter song, the audience will remember the whole song as having been sung at its concluding tempo.

Although the Chancellor is dry and official most of the time, he cannot be so in his scene with Iolanthe. This is tragic and must be played humanly and without exaggeration. Henry Lytton stared dumbfoundedly into the distance. Martyn Green wept into a handkerchief. The two interpretations are equally satisfactory: The point is that nothing must distract from the mood of the scene. When at last the Chancellor is united with Iolanthe, the audience must feel his deep and abiding love for her as he fondles and kisses her with an aged but uncooled passion.

### Earl of Mountararat

Blue blood may be so taken for granted that one feels apologetic about it. Mountararat is conscious of his aristocratic superiority, but also conscious that he lacks many fine qualities. This he accounts for by the natural order of things, by which he means an archetypal, undisturbable relationship between the House of Lords and the House of Commons. The thought of upsetting that relationship is the only thing that disturbs him. It must be observed that he does not register disturbance in the usual way. He is a paragon of *savoir-faire,* having always exactly the right phrase (or song) on the tip of his tongue, and he consequently talks and moves with a grace and assurance that cannot be ruffled. He is a snob, but so vigorous in his snobbery that it does not seem snobbery at all, but rather a cheerful kindliness. He should be a large man with a large, resonant voice, the sort of man who would logically be chosen to sing the national anthem at a public occasion.

### Earl Tolloller

A dry little man of airy condescension, the Earl leads the House of Lords and is consequently somewhat shriveled with aristocracy. He is capable of passion, however, as his song, "Blue Blood," shows, but the passion of love is not so strong as that of friendship. Whereas Mountararat is robust, he is quietly droll, speaking through his nose in a voice that is constantly curling upward at the edges. Like his companion, he is imperturbable.

Although his characterization requires considerable stiffness, his music requires that he have a beautiful tenor voice that can soar easily and suggest that the Peerage is not altogether devoid of the emotions that poets sing of and that are often regarded as the property of the lower classes.

### Private Willis

Gilbert tried in vain to cast this role with a very small man with a very large bass voice. He had to settle for a tall, thin man instead. Today the role is usually given to an actor on the portly side. Gilbert wanted a physique as unlike that of the Fairy Queen as he could manage, in order to lend further absurdity to the fires of her passion.

Private Willis must have a glorious voice, enough musicianship to manage the bass part of the quartet, and enough soldiership to manage his exit in proper cockney fashion. His few lines are spoken in the manner of Dickens' Sam Weller.

### Strephon

An attractive light baritone voice, a pleasing manner, and good stage presence are about all that are required for this role. Strephon takes life easily, and though in his offstage life he has the whole House of Peers in an uproar, things are pretty well managed for him by the Fairy Queen. He finds considerable amusement in Phyllis' jealousy of his mother, and we may take it that his passions do not greatly interfere with his digestion.

### The Lord Chancellor's Trainbearer

It is customary for the Lord Chancellor, on his first entrance, to have a trainbearer who dutifully follows his every step. This character is usually a comic-looking little man, but there is no reason one of his younger wards might not perform this service.

### Queen of the Fairies

The Fairy Queen is among the more attractive of Gilbert's contralto roles. The only jibes about her personal appearance are a few remarks about the surprising things Iolanthe taught her to do. She should be a large, impressive, beautifully dressed woman who can command full attention whenever she is on the stage. No other character in the opera has anything like her dramatic power. It is up to her to create the frightening impression that makes the end of the first act really potent. She must, however, be frightening without ever compromising her attractiveness.

Vocally, the part lies rather low, and a heavy contralto sound is required for it. Almost as important as the singing voice is the speaking voice, which should have a ringing, commanding sound. This is because her lines are unusually important, and because what she has to speak to music in the finale is the dramatic climax of the opera.

## Iolanthe

A much more important role than the length of her part would indicate. Iolanthe provides most of the really serious and human moments in the opera, and should be played by an actress with real warmth and some ability for tragedy. Her songs are not difficult vocally, but they should be sung with great emotion. Therefore, it would be wise to cast this role with an actress who can sing well and project emotion extremely well, rather than with a singer who can act.

## Celia

A winsome character with a singing part that is largely staccato and should be sung lightly and daintily. Her speaking lines are sweet and enthusiastic.

## Leila

Her singing part lies a little lower and is more legato than Celia's where there is a difference. She is the more dramatic of the Fairies, less concerned with delicate phraseology than the others. Of the three, she should have the strongest personality.

## Fleta

She has spoken lines only, and is sweet, but not quite as delicate-minded as Celia.

## Phyllis

She is an Arcadian shepherdess, and closely related to Patience. She does not, however, have Patience's charm and modesty. She is very pretty but somewhat temperamental. Through much of the action she must play the jealous, wronged lover who gives her heart away on the rebound.

Vocally, the role is not too demanding. The most difficult moment is the sustained F with which she surprises Strephon and Iolanthe (p. 94 in the Schirmer score). This must be loud and angry. She never has to sing above G, nor does she have any coloratura. She must have a light, attractive voice; but though there are two love duets, it should not be a passionate one. She should, in general, sing and act like the china figure on which she is modeled. The more figurinelike she seems, the more ridiculous will become the affections of the House of Peers.

## Peers

The opera should not be attempted unless the tenor section is as strong as the bass section, as the entrance of the Peers is the showpiece of the production, is long and tiring to sing, and must be extremely well performed.

The Peers, more than any other male chorus, have an opportunity for individuality in makeup and characterization. This is because they are onstage for so long during Act One, and because each has an opportunity to introduce his character to the audience as they march in single file across the bridge. They should be men to whom dignity is second nature, and who can become interested in Phyllis not with the vulgarity of lower-class individuals, but with the suave sophistication appropriate to their station in life. This will have to be emphasized in rehearsal, as every chorus contains two or three ham actors who think they can get a laugh by doing something rather tasteless, and such activities would be very much out of place in a production of *Iolanthe*.

One quality every Peer should have or develop is the ability to handle his ceremonial robe with grace and aplomb. From time to time a corner of the robe must be tossed over the left shoulder in a manner that suggests years of habit. The Peers, after all, have little except ceremony with which to concern themselves.

## Fairies

If possible, the Fairies should all be auditioned as dancers as well as singers. Precision dancing and gesture while they are singing, with no awkwardness or sloppiness, will greatly enhance the tone of the production. There is less room for individual awkwardness among the Fairies than among any other female chorus, as they must throughout the performance sustain the illusion that they are ethereal, a difficult thing to do if any of them are overweight or particularly graceless.

Another respect in which they differ from most other female choruses is in their authoritarianism. Although they are dainty, they know what they want and how to get it. Falling in love with the Peers creates a dilemma for them, since it is not natural to them to be the blushing, modest Victorian maidens that the Peers would be used to. Although their Queen is more stouthearted than any of the rest of them, they all partake of her Amazon qualities to some extent, and that is what makes it possible for them, in the end, to oppose her.

NOTES ON STAGING

Throughout the opening scenes it is important to maintain a mood of fantasy that does not overemphasize the comic. The lighting can help by carrying the varieties of shading of the landscape onto the stage so that as the Fairies move the light on them continually changes.

At the rise of the curtain, the Fairies are seen tripping across the bridge in single file and making a large circle around the stage. The formation in which they begin to sing, however, should not be a circle, but rather a series of lines in which they can all face the audience and do a dance step that is in keeping with the staccato character of the music and includes elaborate and precise gesturing with the wands. During the solos they continue dancing, suggesting with their gestures the sense of the words that are being sung.

The dialogue that follows the chorus provides quite a change of mood. It is evident that the Fairies have merely been putting on a show with their dancing, that they are actually quite discouraged. Their posture becomes more droopy: They must seem to wilt, like flowers, rather than collapse like tired humans. Throughout the dialogue, all of the chorus should respond with reactions, sometimes vocal ones, to the lines that are being spoken. They should also show, by their behavior when the Fairy Queen enters, how much deference they feel toward her.

The Queen's entrance changes the tone of the scene somewhat. The Fairies cease to droop both because they feel at attention in her presence and because they see her as the source of their problem: She must forgive Iolanthe, and then all will be well. The more positive quality of the scene will be enhanced by brightening the lights a little as the Queen enters.

As the Queen recounts the list of Iolanthe's achievements, she crosses the stage, suggesting each of them in gestures. Her actions are mimicked by the three solo Fairies, not in fun but in sympathy. Each time she says "Iolanthe," she surprises them a little by turning on them.

During the music that introduces the invocation, the Queen moves upstage to the bridge, and the other Fairies group themselves respectfully behind her. Iolanthe slowly emerges as summoned and kneels before the Queen. She is covered with drab waterweeds, which disguise her fairy costume. When the Queen pardons her, she casts off her waterweeds and dances around among all the Fairies, many of whom hug and kiss her.

In the dialogue that follows, the tone should be one of happy reunion and of charm. The scene should move quickly as, apart from the Queen's quip about stoutness, which should get a good laugh, it is entirely exposition. The reference to being a fairy down to the waist should be accompanied with appropriate gestures.

When the Fairies hear the music that heralds Strephon's entrance, they retire to the edges of the stage in order to leave Strephon alone with his mother. He enters, playing his flageolet and dancing as he sings. A basic waltz step with the feet placed in front of each other on the toes and lifted rather high would be suitable for this. As the chorus sings, Strephon takes Iolanthe by the elbow, and the two of them dance across the stage. On the concluding music he continues dancing in front of her and playing his flageolet.

During Strephon's first speech, a rather impassioned one, the Fairies, entranced by him, gradually come out of hiding and stand around him. Most of the scene is played between Strephon and the Queen. The Queen's majesty does not awe Strephon as it does the Fairies, which makes him seem a little oblivious, but all the more charming. Although he speaks of his problems, he seems rather amused than irritated by them, and the smile that characterizes his speaking voice never quite leaves it. The Queen's last line is both majestic and warm, and it is accompanied by a stately motion with her wand pointing down toward her feet.

For the first part of the ensemble the Fairies and Queen remain in place, the Fairies (not the Queen) curtseying to Strephon. Then the Queen gives the signal, and the Fairies circle around Strephon and out a downstage exit, the Queen following them, and then Iolanthe, who has bidden farewell to her son.

On the music for Phyllis' entrance the lights should come up a little. Her entrance is just like Strephon's, except that the two are at center as they begin to sing together, and they dance toward opposite sides of the stage and then back together again, both playing their flageolets.

The dialogue changes the mood greatly, for Phyllis is quite worldly and very much in contrast with the Fairies both in the cynicism of her thoughts and the vitality of her speech. Strephon, who has appeared in the presence of the Fairies a happy-go-lucky creature, suddenly seems to be a slightly henpecked lover who must assert himself in order to hold his own. The staging of the duet should be minimal, the focus being entirely on the singing. While they are singing together they walk slowly across the stage, Phyllis' head on Strephon's shoulder as she looks adoringly up at him.

The chorus of the Peers requires attention to two matters. One is that each of the Peers must be given the opportunity to establish his character as an individual. The other is that the number is quite long and must be given a number of interesting formations. To begin with, the Peers all march across the bridge in a more or less straight line to the opposite side of the stage. They then turn and cross the stage diagonally to the downstage corner. They subsequently march across the front of the stage. This gives each Peer two turns in which to make an impression by the way he turns his head and adjusts his robe. They are all extremely haughty, but each must find his own peculiar style of haughtiness. They should be given no uniform gestures until after this point.

It may be convenient to divide them into tenors and basses so that contrapuntal actions can correspond to contrapuntal vocal lines. In the first lineup across the front the tenors may be a step or two behind the basses, but interspersed with them. It is at this point that they begin to sing. For eight measures they simply mark time. Then the basses move across the

front and upstage while the tenors continue to mark time. At letter D (Schirmer score), the tenors pantomime trumpets and mark time, while the basses pantomime cymbals as they march back and forth behind the tenors. At letter E, the basses are directly behind the tenors and not in view. On the first "bow" the tenors take a step forward and, with the right arm extended downwards inside their robes, they open their robes, revealing their suits. On the second "bow" they bring the right arm back to the left, covering their suits. This entire action is repeated on the next two measures. Measures 5 and 6 each get a step forward and appropriate pantomime. Then the tenors move to the side, again pantomiming, to make room for the basses, who repeat most of the above sequence. While the basses are singing, the tenors move around behind them and intersperse themselves. They are then able to move forward between the basses for their "tantatara's" while the basses mark time. On their last four notes, the basses even up with the tenors. The line now divides in the middle, each group moving upstage at the sides and meeting again one by one upstage center. As the Peers meet they nod to one another in a dignified and individualistic manner.

This should be enough to indicate the type of staging needed for this number. The above suggestions will have to be varied according to the size of the chorus and the dimensions of the stage, but there should be no difficulty working out a series of marching formations that are varied and interesting and suggest the pomp and ceremony associated with British public occasions.

The end of the number finds the Peers lined up in an inverted "V" on opposite sides of the stage. The Lord Chancellor waddles in, peering through his glasses, examining the Lords as he goes, to determine in his myopic way who is where, and essaying the beginnings of the little dance that he will use when the introduction to his song finally materializes. This dance consists of no more than tenderly extending one foot out to the side, retracting it and then following suit with the other foot. While he sings he does not use his feet, but he points at the audience with his glasses and uses sparing but appropriate gestures. As the Peers sing, he nods and smiles to them, turning to one side and then the other. He stamps his foot angrily on "Which is ex*as*perating," and this irritates his gout.

The following dialogue is straightforward

*Peter Pratt as The Lord Chancellor in* Iolanthe: *"The law is the true embodiment of everything that's excellent."* (D'Oyly Carte production)

and must depend on the Lord Chancellor's personality rather than any stage action to make its effect.

Phyllis enters and curtseys to the Lord Chancellor, who moves upstage with her, leaving the center free for Tolloller.

From this point until the entrance of Strephon there is little specific stage action other than the movement forward to center of each soloist in turn. The director should concentrate on the attitudes expressed in face and gesture, particularly of the chorus. They are all very much in love with Phyllis and they feel inferior because they are not of common birth as she is. Phyllis, though she is in love with Strephon, is enough of a flirt to enjoy the attentions of the Peers, and there may be some byplay as she moves among them. This should be kept to a minimum, however, as the stage action here must remain subordinate to the words that are being sung. If the singers project well both their voices and their personalities, the director will have no problem with the scene.

The Lord Chancellor has been engaged in conversation with one of the Peers and does not at first take in the import of Phyllis' declaration that her heart is given. But when he does he is easily the most outraged of the Peers. He confronts Phyllis front as Strephon enters at the rear. Thus the entire focus is on Phyllis, and Strephon's entrance is a surprise to both the audience and the Peers. The *fortissimo allegro* in the third measure of Strephon's declaration is accompanied by the shaking of fists by all the Peers as they turn to see Strephon. He responds by coming down to the center of the stage during the two measures before the *allegro non troppo*.

For their duet Tolloller and Mountararat are in a downstage corner using their capes to express their indignation and to rebuff Strephon. As the chorus begins to sing, the Peers in a double line march around the entire stage and exit across the bridge in the direction from which they entered. Strephon and Phyllis take up the rear, mocking the Peers with an exaggerated imitation of their march. As they are on their way out, they are confronted by the Lord Chancellor, who gestures to Phyllis to leave by a downstage exit and restrains Strephon.

The humor of the following dialogue depends upon the contrast between the unrestrained romanticism of Strephon and the down-to-earth legalism of the Lord Chancellor.

The latter's "No" following Strephon's long speech should be thoughtful but firm, as if the point were really worthy of consideration. If the inflection is just right, the line should get one of the biggest laughs of the evening. From that point on, the Lord Chancellor is very firm in his position, and all Strephon's enthusiasm goes for nothing. During the song, Strephon sits despondently upstage, and the Lord Chancellor sings directly to the audience.

For the introduction to each verse the Lord Chancellor takes a few steps toward the exit as if he were going off. Then, as he begins to sing he turns to the audience as if he has suddenly remembered they are there. By the last verse he is right next to the exit and will rapidly disappear at the end. The effect is of a very busy man who is on his way to an appointment but stops momentarily to answer a question. There is little in the way of gesture: The Chancellor may remove his pince-nez at the beginning of each verse and replace them at the end. His delivery is very dry except that he gets dramatic and does appropriate representative actions for "The Army, the Navy, the Church, and the Stage." Martyn Green sometimes inserted "Alas, poor Yorick" at the end of this line.

The dialogue between Strephon and Iolanthe is simple enough and should be played quite seriously. At the end of it, as the music begins, the two Lords lead Phyllis in with the other Peers behind them. They are all on tiptoe and with their fingers to their lips. Strephon faces Iolanthe and sings his verse. Then, during the chorus, he walks arm in arm with her across the stage until it is time for her verse. This process is repeated until the ensemble, when all are stationary.

When Phyllis reveals herself the lighting should suddenly brighten and all the Peers should step forward so that the stage appears filled. This is Phyllis' most dramatic moment, and she should not compromise the force of her sustained high note. Strephon is not the least subdued by her sudden appearance, being quite certain of the rightness of his position. There should be three distinct attitudes in the characters at this point: Phyllis' anger, Strephon and Iolanthe's self-assurance, and the Peers' vengeful amusement.

The Lord Chancellor enters, and the focus is immediately on him as the characters try to explain what has happened. Iolanthe must veil herself so that he will not recognize her. The two Lords come forward in turn, and then

*Jeffrey Skitch as Strephon in* Iolanthe: *"Can I inactive see my fortunes fade?"*
(*D'Oyly Carte production*)

Strephon takes a commanding position a little upstage and attempts to play upon the sympathies of the Peers. The Lord Chancellor is gradually moved and falls to weeping upon the shoulder of Mountararat. The latter's words momentarily cheer him, but then reduce him to tears and use of the shoulder again "because our Strephon did not die." At this point all the Peers pull out handkerchiefs and try to comfort one another.

The focus now shifts to Phyllis as she renounces Strephon and offers herself to the Peers. Her ballad offers the opportunity for moving among the Peers and singing directly to them as individuals while occasionally directing attention to Strephon. She concludes the number by taking the two noble Lords by their arms.

The ensemble should contain lively stage action as Phyllis escorts the two Lords about the stage and tantalizes them, taking different attitudes in relation to them. The chorus should have specific gestures for their interpolations. The Lord Chancellor, who has been seated off to the side, becomes interested in the situation and tries to let the two Lords know that before anything is settled he must give his consent.

Strephon, who has been merely saddened by the ballad, becomes furious at the ensemble, and immediately following it strides across the stage to up center to call the Fairies. They come in from all sides in several lines that weave in and out among one another and the Peers until they reach final positions in front of the Peers. The Peers, of course, are enchanted at the sight of so many beautiful young ladies, the Lord Chancellor particularly so, and the dominant impression is his flurry of excitement as he suddenly finds himself so attractively surrounded. When Strephon begins to sing he is somewhat upstage, with the Fairy Queen and the Lord Chancellor downstage, facing each other. The Peers and Fairies should have animated gestures including the snapping of fingers on "Oh, fie!" during their choral refrains.

The two Lords line themselves up next to the Lord Chancellor. While Mountararat sings his verse he does the necessary arithmetic in a small notebook while the Lord Chancellor looks on and then checks the results on his fingers. On the following chorus, one line of Peers and one line of Fairies move into positions on the opposite sides of the stage so that all Peers and Fairies are now separate and facing one another.

This attitude of defiance of one another continues throughout the Lord Chancellor's solo and following chorus and ensemble, the Lord Chancellor setting the tone for the action of the Peers, the Queen setting it for the Fairies. When the Queen announces that she is a Fairy, the Chancellor is taken quite by surprise and turns pale and changes his whole attitude. From this point on he is a cowering minion. The Peers are somewhat less taken aback, perhaps because their haughtiness is congenital and not to be cast aside.

Celia and Leila threaten the Lord Chancellor with their wands, increasing his nervousness. The Queen then delivers her sentence, which the Peers write down in their notebooks. The Lord Chancellor places his on Mountararat's back. Rather than keeping his attention on what he is writing, he periodically looks at the Queen. While he is doing so, Mountararat goes down on one knee in order to rest his notebook on the other, causing the Chancellor to topple. Later, on the words "Competitive Examination!," the Lord Chancellor faints away altogether into Mountararat's arms, and has to be borne away by the two Lords, Tolloller first carefully tucking his robe under one arm.

The ensemble that closes the finale offers the opportunity for dancing by the entire chorus as well as several regroupings as lines of Fairies and Peers change positions. At the end, the Fairies threaten the Peers with their wands, the Peers kneeling to implore for mercy. Phyllis rushes in, followed by the two Lords and the Chancellor. She pleads with Strephon, who casts her from him into the arms of the Lords. The Lord Chancellor attempts to reprimand Strephon for this, but the latter is shielded from him by the Queen as the curtain falls.

Act Two opens with Private Willis alone onstage. As he sings, he stands at attention. During the musical interludes he goes through the elaborate series of marching steps that sentries use during the changing of the guard. He is back in front of his sentry box by the chorus that follows.

The Fairies distribute themselves about the stage and do a dance that does not take them far from their initial positions but should be choreographed precisely. The Peers skip in trying to look nonchalant. They end by form-

*Leonard Osborn as Lord Tolloller in* Iolanthe: *"And now, my Lords, to the business of the day."* (D'Oyly Carte production)

ing an inverted "V" inside of the stage from the Fairies. This sets them up for the later duet "In vain to us you plead."

The dialogue should be paced rapidly and should so emphasize the anger of the Peers that the Fairies seem to lose the upper hand. No action is required for Mountararat's solo, other than an appearance of great dignity, giving the effect of a national anthem.

The action for the duet involves simply the attempt of the Peers to make an exit just before the words "Don't go!" each time they occur. The robes are helpful here, as a gesture with the robe and a turning away indicate the intention to leave without the necessity for actually taking steps.

During the dialogue with the Queen, Private Willis maintains rigid attention and in no way yields to the allurements of her voice. The Queen, on the other hand, contrasts as much

*Ella Halman as the Fairy Queen in* Iolanthe: *"When I banished her, I gave her all the pleasant places of the earth to dwell in."*     (D'Oyly Carte production)

as possible the expression of her feeling with the acting out of her control over it. Her song should be filled with gestures that remind one of a classical statue, suggesting the coldness of restraint with which she imprisons her true feelings. On the apostrophe to Captain Shaw it is traditional to gesture toward one of the seats in the audience as the original Fairy Queen did when she addressed the actual Captain Shaw.

If the actor playing Mountararat is particularly good, it may prove desirable to include the scene containing his recitation (see pages 272–273). This scene was used in the opening-night productions in England and America. For the American production it had musical accompaniment, but the English version (presumably representing a later stage in the development of Gilbert and Sullivan's thought) was recited. It is possible that Gilbert was remembering the success of Grosvenor's poem in *Patience* and wished once again to have one of his lyrics attended to without musical distraction. In any event, it is one of his best lyrics and if well projected should add to the effectiveness of the production. If it seems too long, the second verse may be omitted.

In the delivery of the poem Mountararat must be a little less unbending than he is elsewhere in the opera. For once he is not asserting a patriotic fact (as in his previous solo) but attempting to get a point across. His love for Phyllis has caused him to become more human, and he should project the poem to her rather than merely to the audience. This will give her an opportunity to react to it in detail as she follows the fortunes of De Belville with eager anticipation.

The following dialogue is surely the funniest in the opera and depends for its effectiveness on a subtle mixture of snobbery and affection. If both qualities are not projected by the two Earls, the situation will seem forced, but if there is just the right amount of emotion we will almost believe what is being said.

The quartet requires no movement except that the characters turn slightly to acknowledge Private Willis' entrance into it, and then perhaps move in his direction a little so as better to include him. At the end the two Earls exit with their arms round each other's waists in one direction and Phyllis in the other. When they are out, Private Willis snaps to attention, brings his rifle up to his shoulder, marches to his left across the stage, does an about-face, and again marches across the stage and off. On his way he winks and nods his busby at the audience.

Unlike the Major-General in *The Pirates of Penzance,* the Lord Chancellor does not traditionally appear in his nightgown signifying attempts at slumber. The producer might well consider this possibility, however, perhaps having a nightgown designed that will preserve the Lord Chancellor's dignity—and his wig. He might also bring a pillow with him and demonstrate his difficulties with it.

Whether and to what extent gestures should be used in this song depends on how clearly the actor can project the words. Nothing should be allowed to distract from them, because in this song the audience must follow the development of the story line. That means every other consideration must give place to enunciation. The tempo should be held back enough to allow for clarity, even if the singer can take the song at a very fast clip. Martyn Green has suggested that if the tempo is speeded up at the end the audience will remember the closing section as having had the tempo of the entire song. If the song is sung relatively slowly and is encored, it is possible to repeat the last part of it double-time, a trick that greatly delights the audience.

In the following scene the problem is to build to a surprise effect during the trio. The Lord Chancellor must appear dejected and physically in something of a collapse, whereas the two Earls in their attempts to cheer him up are full of energy by contrast. Then, to the music introducing the second and third verses of the trio, the Lord Chancellor suddenly breaks into a wild comic dance.

During the first two verses, the Lord Chancellor comes forward and stands listening to the singer while the Earl who is not singing does a step-halt progression toward the back of the stage and forward again. While the three sing together, and during the interlude music, a relatively simple step is performed. The two Earls do it skillfully, the Lord Chancellor listlessly. During the third verse both Earls go to the back of the stage and forward, one on each side, while the Lord Chancellor sings his solo. Once again the Lord Chancellor's movement is listless—until the words "Nothing venture, nothing win," at which point he again breaks into a rapid and extremely skillful dance.

This number is a good one to encore, perhaps several times. During one of the encores, the Lord Chancellor may hide in the sentry box. The two Earls come on looking for him

*Philip Potter as Lord Tolloller in* Iolanthe, *Act II: "It's a difficult position. It would be hardly delicate to toss up."* (D'Oyly Carte production)

but do not find him until they hear his voice from his hiding place.

In the original version this trio was followed by a song for Strephon. (See pages 273–276) If it is used, the considerations discussed on page 257 apply.

The following duet needs little action, but depends on the singing and the feeling of affection between the two lovers. The director may be tempted to incorporate a dance step while they are singing together, but this is unlikely to be effective. A few steps during the introduction and closing bars should be sufficient.

The dialogue scene is serious, except for the Lord Chancellor's victory speech. This should be comic, but should contain enough genuine emotion so that it does not become difficult for the Lord Chancellor to be convincingly serious in his scene with Iolanthe.

Iolanthe appears with her veil and, in harmony with the wailing of the strings that introduce her, moves desperately toward the Lord Chancellor. He is seated on a bench and does not examine her too closely. She should place herself so that she can appear to be singing to the Lord Chancellor and yet deliver her ballad directly to the audience. During the second verse of the ballad, the Lord Chancellor is much affected. He should communicate this to the audience with restraint. Here, if anywhere, there should be absolutely no clowning, conscious or otherwise.

Iolanthe's response to the Chancellor's announcement that Phyllis is to be his bride should be to run across the stage, desperately making up her mind to her fate. During the singing of the offstage chorus she rushes about as if being pursued by Furies. Finally, she kneels before the Chancellor and lowers her veil. He seizes her face in his hands and gazes at her, kissing her a few times not passionately, but affectionately.

The Queen enters, followed by the Fairies. They remain in a group near the upstage corner, opposite the Chancellor. The Queen raises her spear above Iolanthe, who has kneeled before her. Her action is interrupted by Leila, who rushes forward. Immediately the Peers and Fairies, forming couples, fill the stage, and the Queen moves down center.

The dialogue is simple enough, except that Private Willis speaks in a Dickensian manner, pronouncing "ill-convenience" as "ill-conwenience." The finale requires only a simple dance step that all the principals can perform as they are lined up across the front of the stage.

### SCENERY AND COSTUMES

We have already commented on the main demands of the scenery, and need only add here that very simple settings are possible. A few trees and bushes and a bridge against a blue cyclorama will suffice for the first act. For the second act the sentry box should be provided. The Houses of Parliament might be provided by a slide projected onto the cyclorama. Or an impressionistic suggestion of their outline may prove effective.

If possible, the costumes for the Peers, the Chancellor, and Private Willis should be rented, as they are all standard. If renting is not possible, the Peers and the Chancellor may wear adapted choir robes, the Chancellor's having a border of gold braid, those of the Peers being covered on the outside with colored cloth of blue and light purple. Coronets for the Peers may be made of cardboard with cotton brims. During the second act, the Peers wear formal evening dress.

The Fairies may wear uniform-style evening gowns with wings attached. Originally the Fairy Queen was dressed in Wagnerian splendor with a corset of chain mail and a winged helmet, but this has been dropped in recent productions, though there can be no question that it adds to the power of the characterization. Phyllis and Strephon should look like china figurines. They wear white powdered wigs and costumes with matching floral designs. Strephon has a lace collar, a jacket with a vest, knee breeches, white stockings, and shoes with buckles.

# Chapter XI

# PRINCESS IDA, OR CASTLE ADAMANT

## PRODUCTION NOTES

Three primary problems beset a production of *Princess Ida*. The stage effects are more demanding than usual. These include the necessity for at least two and possibly three separate sets, the acting out of the storming of the castle, Ida's fall into a stream and rescue by Hilarion, and the fight in which Hilarion and his friends defeat Gama's sons. The second problem is that the dialogue is in blank verse and is somewhat difficult to make appealing. The third problem is in the casting. Two good tenors are necessary as well as a soprano of unusual dramatic force. If all of those problems can be solved, *Princess Ida* will provide entertainment far superior to its reputation.

The imaginative producer will find *Princess Ida* an unusually rewarding opera to work on. If sufficient resources are available, its liabilities can be transformed into assets.

Begin by considering the storming of the castle. Gilbert's directions set Act Two in the gardens of Castle Adamant. According to that plan, the soldiers enter after they have already scaled the walls. A much more exciting approach is to design the set so that walls and battlements are part of it and can be approached from the outside, perhaps by having the soldiers march up through the audience. Girls on the battlements, ladders for the men, which can be pushed over, a battering ram that splinters, and other humorous effects can add greatly to the scene. Use of the battlements also makes possible more effective groupings at other points in the opera, as it means that more than one level is available for the staging.

Next consider the blank-verse dialogue. It is taken almost without change from a play that Gilbert wrote before he had developed the aesthetic sophistication that guided him in all his other operas except *Thespis* and *The Grand Duke*. The play, entitled *The Princess*, was technically a burlesque in that it made fun of a serious subject, was filled with comic songs derived from Italian opera, and was played by actors trained in low comedy. It contains a number of rather poor puns and a few sight gags that are of low-comedy character. If the director will accept it for what it is and use the sort of staging often associated with the production of Molière plays, he can have a great deal of fun with it. If, on the other hand, low comedy is studiously avoided in the production, the dialogue becomes rather stiff and tedious.

Musically, *Princess Ida* is one of the more difficult of the operas, and it requires an extremely well-trained chorus. Their efforts will be well rewarded, as the music is excellent throughout and may well constitute Sullivan's finest score.

## CRITICAL DISCUSSION

In evaluating *Princess Ida* one must take into account both that its libretto is inferior to many of Gilbert's other works and that its music is generally superior. The chief problem, however, lies in its subject. The question of higher education for women was hardly a new issue even in Gilbert's day and certainly seems outmoded as a subject for satire at the present time.

In understanding *Princess Ida* it helps to consider its genesis. It began as a long and somewhat tedious narrative poem by Tennyson on which Gilbert based his early play. The characters were transformed from the rather ponderous figures of Tennyson into characters in a burlesque. They were subsequently dignified with the greater sophistication and restraint characteristic of the later Gilbert, but they retained elements from both of their earlier incarnations. Thus it is not surprising that we sometimes find them sounding sentimentally heroic, sometimes farcical, and sometimes genuinely witty.

The wit is chiefly found in the lyrics, some of which are among Gilbert's best. Gama's two songs have often been considered somewhat autobiographical, as they seem to reflect many of Gilbert's own characteristics. In any event they perfectly capture the rather paranoid frame of mind of the man who is critical of everyone except himself in order to defend himself from the very criticism to which he is so susceptible. Brilliant, too, is Lady Psyche's evaluation of Darwinian Man, an evaluation that probably seems truer to the modern anthropologist than it did to the Victorian. The plodding, hulking helplessness reflected in the lyrics for Gama's three sons raises the level of their characterization to genuine comedy.

Somewhat sillier in concept are the lyrics for Hilarion and his friends. Their masquerade as ladies, Cyril's kissing song, and their song about how to win a war against women are in the worst tradition of the chivalric fashion of keeping woman in her place. If examined carefully in the light of modern social attitudes, they seem in bad taste. Played in the theatre in an atmosphere of fantasy, however, they make excellent entertainment.

If Gilbert's intention is to denigrate woman, he falls short of that intention in the characterization of Ida, as she, alone among Gilbert's characters, is predominantly a tragic figure. She is free of the dictatorial malice and misanthropic fanaticism of Lady Blanche. She is, rather, a genuine revolutionary, who, resenting the early marriage to which she did not consent, has acted on what later turns out to be a mistaken view of mankind. Her first aria, "Oh, goddess wise," makes her appear sincerely and nobly dedicated to a cause. Her second aria, "I built upon a rock," beautifully captures the resentment and despair of a deserted heroine. In both of these arias Sullivan reflects the seriousness and power of Gilbert's words. Finally, Ida is given music in the second-act finale that makes her appear far nobler in courage and vitality than her male opponents. The simpering Hilarion, the hulking Arac, and the malevolent Hildebrand all seem insignificant beside her. Here again, Sullivan has emphasized character traits that Gilbert's words merely made possible.

We have earlier suggested that Gilbert's relationship to women was paradoxical: that he both condemned and idolized. Lady Blanche is the least attractive of his contraltos, and also the least important of them. Ida, unlike the other heroines, seems a Blanche transformed into nobility. The power, decisiveness, and leadership ability that one finds objectionable in so many of Gilbert's female characters are in Ida entirely admirable. It is as if Gilbert were unconsciously apologizing for his lampoons. And to top it all off, Ida, the fanatic and revolutionary, is instantly ready to acknowledge her mistake. If her acceptance of Hilarion as a husband occurs a little too quickly, we can easily imagine that she will never allow herself to become tyrannized by her husband.

Thus, *Princess Ida* can almost as easily be made to seem a eulogy of woman as a condemnation of her. True, the sillier characteristics of females are often mentioned and harshly dealt with. But those references do not summarize and dismiss women as they might do in a lesser work. The dimensionality of the characterization lends specificity to the satire. Only certain female characteristics are lampooned.

Beyond that, we must see the satire as more abstract. Fanaticism in all its forms is the real target. Those who isolate themselves from reality and create a fiction as the basis for their action will surely lose effectiveness once reality impinges upon them. Not simply women's education, but all education when it becomes too one-sided and retreats into an ivory tower, will fail to maintain its ideals. *Princess Ida* may be taken as a plea for objectivity and understanding in all human endeavors.

The score invites special attention because of its unusual complexity. The finale of Act Two contains several examples of counterpoint, more subtle and interesting ones than the more famous examples in *Pirates, Patience,* and *Yeomen.* The wailing of the girls against the attacking vigor of the men contrasts the attitudes of both sets of characters and also suggests the pandemonium that has broken out. The comments of the hulking brothers during the singing of Hildebrand are musically humorous at the same time that they contribute to the characterization.

Also to be noted is the succession of delightful numbers in Act Two, which keep up a steady stream of gaiety in contrast to the rather somber mood with which the act begins. Here the music suggests the carefree joyfulness of life unhampered by dogma and overzealousness. The single exception, "The world is but a broken toy," does not decline into the churchiness of which Sullivan was so often guilty during his more serious moments, but becomes one of his best part-songs, combining Elizabethan directness with Mendelssohnian melody of line.

The one number that fails to meet the demands of the occasion is the third-act finale. This reprise of "Oh, dainty triolet!" is too saccharine, and neither lighthearted nor weighty enough to bring the evening to an effective close. Some amateur musical directors have made slight alterations in it in an attempt to give it more sparkle. One solution is to change the rhythm to that of a waltz by lengthening the fourth and possibly the second notes of the melody and making the third and fifth notes correspondingly shorter. With this change the melody can be played faster. Most productions prefer to leave the music as it is and sing it so well that attention is drawn to the quality of the performance. In any case, the defect is hardly a serious one in the light of the abundance of oustanding music throughout the rest of the score.

## CHARACTER SKETCHES

### King Hildebrand

Rutland Barrington, the original Hildebrand, attributed the comparative lack of success of *Princess Ida* to the relative shortness of his role, and there is some truth in this. Hildebrand is relatively humorless, but he appeals because of his imposing nature and the vigor of his few songs. He is the only male character of any real stamina, and it is he, not Hilarion, who really opposes the Princess. To a certain extent, therefore, his dignity will help to establish hers. He should be played by a large man with a deep voice and the ability to sing patter clearly. Most of his lines require rapid and authoritative delivery. He has no patience with either Gama or Ida, and as Gama's sons point out, "When he says he'll hang a man, he'll *do* it!"

### Hilarion

This is an unusually demanding tenor role, as Hilarion has two important (though perhaps second-rate) solos. Like his father, he is somewhat lacking in a sense of humor, and furthermore many of his lines are so pompous and

sentimental that they would be difficult for even the best actor to make convincing. Hilarion attempts to win the heart of Ida with expressive glances, flowers, etc., but in truth it is his father who wins her heart for him with his superior logic. The actor will have something of a struggle to make Hilarion appear anything other than ridiculous, as he is troubled with puns in unfortunate places, his first song is based on mathematical idiocy, and his second song is a plea for mercy at the hands of a woman who has imprisoned him. Furthermore, he manages to convince himself that he is in love with Ida before he has seen her and even after being exposed to the unseemly behavior of her father. The only way to overcome such deficiencies is to play the part with such gusto and eagerness that the audience will accept the feeling of the moment without attempting to relate it to anything else that is happening. Hilarion must not appear absurd, after all, since he has been given the task of being, under very discouraging circumstances, the romantic lead.

### Cyril

Here is a tenor role that is far more rewarding to play. Cyril has a sense of humor. He has also the pleasure of getting tipsy under somewhat improbable conditions and of singing a kissing song while pretending to be a woman. A good performer can make this song one of the high points in the production.

Actually, Cyril is something of a foil to Hilarion, since he is the least serious of the three friends and the most obviously attracted to flirtation. It is therefore important that he be played by an actor with a strong personality. Vocally, the part is not especially demanding and might even be sung by a high baritone. Dramatically it provides the spice needed to make the second act really enjoyable.

### Florian

Florian is more restrained than Cyril, but more fun than Hilarion. The role requires an attractive baritone voice and good musicianship. Along with the other two he must be a good dancer as well as a good actor, since several of his numbers in Act Two depend on dancing for their effectiveness.

### King Gama

Physically, Gama is a descendant of Richard III. One of his arms is withered and useless.

His leg is twisted so that the toe turns in. His shoulder wears a hump. His speech, however, lacks Richard's diplomacy, for his tongue is so barbed that no greater torture can be found for him than to deprive him of anything to grumble at.

Although Gama has brief appearances in only two of the acts he is one of the most important characters psychologically. He makes it easy for us to understand why Ida should despise mankind. He makes it acceptable that Hildebrand's forces should attack Castle Adamant. He makes Hilarion and his friends appear more attractive merely by being so unattractive himself.

Finally, he is among Gilbert's greatest characters, as his perplexity at being called a disagreeable man is genuine. His blindness to his own defects is matched only by his brilliance in pointing out those of others. He has most of the best lines in the dialogue, and while he is onstage all attention is entirely on him.

### Arac, Guron, Scynthius

These three hulking brothers are identical except that Arac must have an excellent singing voice, capable of handling the Handelian coloratura of his second solo, whereas the other two may have chorus voices. Dramatic ability is not important, as they have virtually no lines, and all that is required of them is that they look big, stupid, and helpless. Their fight in Act Three will require careful rehearsal, but other than that they merely stand around. They are aware of their lack of intelligence. They also feel rather helpless on the battlefield. But they have enough horse sense to take off armor that merely gets in their way. They are prototypes of all stupid people who are pushed by ambitious and brilliant parents well beyond their capacity.

### Princess Ida

It is no coincidence that three of the four D'Oyly Carte recordings of this role have been made by genuine opera singers. It is the most difficult dramatic-soprano role in the series and requires a singer who can project with unusual force. Once that is accomplished, most of the difficulties with the part have been overcome, since Ida's best acting occurs while she is singing. She is totally without humor, and her lines can thus be given no more than a well-projected reading. Since the only moment that approaches a love scene for Ida comes right at the end of the opera, there is little need for the role to be played by a sweet young thing. An Ida whose appearance is as hefty as her singing will triumph through most of the opera, and if she happens to tower over Hilarion at the end, the audience will certainly forgive her.

Perhaps her most important scene is the one in which she realizes that all her trusted forces have abandoned her. At that point she becomes a tragic heroine. Although much of the action has made fun of her principles, the audience is now asked to side with her. It will be difficult for the actress to obliterate all the comic nonsense of the second act in order to make her plight seem real. There must be no absurdity—nothing to remind us of how we have previously seen her objectives. This means that the lines preceding her solo, brief though they are, must be absolutely sincere and believable.

### Lady Blanche

Although this is not a lengthy role, it is a difficult one. Blanche can easily become unbearable, and it is only when she is given dignity and gusto that she can overcome the deficiencies of her role. In any event, she is meant to be terrifying. If possible, she should be massive, so that she towers above the other ladies. Her helping verbs are ubiquitous, and some dramatic device must be found for projecting them. A suitable gesture identified with each one may make the business quite humorous if the actress does it shamelessly. Her song, "Come, mighty Must!" is often omitted because it slows down the action and is in itself undistinguished. In the hands of a good actress it can, however, be a most effective number. The role is an opportunity for an imaginative performer to make a great deal out of very little.

### Melissa

Melissa is the least committed of the lady students, possibly because, being Blanche's daughter, she has been bullied into living at Castle Adamant. Her ideals break down as soon as she sees her first man, and she becomes charming and wistful. Her mother's discovery frightens her, but she has enough backbone and imagination to find a clever way out of the difficulty.

*Lady Psyche*

Psyche, being a professor, is not as girlishly delighted as Melissa, but she is nevertheless easily captivated on her first contact with males. She has one of the most delightful songs in the opera, but it is not a difficult one and can easily be projected by a light soprano voice with a certain amount of charm. Psyche should be pleasant but dignified, without being pompous.

*Sacharissa*

She is a student who during the battle becomes the lady surgeon. She has a single line to sing and scattered lines of dialogue. She must be able to appear terrified at the thought of cutting off real live arms and legs. Her role presents something of a problem, since it was her reaction to surgery that caused critics to chide Gilbert for failing to remember Florence Nightingale. Consequently, the more she appears to be part of a fantasy, the more her reactions are abstracted, the more tasteful her role will seem.

*Chloe*

Another student, who later becomes captain of the fusiliers. She is a careful soul who refuses to arm her band with rifles for fear they might go off.

*Ada*

She is the bandmistress and might be costumed as such. She is without a band, as they do not feel well enough to come out into the heat of battle.

*Chorus*

During the first act the ladies appear as courtiers in King Hildebrand's palace. During the second and third acts they are girl graduates and a few Daughters of the Plough (farmer women who act as servants and guards). They must change character somewhat between the first and second acts. In the first act they are constantly interested observers who play little part in the action. In the second and third acts they are very much involved and must react according to their changing fortunes. Thus they establish dignity at the beginning of the second act, become more robust during the luncheon scene, fascinated and terrified by the presence of the men, and ultimately both cowardly and infatuated.

The men are soldiers throughout. They also merely observe during the first act and have little to do during the second and third acts except for the storming of the castle, which they thoroughly enjoy. It will be seen that *Princess Ida* can be performed by a chorus that is much better equipped with women than with men, as choruses often are.

## NOTES ON STAGING

The humor of *Princess Ida* may be intensified if its absurdities are underlined with visual details. Gama's physical deformity is clearly outlined in the dialogue and can be made humorous rather than merely grotesque. The three brothers in their armor are also a visual absurdity. It is easy to devise costumes for the courtiers and soldiers that have their own kinds of absurdities, and to give the ladies academic gowns more picturesque than scholarly. Visual absurdity can be carried over into the staging by postures and groupings of characters that are amusing to look at. That is particularly true during the opening chorus, when the courtiers and soldiers are discovered surveying the landscape with opera glasses and telescopes. One group of about four or five can be crowded around a large telescope taking turns with it. Others can be peering out of windows and from behind objects. They might move their telescopes together in rhythm, sweeping across the horizon and back again. Occasionally someone thinks he sees a sign of life and indicates this to others, only to have his enthusiasm quelled by a more critical observer. Florian, of course, is prominently placed, and should be in a particularly interesting posture—leaning over a wall, or kneeling and leaning forward. During his solo he stops looking through the spyglass while the others continue to look, then looks while they sing, so that there is alternate looking between him and the chorus. At the section beginning "No, no—we'll not despair," the chorus become warlike, using their optical instruments like weapons, and line up defiantly, only to go. back to their looking action as soon as the words indicate the change.

Hildebrand strides in and seizes Florian's sypglass, looking through it as he says, "See you no sign of Gama?" Florian has to take it back from him and look again before he can reply. Hildebrand's aside to Cyril takes him across the stage to where he has left the latter and establishes a close relationship between them. Meanwhile, one of the chorus has discovered something on the horizon. The news gets around, and soon all are looking. Florian, the last to see the approaching Gama, tries to bring the matter to the attention of Hildebrand. But Cyril and Hildebrand are so wrapped up in their aside that nothing will break through to them. Soon all the chorus are buzzing among themselves, and Florian has several times got as far as "But stay, my liege." Hildebrand gets to his awful pun about "sting" and "stung" and finally looks up to see if anyone is laughing. Angrily he cries out, "attention" and all the soldiers fall into formation. He repeats the awful pun and one by one the soldiers double up with laughter. Having satisfied himself, he dismisses them. Florian, now vexed, says, "But stay, my liege" in a monotone. He indicates the spyglass, which Hildebrand seizes and looks through to no avail. Florian then takes back the spyglass and begins the description of what he sees. After each part of his description, Florian allows Hildebrand to look through the spyglass and nod with satisfaction. When Hildebrand says "Is the Princess with him?," it is he who is looking through the spyglass, and Florian cannot reply until he gets it back. Hildebrand's "One never knows" is extremely thoughtful and meant quite seriously.

The efficiency of Hildebrand's court is revealed in the next speech, for as each thing is demanded a courtier rushes offstage and soon returns with some token of the thing demanded. Tokens of hospitality and imprisonment are placed on opposite sides of the stage. During the first chorus of the following song, the tokens of hospitality make their way among the chorus, who react to them and enjoy them. During the second chorus it is tokens of imprisonment and instruments of torture that are passed around.

Incidentally, "hurrah" is pronounced as written in the first chorus, and as "hurray" in the second chorus. The change is because of the rhyme scheme and adds a touch of humor to the song. The "hurrah" pronunciation returns at the end of the second chorus, to rhyme with "papa."

An interesting way to end the song is as follows. If it has been possible to wheel onstage two tables, one for the banquet items, one for instruments of torture, the chorus can crowd around the banquet table grabbing for food. Hildebrand then picks up a whip off the other table and cracks it above their heads. All of the chorus disappear. Hildebrand pauses and selects a large bunch of grapes, which he munches as he exits, as the two tables are wheeled off.

Hilarion's solo requires nothing more than the conventional movement for such a song. Many of Gilbert's leading men carry musical instruments and there is no reason Hilarion could not be given a lute for this song. This would allow him to relate to the instrument in a number of interesting postures as he strums on it.

During the following dialogue Hilarion picks up a telescope left on the stage by one of the chorus. He gazes through it on "I think I see her now." At this, Hildebrand rushes to seize the telescope. Hildebrand is somewhat bored with Hilarion's narrative and walks off in a huff after the quotation. Hilarion has not seen him go, and at the conclusion of his speech turns to share the joke with his father, only to discover that he is not there.

*Princess Ida* is perhaps the best opera in which to have entrances up the aisle through the audience. This is because the chorus spends so much time looking through glasses, and the glasses are best pointed toward the audience. If the characters then make their entrances from the back of the stage, the effect is a poor one. If entrances through the audience are not possible, Gama and his sons should enter from a downstage side, in which direction the glasses will have been pointing. If, however, the entrances are made through the audience, the three sons can begin marching up the aisle at the beginning of the next chorus. They walk slowly, clad in heavy armor, which makes appropriate noises with every step. They may be accompanied by attendants. It would be most effective if they were mounted on horseback (people dressed as horses are quite adequate) and had to dismount before their solo. This could be accomplished in a way that exaggerates the heaviness and awkwardness imposed on them by their armor.

Naturally the interest of the chorus in these characters is great. Some of the more curious girls try to sneak up and examine their armor, but are never quite brave enough. Attempts are made to get the village idiot or court jester to approach with a rapier and challenge them to a duel, but somehow this idea is never quite conveyed to the armored one who is being approached. For their own part, once they are in position, the three brothers simply stand and look big, except that they raise their huge

*Jeffrey Skitch as Florian in* Princess Ida: *"Will Prince Hilarion's hopes be sadly blighted?"*                    (*D'Oyly Carte production*)

swords off the ground with some difficulty when they all sing together at the end.

Gama, being a king, is naturally accompanied by courtiers of suitable character. He comes down the aisle riding on a large rocking horse that has been mounted on wheels and is pulled by serfs. He may begin singing before he has reached the stage, which lends variety of positioning to his song.

Gama's song lends itself to being addressed to various groups of choristers from time to time. The reaction is always the same: Everyone shudders with horror at the sight of him. There is to be no complexity, no psychiatric sophistication on the part of the chorus. They universally and obviously dislike him. Thus, his remarks call forth continued reactions from them during his dialogue. It will be the chorus reactions rather than bits of stage business that will make this dialogue scene interesting, since Gama is always the center of attention, and his lines rather than his actions are the source of humor. The one exception is that both Hildebrand and Gama have their retinues. Hildebrand is always on the verge of calling forth his guards to seize Gama. Gama's followers invariably react to this by taunting Hildebrand's guards. The effect is of almost constant brinkmanship.

At the beginning of the duet the focus shifts to Hilarion, who is being addressed. Gama's attitude is mocking and he suggests with his actions a distorted version of the etiquette to which he refers. On the chorus the ladies curtsey to Hilarion—down on "po-" and up on "litely." Hildebrand's tone is threatening, particularly when he threatens to hang Gama. As the chorus ladies curtsey to *him,* they are delighted at the prospect.

Gama and his sons are marched off by Hildebrand's guards, their retinue having wilted when the threat of action was carried out. This leaves the center of the stage for Hilarion, Cyril, and Florian. They form a picture, two of them kneeling while the other sings. The beauty of the music should not be marred by any further staging than this.

On their entrance music, Gama and his followers, now wearing chains, burst through the crowd, Gama shaking his fist, the three brothers plodding in doggedly. It is amusing to observe that though the chains for the three brothers are heavy and black, the chains for Gama and his retainers match the colors of their costumes. The three brothers take their places near the center of the stage and sing their verse. During the chorus the courtiers mock them by marching around them in soldierly attitudes, imitating the beating of drums, but showering them with flowers and other emblems of peace. During Hildebrand's verse, the chorus line up in strict formations and execute a disciplined and intricate march suggesting Hildebrand's superior military forces. This discipline they break for the chorus, during which they repeat their previous activity. On the concluding chorus of the act they again fall into formations, this time intricately lining up. At a signal, the prisoners are marched off, followed by a final shower of peace emblems.

The second act opens with an atmosphere of classical repose. The girl graduates are grouped about the stage in attitudes of learned adoration, gazing at Lady Psyche, their source of wisdom. Psyche walks among them carefully observing that they are taking proper notes. All of the girls have notebooks and write down everything she says.

Lady Blanche creates quite a different effect from Lady Psyche, who is loved and admired. Blanche is the disciplinarian, the conniver, and she is feared and hated. The somewhat relaxed attitude of the girls immediately changes as she enters. All stand up respectfully and try to look inconspicuous. Blanche strides across the stage like a pompous martinet. As she reads off each of the punishments, she circles about the victim she is addressing. Although the girls might secretly feel sympathy for their peers, in the presence of Blanche they can express only scandalized shock at each of the crimes.

Once again the atmosphere changes as the entrance of Ida is announced. The girls are formal in the presence of the Princess, but they love and admire her. As they sing their chorus they move slowly into a formation of rows on one side of the stage in order to welcome her. It may be desirable to delay the Princess' entrance until the end of the chorus, so as to give her initial appearance more dramatic impact. Since she must be played seriously throughout the piece it is not possible to have her enter while they are singing and engage in comic business in order to make her presence interesting to watch. The alternative of having her stand in one place for several minutes dulls the entire effect of her role.

If it is possible to include in the set a suitable statue of Minerva that does not distract from the action of the later scenes, Ida may address her recitative to the statue. Otherwise she is assumed to be addressing the goddess in the heavens and will look out over the heads of the audience. The aria requires no more than a little conventional stage movement and should not include any chorus action.

Ida's long speech is perhaps the most difficult piece in the entire series of operas. It is a delicate combination of dignity and humor that must never be allowed to become distasteful. Without losing her dignity, Ida must exude the charm that the lines imply, so that her kind of victory over man is enacted in the very way she speaks. There must also be the fervor of oratory together with sufficient movement about the stage to keep the scene interesting. Conventional gestures would be expected in such a lecture, but they must not be allowed to become irritating. The girls should take notes on the lecture and listen attentively to it, but should never react in a way that distracts from their assumption of the dignity of the occasion. Trying to make the scene into low comedy would not only destroy its point but largely ruin the style of the entire production, because if we do not take Ida seriously there is no target for the satire.

The subtlety of acting skill implied in the above is difficult to find in a performer who is also a singer of sufficient musicianship for the music. Inasmuch as there is little else in the opera that calls for acting from Ida, it is possible that the director can teach an unskilled actress to get the proper effects by having her learn the manner of the speech by rote. Such an approach should be used only if he is forced to work with a singer who is a weak actress.

Since the department stores to which Ida refers are not generally known to American audiences, it may be possible to have her refer to local dealers in women's fashions. Care should be taken, however, to make the names chosen fit the rhythm of Gilbert's blank verse.

Lady Blanche's references to the Is, the Might Be, and the Must will become tedious, particularly if her song is included, if some way is not found to make them interesting. One device is to give her a particular comic gesture that is associated with each word. When she reels them off in rapid succession the effect is quite amusing and not out of keeping with her pompous character.

The conflict between Blanche and Ida is made quite clear in this dialogue scene, and is an important part of the motivation for later events. Ida's dignity should be strong enough to offset Blanche's oppressiveness, making the exit of Ida and her maidens not simply a straggling off the stage of the chorus, but a repudiation of Blanche. This will be clearer if the maidens, in quiet dignity, turn their heads away from Blanche as they exit. She, during this exit, can gradually build to a climax of antagonism that culminates when she begins to speak.

The song "Come, mighty Must!" is cut from current D'Oyly Carte performances. It is not a particularly good song, but it can be a show-stopper if it is well performed. It should therefore be included if the performer playing Lady Blanche is a very good actress. (Acting, much more than singing, is important in putting it across.) The secret, again, is to use elaborate gestures with each of the helping verbs. The more melodramatic the gestures the better. Also, in contrast to Ida's aria, this song will sustain a great deal of purposive movement about the stage as Blanche identifies herself with each of the conflicting forces about which she sings.

Hilarion and his friends enter climbing over the wall at the back, according to the stage directions. Many modern sets do not include such a wall, and it is quite acceptable to have the three men come in from a side of the stage, one of them first and gesturing to the other two to join him. The song is interesting to stage because of its many sections that allow for various groupings. The cautious attitude of the introductory music and the opening words change to bravado by the words "In this college." Then each of the friends tells what he has learned. He will do so by taking a position some distance from the others and they will join him on their words that echo his. The gestures will indicate the physical nature of the unpleasant thing that has been learned. Florian, for his recitative, stands facing the other two and gesturing comically. Hilarion answers him by leaping onto a stool or a platform so that he seems to be declaiming profundities. His solo should have appropriate gestures that can be imitated by the other two when they echo his words. The chorus "These are the phenomena," is effective if the three line up very close to one another, their bodies facing the side of the stage, their heads facing the audience, and with their downstage hands they touch their chests and then extend their hands toward the audience in rhythm, meanwhile moving forward in the same rhythm, with a little bounce in their step, so that they resemble a group of chorus girls. On the repetition of the words, they quickly about-face. At the end of the song they are so enjoying themselves that they strut about the stage looking overconfident.

In the following dialogue, three academic robes are discovered. Martyn Green's note on the staging here reads: "To overcome the glaring coincidence of these opportunely placed academic robes, three of the young ladies are discovered stitching away at them as the curtain rises." The "coincidence" is not unusual for Gilbert, and is the sort of thing that is better ignored than explained. The effect of having the ladies stitching during the opening chorus rather than attentive to Lady Psyche will diffuse the focus of the scene unless the ladies are all engaged in similar tasks. Thus it seems to this writer hardly to matter that the robes are discovered without their having been prepared for.

It is important to rehearse the putting on of the academic robes well before dress rehearsal, as many a performance has been slowed by actors struggling with robes they could not immediately get on. The effect of the sudden transformation is a good one, and on the last three lines the three men assume maidenly poses that set them up for the opening of the following trio.

This trio almost stages itself because of the humorous effect of the men posing as maidens. It should not be given choreography that is complicated enough to compete with the humor of the situation. A simple step combined with appropriate female gestures is quite enough for the dance section. When the three characters sing together their gestures should be uniform. During each of the solos the singer can depend entirely on acting and spontaneity to put the song across while his two accomplices merely look on.

The discovery of the three "maidens" by the Princess in the dialogue that follows is in many respects highly improbable. The audience, however, will take it at face value if it is played straight and without clowning. No attempt should be made to mimic female voices. Nor should the three men be more than quietly subdued in the presence of the Princess. Evidently she is more concerned with maintaining the proper decorum in dealing with applicants than with the possibility that they might be male. She is also, we suspect, a little nearsighted. In any event, too much clowning during this scene will blunt the humor of similar scenes that come later and spoil the effectiveness of the beautiful quartet. Cyril is a little obstreperous,

but is for the moment kept under control by the efforts of his companions.

The quartet is musically so designed that some movement during it is appropriate and will help to avoid monotony of effect. The Princess is carried away by her philosophy, and the three men momentarily partake of her mood. Thus she may move at one or two points across the stage, almost in a trance. The others a little later will slowly follow her, as if drawn unconsciously toward her. If this effect is well handled it will contribute greatly to the dignity of the work and help to suggest that the attitude of the three princes toward women's education is not as narrow-minded as we might otherwise think.

Upon the Princess' exit the quality of the acting changes. The three friends have passed their original test and expect to be victorious in their attempt. This makes them a little less cautious than they were before, and quite exuberant in their attitude. Psyche is quickly won over to their cause, so that there is barely an intermission in their levity. The recitation of Psyche's learning is with mirth, which is joined in by Psyche herself, as she is intoxicated by the spirit of these gentlemen and immediately enjoys their company. She is also, however, beginning to assert herself by charming Cyril into love and at the same time indicating that she will take him with no illusions. When she speaks of Man being Ape, she looks pointedly at Cyril, who immediately feels on the defensive. Her song, then, becomes a flirtation with him, and, to a lesser extent, with the other two. It is possible to have her indicate some of the actions of the song by using Cyril as a halfway willing actor of the story.

The entrance of Melissa raises the mirth of things to an even higher level, since she has none of Psyche's irony, but takes the men immediately on their own terms, shamelessly rubbing her fingers across Florian's chin. The quintet is spirited and provides an opportunity for the choreographer, since it does nothing to advance the story, but expresses a mood of general gaiety felt by all the characters at this point. The dancing should be elaborate and intricate.

Suddenly a dark cloud descends upon the mood, as Blanche has observed the gaiety and demands an explanation from her daughter. Melissa, though confused and terrified, is clever enough to remember her mother's ambition. Blanche, who has been pursuing her daughter like a cat stalking a bird, suddenly changes,

*Leonard Osborn as Cyril in* Princess Ida: *"When day is fading, with serenading and such frivolity we'll prove our quality."*                    (D'Oyly Carte production)

becoming more like a cat contentedly licking its paws. A spirit of conniving enters the scene. The stately dance with which the two characters relate to each other in their duet is a way of saying, "We understand each other and will keep everything secret so that each of us will have what she wants." There should be slyness in their expressions and movements, which neatly works against the innocent sound of the melody. Their actions should be formal, somewhat in the style of the minuet.

In Melissa's dialogue with Florian there is an awkward and farfetched pun based on a reference to *Macbeth*. Unless the audience is highbrow enough to catch the reference, it might be well to shorten the line to read, " *'Are men,'* she cried. She keeps your secret, sir." If the relationship between Florian and Melissa is clearly between two charming young lovers, the scene should be played straight. If, however, the actors feel a little awkward with the lines, the scene can be made humorous by exaggerating it. Florian's reaction can be exaggerated fear. When she says "fly from this," he can start to run off, halted by her added, "And take me with you." When he turns and attempts to embrace her, she pushes him away with her "no—not that!" Florian then attempts to drag her off on his line. The luncheon bell causes him to stop and smack his lips over the thought of food.

Hilarion and Princess Ida come in, conversing together, and take their places across the stage from Melissa and Florian. The other ladies follow, the leading players taking prominent positions. When the chorus are in place, the Daughters of the Plough enter with the food and set the table. When the table is set some of the ladies rush forward to get food. Blanche reproves them with her solo, and two or three of them put back some of what they have taken. As Cyril sings, he inspects the table, trying to determine which of the delicacies he should select. On the appropriate words he seizes a huge leg of lamb and takes a bite out of it. The ladies are delighted and follow his example. Blanche, with a sigh, realizes that she is not going to be listened to and consoles herself by selecting the largest leg of all. As the music ends, the Daughters of the Plough collect the remainder of the food and the wineglasses and exit.

Ida and Hilarion walk slowly to the center of the stage. The passionate tone in which Hilarion declaims "Oh, Ida! Ida!" contrasts humorously with the conversational tone he adopts elsewhere in the speech. When Ida asks "is the booby comely?" Cyril, who has retained his glass of wine, nearly chokes in the middle of a swallow. Hilarion gives him a murderous glance, which so unnerves Cyril that he retreats to Psyche and throws his arm around her shoulder. This causes Blanche to cough suspiciously, and Cyril, realizing what he has done, removes his arm from Psyche and slaps his own hand reprovingly. Hilarion then continues. His reference to dressing himself in Hilarion's clothes causes a shocked reaction from everyone, which Hilarion hastily and rather clumsily covers with his parenthetical remark.

Cyril, in his embarrassment, has hastily finished off his wine and is now quite high. His actions become increasingly obstreperous until he has revealed nearly everything. Undaunted, he pours himself another glass during the introduction to his song. During the first stanza he sings the song to all the ladies, addressing them as individuals in turn. At the end of the stanza he suddenly finds himself confronting Blanche. This causes him to retreat into another large draught of wine. The effect is to make Blanche seem quite attractive to him, and he addresses the second verse to her, gradually approaching her, until on the "kiss me," section he throws his arms around her and gives her a large smack on the cheek, missing a word or two as he does. This draws a loud scream from Lady Blanche, which merely adds to Cyril's mirth.

Hilarion, breaking away from Florian's restraining grasp, strikes Cyril on the breast, causing him to fall down. Ida, recognizing Hilarion, runs onto the bridge and falls off it. For comments on the staging problem here, see the section on scenery (p. 128). After Hilarion springs into the stream, the girls crowd around it, shouting back to others behind them what is happening. Hilarion enters, carrying Ida in his arms, and sets her down in the center of the stage. She signals to one of the girls, who holds a looking glass for her, and to another, who presents her with a brush. Angrily, she brushes her hair and makes herself presentable, turning to the three men just as she begins to sing. At her command, the Daughters of the Plough come forward and arrest the three men. For his solo Hilarion stands somewhat upstage and to the side, where he is held prisoner. The grouping of the other characters is such, however, as to focus all attention on him, some of the ladies on the downstage side opposite him turning their backs to the audience in order to face him. On their plea for mercy Cyril and Florian kneel and remain in that position until they are marched off.

If an entrance from the front is used, Melissa will see from the front of the stage the soldiers marching down the aisle. At that point many of the girls can mount the battlements while others guard the gate. Ida herself takes the highest platform from which she can command her troops and observe the action. A Wagnerian helmet and spear would not be inappropriate for her at this point. The soldiers rush up onto the stage, several of them with a battering ram, which shatters when used on the gate. King Hildebrand, who has commanded this operation, disgustedly orders the soldiers who have executed it to leave, which they shamefacedly do. A ladder is put up and a soldier climbs to the battlements, where he is seized by three ladies and kissed. Wounded, he climbs back down and is carried off on a stretcher. Now at a command the soldiers begin throwing flowers up at the girls, who catch them and place them in their hair. Several mirrors come out, and the girls admire one another.

The gate is forced open. Hildebrand enters it, followed by Arac, Guron, and Scynthius, who are handcuffed and guarded. Lady Blanche confronts Hildebrand, who snaps his fingers under her nose and walks past her. Blanche gesticulates angrily to the three brothers, who all pull out handkerchiefs and weep in their defenselessness. Hildebrand is now across the stage from Ida and below her, almost ready for his song. Just before the introduction to it, while they are singing, the soldiers line up in formation behind Hildebrand. Little action is needed for the song. The air of defiance and challenge will be better communicated if Hildebrand holds his ground than if he moves around a great deal.

For their trio Arac, Guron, and Scynthius march forward sadly and face the Princess, standing between her and Hildebrand. On "Yes, yes, yes" they nod to one another as though in consultation.

When Hildebrand sings "I rather think I dare," he moves in front of the brothers, again challenging the Princess. At the conclusion of this recitative he turns his back on her and marches across the stage, followed by all the soldiers. They now line up on one side of the stage, the girls on the other, and the Princess moves into her final position either at the front center of the stage or on the battlements. From here to the end, the chorus hold their positions but use frequent gestures and (if the scenery allows) dance steps in place, to give the final

moments of the act sufficient animation. On their last note the girls kneel to Ida, pleading with her to relent and marry Hilarion. She stands with her spear raised in defiance as the curtain falls.

The idea of the third-act opening is to develop contrast between the warlike actions of the girls and their retiring sentiments. They are armed with battleaxes since, as Chloe says later, they were afraid that rifles might go off. The visual effect of the opening can be funny if the girls have dressed themselves in garments designed for protection but not uniform in appearance, and if they hold their battleaxes in individualized ways and stand in postures that are humorously threatening. During Melissa's solo the girls hold their battleaxes daintily. The battleaxes, by the way, should be made out of styrofoam or some other light material. When the girls hold them during the first part of the chorus they do so in such a way that they will look heavy. They now suddenly appear light and unthreatening. When, at the end of the number they are again held threateningly, the effect is entirely different.

In the following dialogue the girls should maintain the semblance of militarism as they answer to the Princess. Their replies to her questions are authoritative, not squeamish, as if they thought their behavior were perfectly in order under the circumstances. Only Lady Psyche sounds human, even flirtatious, rather than official. On command from the Princess, the ladies exit, singing a refrain of "Please you, do not hurt us."

Left alone, the Princess becomes a tragic figure. If the preceding scene has been particularly funny, the Princess should allow the audience time to adjust to the change of mood, not rush into her next line. Also, the lights should be dimmed as the chorus exits. It might be well to use only a follow spot on the Princess.

For the song the Princess should take two or three varying positions on the stage. Her posture should suggest that she is defeated, yet noble. Some gestures may be used, but they should be dignified and not pictorial.

The sincere tragedy of the Princess' solo is followed by the mock tragedy of Gama's torment. This scene should be played genuinely and with simplicity. It will be funnier if the audience really believes that Gama is suffering than if he either overplays his torment or seems to be laughing at the situation along with the audience. The song must be played directly to

*Donald Adams as Arac in* Princess Ida: *"Like most sons are we, masculine in sex."*
*(D'Oyly Carte production)*

the audience and should contain lots of movement. Gama must not forget his physical deformities here, but rather use them to help suggest the extent of his torment. His attitude is one of righteous indignation followed by self-pity. He seeks by any means available to elicit the audience's sympathy for his plight. His delivery should be the exact opposite of the introspective quality the Princess uses in her previous solo. The reaction of the girls to Gama is completely sympathetic, and a comic effect can be achieved if their attention to him is so complete that they unconsciously imitate some of his actions. Their singing should be as animated and well projected as his. This song should be encored. In D'Oyly Carte performances, several encores are used, a new verse each time.

The Princess' line in which she yields is a difficult one because of its sudden change of mood. It will help if the Princess has reacted sympathetically throughout the song, and if she pauses and sighs before she announces that she will yield. In any event, the impression should be created that she does so not lightly, but as a result of the series of disappointments she has suffered in this act.

If the central aisle is used for staging, Gama may leap off the front of the stage and run down it, laughing hysterically as he goes. The soldiers may subsequently make their entrance up the aisle, singing as they go. This means that there is less of a problem keeping the staging animated while they sing the chorus, since only the last part of it will be sung from the stage. During that part they move in battle formation, taking up positions at attention about the stage. The girls show great interest in the men as they enter, and finally mingle with them, ready to watch the fight along with them.

Gama rushes up the aisle crying out to Hilarion, Cyril, and Florian, who have entered at the conclusion of the chorus, brought in by Daughters of the Plough. His jeering lines go with his bouncing, toadlike quality as he leaps onto the stage and rushes about in a frenzied manner, driving the three youths to a fury of anger. Hilarion is so angry that he pulls his sword and is about to attack Gama until restrained by the menacing sight of the three brothers.

Gama rushes off one side of the stage, the three youths are led off the other side, and the three brothers move forward to center for their song. Each has an attendant beside him who will take the pieces of armor as they are re-moved. The actions for this song are stiff, the situation and the massive appearance of the characters carrying it completely.

At the conclusion of this number the six characters move into positions for the fight, each duo having roughly one third of the stage area. Each is handed a small sword by one of the Daughters of the Plough. The fight should be choreographed so that the effect is more like dancing than swordplay. At the conclusion of the number, Arac, Guron, and Scynthius simply collapse without having actually been struck at all. The three youths stand over their victims, swords raised above their heads in victory.

The conclusion of the opera presents a major problem, since it suddenly becomes serious in tone, with the exception of a couple of witty remarks. It is as if Gilbert has decided that the fun is over, and it is time for philosophy. The director has no choice but to play the seriousness of the text, but he must avoid stuffiness in doing so. Blanche and Hildebrand retain their overbearing comic characters, each achieving a kind of triumph. Basically, however, the scene belongs to Hilarion and the Princess, who must speak their lines with eloquence and power. If there is sufficient energy in the concluding dialogue, the change of tone will not be noticed.

The energy must carry over into the finale, which can easily drag if it is not sung with complete conviction. The focus is entirely on Ida and Hilarion, and there is no need to move the chorus or to introduce dance steps, though the cast may be brought in a little closer to the front of the stage just before they begin to sing. Especially to be avoided is to have the chorus sway in rhythm to the music, a device that would merely emphasize the too-sentimental quality of the ending.

The one sideshow is provided by Gama and Blanche. Gama attempts to propose to Blanche, the only woman he has met recently who might, out of desperation, be interested in him. He kneels beside her and draws her attention. She, however, is thoroughly committed to her aversion to men and gives him a discouraging sneer. Giving up, he turns to watch the affections of Ida and Hilarion, and for the final tableau is leaning sadly against the pillarlike Blanche.

## SCENERY AND COSTUMES

*Princess Ida* provides an unusual opportunity for imagination on the part of the designer. Most Gilbert and Sullivan operas have costumes

*Princess Ida: "Your theme's ambitious: pray you, bear in mind who highest soar fall farthest."*

*(D'Oyly Carte production)*

and/or settings that represent real dignitaries and places. Consequently the imagination of the designer must take into account certain historical and geographical considerations. The locale and time of *Princess Ida* are not specifically identified, though the best evidence suggests Hungary during the Middle Ages. Nowadays the opera is most effectively played as pure fantasy, which means that the castles can be fairyland or dream castles, and the characters can be costumed in whatever colorful and amusing way appeals to the designer. Some inspiration might be derived, for example, from the costumes and characters of the figures on playing cards.

We have suggested that in Act Two it is possible to show the actual storming of the castle and to create several levels through the use of battlements. In all the acts there is an opportunity for lavish decoration, using flags, statues, fountains, and the like, or perhaps including in the castle the colorful sort of park one might find in a zany children's book. The one requirement is that some provision be made for Ida to fall into water and be rescued. If the resources of the company are modest, this

*Martyn Green as King Gama and Evelyn Gardiner as Lady Blanche in* Princess Ida. *At the end of the opera, Gama, unable to interest Blanche in a romance, uses her instead as a leaning post.* (D'Oyly Carte production)

action can take place offstage, but it is much more effective if handled onstage. One solution is to locate the stream in front of the apron, so that Ida falls down behind the orchestra pit. This will bring the subsequent action to the front of the stage. Usually, however, the stream is located at the rear and is created by having the acting area in front of it be on raised platforms.

From the point of view of costumes, the two absolute requirements are the armor for the three brothers and academic robes for the women. Otherwise, the designer may follow his own inclinations almost completely. The more oddly shaped and funnier the costumes the better, provided they do not make it difficult for the actors to project their characters.

Despite its opportunity for colorful scenic effects, *Princess Ida* can be very effective on a stage that is almost bare. With few exceptions, the actors are not dependent on the scenery to make an impression, and clever staging along with the extremely tuneful music can carry the evening.

Chapter XII

# THE MIKADO, OR THE TOWN OF TITIPU

PRODUCTION NOTES

The primary consideration that must enter into your decision on whether to do *The Mikado* is its immense popularity. The fact that it is performed more often than any other light opera of any kind means that it is easy to find the resources you need in order to do it. Almost all costume rental companies can provide a complete set of Mikado costumes, including wigs; there are likely to be many people around who have seen the opera and have ideas about how to do it; and it should be easy to attract an audience. On the other hand, because the work is performed so often, audiences are much more likely to be critical of any given performance. If a traditional manner of performance is used, many people will have seen the same thing done better. If an attempt at originality in production style is made, some of the audience are likely to have strong objections to what they will feel to be a wrong interpretation. In short, it is well to accept the fact that if you do *The Mikado* you had better have an extremely good production or resign yourself to a lukewarm reaction from many people who see it.

The next consideration is that though the work is thoroughly English in its satire and in the manner in which it should be acted, it must have a convincing veneer of Japanese mannerisms laid upon it. The following comment by S. J. Adair Fitz-Gerald on the original production sets a standard in this respect that is worth remembering:

Gilbert and Sullivan always did things properly, and D'Oyly Carte never did them by halves, and as they found almost everything they wanted at Knightsbridge to assist them in the correct representation of the work in hand, they secured the cooperation of the managers of the Japanese village, who willingly lent them a Japanese male dancer and a Japanese waitress or tea-girl to attend the rehearsals and coach the company—a charming Japanese tea-girl, whose knowledge of English was limited to "Sixpence, please"—the charge for a cup of tea at Albert Gate, Knightsbridge. She very quickly, however, picked up the language, and was engaged to teach the Savoyards Japanese deportment, and how to walk or run with the funny little footsteps necessary for their parts. Others of her nation gave them lessons in the art of manipulating the fan, and also in the science of make-up. The Japanese terpsichorean artist and John D'Auban between them arranged the incidental dances. And thus to the minutest detail the Savoyards studied to become Japanesy in every way, and succeeded to such perfection as to win high and agreeable praise from their monitors.*

Once the appropriate scenery and costumes and Japanese training have been obtained, *The Mikado* is not difficult to do. The following casting problems should be kept in mind: Ko-Ko is the most demanding of the comic roles. He must be able to handle his patter songs in a light comic style. He must be able to sing the "titwillow" aria beautifully. He

* S. J. Adair Fitz-Gerald, *The Story of the Savoy Opera* (London: Stanley Paul, 1924), pp. 108–9.

132

must be a comedian with a good sense of timing, as he carries the major responsibility for making the dialogue effective, and he must be an excellent dancer and to some extent a gymnast. Nanki-Poo is an unusually demanding tenor role, requiring a beautiful voice and plenty of charm. His opening solo should not be attempted by anyone who is only just learning to sing. The Mikado should be an actor of extremely commanding dimensions with a heavy baritone voice. If these requirements can be met, the other roles should not be difficult to cast.

Although the libretto calls for two settings, nothing in the action makes it impossible to perform the opera with a single set. A typical Japanese landscape with a volcano in the background is the sort of thing that is most often used. All you need have in addition is a couple of benches.

The chorus play a leading role in the opera, but their music is never exceptionally difficult. More than in many operas it is important that the chorus have acting ability, since they are constantly responding to rapidly changing emotional situations. In fact, the ability to project emotions should be tested in the chorus auditions.

## CRITICAL DISCUSSION

A large part of the success of The Mikado may well lie in an aspect of it that is rarely discussed: its appeal to our subconscious aggressive instincts. The two taboos that tend to create the most anxiety in our lives, death and sex, are not only frequent sources of humor in this opera, they are also made central to its plot. The idea that flirting should be punishable by death, and that the highest office in town should be the Lord High Executioner, creates a comic framework within which laughter may help to release hidden anxieties. Once the Lord High Executioner is accepted as a public official, one can imagine the ease with which undesirable members of society can be discarded. The undesirables the Executioner has selected for his attentions are not hardened criminals, but rather the people who are responsible for petty irritations against which there is normally no recourse.

But execution is not the only punishment we are permitted to contemplate. The Mikado, with keen psychological insight, has devised many ways of letting the punishment fit the crime. His hypothetical punishments are imaginatively delightful. His actual ones are humorously bloodcurdling. The three who have mistakenly compassed the death of the heir apparent are to be treated to something "humorous, but lingering," with either boiling oil in it or melted lead.

This kind of frolicking with the pseudo-sadistic is so appealing because it allows us to have our cake and eat it too. As civilized people we have to keep our aggressive impulses under control. Any direct expression of them would cause us to feel unendurably guilty. When they are expressed entirely in fun in an atmosphere of light music and sparkling dialogue, as they are in The Mikado, the effect is most satisfying and in no way unsettling.

The humorous expression of the bloodthirsty is for that reason widely practiced. Gilbert himself had already used it a great deal in the Bab Ballads, most notably in "The Yarn of the Nancy Bell." But in The Mikado, Gilbert explored with true genius the complexity of our hidden aggressions and some of the social practices that are based on them. The ambivalence and ambiguity with which society rewards and punishes are implicit in almost everything that happens in The Mikado. First of all, we have an ideal solution to the problem of authoritarianism. The official who metes out the punishments must punish himself first. What more ideal protection from governmental intervention could one seek? The executioner who can take our lives is deprived of his sting if he must first take his own life. Such an executioner may be depended upon for benignity, and Ko-Ko is the most benign of humans. "I never even killed a bluebottle!" he weeps. So in the midst of aggression there is tenderness. For all its arbitrariness, the Town of Titipu is a place where mercy seasons justice. That is a prime characteristic of topsy-turvydom, since if you are always going to see to it that everyone gets married and lives happily ever after at the end of things, you may meanwhile get as bloodthirsty as you like.

We get at the structure of society, however, when we point out that all societies have their kings and desperate men. The kings are admired and given power, the desperate men are punished and made scapegoats. For "kings" read everything from streetcorner gang leaders to gods. On some people we bestow our love and respect, on others our hatred and contempt. But society is ambivalent about its kings and scapegoats, and frequently mixes up or interconnects those roles. Kings may be deprived of the joys all their subjects have. As Henry V so eloquently puts it, "What infinite heart's-ease must kings neglect, that private men enjoy!" Scapegoats, on the other hand, are sometimes given the opportunity for riotous living not permitted the common man before they go to their deaths. In primitive societies this is a ritual. As civilized people we often turn our outlaws into folk heroes, such as Robin Hood, or objects of affection, such as Falstaff.

In any event, since nearly every member of society has committed acts for which he could be sent to prison, and only a small number of us actually are sent to prison, we must regard our criminals as in some sense scapegoats, and our feelings toward them as a purging of our own sins, projected onto them. As we become more sensitive to the complexities of human nature, we become more tolerant of our criminals and more critical of our public officials. Ultimately the roles of king and scapegoat may be combined in the same person. In primitive societies that is accomplished through religious mysteries. The supreme example of the scapegoat-king is Jesus Christ, who was the total scapegoat in that he took upon himself all the sins of all mankind, and who was also the King of Kings. In America in recent years we have had an increasing tendency to divide into factions in which one man's criminal is another man's leader, Lyndon Johnson and Malcolm X being cases in point.

*The Mikado* happens to be one of the most sophisticated and brilliant explorations of the theme of the scapegoat-king in all of literature. No less than three of its characters play this role, with varying consequences for themselves. Ko-Ko, the cheap tailor, is condemned to death for flirting. He is thus clearly a scapegoat, since many other citizens of Titipu do in fact flirt during the course of the action, though they are not arrested for it. He is then promoted to the highest rank a citizen can attain, and is given the kingly powers of life and death over everyone in the town. This is by the logic of the Mikado himself, who sees "no moral difference between the dignified judge who condemns a criminal to die, and the industrious mechanic who carries out the sentence."

Ko-Ko solves his dilemma by appointing Nanki-Poo substitute. Unknown to Ko-Ko, Nanki-Poo is a prince, and thus qualifies for the kingly half of the equation. He is furthermore fleeing his father's wrath for refusing to marry Katisha, and is thus already something of a scapegoat. Adopting this role formally, he is given a month to live, and, says Ko-Ko, "you'll live like a fighting cock at my expense."

We have yet another version of the equation in the role of Pooh-Bah, who seeks in an extremely ambiguous way to mortify his family pride. (He is, by pedigree, the most respectable individual who has ever lived.) Since all the official posts in the town were resigned by people who were too proud to serve under an ex-tailor, Pooh-Bah has accepted all these offices and has thus attained the role of Lord High Everything Else. Are we to interpret his offices as privileges of a kingly nature or burdens suited to a scapegoat? Pooh-Bah manages to have it both ways and keep us completely in doubt on this point.

How does this matter of scapegoating relate to our individual private lives? Each of us sees himself both as a king and as a desperate man. Each man is the center of his world, the most important person in it. But most civilized people are rather harsh in their judgment of their weakest points and see themselves as in many ways secretly sinful. In the Middle Ages this drama of identity was played out in the contest between Heaven and Hell for the allegiance of one's soul. Nowadays it is more a matter of social respectability versus public censure. We are likely to try to be Pooh-Bahs, to see ourselves in our self-pitying moments as Nanki-Poos, and in our self-condemning moments as Ko-Kos.

Behind all this turmoil of moral self-assertion and doubt is the father image. We tend to be loved by our mothers and judged by our fathers. Thus the question, How good a person do I think I am? may be answered somewhat in terms of, How good a person does my father think I am? The father rewards and punishes. He is wise, virtuous, and without defect. He is a source of sympathy and of condemnation, sometimes both at once. As one judges oneself, an image of him is always lurking in the background.

Just so, over the lives of our three major characters lurks the shadow of the Mikado. There is no question about *him:* he is the lawgiver, and his judgment is final. He manages at the same time to be the most sympathetic and forgiving of monarchs ("It really distresses me to see you take on so. I've no doubt he thoroughly deserved all he got.") and the most unrelenting of despots, ("I forget the punishment for compassing the death of the Heir Apparent.") He is just what the father must actually seem to the young child who is both loved and punished.

If we examine the structure of *The Mikado,* we find that Gilbert's best and deepest social satire is also his best-designed work theatrically. The action of the plot begins almost immediately and moves forward continuously, each dialogue scene marking an important step forward in the complications of things, and each song providing an opportunity to comment on the universal significance of what has just happened. So artful is the sensing of the universal in the particular that *The Mikado* is filled with lines that have made their way into the language. Yet the work is not so epigrammatic that we lose the individuality of the characters, three of whom are masterpieces in their own right.

The interweaving of Ko-Ko's story with Nanki-Poo's has been so managed that the romantic and satirical elements of the plot constantly put one another into perspective and at the same time help to heighten the tension. The characters are introduced in a sequence that continually intensifies our interest. We are allowed to get used to Nanki-Poo in the company of the rather neutral Pish-Tush before Pooh-Bah is introduced. His character is in turn fully stated before the entrance of Ko-Ko. These three characters are allowed to compete for our attention through most of the first act until Katisha is introduced as a surprise right at the end of it. The entrance of Katisha in Act One means that she does not compete for our attention with the Mikado when he enters in Act Two. Of all the characters he is the most powerful, the more so because his entrance has been anticipated almost from the beginning of the opera. Such an entrance would be a dramatic liability if the character were any less fully realized than he is. As it is, he dominates the whole last section of the opera, giving the final moments an added impact that would otherwise have had to be an anticlimax.

The music, considered purely as music, is not so fine as that of *Iolanthe, Princess Ida,* or *Ruddigore,* but it serves its function perfectly. The macabre proceedings that Gilbert has provided are always prevented from becoming overwhelming by the tunefulness of the score. This is achieved despite the fact that the music almost never contradicts the words. (There is one exception: Yum-Yum's aria, whose words are self-centered and somewhat cynical, is given music that in its romantic winsomeness seems to deny both these qualities.) What the

music does do is reassure us that everything is entirely in fun and no harm is intended.

Sullivan ironically used this Japanese setting for some of the most thoroughly English of all his music. Here, more than in his earlier operas, he casts back to the Elizabethans, and to Purcell and Arne for inspiration in writing ballad, madrigal, and glee. Yet there is enough oriental flavoring so that the music never seems inappropriate. This is found in the opening chorus, the finale of Act One, and the entrance of the Mikado, for which Sullivan used an actual oriental tune.

Sullivan's ingenuity is reflected most in his ability to hold the music back so that it does not compete with the words. Time and again characterization and verbal ingenuity are in the forefront, and the tune provides a background. The professionalism of the orchestration is reflected as much in what is left out as in what is included. There are brilliant touches such as the little tune that the piccolo whistles underlying Pitti-Sing's words to that effect in her verse in "The criminal cried," but there are many other places in which the words are allowed to make their effect without an underlining from the orchestra which would be obvious or even banal. One has an opportunity for appreciating Sullivan whenever one hears one of the nonauthentic orchestrations that are so frequently used by amateurs. It is worth noting also that, although Sullivan's motto evidently was "When in doubt leave it out," the orchestrator for the average Broadway musical seems to have decided, "When in doubt put in a whole lot more to make sure nobody misses the point." Such a difference is an important clue to the distinction between a good production of a Broadway musical and a good production of a Gilbert and Sullivan opera.

## CHARACTER SKETCHES

### The Mikado of Japan

A dark baritone voice and a macabre sense of humor are needed for this character, along with an imposing stature. The dialogue requires not merely good diction, but the ability to smack one's lips over the words. The Mikado thoroughly enjoys every moment of the action, and nothing conveys this better than his technique of deliciously overpronouncing everything.

Nanki-Poo describes his father as "the Lucius Junius Brutus of his race," in other words, a man so devoted to his concept of justice that he would kill his own son in its cause. To the Mikado, people are abstractions and the law is a reality. The necessity for executing three charming citizens is looked upon as a mild inconvenience, but the "fool of an act" that brings this about is the object of his personal wrath. The delightful punishments he has concocted for his erring subjects call forth a bloodcurdling laugh at the end of each verse of his song.

He moves somewhat like a toad, hunching himself within the folds of his costume in such a manner that he can extend his hands or his head suddenly in the presence of a victim. Other animals are called to mind by his behavior: the praying mantis hovering thoughtfully over its still-living meal; the cat, perfectly relaxed one moment and hissing and spitting the next; the rattlesnake about to strike. His use of his fan helps to create these impressions. When it snaps open suddenly, everyone falls to the ground in terror. When it is opened gradually, uncoiling itself like a snake, the spectator shivers with dread. When it is held in the air spread open, it is a command to bow. The Mikado also uses his wrists to characterize: they are held slightly up, the hands extending down gripping his fan like claws. The eight or ten rings that he wears help to make his fingers appear threatening.

### Nanki-Poo

One of Gilbert's few tenors who are completely likable, Nanki-Poo must have charm and grace, but needs little comic ability. The main thing is that he must be able to sing extremely well, as his opening song is demanding in range, variety of mood and vocal shading, and coloratura. Subsequent demands on his voice are moderate, so he can afford to put all he has into "A wandering minstrel."

Nanki-Poo has two characteristics that predominate. He loves Yum-Yum, and he is pleasantly careless about the prospect of dying. Throughout the action he gives the impression that, for him, existence is "as welcome as the flowers in spring."

### Ko-Ko

One of the greatest of all comedy roles, Ko-Ko is relatively easy to play because it is so well written. Although an artist of versatility is required to realize all the values of the role,

it would be difficult to make Ko-Ko unfunny.

The first thing to observe is his seriousness. He wants to marry Yum-Yum, an objective that he feels he probably shares with the rest of the world. He wants to find someone to execute. He wants to learn how to be a good executioner. And, finally, he wants to put one over on the Mikado. He is the essence of a petty official assuming a competence beyond his reach. He is shortsighted, irritable, and continually perplexed.

Like many comic figures, Ko-Ko parodies the concept of the tragic hero. He suffers from the sin of pride, thinking that he controls a situation that is in reality out of his grasp. He is made to realize his error and take upon himself the consequence: He must marry Katisha. This fate he addresses as willingly, albeit unenthusiastically, as Oedipus accepts his blindness.

Although the role is comic, and at times farcical, it has its moments of pathos as well. The "titwillow" song is best rendered in a manner that brings the audience close to tears. Again, when Ko-Ko realizes he can't kill anyone or anything his despair should seem genuine.

A Ko-Ko who can dance imaginatively has many opportunities to do so. There are several ensemble numbers in which his lightness of foot can underline the lightness of the music and help to contrast him with the stiffer souls who usually accompany him. "Here's a how-de-do!" provides wonderful opportunities for comic dancing, particularly if it is encored several times.

### Pooh-Bah

This character is heavy in every sense of the word. If the actor who plays him is not, then the costume should be padded. Pooh-Bah does not walk, he waddles. In his pride and smug self-satisfaction he is the antithesis of Ko-Ko. There can be little confusion about his character, actually, because he himself discusses it at some length: "I am in point of fact a particularly haughty and exclusive person of pre-Adamite ancestral descent. You will understand this when I tell you that I can trace my ancestry back to a protoplasmal primordial atomic globule. Consequently, my family pride is something inconceivable. I can't help it. I was born sneering."

A heavy baritone voice is required for the singing, and for the dialogue a booming overpronunciation of the words that makes of each syllable a miniature lecture on the superiority of the person who utters it.

Because of his enormity, Pooh-Bah has maneuvering problems, and he does not fall suddenly to his face in front of the Mikado, but lowers himself by degrees. He is equally slow about getting up, a fact that sometimes puts him into an awkward position at just the right moment.

### Pish-Tush

This character serves as a foil to Ko-Ko and Pooh-Bah and has little individuality. If he were acted too imaginatively, he would throw the opera out of focus by drawing attention away from other characters who make things quite interesting enough. He should have an attractive baritone voice and a quiet dignity.

### Go-To

This character is introduced to sing Pish-Tush's part in the Madrigal if the latter cannot sing low enough. He is simply that member of the chorus with the finest bass voice.

### The Mikado's Umbrella-Bearer

A little man, or perhaps a child, who follows the Mikado around at his first entrance, bouncing along with the Mikado during "My object all sublime." He also appears for the finale.

### Yum-Yum

An important part of Yum-Yum's character is suggested by her name. Besides being so beautiful as to cause most of the trouble in the opera, she is extremely self-centered. This quality is disguised by her lively charm, which helps her deal with any situation without becoming ruffled. In her scene with Nanki-Poo she manages to avoid flirting by demonstrating with him all the things that one should not do. When Katisha arrives, it is she who quickly alerts the chorus to drown out the latter's pronunciamento. When she learns that her husband's death will cause her to be buried alive, she begs off with a charm that makes her position seem perfectly understandable.

The singing for this role is not as demanding as that of many soprano leads. The aria beginning "The sun, whose rays" must be sung with beauty and tenderness, but it requires neither dramatic nor coloratura effects. Her other singing is mostly of an ensemble character.

### Pitti-Sing

This is a relatively small role that should be given to a fine actress who can sing adequately. Much of the sparkle in the opera derives from Pitti-Sing, who gets to rescue the mood of things at the end of Act One with "For he's going to marry Yum-Yum." Whereas Yum-Yum is charming, Pitti-Sing is vivacious. One of her finest moments is in the taunting of Pooh-Bah in Act One. This makes it all the funnier for her to be so closely associated with him in the concocted story about the executed criminal in Act Two.

### Peep-Bo

The primary consideration for casting this role is that she blend well with Yum-Yum and Pitti-Sing. She has some solo work in the "Three little maids" trio, and some dialogue in the first act, but that is all. She should be as pretty and vivacious as they are, and emphatically not more so.

### Katisha

Katisha represents the cruelest of Gilbert's jibes at aging women. She is meant to be repulsive completely without qualification. Furthermore, much of the action of the plot stems from her repulsiveness, and so does the reaction to her by all the other characters, including the chorus.

Although she is unattractive, Katisha is a most interesting role to play. She has moments of comedy, moments of intense drama, and moments of introspective tragedy. No actress should attempt the part who is not comfortable with all three, as they are all equally important. Her comic moments are in the scene with Ko-Ko, when she must be flirtatious without being disgusting or pathetic. Her drama is in the first-act finale, when she must make an entrance that terrifies everyone onstage, and hopefully the audience as well. Her terrifying appearance must be sustained all the way to the end of Act One. Introspective tragedy is found in the brief song "The hour of gladness" in the Act One finale, and in "Alone and yet alive" in Act Two. In these places she must tempt us to feel pity for her, but not become so serious that we lose perspective. The balance between pathos and bathos in the role is indeed a delicate one.

The only time when Katisha is onstage and does not dominate the action is in her scene with the Mikado. Here she becomes a secondary character and must not distract attention from him. This is hard to do, because she must still appear domineering, appear to be the only one who is not afraid of him. A Katisha who "upstages" the Mikado can be a serious liability to the production.

The singing is as demanding as the acting. Katisha should have a powerful and sensitive contralto voice. Even among professional companies too many Katishas have hooted their way through the role, making the second-act solo tedious or unbearable. Although the voice should suggest unattractiveness, this impression must not be allowed to contaminate the music.

This is also a role in which makeup is all-important. Like Dick Deadeye and King Gama, Katisha is physically not quite human. She must be terrifying and grotesque, her ugliness of the realm of comic opera, not of real life, and therefore not provocative of sympathy.

### Gentlemen of Japan

Court etiquette makes these gentlemen look like marionettes. Their chins are up, their expressions dignified. Their backs are absolutely straight as they rise or sit, and they turn their whole bodies rather than their heads. Their fans are more expressive than their faces, and indeed are their chief means of communicating emotion.

### Chorus of Schoolgirls

Giggling, which sounds to the occidental ear like hissing, is their trademark. They are more vivacious than their male counterparts and do most of the reacting in the Act One finale, in which reactions are crucial. Although they are silly, like all schoolgirls, they are also pensive. In their own words, "Each a little bit afraid is,/ Wondering what the world can be!"

### NOTES ON STAGING

*The Mikado* requires more energy and sparkle in production than any of the other operas. It is both bloodthirsty and gay, and the two qualities balance each other, the one bringing the other into relief. Therefore the director should seek vivacity as well as precision from his company, remembering that precision must never be sacrificed: its importance is clearly stated in the opening chorus.

All of the characters except Nanki-Poo, Pooh-Bah, the Mikado, and Katisha will use the Japanese shuffle whenever they walk. This will take some practice, and it would be well to begin staging rehearsals by learning to get across the stage at a normal speed without ever lifting the feet from the floor. In addition, fans should be used at all rehearsals, and everyone should practice snapping them open and shut until the action becomes second nature.

The impression created by the opening chorus should be one of movement within a tableau. The nobles are grouped about the stage, some sitting, some standing, a few talking together, here and there one quite alone. At various times during the number a group can move from one part of the stage to another. The important thing, however, is that there be certain specific moments in the music when everyone quite suddenly assumes a different position. Those who are sitting may stand, others may sit, still others may snap open their fans. The impression should be that suggested by the song: a picture on a vase or screen made up of marionettes who suddenly change their positions.

Into this very stilted picture runs Nanki-Poo, appearing by contrast quite human. During his song he strums on his guitar. The song is in reality a collection of several songs, each of which should have its own kind of staging and a separate stage picture. For the first part, the gentlemen retain their original configurations. At "Are you in sentimental mood?" Nanki-Poo puts one foot up on the bench and several of the nobles gather around him. They express on their faces the emotions of which he sings. Beginning "I'll charm your willing ears," Nanki-Poo crosses the stage to join another group of nobles. On "If patriotic sentiment," the men move into ranks like an army and begin marking time to the music. They may use their closed fans to suggest trumpets. Nanki-Poo acts the role of a general leading his troops into battle. At "And if you call for a song of the sea," the chorus pretend to uncoil ropes, polish brass, and engage in other sailorlike activities, while Nanki-Poo walks among them like a supervising midshipman. An interesting touch is to bring in a few Japanese women at this point as onlookers, so that when Nanki-Poo sings, "With his Nancy on his knees," he can put his arm around one of them. This would

*Nanki-Poo in* The Mikado: *"A wandering minstrel I."*    (D'Oyly Carte production)

also lend more variety to the final stage picture when Nanki-Poo returns to the beginning of the song and the groupings should again appear formal.

For Pish-Tush's song, "Our great Mikado," the primary staging problem concerns the musical introductions and interludes. During these, Pish-Tush and Nanki-Poo may do variations of walking toward each other in rhythm, bowing, and then walking away again, perhaps exchanging positions on opposite sides of the stage. Alternatively, if Pish-Tush is expert enough with his fan, he can use this music as an opportunity to display his expertise. The chorus should move, too, but much less noticeably, as they are completely in the background for this song, which is addressed solely to Nanki-Poo. A few minor changes of position among them while the major characters are moving across the stage will keep them from appearing static. On the refrain, when the chorus joins in, elaborate fan work is called for, Pish-Tush's working contrapuntally to everyone else's.

Pooh-Bah's entrance changes the tone of the scene. Until now everything has moved briskly and has been concerned with developing the plot. Pish-Tush's song has been important exposition and has been so staged that the words are no more than clearly stated. Pooh-Bah does more with words than state them; he illustrates them. With hands and facial expressions he virtually choreographs his dialogue, so that the interest shifts from the development of the plot to his peculiar character. For example, when he says "rolled the two offices into one" he makes a rolling gesture with his fan that suggests the action was performed literally.

In recognition of each of his offices he has received a decoration, and he points out each of the medals as he recites the office it stands for. Nanki-Poo and Pish-Tush bow obsequiously upon hearing each of his titles.

When Pooh-Bah receives a bribe, there is nothing surreptitious about it. Accepting bribes is a ritual with him, and he does so by extending his hand slightly behind his back, which is turned to the briber, and by raising his nose even higher than usual, to show that his dignity will survive the assault. Having been "insulted," he weighs the insult thoughtfully in the palm of his hand and sighs at its insubstantiality.

The staging for "Young man, despair" is somewhat similar to that for the song that preceded it. Movement of the three characters occurs during the orchestral introductions. Now, however, Pooh-Bah's huge waddle creates a comic contrast to the relatively graceful movements of the other two characters. For the refrain the obvious pictorial gestures are appropriate, and they should be performed with gusto, Pooh-Bah using slightly more elaborate ones than the other two.

When the men enter for "Behold the Lord High Executioner," they form an inverted "V," not completely closed at the top. They remain in this position, but bow whenever they sing the word "Defer." Ko-Ko enters just before his solo, followed by a small boy who carries his "snickersnee" on a pillow. During his solo, Ko-Ko moves back and forth across the front of the stage in time to the music by alternately putting his toes and then his heels together, so that his feet are always in a regular or inverted "V" formation. While moving thus he looks straight out at the audience and uses appropriate gestures and fan motions. At the conclusion of his opening solo he seizes the snickersnee from his attendant and bows to the chorus as they sing "Defer." Each time he turns from one line of men in order to face the opposite line, he nearly decapitates several choristers. On the concluding measures of the number, when the singing is completed, Ko-Ko moves around the semicircle of choristers with his snickersnee, just barely missing each man's neck as each one in his turn bows. He concludes by raising the snickersnee above the neck of his attendant, who is kneeling prone on the floor, as if he were going to decapitate him. The blade comes down just above the head of the attendant, who picks up the snickersnee and runs offstage with it.

In the following speech there are some chorus reactions. After the word "reception," the gentlemen all bow with a bleating sound like "Ma-a-a-a." Ko-Ko replies by doing the same thing before continuing his speech. At the end of the speech, the same action occurs and is repeated once while the introduction to the song is played. This gives Ko-Ko just time enough to get out his little list before beginning to sing.

The little list has been handled in a number of ways. Sometimes Ko-Ko simply refers to his fan as if it were the list. The most common approach is to have what appears to be a very short scroll, which, unwound, turns out to be extremely long. If this approach is used, Ko-Ko

*Peter Pratt as Ko-Ko in* The Mikado: *"Taken from a county jail."*
(*D'Oyly Carte production*)

will have to practice the business enough so that he doesn't get the scroll badly tangled up in performance.

During the choral refrains, Ko-Ko reads his list. This is done in the Japanese style, bottom to top and right to left. For this purpose, Ko-Ko has black horn-rimmed glasses.

It is relevant at this point to discuss the matter of topical interpolations. First, the word "nigger" must be changed, since Gilbert meant by it, not "negro," but minstrel. D'Oyly Carte uses the word "banjo," but "minstrel" might be more meaningful to American audiences. Today, however, some other word might be used, reflecting the current popular music.

Gilbert repeatedly changed the words "lady novelist," and they have continued to be changed up to the present time, reflecting changing topical interests.

Some amateur performers have replaced the third stanza with one of their own. Such a practice is frowned upon by traditionalists, and definitely should not be used if the production is meant for the general public. If, however, a school or some other small group is producing the opera, so that nearly all of the audience will have a common interest, a third stanza referring to personalities known only within the particular audience can add to the enjoyment of the evening, provided the stanza is clever enough so that it does not seem awkward compared with the two that have preceded it.

During the song, appropriate gestures and poses must be used. For example, the "lady from the provinces" is given a stance that suggests the giggling, timid, but eager gaucheries of one out of place at a fancy ball. "You-know-who" in the third stanza is accompanied by a gesture or pose suggestive of some public figure currently in the news. Those gestures that are fully realized in this way should be far enough apart so that they do not compete with one another for attention. Two, or at the most three, to a stanza is quite enough. Other gestures will be only vaguely suggestive motions of the hand.

The dialogue that follows provides an excellent chance to establish the contrast between the light-footed Ko-Ko and the waddling Pooh-Bah. Each time they cross the stage to avoid the hearing of an official, Ko-Ko moves quickly to the spot and then beckons Pooh-Bah, who follows ponderously after. Again, when Ko-Ko shakes hands with Pooh-Bah, he turns to go. But Pooh-Bah does not release his hand, since he has more to say. This nearly trips up Ko-Ko. Near the end of the scene Pooh-Bah extends his hand in his characteristic manner to receive a bribe. Ko-Ko looks at it, has no money, and so substitutes a handshake. During the remainder of Ko-Ko's speech, Pooh-Bah slowly brings his hand into focus, discovers that there is no money and digests this information just in time to add to the end of the scene a line that is traditionally written in: "No money, no grovel."

The chorus "Comes a train of little ladies," has a somewhat melancholy melody compared to other female chorus entrances. This quality should be reflected by choreography that emphasizes the beauty and pensiveness rather than the sprightliness of the young ladies. One helpful device is to give each of them a Japanese parasol. These parasols, opened and pointed toward the audience, can be rotated to achieve a kaleidoscopic effect. A number of beautiful effects can be achieved by moving the ladies around into groups in which some are kneeling and some standing in various pensive poses. Two or three such groupings will suffice for the song if interesting work with

fans and parasols is developed during each of the tableaux.

The introduction to "Three little maids" allows each of the three soloists to move from up center to down center individually in sequence. They should prepare for this by entering up center just at the conclusion of the previous chorus. When they begin to sing they hold their fans closed in both hands and bend their knees on the words, "school," "well" and "girlish," coming up at the end of each line. During the part marked *"Chuckle"* they open their fans so that their mouths are covered, and look at each other, making a hissing sound, which is their way of giggling. On the refrain they do a dance variation of step-halt across the front of the stage, all together at one side.

On the second stanza, Yum-Yum runs to the center of the stage on her first solo line. She is followed in sequence by the other two. This action is repeated, taking them over to the other side of the stage, so that their dance on the second refrain returns them to the center of the stage for the conclusion of the song.

Ko-Ko rushes on from one side followed more slowly by Pooh-Bah. He intends to kiss Yum-Yum, but she restrains him with fingers directed neatly to his chest. His lips are still extended and puckered when he says, "Well, that was the idea." When he finally does kiss her, Ko-Ko gives Yum-Yum a peck on the cheek, which elicits the expected hissing from all three girls.

Nanki-Poo enters, and all three girls rush to him, jumping up and down with enthusiasm, and speaking rapidly and loudly. Ko-Ko, trying to see who it is, stands on tiptoe and tries to look around them unsuccessfully. Finally in frustration he interrupts them. After he says "One at a time, if you please," he flicks open his fan. Rapidly in succession the three girls, Nanki-Poo, and Pish-Tush flick theirs open. This is followed by the slow and noisy unfolding of a very large fan by Pooh-Bah.

When Nanki-Poo admits to loving Yum-Yum, he kneels, placing his face quite close to the floor. Ko-Ko, about to reply, looks around to where he was and no longer sees him. After clearly not knowing where he has gone, he discovers him kneeling. Ko-Ko then gets down on his back and slides his face under Nanki-Poo's. The latter, startled, raises his head a little, but does not get up. Ko-Ko delivers his next line from this position, getting up on "Thank you very much."

While Ko-Ko has been interviewing Nanki-

*Cynthia Morey as Yum-Yum in* The Mikado: *"Sometimes I sit and wonder, in my artless Japanese way, why it is that I am so much more attractive than anybody else in the whole world."*                    (D'Oyly Carte production)

Poo, the three girls have been investigating Pooh-Bah. When Pitti-Sing touches him, he moves his arm as if to wave away an irritating insect. This causes her to scream: "Oh, it's alive." During the ensuing dialogue, Pooh-Bah does not look anywhere except straight ahead. When he says "How de do, little girls," he speaks in a quick falsetto, bowing slightly toward them, then snaps open his fan, turning his back on them and fanning himself hastily. It has been a grave ordeal for him. When he is forced to repeat the remark in commenting upon it, he also repeats the action that went with the remark.

On the introduction to the quartet the three girls skip happily around Pooh-Bah while the chorus in groups of two or three execute the same sort of dance more or less in place. When the singing begins, the three are lined up facing Pooh-Bah, and as two of them sing solos, they in turn run up to him a little tauntingly. Pooh-Bah is immobile throughout this. When his turn to sing comes, he moves from his position to one roughly equivalent to it on the other side of the stage, walking with slow dignity. This dignity is somewhat compromised when Pooh-Bah gets to the "Tra-la-la" section and does some delicate footwork along with marvelously dextrous fan gyrations.

The scene between Nanki-Poo and Yum-Yum should be acted rapidly and with energy, or it can easily become dull. The staging is obvious, except that Yum-Yum should fall prostrate at Nanki-Poo's feet upon discovering that he is the son of the Mikado. He then helps her up at the beginning of his long speech and seats her on the bench. His anger at his father's action carries him away from her, but then at the end of the speech he moves back to her again as indicated.

The duet is staged as a conventional love duet, except that all kissing is carefully concealed by the two lovers behind their fans. The last time they kiss, the fans come apart and reveal what is happening. Yum-Yum discovers this and quickly pulls them together again. When they exit in opposite directions, they turn and throw each other a kiss just before going into the wings.

Ko-Ko enters and is followed by Pish-Tush and Pooh-Bah, the former bearing a letter from the Mikado. Ko-Ko sits cross-legged on the floor stage center to read the letter, and the other two sit on either side of him. The scene has the tone of a legal argument, Ko-Ko proceeding with self-righteous logic. The tone becomes a little bloodthirsty only when Pooh-Bah suggests, smacking his lips, that "A man might try" cutting his own head off. Ko-Ko, declaring that he is adamant, gets to his feet, and the other two follow suit. This process is somewhat drawn out for Pooh-Bah, who is still only halfway up on the remark that he is in "an awkward position." Pish-Tush is somewhat nearer Ko-Ko than Pooh-Bah is when he suggests finding a substitute. Ko-Ko is prepared. Searching about in his sleeve he finds another medal for Pooh-Bah, which he proceeds to pin on him. Pooh-Bah admires it fondly, but hands it back to Ko-Ko on the word "no." Ko-Ko handles it as if it were a dangerous object, and looks about helplessly for someone to give it to, quickly finding that Pish-Tush is unwilling to take it.

The following trio offers many opportunities for humorous staging. Whatever is done with it, it should be practiced enough so that there is no confusion of words or music as a result of trying to remember the staging, and so that the diction is not obscured. The suggestions here may easily be varied, as there are numerous other possibilities.

On the opening chords Pooh-Bah sits down solidly on one of the benches while the other two watch him, Ko-Ko somewhat more distant. The music leading into Ko-Ko's solo suggests pacing, and this he does, ending up next to Pooh-Bah in time to sit next to him, chin in hands as he begins to sing. Pish-Tush's solo is executed largely before he sits down. To the extent that the acoustics allow, he should sing to Ko-Ko and Pooh-Bah, who are upstage of him, rather than to the audience, as their reactions to what he is saying should be much funnier than his delivery. Ko-Ko is mentally experiencing everything he mentions, while Pooh-Bah has a look of glowing satisfaction on his face. Pish-Tush sits next to Pooh-Bah in time for the ensemble. They sit in three distinct postures, Pooh-Bah erect and proud, Ko-Ko wilted, chin in hands, and Pish-Tush leaning forward a little, in a lecturing pose.

The next section of the trio is introduced again by three solos, Ko-Ko first this time. Now each moves in his turn downstage center, Pooh-Bah and then Pish-Tush clapping Ko-Ko on the shoulder and giving him advice, which causes him to wilt always a little more.

Then, on the first word of the patter trio they all collapse together on the floor. Their closed fans are used together in precise gestures on the last three beats of each line, suggesting in turn the dock, the lock, the shock, and the block. On the last note, all rise. Pooh-Bah and Pish-Tush happily leave, but Ko-Ko remains, sadly caressing his neck.

Ko-Ko is downstage soliloquizing when Nanki-Poo enters upstage with a rope, the noose already around his neck. He throws the other end of it up toward the top of the scenery. Ko-Ko's first remark is only a momentary interruption of this process. When Ko-Ko realizes what Nanki-Poo intends to do, he rushes up to him, grabs him by the arm, and leads him downstage. When Nanki-Poo produces a knife, Ko-Ko attempts to take it from him and, not finding this easy, bites Nanki-Poo's hand to make him let go. His horror gives way when an idea strikes him, an idea that he smugly confides to the audience.

Ko-Ko then attempts to sell Nanki-Poo on the idea of being beheaded, and Nanki-Poo offers to do so in exchange for Yum-Yum. When Ko-Ko draws the line, Nanki-Poo does too—his rope. The noose is still around his neck, and he coils the other end and throws it as he did before. When the loose end falls behind him, Ko-Ko picks it up and drags Nanki-Poo back downstage, pulling him by the neck. Ko-Ko agrees to the bargain, and Nanki-Poo agrees in his turn that Yum-Yum shall never find out from him that Ko-Ko is not a wise and good man. The thought pleases Ko-Ko at first, but then he does a double take when he realizes its implications.

The finale of the first act represents a peculiar kind of problem in that it is dramatic but at the same time quite static. The chorus remains onstage the whole time watching the acting and reacting to it, but seldom playing a part in it. That means there is little the director can do in terms of moving the chorus about, and he must concentrate his energies on three things: reactions, gestures (including fan work), and dancing in place. All of these things must be carefully drilled, as a listless or imprecise chorus can spoil the effect of the action. It does not matter so much what the chorus does as that it be sure of whatever it does do. Therefore, if the chorus people find it difficult to learn complex gestures or dance steps, these should be simplified, so that every member of the chorus will, by performance time, be absolutely certain of his part throughout.

As the chorus enters, Ko-Ko and Nanki-Poo are seated downstage center, Ko-Ko measuring Nanki-Poo's neck and taking some practice shots at it with his fan. Pooh-Bah and Pish-Tush lead the chorus in and take positions near the seated figures. The ceremonial dignity of their entrance should be complete and in humorous contrast to the figures seated at the front of the stage, who seem to be the best of friends, laughing and joking about the coming execution. Ko-Ko rises to introduce Nanki-Poo, who also rises and takes a bow. The three wards arrive just in time for Ko-Ko to offer one of them to Nanki-Poo. (He picks Pitti-Sing first, being unable to see very well through his tears, and pushes her aside with the words, "Not you, silly!") Then Ko-Ko rushes off, weeping.

Yum-Yum and Nanki-Poo rush into each other's arms and there is a spectacle of fan waving in celebration of their happy union. Aside from the stepping forward of principals as they sing to the happy couple, the only action in this section of the finale is the choreography of fans and feet. This choreography should be brilliant, but should not involve too much motion of people about the stage, as that

would detract from the shock of Katisha's entrance.

Too many Katishas limp on like tired housewives and produce only the faintest tremor from chorus or audience. The effect, rather, should be one of a tigress breaking forth from her cage. At the proper moment she should suddenly appear upstage center, terrifying the entire chorus, who retreat screaming from her presence. Nanki-Poo should be placed so that there is plenty of space between them, and she can convincingly stalk him throughout the rather long sequence that follows. Nanki-Poo's attempt to retreat separates him from Yum-Yum by some distance, so that the two stanzas of Katisha's solo will be addressed in opposite directions.

Katisha's stalking (the image should be of a large cat whose tail is waving with slow, boiling anger) is interrupted by the high spirits of Pitti-Sing, who completely distracts her with her song. Pitti-Sing's light-footed darting around her makes her appear more like a creature attacked by a fly. She hisses and snaps her fan, and Pitti-Sing thoroughly enjoys the game.

Katisha attempts to reveal the true identity of Nanki-Poo, but her revelation is drowned out by the chorus, who have been whisperingly prepared for their action by Yum-Yum and Pitti-Sing, working from opposite sides of the stage toward the center just in time to tell everyone what to do. Each of the Japanese interjections is accompanied by the waving of fans and a few steps forward, closing in on Katisha. At the end of this sequence, she bursts through the chorus and takes a position upstage center (on the steps at the back, if there are any), now with a coolie on either side of her. As the curtain falls, we have two distinct impressions: Katisha is at the back, threatening, and Nanki-Poo and Yum-Yum are at the front, rejoicing. The chorus, having turned their attention away from Katisha, are now sharing in the joy of the two lovers.

It may be effective to raise the curtain again immediately after it has fallen, to show Katisha still in her threatening pose and the two lovers with their backs to the audience pointing their fans at her. She then rushes off, and they turn and embrace happily, as the curtain falls again.

As the second act opens, Yum-Yum is discovered seated at her bridal toilet with Pitti-Sing and Peep-Bo dressing her hair and painting her face while she watches in a mirror. The other girls stand or sit in various groups around her. The director should be concerned in this

*Ella Halman as Katisha in* The Mikado: *"My wrongs with vengeance shall be crowned!"*
(*D'Oyly Carte production*)

number with the interesting grouping of figures, and should at several points have a small number of choristers move into different positions. In addition, a number of pictorial gestures should be used. These will be more interesting if they are the same within each group, but slightly varied from group to group. They are particularly important during Pitti-Sing's solo.

Yum-Yum's soliloquy and song should, in their delivery, suggest nothing of the self-centeredness that the words imply. Yum-Yum is too naive to believe that there is anything unusual about reacting to one's own beauty as she does. As she sings, she should let the words speak for themselves and give the song neither passion nor satirical point. A Yum-Yum who is a good dancer may give an added effect to the song with a *very* restrained dance interpretation of it as she sings. This would help to make clearer and more credible her identification with the sun and the moon.

Yum-Yum's joy is turned to sorrow by the entrance of her sisters, who remind her of the shortness of her anticipated marriage. When Nanki-Poo enters, he is greeted by three girls in tears. Yum-Yum runs to him and puts her head on his shoulder. Pitti-Sing and Peep-Bo then follow suit, so that Nanki-Poo is simultaneously comforting three girls all in a row, the latter two each with her head on the shoulder of her sister.

Traditionally the madrigal is given no staging at all, probably because Sullivan insisted in the original production that it was a musical number and should be treated as it would be in concert. Some combination of bows and do-si-do's* during the introduction to each stanza would make things more interesting and provide for regrouping during the second stanza.

During the following dialogue, Ko-Ko has some traditional business that is quite amusing. When he says that married men never flirt, he catches his breath, glances at the audience, and quickly sits, hiding his face behind his fan and then peeps over it, counting the married men in the audience who are at that moment engaged in flirting. He then retreats behind his fan and from that source a distinct "me-ow" is heard when Yum-Yum utters the word "pet."

The following trio is the high point for comedy in the entire series of operas. In D'Oyly Carte productions it is always encored several times. Martyn Green averaged six encores with it, and his record was eight. The action is en-

tirely Ko-Ko's: The other two just stand in one place and sing.

During the introduction Ko-Ko leaps up and dances offstage. He is gone until a split second before it is time for him to sing, at which point he appears on the opposite side of the stage from which he exited. During the rest of the trio his elaborate dancing in and out among the lovers is a primary source of fun. On the sequence of three solo "Here's a how-de-do's," each character in turn snaps open a fan. Ko-Ko's fan will be a surprise each time. It is broken one time, next it is very large, then very small, and so on. A good way to end the number is to have a huge fan big enough to hide all three characters completely. This has been lying folded up onstage from the beginning of the act and is, on the last note, opened and carried off by the three of them.

If encores are used, two of Martyn Green's best devices should not be missed. For one encore, just before it was time for him to sing, he appeared from one of the rear wings in the strangulation grasp, apparently, of someone offstage. His repeated efforts to inform this person of his need to go forward and sing were to no avail—until he fell backward, released by the grasping hand, and revealed that it had been his own. The illusion was accomplished by using his downstage hand to try to free himself from the offending grasp, and by pushing his sleeve back to the elbow so that the arm reaching out from the wings was bare. His active dialogue with the person offstage also helped.

The second device was the famous "kiddy car." While the lovers were singing their part of the trio, Ko-Ko appeared to be riding back and forth across the stage on a tiny vehicle. When it was his turn to sing, he simply stood up, revealing that there had been nothing there. His fan had supplied the handle bars, and his costume fell to the floor in such a way that it seemed to conceal the seat and wheels. Actually, as he squatted, his feet, placed directly under his body, moved so rapidly and evenly as to give the illusion of being wheels. This trick looks and sounds impossible, but it is actually relatively easy to learn.

Now that Nanki-Poo is no longer going to marry Yum-Yum, he wants to die at once. He bends over, offering his neck to Ko-Ko. "Chop it off, Ko-Ko! Chop it off!" says Pooh-Bah, in a line that traditionally differs from the printed version. Ko-Ko, in describing his intended apprenticeship, has a choice of two possible bits

---

* As in a square dance.

of business. One is to use the fingers of his left hand to represent the heads of the unfortunate animals. He holds this hand up, palm facing him, and taps each finger in turn with his fan, beginning with the little finger. Each finger bends and then reappears. The index finger, representing the Second Trombone, does not reappear. Whereupon Ko-Ko goes searching for it, eventually finds it behind the footlights, and carefully replaces it.

If Ko-Ko is not a gifted mime artist, it may be better to have him use his fan as an axe, chopping his way through the air until he almost hits Nanki-Poo's neck, from which he retreats, screaming in terror. In any event, when he weeps, he weeps upon Nanki-Poo's shoulder, and the latter has to comfort him.

When Ko-Ko promises to bribe Pooh-Bah, he pulls out a small purse, which he dangles in front of him and subsequently gives to him, so that Pooh-Bah on the "useful discipline" line is thoughtfully weighing the purse in his palm.

The chorus enters to herald the entrance of the Mikado. As the audience views the stage, the chorus makes two or three diagonal lines across the left. All go down into a prone position to sing "Miya sama." It is sung in a nasal tone, to give an oriental sound. The Mikado and Katisha enter on the repeat.

Martyn Green has suggested that the Mikado should enter in a litter carried by coolies, as was done in the 1938 film. This would certainly add to the glamour of his entrance, particularly if entrances from the front are used and the litter can be carried down the center aisle. It is the personality of the Mikado himself, however, rather than ceremonial display that must be the center of attraction at this point. No entrance was ever better prepared than this one, and the Mikado must certainly live up to what is expected of him. His full costume, large fan, and towering headgear all help, of course, but it is his sneer that predominates. Shortly after he begins to sing, Katisha interrupts him. This interruption does not diminish him, for with a snapping open of his fan and a scowl he stands aside with unblemished dignity. He will have his big moment in the solo that follows after Katisha has been seated and has become a mere accessory.

On the introduction to his song, the Mikado breaks into a dance that carries him across the front of the stage. Both hands are up, palms facing the audience, the opened fan in one of them. As he dances there is considerable bounce in his movements. The singing is ac-companied by illustrative gestures, usually made with the fan, such as the tracing in the air of elliptical billiard balls, or the use of the fan as a vocal score for the amateur tenor. At the beginning of the refrain he assumes the same pose he used for the introduction and does a slower version of the same dance. While the chorus sings he points the folded fan at them with his right hand, while the left hand remains up, and he moves along their line facing them and hissing at them. When he has completed this circuit, he wheels around suddenly, as if to see whether they are still bowing.

One of the most important touches in the entire production is the Mikado's laugh, which occurs at the end of each stanza just before the refrain. This cannot be a mere casual snicker, it must be a carefully designed eruption that seems as if it might take the top off the theatre building and must certainly be the ruination of the singer's vocal cords. Careful study is needed to achieve this effect, and the best recordings, though they need not be imitated, should at least set a standard. Darrell Fancourt and Donald Adams on the D'Oyly Carte recordings are definitive, with Anthony Raffell on the *Reader's Digest* set running a close second, and Owen Brannigan in the set conducted by Sir Malcolm Sargent managing the laugh with artistry but insufficient gusto.

At the conclusion of the song, Ko-Ko, Pitti-Sing, and Pooh-Bah rush in and kneel before the Mikado in a prone position. Although the first two seem to dive into it quite naturally, Pooh-Bah has his usual difficulties, caused by corpulence aggravated by dignity, in getting to the floor. Ko-Ko announces that the Coroner has just handed him the certificate of death, at which point Pooh-Bah hands Ko-Ko a scroll, which Ko-Ko then hands to the Mikado. As the Mikado reads the list of those present, Pooh-Bah bows in acknowledgment of each of his titles. Ko-Ko goes a bit too far in mentioning a "remarkable scene" and is told to describe it. At this he faints into Pooh-Bah's arms, but is quickly revived by Pitti-Sing in time for his song.

Ko-Ko's acting out of the scene is complete with the baring of the big right arm and the drawing of the snickersnee. He is in such terror, however, that he all but accompanies the criminal to his knees. Having completed his part of the narrative, he pushes Pitti-Sing out to do hers. She relies on her attractiveness and attempts to distract the Mikado by a mild flirtation with him, to which Katisha reacts by snapping open her fan violently, reminding the Mikado of his own law! Pooh-Bah is next, and there is little that he can do except try to preserve his dignity by making it legendary.

The staging for the following dialogue is generally obvious. The reference to Knightsbridge is usually changed to indicate the local Japanese part of town, if there is one, or some other location that will have unusual meaning for the audience. When Ko-Ko mentions pocket handkerchiefs, he is standing right next to the Mikado. He does not laugh, but the Mikado does, and digs him in the ribs. Ko-Ko then laughs and digs the Mikado in the ribs. This produces an explosion of wrath from the Mikado, which gets everyone immediately onto the floor again with such awkwardness that they bump into one another and Pooh-Bah rolls over on his back and has to be surreptitiously righted by his two companions. As the Mikado describes the punishment, there are mournful groans from the kneeling three at appropriate moments. They remain prone except on the word "yes," when all three sit up hopefully, only to have their hopes dashed, and when Pooh-Bah raises his head to announce that he doesn't want any lunch. All then rise for the glee.

"See how the Fates" is one of those numbers that really should have no staging, but should be concertized. Both for the musical effect and the sense of the words, the Mikado and Katisha should not be close to the other three. Incidentally, if cuts are made in *The Mikado,* this number is usually the first to go, on the grounds that it slows down the action. Quite the contrary, the act has been paced so rapidly up to this point that it is time for a breather, as what follows will be equally rapid. The scenes that follow will actually be funnier if this "interruption" is allowed to remain.

Nanki-Poo enters, and it transpires that the only thing that can save Ko-Ko is marriage to Katisha. This brings loud laughter from Pooh-Bah, and causes Ko-Ko to faint, momentarily. Having recovered, Ko-Ko sits on the floor in a pique, declining to pin his heart on any lady's right heel.

This time it is Ko-Ko who remains stationary for an ensemble. He sits on the floor and watches the other characters do a lively dance during the introduction to "The flowers that bloom in the spring." The dance is resumed as all join in the refrain. Ko-Ko does not rise until the introduction to the second stanza, when he stands apart from the other characters and

sings rather dolefully and sarcastically. His comic business associated with this song is normally saved for the encores, but if the production does not anticipate encoring this number, the comic business may be introduced at this point.

The first encore business originated by Henry Lytton and developed by Martyn Green involved a double-jointed big toe that rose in the air while Ko-Ko was seated. Several times he pushed it down with his fan, but each time it again rose in the air. Finally he stood and pushed down on the toe with his fan, only to find that the one on the other foot rose in its place.

During the second encore Ko-Ko drew a caricature of Katisha on his fan, showed it to the audience, and then made of it a bonnet around Pooh-Bah's head.

The recitative and song, "Alone, and yet alive!" should be treated as serious drama. The recitative should involve gestures and movement, but the song is best sung from a single position, or at most two positions, and with relatively few gestures. Katisha is introspective in this song, and the effect should be conveyed by sensitive singing rather than by external action.

The following dialogue should be the funniest scene in the opera. Ko-Ko enters, takes a quick look at the woman whose back is to him, recoils, decides he'd better get down to business, and takes off his jacket, which he deposits in the wings. He then crawls up behind the bench across the stage from her and makes several attempts to address her. At first all he can manage is a falsetto "Kat!" When she hears it and turns, he ducks down behind the bench. Finally he works up his nerve, comes out from behind the bench, and approaches her. When she hears him utter her name, she moves slowly forward. Quickly he cries, "Behold a suppliant at your feet!", running forward on his knees. On "mercy" he flings himself prostrate at her feet. She paces around him, and on "You have slain my love," she grabs him by the collar and shakes him up and down three times. Then she abandons him and moves sadly downstage. When he says, "Here," Ko-Ko has trouble getting the word out. He is up and pointing to himself with his thumb, but for a moment all that will come is a squeak. When he finally utters the word, she wheels on him. As he starts talking, she moves forward and he moves backward, talking more and more rapidly. Finally, he leaps onto the tormentor at the side of the stage and climbs halfway up it. When the audience's laughter has died down, he utters the line "Ah, shrink not from me!" Getting down from his perch, he adopts a dedicated but businesslike tone, and gritting his teeth gets through his long speech. His "Darling!" has the tone of one who has just put a piece of candy in his mouth and finds it to be burnt rubber. When he threatens to perish on the spot, he pulls his folded fan from his belt as if to stab himself. Katisha screams, and he opens the fan and smiles sheepishly.

"Titwillow" should be sung with greater musical accuracy than is usually found—even on the recordings of it, and should be treated seriously. Gestures are appropriate, but no clowning. One device that may be found effective is for Ko-Ko to use his right hand as a puppet impersonating the bird. He can then carry on a dialogue with the poor creature and perhaps lend it even more sympathy than it acquires in mere narrative.

The following dialogue requires no comment other than the stage directions in the printed text. The duet, "There is beauty," requires the services of a choreographer and should be both sprightly and comic. Ko-Ko will probably have to do most of the dancing in it, and this can be accomplished by having him dance around Katisha and taunt her by continuously eluding her embrace. At the end of the duet they fling their arms wide and go straight for each other, but Ko-Ko goes right past Katisha and off into the wings.

Neither the closing dialogue nor the finale present any staging problems. The fun is just about over, and all that is required is to sustain the pacing and the mood and finish with a flourish of fan waving. It is well, however, to be careful about two things. For some reason amateurs are more likely to forget lines and introduce ad-lib clowning during the closing moments of the opera than at any other time in it. They should be restrained from this both through adequate rehearsal and through the in-junction to maintain their characters until the final curtain. Nothing is more tasteless than spoiling the effect at the very end.

## SCENERY AND COSTUMES

The sets are the courtyard and garden of Ko-Ko's palace. The courtyard usually has an archway at the center of it, with a pagoda-style top. There is a raised area at the back that is at least partly obscured, so that an entrance can be made virtually from up center. The chief characteristic of Ko-Ko's garden is that it looks out on a body of water with a circular bridge across it.

Since the scene is not Japan as it really is, but the Japan imagined by Victorian England as a result of seeing a few teahouses and old prints, the set should be stylized in the manner of such prints.

The original production made little attempt at artistic unity. Japanese costumes were gathered from many sources and put together on the stage as they happened to be available. A turning point in *Mikado* design occurred in 1926 when Charles Ricketts designed a set of costumes based on the Japanese eighteenth-century style and carefully interrelated their colors. Included were such touches as the cap for Ko-Ko, which looked like a headsman's block.

Most amateur productions rely on rented costumes, which are seldom designed with a single production in mind. In general, it will be difficult for the amateur production to achieve visual unity unless a gifted designer is available to the company who can provide the kind of imagination that Ricketts displayed.

As far as detail in costuming is concerned, there is little that goes beyond the standard Japanese dress, except for the bald wigs for Ko-Ko and Pooh-Bah and several of the chorus, and the Japanese-style wigs for all the female characters and chorus.

# Chapter XIII

# RUDDIGORE, OR THE WITCH'S CURSE

PRODUCTION NOTES

Two major problems must be solved by the producer of *Ruddigore*. The first is technical, the second, aesthetic. The most important scene in the opera is the Ghost Scene, when the Murgatroyd ancestors step down from their picture frames and question their descendant on the matter of his crimes. This scene requires painted portraits of the members of the male chorus in costume, as well as some way of exchanging the canvases for living people during the progress of the performance. The problem is not easily solved, and even caused difficulty during the opening performance of the opera. It is often solved by having only the portrait of Sir Roderic onstage and having the other Ghosts enter from the wings. Nevertheless the presence on the scene-painting staff of a portrait artist is required. That problem is eliminated if the Ghosts stand rigidly within their picture frames until the time for their descent. Unfortunately that is uncomfortable not only for the chorus members but also for the audience, who are compelled for nearly a half hour to observe actual people pretending to be scenery. The effect is distracting to say the least.

Then there is the question of how to remove the portraits quickly in order that real actors may appear. At one production staff meeting the idea of using window shades was suggested and adopted. "But," quipped a stagehand, "have you ever seen a window shade that would always go up when you wanted it to?" His remark turned out to be unfortunately prophetic. Probably the usual solution is to use actual canvases that can be slid into place in grooves at the top and bottom. Little can go wrong

with this solution mechanically, but special precautions will have to be taken so that the actors do not reinsert them backwards or upside down, or fail to find the grooves in time in the dark.

We now come to the aesthetic problem. In its original production *Ruddigore* was something of a failure. This was attributable in part to the structure of the piece, which has an excellent (though possibly overlong) first act, followed by a second act that is not as carefully developed as it should have been. Thus, though much of the opera represents Gilbert and Sullivan's finest work, the directors of the production will have to work hard to compensate for those faults that tend to show up more in performance than under piecemeal investigation.

The problem is complicated by the fact that, because objections to the work involved a certain amount of Victorian queasiness, Gilbert's rewriting was more designed to tone down certain scenes than to make them artistically better. Thus it may be valid in this case to return to the first-night edition in a number of places. We have included in our text some additional lyrics and dialogue to help make this possible.

An additional production consideration is that there are five or six places in the opera where dancing is extremely important (including the ends of both acts). Thus it will be necessary to have among the directors a good choreographer who is in agreement with the general aesthetic aims of the production.

CRITICAL DISCUSSION

*Ruddigore* is that sort of theatrical parody represented more recently on the musical stage by such shows as *Little Mary Sunshine* and *The Boy Friend*. That is, it mocks the absurd conventions of a type of popular entertainment. Unlike many parodies, however, it goes beyond the mockery of convention to make fun of human foibles not really suggested by the melodramas from which it draws its primary inspiration.

The baronet who is represented as being a villain but turns out to be really good in the end, the sailor who swaggers and attempts to reduce all human experience to the language of the sea, the girl driven mad from rejected love, and the supernatural effects all fall in the category of parody. Rose Maybud's dependence on her etiquette book, Robin's shyness and his blundering attempts at crime, Richard's subservience to the dictates of his heart, and the Bridesmaids' love of weddings, no matter whose or under what conditions, are examples of Gilbert's wit transcending the parody with which he begins.

Possibly relaxing after the success of *The Mikado,* on which he had lavished the greatest care, Gilbert contented himself with a great deal of inspiration and too little discipline when he wrote *Ruddigore.* Structurally it is poorly balanced in several respects. First, the opening scenes are rather slow to develop content or excitement. They are clever enough in their way, but there is nothing really spectacular until the entrance of Richard and the hornpipe that follows. The act then quickly reduces in tension again until the entrances of Mad Margaret and Sir Despard, two of the most brilliant pieces in the opera, right in succession. From the entrance of Mad Margaret until the end of the first act, the opera plays flawlessly. Difficulties quickly develop in the second act, however, in that the tone of the work changes drastically, and the tempo of the action is speeded up so that the audience has a difficult time adjusting after the first act. No other opera in the series makes so great a change in general atmosphere between the first and second acts as does *Ruddigore.* Furthermore, the second act is a series of scenes, each of them excellent in itself, that do not fit together very well. The problem has been somewhat exaggerated in Gilbert's revision, which tends to shorten everything enough so that the juxtapositions seem even more awkward. The opening duet has been cut from four stanzas to two, which makes it seem distinctly too short. The duet that follows, between Richard and Rose, has also been

truncated, giving that scene too little chance to develop its contrasting mood. There follows a short, somewhat violent dialogue scene contrasting rather dangerously in mood with the music that precedes and follows it. The latter, a ballad for Rose, has been cut from two stanzas to one, which means that the first three numbers in the act are too short to sustain their various moods.

There follows the long and well-sustained Ghost Scene, which by its very excellence creates problems. Some transition is needed following it, so that Robin may digest and react to the ordeal he has just been through. For this purpose Gilbert supplied a recitative and lyric, the latter beginning, "For thirty-five years I've been sober and wary—." Sullivan, unfortunately, set this to music entirely too unsubstantial to support the transition needed. Gilbert, unsatisfied with the setting, requested that it be redone, but Sullivan did not comply. Gilbert then wrote a new lyric beginning, "Henceforth all the crimes," which was satirical enough, but hardly an improvement on what he had originally written. The music Sullivan supplied for this was not satisfactory by any criteria. Thus the most important problem in the structure of the second act still remains unsolved.

The following duet and dialogue between Sir Despard and Mad Margaret, which is Gilbert and Sullivan at their best, would be even better were it not for the unresolved nature of what precedes it. The patter trio that ends the scene is a classic of its kind and goes far toward making the second act seem successful. Unfortunately, the duet for Hannah and Sir Roderic, which comes next, though certainly one of Sullivan's best ballads, would be far more effective if it had been placed somewhere near the middle of the act. Whatever damage its extremely slow pace does to the act is compounded by the cut that Gilbert made following it. The dialogue for these two characters that originally followed the duet helped provide the right sort of satiric mood needed to lead into the ending. As it stands, the ending seems very abrupt, even more so because Gilbert was dissuaded by audience reaction from bringing back to life the entire chorus of Ancestors. Although modern revivals have generally followed the revised version in this respect, it seems silly to do so, as what was mildly shocking to Victorian audiences could hardly be expected to raise even the slightest tremors of concern in a modern audience. Bringing the

Ancestors back to life serves the useful function of providing partners for the Bridesmaids in the long closing dance.

The last cut served to shorten the finale so much that it serves as little more than a punctuation mark at the end of the evening. Although the song that originally opened this finale is not particularly imaginative, it does help to bring the evening to a close at the proper pace and should be retained for that reason. The Schirmer score offers a choice of finales, the second one containing only "Happy the lily," but in a longer version. The best solution is to combine the two finales in order to achieve something like moderate length.

The foregoing discussion of the structural defects of *Ruddigore's* second act may perhaps give the impression that it is less than an extremely fine opera. It is intended rather to help explain why it was not revived for more than thirty years after its original production and is still not considered in the front rank of Gilbert and Sullivan's efforts. The fact is that, though it was certainly not one of Gilbert's best works, it was one of his favorites. And Sullivan provided music that is always highly satisfying and sometimes rises to imaginative heights unequaled anywhere else in the series. The madrigal is probably the best of his part-songs, "When the night wind howls" his most imaginatively orchestrated number, and the duet for Despard and Margaret his funniest piece of music. There is relatively little in the score that does not meet high musical standards, and the music is in general more subtle than almost anything he wrote before *Iolanthe.*

Gilbert's lyrics do not have the quality that makes them seem applicable to many situations and consequently leads to their being quoted out of context, as do those in *The Mikado.* They are, however, generally appropriate to the situation and often quite skillful in their development of character. Much of the humor is more sophisticated than that to be found in *The Mikado.* For example, Ko-Ko's need to find someone he can execute does not have quite the satiric implications of Robin's need to avoid committing a crime every day. Then again, the Mikado's lavishness with punishments for all sorts of crimes is not quite as droll as the concept of a picture gallery with a recalcitrant descendant. Thus, if audiences do not find *Ruddigore* as immediately appealing as *The Mikado,* it is quite possible that performers will find it more delightful in constant repetition.

## CHARACTER SKETCHES

### Sir Ruthven Murgatroyd

Robin, as he is more likely to be thought of, is one of the more difficult comedy roles to act, not only because of the contrast it provides, but also because the details and motivations of Robin's character are not as immediately clear as in other cases, and must be clarified by the actor. During the first act Robin is dominated by his shyness. In the second act he becomes, under duress, a bad baronet—not an altogether effective one, admittedly, but at the same time not lacking in melodramatic enthusiasm.

Robin is subjected to almost continual frustration. At first it is his shyness that gets the better of him. Then it is his half brother, Richard, who, finding all to be fair in matters of love, does him in. Finally it is his uncontrollable picture gallery that makes his life difficult. Subjected to so many unpleasant situations, Robin finds it difficult to maintain that appearance of dignity on which comedy depends, and there are many moments in the action when he is in real danger of arousing our sympathy rather than our mirth. Inasmuch as good comedy should be played sincerely, the matter is a very delicate one in this case. The problem is best solved if to Robin's other qualities is added a naïve *joie de vivre* that carries him through his various frustrations. Otherwise, he can become merely funereal and cast a shadow over an otherwise frolicking entertainment.

### Richard Dauntless

This is an unusually demanding tenor role, not so much because of the music as because it must be delivered with consistent gusto of a sort many tenors find difficult. Furthermore, Richard must be an excellent dancer, as his hornpipe should be one of the highlights of the evening.

Richard sparkles with the bravado of the braggart sailor and with the glad-handedness of the man who is out for himself and accomplishes his aims best by winning the affections of others. He is light-footed, light-headed, and lighthearted. These qualities make him an important foil to the gloom that hangs over the

Murgatroyds, and if he becomes tedious he not only spoils his own part, he throws the whole opera off balance.

## Sir Despard Murgatroyd

Here is the melodramatic villain *par excellence*—the more delightful because his crimes are compensated for by charitable actions, themselves crimes, in this world of topsy-turvy-dom, indulged in with sanguinariness known only to the stage. Ferocity is the keynote in the first act, and this same ferocity is enlisted in the cause of virtue in the second act. Sir Despard is in every way the opposite of his elder brother, Ruthven, as there is no caution here, and one can see why he is attracted to poor Margaret with her strange, mad ways: He *loves* making a scene.

Sir Despard's character down to his makeup is described in his opening song. Every gesture, every line of his countenance, every nuance of his voice is picturesquely exaggerated. He might be the Mikado dethroned and traveling incognito, he is so thoroughly theatrical. To capture these qualities, both an imposing physique and a voice capable of etching the darker qualities of the music are essential.

## Old Adam Goodheart

The first name is pronounced with the accent on the second syllable, and was originally changed to Gideon Crawle in the second act, an inspiration that might be restored in a modern production. Old Adam is the faithful retainer who follows his master through all his misfortunes and helps him in crime exactly as he did in virtue. He is old and decrepit, but should not be exaggeratedly so. Although he need not have a beautiful solo voice, it should be a musical one, as his ensemble singing is quite important.

## Sir Roderic Murgatroyd

This specter conjures up another world in his demeanor, as he has been given words and music that transcend light opera, and if the performance takes on a new dimension with his appearance, he will contrast effectively with the more mundane villainy of Sir Despard. Sir Roderic stands for the laws of the supernatural, and though he is perhaps an unwilling victim of the witch's curse, he is nevertheless a conscientious one. He should have a bass voice of almost operatic quality, and the charisma of his acting should transcend the irritability of his character. His scene with Dame Hannah allows him to come down to earth somewhat, but he does so a little uncomfortably as though out of practice at mortal frivolity. The spookier he seems when we first meet him, the funnier he will be when he comes back to life.

## Rose Maybud

Vocally this role lies a little lower than most leading soprano parts. The singing voice should be bright, clean, and devoid of the sensuous. Scooping her way into her high notes will make Rose seem entirely too much a woman of the world. As she is in fact ruled entirely by her book of etiquette, which gets her safely through all situations, she should communicate a picture-book atmosphere wherever she goes. The actress should not attempt to underline the humor of the lines by making Rose seem idiotic or self-satisfied. She fully captures her own character in a single reference: "sweet Rose Maybud." And because she is sweet she gives herself fully, whether offering an apple to a blighted soul or her heart to some lover or other. She offers herself fully without effort, because there is so little of her to give. Indeed there is less flesh and blood in Rose than in any of Gilbert's other females, bloodless as some of them are. Her storybook language, syntactically similar to that of Elsie Maynard in *The Yeomen of the Guard,* but totally without the latter's sense of pathos, will seem merely cumbersome if Rose becomes too human.

## Mad Margaret

Evidently Gilbert had Ophelia in mind when he wrote this part, and the observation leads to several consequences. First of all, the general impression is of wildness of behavior along with the association with flowers. Secondly, there is an essential nobility in Margaret that is perhaps emphasized by her madness. Third, and perhaps most important, her insane fantasies are real to her, and that reality must be carefully worked out by the actress. When she leaps from one idea to another, the actress must have thought about the possible connection between the two ideas that links them in her mind. If this connection is not clear to her, the character will not seem mad at all, but merely bizarre. The audience must sense of Margaret, as Polonius does of Hamlet, that "though this be madness, yet there is method in't."

In the second act, Margaret's madness is restrained with difficulty, and she alternates between the proper Victorian charity worker and the raving vixen that she is always threatening to become. Margaret thus contrasts with Rose much as Despard does with Robin, as she has all the sensuousness and vitality that Rose lacks.

The singing is not difficult, and is within the range of either a soprano or a mezzo. The voice should have character and musicianship, but it need not be a beautiful one.

### Dame Hannah

This role comes closest to Anna Russell's description of the "large, fat contralto with a voice like a foghorn that you always have to have in these operations." It seems almost gratuitous, almost an afterthought, and it can, therefore, in the hands of an unskilled performer, become unbearably drab.

This is despite the fact that Hannah has two excellent songs and a couple of good comedy scenes. Probably the trouble is that her role is confined almost entirely to the beginning and the end of the opera with little chance to make an impression in between. Here, as with some of the other parts, charisma is essential. A Hannah who seems in some strange way to be identified with the curse of which she sings will prevent the audience from forgetting about her before she makes her second appearance. Gilbert may have been thinking of Azucena when he wrote her first song, and the image may help the actress rise above the impression of a good-hearted but dull old maiden aunt.

### Zorah, Ruth, and Chorus of Bridesmaids

The continual repetition of "Hail the bridegroom, hail the bride" that runs through the first act is very funny and helps to characterize the mercenary nature of their activities. It is Ruth who, in her dialogue, gives vent to this quality most clearly. These Bridesmaids in their attitude anticipate the development of our modern glamour industry, and this observation should help to clarify their characterization. They are all smiles and beauty, but underneath the surface they are thoroughly and impatiently businesslike.

Zorah has some beautiful music to sing in the opening chorus, and the purer her voice the greater will be the satiric effect once the dialogue begins.

### Chorus of Bucks and Blades

These are playboys of the upper classes looking for a bit of fun among the lower classes. Their behavior should suggest both their superior social status (such symbols as the monocle will help to communicate this impression) and their intentions toward the young ladies with whom they intend to spend the day. Lest the effect of this scene be too off-color, we should keep in mind the pastoral tradition and the idea of Marie Antoinette cavorting in shepherdess outfit. The eyes with which these Bucks and Blades view the girls are influenced at least as much by the spirit of Rousseau as by that of Hugh Hefner.

### Chorus of Ancestors

The easygoing aplomb of the Bucks and Blades is a far cry from the stiff fogginess of the Ancestors, dutifully cross-examining and tormenting their unfortunate descendant. The only similarity between the two sets of characters is the relatively high elevation of their noses. The Ghosts are humorless and ethereal. Nothing about them suggests liveliness.

There remains the question of the Act Two finale. Should the Ancestors be revived, as in the original production? Or should the Bucks and Blades appear on the scene as companions for the Bridesmaids? Musical balance requires one of those solutions. There is a third possibility: The Ancestors might step down from their frames and, upon discovering that they are actually alive, remove their outer garments to reveal the fact that they have been enjoying existence on the side as Bucks and Blades. That should provide a touch of Dracula and thoroughly confuse everyone!

### NOTES ON STAGING

*Ruddigore* depends for its effect largely on scenes between small groups of characters. It is therefore necessary to concentrate on clarity of characterization much more than spectacle when staging this opera. Remember that the characters must all sparkle above and beyond the specific qualities dictated by the script, and that they must be kept simple enough so that they do not confuse the parody and thus destroy the humor. Because of the tendency of the action to drag in certain spots, it will also be necessary to work extra hard on maintaining the pace of the music and dialogue, and adding imaginative touches that will keep the action interesting. Finally, though spectacle occurs less often in this opera than in most of the others, what there is should be so handled that it is memorable. A Ghost Scene that does not quite come off is a disaster.

The opening chorus represents a group of Bridesmaids ranged in front of Rose's cottage. In the D'Oyly Carte production they do not enter, but are discovered already onstage. It might be interesting, however, to bring the curtain up earlier than is indicated in the score and to suggest life in the village of Rederring by having a few picturesque characters cross the stage before the Bridesmaids assemble. The professional and public nature of their duties might be accentuated by having a few villagers looking on as they sing the opening chorus. In any event, it is customary to have Dame Hannah seated onstage knitting as the curtain rises.

There is some difference between the sense of the words and that of the music in this opening chorus. The words suggest that the Bridesmaids are irritated with Rose for keeping them waiting so long. The music suggests that they fully expect her to get married today, and are happy and excited at the prospect. In order to create a pleasant mood in the audience it is best to follow the lead of the music and make the Bridesmaids glow with happiness. Their irritations will be given ample scope in the ensuing dialogue. It is also wise to give the Bridesmaids more than one placement onstage during the song, but to keep them in the sort of formation associated with Bridesmaids rather than break them into groups.

Dame Hannah's remarks return the girls to their customary torpor. They sigh and cast down their glances, discarding the hopeful appearance they had had earlier. They also break into small groups to discuss the problem. There is a moment of renewed hope, however, when Zorah approaches Hannah and suggests that she marry. Hannah looks pleased for a moment at the idea, but then works herself into a melodramatic declaration. When she says, "I am pledged!" all the girls turn eagerly toward her and shout with glee. On the following line they sadly and in unison resume their downcast glances. Hannah now moves forward to tell her story and that of the bad Baronets of Ruddigore. The focus shifts from the Bridesmaids in general to her in particular, and it might be

well to dim the lights as she rises, and put a follow spot on her.

Hannah's song is a fine one, although not ordinarily very interesting from a staging point of view, as it is pure narration. One production brilliantly solved the staging problem by moving Hannah over to the side of the stage to sing while a group of dancers entered and, dressed in black with red backlighting, they danced the story of the witch's curse. This helped to increase the spectacle in which this opera is weak, and also to provide something in the first act that would help to balance the macabre elements that come later.

When Rose enters, the quality of the scene changes completely. The lights should come up, and the general atmosphere appear warmer than before. Rose's reactions to Hannah's suggestion that there must be someone she could love plainly tell the audience that there is someone, and that she is having difficulty concealing the fact. Her song is easily staged, as the business of checking the book of etiquette and showing each point to Hannah is all that is needed to make it effective. Rose's speech following the song can be funny if she moves from a tone of idolization on the name of Robin to real frustration on her problem of bringing him "to the point."

The scene between Robin and Rose is a beautiful one and should be played with utmost sincerity. The two should be simple country folk and no more. If any hint is given at this point of the fact that Robin is a bad baronet in disguise, the effect is spoiled. Robin enters wearing a hat, which he takes off upon seeing Rose and toys with nervously while speaking to her. Each remark he manages is a triumph for both of them. There are long, pregnant pauses between the lines. The business established during the dialogue is carried over into the duet.

Robin's character is given an added dimension in the next scene when Old Adam enters and utters his real name (which is pronounced "Rivven"). The melodramatic exaggeration of the dialogue really makes its first appearance here with Adam's adulation of his master. Given permission to utter Robin's real name, Old Adam laboriously gets to his knees. Having done his bit, Adam pulls out a pocket handkerchief and wipes his brow. Then Adam announces the return of Richard. Robin, rejecting the idea, walks offstage, leaving Adam to rush after him, calling, "See, he comes this way!"

*Martyn Green as Sir Ruthven Murgatroyd in* Ruddigore: *"As you love me, breathe not that hated name."* (*D'Oyly Carte production*)

Richard's entrance is one of those that can be made effectively from the back of the auditorium. If it is, the girls rush to the front of the stage peering off and trying to see Richard. If it is not, the entrance of the girls must suggest that they are bringing news. Some villagers may stroll onstage at the beginning of the number, perhaps including Dame Hannah and Rose. The girls rush in to tell the villagers, and there is much jumping about and waving of handkerchiefs. Dame Hannah whispers to Rose, perhaps suggesting that Richard is the man for her. Rose, horrified, rushes offstage, and Dame Hannah, upset that her suggestion has not proved a good one, rushes after her, just as Richard makes his appearance. He has several good friends among the Bridesmaids whom he picks up and spins around before beginning to sing.

One production, having a weak singer in the part of Richard, and an excess of men for the

chorus, created a chorus of sailors to accompany Richard onstage at this point. His solo music then was divided between him and the men's chorus, with the women entering as indicated and the men singing along with them. If the sailors' chorus is used, of course, each sailor will have a Bridesmaid to whom he is returning.

Following Richard's song comes the hornpipe, one of the high points in the opera. Richard is the star of it, but the girls join in too. Richard uses about twelve steps, and his most sensational ones are greeted by the girls with cries of delight. If the sailors' chorus is used, the men lead the girls off at the end of the number, presumably for a quick good time before the Bucks and Blades make their appearance.

The reunion between Robin and Richard is played rapidly and warmly. At his mention of the oath, Robin becomes very intense, placing his hand over his heart and raising his hat above his head. At the conclusion of his line, he replaces his hat on his head so forceably that it comes down over his eyes. Dick's next speech, with its sailing terminology, is accompanied by gestures suggestive of actions on board ship. By the end of the speech his gestures have become so involved and difficult to follow that Robin gets quite wrapped up in them and has to be nudged by Richard before he realizes that he has finished his speech.

Robin feels Richard's pulse and pulls a watch out of his vest pocket in order to time it. The watch evidently doesn't work, and he shakes it, producing a clearly audible clanking, thereby restoring it to working condition.

Robin's song is about his modesty, but there is nothing modest either in the words or in his delivery of them. The song should have a great deal of bravado with Robin stomping about and using elaborate gestures. When he says, "I fail in—and why, sir?," Richard interpolates, "I dunno." Following "You ask me the reason?" Richard replies, "No, I didn't," to which Robin rejoins, "Oh, pardon me, I thought you did." On the final refrain when the two sing together they start out at opposite sides of the stage and dance in toward the center, ending up nose to nose. They then shake hands warmly and pat each other on the back, and Robin runs off.

Rose's entrance sends Richard into a paroxysm of nautical language, corresponding gestures, and moving back and forth, so that her "Sir, you are agitated" appears very much an understatement. The apple she offers him has

*Marjorie Eyre as Mad Margaret in* Ruddigore: *"Cheerily carols the lark over the cot."*
*(D'Oyly Carte production)*

already had a large bite taken out if it. He examines it hungrily and is about to take a bite when he discovers its condition and returns it sheepishly.

Whenever Rose refers to her etiquette book she moves forward and faces the audience while flipping through its pages. Richard's consultations with his heart are similar enough to this so that some parallel between the two sources of guidance is suggested.

Richard receives Rose's permission to kiss her once. This, it is clearly indicated, is to be be a kiss on the cheek. But Richard is not so unambitious and he grabs her and bends her halfway back to the floor.

Their duet has been omitted from most D'Oyly Carte performances, though it is present on the most recent recording. There is no possible excuse for cutting it, however, as it is one of Sullivan's finest duets. The staging should make it clear that Rose has no qualms about immediately surrendering her heart to the firstcomer.

Robin enters, followed by the Bridesmaids, whom he has obviously prompted to appear and herald his approaching marriage. On "Hail the Bridegroom—hail the Bride" each time they sing it, the Bridesmaids all join hands and swing their arms back and forth mechanically. Robin's attempt at an embrace is neatly stopped by Rose's index finger to his breastbone, while she turns to consult her book. After it is clear that Richard and Rose are happily united, Robin chases the Bridesmaids away. The last one to exit sticks out her tongue at him, causing him to remark, "Vulgar girls!"

Robin now attempts to paint a picture of Richard that will be unattractive to Rose. When he mentions his hornpipe, Richard obliges with a step or two, accompanying himself with a little whistling. When he finishes, Robin says, "There—and that's only a bit of it!"

The following trio is the means whereby Rose switches from Richard to Robin. In the opening ensemble the three stand together in a line. As Richard sings, he puts his arm around Rose, who is not responsive. Robin then takes Rose by the hands and seats her while he sings his proposal. Richard comes around behind her and again attempts to embrace her as she begins to sing, but she pushes him away and indicates her preference for Robin. By the end of her stanza she is embracing Robin. For the concluding ensemble Robin and Rose cross the stage arm in arm, while Richard, behind Robin's back, indicates in pantomime his intention of getting even. The sight of them together is too much for him, however, and he pulls out a long sailor's handkerchief and sobs into it as he rushes offstage.

panion will momentarily place her in the same world as that of the squirrel who had a mother and the fly that died—pop!

The song Margaret sings has the following tune:

The cat and the dog and the little puppee, Sat down in a-down in a-ina—

Mad Margaret's entrance should be staged with close attention to the orchestration. The various instruments suggest her wandering fantasies, and she should pursue these, now running after something invisible, now turning sadly away. When she begins to sing she should create fully in her imagination each of the images suggested by the words and react to it as if it were present onstage. No simulation of these things will work unless they are actually visualized, as Margaret's eyes are her most important means of communication, and if they are blank her gestures will be meaningless.

Her laugh is most important and is too often slighted. Unfortunately the two most recent D'Oyly Carte recordings do not do it justice, and one must go all the way back to Nellie Briercliffe's rendition made in the 1930's to hear it the way it should sound. It is an hysterical fountain of sound, leaping to the top of her range and descending rapidly all the way to the bottom. Anything less mercurial, passionate, and impulsive will do little justice to the opening musical setting, which has the same quality.

The ballad, although beautiful, is something of an anticlimax after the opening scene. It can be redeemed by a sensitive actress who carefully pantomimes all the action of the words so that the original hysteria seems merely a preparation for the deeply human sadness that underlies it.

The following dialogue scene is extremely funny, but it must be played sensitively. Rose remains naïvely innocent all the way through and must never try to take the scene away from Margaret. Her helplessness will provide the foil that makes the latter's cavorting seem really funny. Here again it is important that Margaret visualize each situation fully, that she let her eyes take the lead and her gestures follow, and that she become fully and genuinely involved in trying to solve each of the pseudo-problems that her mad fantasies present her. Thus when she finally realizes that she is talking to Rose Maybud, her careful examination of her com-

The welcoming of the Bucks and Blades is quite different from the welcoming of Richard Dauntless, a distinction that is made clear in the musical setting of each. Richard brings out their spirit of adventure, the Bucks and Blades their elegant manners. "Welcome, gentry," therefore, should contain much curtseying and stylized behavior something in the manner of the minuet.

Again, if entrances are to be made from the back of the auditorium, this one may originate from that source. In the original production the Bucks and Blades were all dressed in military uniforms, a device that has no particular logic behind it, but produces a spectacular effect. This allows the men to march in in military formations much as do the Dragoons and Peers. If civilian clothing is used, the entrance will have to be more relaxed and concentrate more on individual characterization. In that case, care must be exercised not to allow the effect to become chaotic. The director should arrange things so that the focus shifts from group to group as the ladies and gentlemen get acquainted, so that each group has a few moments of business accompanied by more movement than occurs elsewhere on the stage.

The union between ladies and gentlemen may be effectively delayed until the gentlemen have marched in front of the ladies several times, and the ladies have waved and smiled at their favorites. During the section in which the ladies characterize the villagers that they are accustomed to, a somewhat awkward dance in unison may help to get the idea across.

The entrance of Sir Despard produces terror among the choristers. They scream and shrink to the sides of the stage as he approaches, whip in hand. With each question he accusingly addresses a small group of the chorus, who react with trembling. Seeing their reactions he becomes more introspective and moves to the front of the stage, while the chorus close in behind him. Then, on "Oh, innocent, happy though poor!" he turns again to the chorus and becomes gradually more involved with them

*Fisher Morgan as Sir Despard Murgatroyd in* Ruddigore: *"When in crime one is fully employed, your expression gets warped and destroyed."* (D'Oyly Carte production)

until the end of the song, when on the last three phrases three groups of girls in succession flee from him screaming.

The humor of the following dialogue lies in the contrast of manner and similarity of purpose of Richard and Despard. Sir Despard feels compelled to remain aloof from Richard because of his breeding, but nevertheless is drawn to him because of the situation. His struggle with this problem should remain subliminal but affect the entire scene. It is much more subtle than the similar scene between Captain Corcoran and Dick Deadeye in *Pinafore*.

The duet requires the nimblest of feet from both characters, because it is accompanied throughout by rapid skipping, which leaves both of them completely breathless at the end. It would be well to rehearse this number quite early, as it will require considerable practice to coordinate the singing and the skipping in such a manner that it is possible to get through the number at all. During the long musical interlude at the end of each stanza they separate and dance around opposite sides of the stage, passing in the middle and shaking hands as they go by.

The opening of the finale is fairly staid. The Bridesmaids enter, strewing flowers as they come. They are followed by the Bucks and Blades, whose buttonholes now contain white carnations. They bow to their ladies and then join them for the ensemble of mixed voices, perhaps doing a dignified dance step in place.

On the introduction to the madrigal the leading characters enter and take their places across the stage, Robin and Rose meeting and embracing. This is a purely musical number, and once everyone is in place there should be no further movement. It is followed by the gavotte, in which the entire company take part. This should be staged in such a way that Rose and Robin are gradually brought together, meeting just at the point of Sir Despard's entrance.

Sir Despard enters upstage center. On the interlude between his first and second couplet he moves in slow motion downstage as Robin and Rose in the same slow motion back away from each other, moving as if under enchantment, reaching helplessly and longingly toward each other. On learning the sad news, Rose falls weeping upon Dame Hannah's breast. The first stanza of Robin's solo is all innocence, but in the second stanza he is already beginning to reveal his new character, assuming the posture

and voice of a villain. Sir Despard, meanwhile, is drooping some of these characteristics in himself. The scowl and stoop that he had earlier give way to a self-satisfied smile and dignified square-shouldered stance as he gradually becomes a paragon of virtue.

The action immediately preceding Richard's solo should be obvious. The solo itself can easily bring the finale to a standstill if it is sung too slowly or with insufficient passion. Although Richard has earlier made the connivance of his heart seem on the frivolous side, his dedication to truth now takes on Wagnerian proportions. It is one of those moments that is funny only if we are tempted to take it seriously.

Rose says farewell to Robin and he turns his back sadly and moves to the corner of the stage, a Hamlet-like figure, as Rose offers herself to Despard. Margaret's entrance a moment later is on the side of the stage opposite from Robin, and for a few seconds the two figures are balanced in their loneliness, Robin's eyes cast down in despair, Margaret looking up toward Despard with lost hope.

In the following "happy the lily" section the soloists of the moment take the center of the stage. When Robin has finished singing, Zorah offers to dance with him, but he casts her aside angrily and rushes off. The dance that follows the singing should be a folk dance. At the end of it Robin reappears upstage center. He has changed his wig and hat, and is wearing a cape. He cracks a whip, driving the chorus from the stage. Old Adam rushes forward and Robin threatens him with his whip. But Old Adam pulls out a collapsible top hat, opens it, and puts it on his head. At this Robin breaks into villainous laughter, which is echoed by Old Adam as the curtain falls.

Act Two finds us in the picture gallery. Robin and Old Adam have been even further transformed. Both faces are deeply lined with villainy, and the costumes are more somber. They enter stealthily, but as the music strikes a loud chord, each takes a step or two backward in terror. The "ha! ha!'s" should be given careful attention. Robin's are light, Adam's deep and booming. They explore the possibilities of villainy throughout the range of the voice and should not be limited to one note. In the song, the name "Ruthven" is pronounced as written, with a long "u."

The second half of the song as sung in the original production should be incorporated into

Ruddigore: *Finale, Act I.*        (*D'Oyly Carte production*)

the production, but this necessitates changing Old Adam's name to Gideon Crawle throughout the act. The deleted words are as follows:

ROBIN.  My face is the index to my mind,
All venom and spleen and gall—
ha! ha!
Or, properly speaking,
It soon will be reeking
With venom and spleen and gall—
ha! ha!

ADAM.  My name from Adam Goodheart you'll find
I've changed to Gideon Crawle—
ha! ha!
For a bad Bart.'s steward
Whose heart is much *too* hard,
Is always Gideon Crawle—ha! ha!

BOTH.  How providential when you find

The face an index to the mind,
And evil men compelled to call
Themselves by names like Gideon Crawle!

The following dialogue may also effectively be restored:

ROBIN. This is a painful state of things, Gideon Crawle!
ADAM. Painful, indeed! Ah, my poor master, when I swore that come what would, I would serve you in all things for ever, I little thought to what a pass it would bring me! The confidential adviser to the greatest villain unhung! It's a dreadful position for a good old man!
ROBIN. Very likely, but don't be gratuitously offensive, Gideon Crawle.
ADAM. Sir, I am the ready instrument of your abominable misdeeds because I have

sworn to obey you in all things, but I have *not* sworn to allow deliberate and systematic villainy to pass unreproved. If you insist upon it I will swear that, too, but I have not sworn it yet. Now, sir, to business.  (etc.)

This scene should be played in semidarkness, with Robin gradually increasing his melodramatic manner. This reaches its pinnacle in the ridiculous overpronunciation of the words describing his proposed threat to Richard.

Robin and Adam exit in time to the following music, swirling themselves into their capes as they go. The lights come up, and the Bridesmaids dance on and continue to dance while Richard and Rose sing their stanzas.

The effect of Robin's entrance will be intensified if the first sentence of his speech is spoken offstage and run through an echo chamber. Richard and Rose then cower as if being attacked by some unknown force. Robin then enters, hands up, fingers out, Dracula fashion, terrifying Rose. But Richard is prepared and waves his flag over Rose's head, causing all to kneel.

Rose's song appeasing Robin originally had a second stanza, which should be restored. It is as follows:

> My heart that once in truth was thine,
>> Another claims—
> Ah, who can laws to love assign,
>> Or rule its flames?
> Our plighted heart-bound gently bless,
> The seal of thy consent impress
> Upon our promised happiness—
>> Grant thou our prayer!

After the chorus dance off it is up to Robin to produce the gradual change in mood that makes the Ghost Scene most effective. This is accomplished if he performs the opening part of his soliloquy in the manner he has already used in this act, but enhances the quality of his voice when he addresses the portraits directly, so that the effect is almost Shakespearean. The supreme effort he makes in rendering this speech causes him to fall senseless at the foot of the portrait of Sir Roderic.

The stage darkens as the music crescendoes, and when the lights come up the portraits have come to life. All stand rigidly for a few moments to establish their effect as portraits, and then they descend from their frames and form a line. Robin, gradually resuming consciousness,

is at first paralyzed at the sight of the Ghosts. Then he leaps up and runs for the exit. At that all the Ghosts extend their forearms, and he freezes in place. Their forearms drop and he moves zombielike toward them. They move around him in a ring, and he cowers in terror at the center of it.

Sir Roderic, who has stood rigidly in place, leans forward and points toward Robin as he says "Beware." He then identifies himself as he steps down from his frame, leaving behind him a silhouette of red light. Robin expresses sympathy, and Sir Roderic and the chorus reject it with a line that is followed by a bloodcurdling laugh from Sir Roderic as the music to his song begins.

Sir Roderic will need virtually the entire stage for this song, as during the musical introduction to each stanza he must swoop about like a bat, using his cape to suggest wings. As he sings the words his gestures, again with the help of the cape, suggest the grisly activities of which he sings. The total effect of the lightness of foot, the gusto of the voice, and the exaggerated gestures and cape movement should be entirely otherworldly, so that one doubts that anyone of real flesh and blood could accomplish all that Sir Roderic is doing.

Although Sir Roderic's song has been ghoulish, his dialogue is merely snobbish, and is best rendered so. No longer does he suggest the macabre: rather he establishes himself as the leader among a group of connoisseurs of crime. His contempt for Robin is not so much that he is violating the conditions of the curse as that he is a bad practitioner of the art. The effect of the scene, then, should be that Robin is educated by those who know far better than he wherein excellence in their chosen field consists. The dialogue should be quick and sparkling, Robin always feeling that he has the upper hand and seldom finding that to be the case. When he is tortured (the Ghosts merely extend their hands and Robin writhes on the floor) the effect on him is one of humiliation. By the end of the scene he vaguely knows that something is wrong, but he is far too dense really to have appreciated what the Ghosts are trying to teach him. He is among that group of students who spend their scholarly lives in remedial classes.

Other than the movement that tortures Robin, there is no need for movement from the Ghosts until they return to their frames. Their transformation into pictures is accomplished in exactly the same manner as their earlier trans-

*Fisher Morgan as Sir Despard and Joyce Wright as Mad Margaret in* Ruddigore, *Act II: "We only cut respectable capers."* (D'Oyly Carte production)

mogrification, and Robin once again falls senseless on the floor.

Old Adam enters to find Robin in that condition and revives him. The poor old man is much taken aback by Robin's sudden desperate manner and flies in terror at his command.

The duet for Mad Margaret and Sir Despard is the essence of macabre propriety. They enter arm in arm, walking very stiffly, Sir Despard carrying an important furled umbrella. While they are singing they alternately bend both knees, keeping their backs straight and maintaining a perfectly deadpan expression. The real fun is in the graceful dance that punctuates each stanza. What is done is not nearly so important as how it is done. Their dignity of manner is in strange contrast to their stiff antics. Such simple things as Margaret turning under her raised arm that grasps Despard's raised arm can be quite hilarious if the attitude is right. For the third dance the umbrella is stuck into the stage and remains upright while the two dance around it.

In the ensuing dialogue Sir Despard always remains funereal, but Margaret alternates between that quality and mild to severe hysteria, depending on the circumstances. Once Robin enters, the scene is carried entirely by the interplay of the three contrasting characters. Margaret's dependence on Despard is illustrated by the ease with which he can unbendingly restore her to calm simply by raising one hand and uttering a single word.

An amusing staging of the patter trio is the following. The three singers begin lined up together. As Robin begins to sing, Despard and Margaret move to the sides of the stage by rapid little steps on the toes, crisscrossing their feet as they go. When they get to the sides of the stage they move toward the back. One of them turns around, and the other simply moves backward. When they get to the back of the stage they move in toward the center, and when they pass each other they reverse their positions so that the one who had his back to the audience is now facing forward, and vice versa. They continue this movement until they are back where they started, only on opposite sides of Robin. This action is repeated for the next two stanzas. At the very end, when all three are singing at once, they repeat this step, the two outer ones moving to the sides of the stage and back, and Despard, who is in the center, moving straight back and then forward again.

This step is easy to master, but it will require a great deal of practice to make it look effortless and to do it efficiently enough so that sufficient breath remains to sing the song clearly. Once the effect has been achieved, the illusion should be of three dignified puppets.

In the D'Oyly Carte production Old Adam simply leads in Dame Hannah, who stands glowering as Robin confronts her. The following idea, however, has proved effective in other productions. Old Adam drags on a huge canvas bag. Robin looks at it for a moment and scratches his head. He then approaches it cautiously. He has just about worked up enough courage to reach out and touch it when it moves. He retreats to the corner of the stage, cowering in terror, but as nothing further happens, he moves toward it again. The same thing happens. The third time he approaches it, a hand reaches out through the opening in the top and gropes for a means of undoing the sack. Robin then retreats and watches the gradual disclosure of Dame Hannah, completely disheveled, and thoroughly prepared for the ensuing fight. The fight itself should be carefully staged with all the excitement of real swordplay, except that, of course, Robin has only a dagger, whereas Hannah is armed with a battleaxe. After he has narrowly missed being decapitated several times, each time with an athletic escape worthy of Douglas Fairbanks, Jr., he throws himself upon the mercy of Sir Roderic, who obligingly steps down from his frame. From then on we have a love scene, and Robin becomes so extraneous that he exits sucking his thumb.

Hannah's ballad requires little movement, except that when both sing together they do a stately dance, perhaps a minuet. After the duet the following dialogue should be restored:

SIR RODERIC. Little Nannikin!
HANNAH. Roddy-doddy!
SIR RODERIC. It's not too late, is it?
HANNAH. (*Bashfully.*) Oh Roddy!
SIR RODERIC. I'm quite respectable now, you know.
HANNAH. But you're a ghost, ain't you?
SIR RODERIC. Well, yes—a kind of ghost.
HANNAH. But what would be my legal *status* as a ghost's wife?
SIR RODERIC. It would be a very respectable position.
HANNAH. But I should be the wife of a dead husband, Roddy!
SIR RODERIC. No doubt.

HANNAH. But the wife of a dead husband is a widow, Roddy!

SIR RODERIC. I suppose she is.

HANNAH. And a widow is at liberty to marry again, Roddy!

SIR RODERIC. Dear me, yes—that's awkward. I never thought of that.

HANNAH. No, Roddy—I thought you hadn't.

SIR RODERIC. When you've been a ghost for a considerable time it's astonishing how foggy you become!

Robin enters, this time quite authoritatively, and reveals the logic that redeems the situation. If this logic is valid, it revives all of the Ancestors, not just Sir Roderic, and so the revision that leaves the rest of them dead seems pointless, at least by modern standards. Here is the final dialogue sequence as originally written:

ROBIN. But suicide is, itself, a crime—and so, by your own showing, you ought none of you to have ever died at all!

SIR RODERIC. I see—I understand! We are all practically alive!

ROBIN. Every man jack of you!

SIR RODERIC. My brother ancestors! Down from your frames! (*The Ancestors descend.*) You believe yourselves to be dead—you may take it from me that you're not, and an application to the Supreme Court is all that is necessary to prove that you never ought to have died at all! (*The Ancestors embrace the Bridesmaids.*)

*Enter* RICHARD *and* ROSE, *also* SIR DESPARD *and* MARGARET.

\*     \*     \*

ROBIN. My darling! (*They embrace.*)

### CHORUS.

Hail the Bridegroom—hail the Bride!—

RICHARD. (*Interrupting them.*) Will you be quiet? (*To* ROBIN.) Belay, my lad, belay, you don't understand!

ROSE. Oh, sir, belay, if it's absolutely necessary.

ROBIN. Belay? Certainly not. (*To* RICHARD.) You see, it's like this—as all my ancestors are alive, it follows, as a matter of course, that the eldest of them is the family baronet, and I revert to my former condition.

RICHARD. (*Going to* ZORAH.) Well, I think it's exceedingly unfair!

ROBIN. (*To* FIRST GHOST.) Here, great uncle, allow me to present you. (*To the others.*) Sir Ruthven Murgatroyd, Baronet, of Ruddigore!

ALL. Hurrah!

FIRST GHOST. Fallacy somewhere!

The only staging problem here is the descent of the Ancestors from their frames. This may easily be accomplished by a drum roll accompanied by a moment of darkness. Better that than destroying the illusion created earlier by having the Ancestors remove the portraits in full view of the audience.

During the final chorus Old Adam enters with a tray of sherry glasses, one of them only half full. Robin passes these out, two at a time. To Richard he gives a full one and the one that is only half full. Richard, after comparing them, hands the half-full one to Zorah.

The concluding dance resembles the one that concludes the finale of Act One.

### SCENERY AND COSTUMES

We have already discussed the problems attending the portrait gallery. If these are solved, there is little difficulty, as the portraits fill most of the stage during Act Two. If possible, there should also be a coat of armor present on the stage, with a battleaxe attached for Dame Hannah to use. The baronial hall should be somber, but not so depressing that the final chorus cannot appear spirited.

The first act represents a fishing village, the only necessary element of which is Rose's cottage. Even this could be omitted if necessary, and the setting could be purely abstract.

The costuming of the Bucks and Blades has already been discussed. That of the Ancestors is also elaborate, as they should represent different periods in history. If the production is to be an inexpensive one, it is possible to dress Sir Roderic in a fancy costume with a cape and have the other ancestors all in hoods and sheets so that they look like ghosts. This is assuming that they enter from offstage and only one portrait is used.

The costuming of the principals is generally simple. Richard's sailor costume is of the most common kind. Robin is dressed as a farmer in the first act, and his second-act costume can be any combination of baronial majesty and theatrical villainy. Robin's costuming will determine that of Old Adam, who wears an inferior version of the same thing. Dame Hannah wears the customary Victorian middle-aged woman's outfit. Rose Maybud would logically be dressed in a simple country girl's dress, but it seems wise to make this fancier than would be worn ordinarily, as she is so often being hailed as a bride. She does not, however, wear a wedding gown. Sir Despard's baronet costume should be elegant, and he should carry a whip. In the second act he is dressed entirely in black with a top hat and tails and even black gloves. Mad Margaret wears a dress that suggests a distraught Grecian robe and is decorated with flowers. Her hair is completely uncombed. In the second act she is dressed in black with only a collar that is white. She wears a black bonnet.

We come now to the Bridesmaids, who are dressed either as conventional bridesmaids of the period or in specially designed costumes suggesting their unique status as the only corps of professional bridesmaids in the world. They are usually uniform in color, but need not be so.

# Chapter XIV

# THE YEOMEN OF THE GUARD,
# OR THE MERRYMAN AND HIS MAID

## PRODUCTION NOTES

The producer of *The Yeomen of the Guard* should take into account the fact that it requires a great deal of spectacle and that it makes heavy demands on the men's chorus. Let us begin by considering the problems and rewards of the visual side of the production. First of all, it is absolutely necessary to have reasonably accurate Yeomen costumes. They are difficult to make and should probably be rented. Any inaccuracies are likely to be recognized by the audience because of the widespread identification of the costume with Great Britain. Secondly, though it is possible to produce the opera without reproducing the Tower of London accurately (the current D'Oyly Carte production takes that liberty), it is generally conceded that the production is significantly enhanced if a reasonable facsimile of the Tower is on view. Thirdly, in the scene of the intended execution there is an opportunity for beautiful lighting effects. Any company capable of meeting these three visual demands effectively should also be capable of producing a show that is splendid and exciting to watch.

The chorus music in *Yeomen* is the most rewarding to work on of any chorus music in the series, but it demands a large and well-trained company. The chorus of Yeomen must be strong, particularly in the tenor section, and must be supplemented by additional men who represent townspeople. The demands on the women's chorus are not nearly as great, but their music is also rewarding to sing.

Since *The Yeomen of the Guard* is the single Gilbert and Sullivan opera that is generally rather serious and human throughout, it lends itself to a greater variety of production styles than do the other operas. In general, the absurdity of Gilbert and Sullivan is enhanced by realistic scenery and polished, highly mannered acting. In *Yeomen* the acting can be more naturalistic and the scenery more abstract. It is also an opera that lends itself to being opened out into the auditorium. One effective production of it placed some of the scenery and action in the center of the area in which the audience sat, much in the manner of arena staging, but also used the proscenium stage for most of the action. The central area represented a well at which Phoebe sang her first song while filling buckets with water. The same area was used for the Headsman's block. The movement of masses of people between the two areas added greatly to the dimensionality of the production.

## CRITICAL DISCUSSION

It is strange that Gilbert's most human story should also be one of his most improbable. Many events in *The Yeomen of the Guard* are either explained inadequately or not at all, and some of these are central to the development of the plot. In addition, the story is rather complicated and difficult to follow on first exposure. Plot inconsistencies are easily forgiven in the world of topsy-turvydom, but in the more realistic world of the Tower of London they suggest haste and carelessness on Gilbert's part.

What we learn from this observation is that Gilbert was much more a master of the development of theatrical mood than of plot structure. Difficulties that appear major on close examination tend not to bother us in the theatre because of the inspired quality of the songs and the interrelationships between them. Looked at from that point of view, *Yeomen* is one of Gilbert's best libretti and provides the inspiration for Sullivan's best serious music in addition to many comic gems.

Gilbert himself was troubled by the opening sequence of numbers, all of which are rather serious or sentimental, and in order to keep the opera from becoming top-heavy he wisely cut a rather undistinguished number for Sergeant Meryll after the opening performance. Yet he need not have worried, since even among those first few numbers are many shades of contrast, Phoebe's opening solo being a world apart from the pageantry and counterpoint of the entrance of the Tower Warders, which is in turn followed by a grimly foreboding contralto solo and a trio of grand-opera proportions.

The key to the song structuring, however, lies in the duet for Jack Point and Elsie Maynard, the story of the Merryman and his Maid, which parallels in miniature the story of the opera itself. In this song, which is brought back in the finale of the second act, are the elements of gaiety, sentiment, and pageantry perfectly blended, and in its simple folk-song manner it manages to suggest not only the plot but the general quality of the rest of the opera.

Point and Elsie are the perfect couple upon which to center the action of the opera, as Point is the essence of the opera's wistful humanity and Elsie of its sentiment.

Gilbert many times failed as a serious playwright, because in trying to be tragic he became merely sentimental and banal. His great success with the absurd and grotesque was partly owing to the shallowness with which he observed human feeling, though his observations of human nature were profound indeed. Sentiment seldom endures in the theatre because it is so vulnerable to changing values and to parody, and for the latter reason it is usually carefully insulated from real comedy. The singular success of *Yeomen* is that it is able to mix the sentimental and the comic without damage to either, and the sentimental qualities of the opera are thereby rendered invulnerable to the ravages of time. Furthermore, because the sentimental must hold its own in the presence of comedy it is subjected to unusual restraint, and what from the pen of a lesser dramatist, or Gilbert himself in a less auspicious mood, might easily have overflowed into the banal, is held back so that heartbreak and suffering are suggested rather than overstated, and the characters consequently seem perhaps more human than they really are.

Many little touches in the dialogue help to achieve this effect. For example, Point's sampling of "The Merrie Jestes of Hugh Ambrose" serves as a vehicle for suggesting both his heartbreak at Elsie's marriage and his difficulties with his new employer. Then again, Phoebe's promise to marry Wilfred in a year, or two, or three, in order to keep him quiet, helps us to see a way out of her plight that relieves us of excessive sympathy for her.

Sullivan's music captures this same quality, particularly in the orchestration, as Gilbert gives him ample opportunity for suggesting character or situation through the voices of various instruments. Excellent examples of this technique will be found in Phoebe's "Were I thy bride," Point's "I've jibe and joke," and the Funeral March. The first two manage to suggest a humanness beneath the humor of the situation, and the third is a powerful evocation of the reality of death that hangs over the plot.

It is evident that Gilbert was exploring in *Yeomen* more than he himself knew, and that to the last he was uncertain of the exact value of what he had done. Probably Point's character is developed beyond Gilbert's original plans for it, as he is the pivotal figure in the opera. One imagines Gilbert attempting to work up a typical opera plot set in the England of Henry VIII and introducing Point, the strolling jester, more for local color than anything else. After all, it is Elsie to whom things happen, and Point is merely her disappointed lover to whom she had probably never promised her hand in the first place. Yet Point's sorrow at this unintended rejection of his love becomes more important than any of the convolutions of plot. Time and again he refers directly or obliquely to his sorrowful state. Even in the purely abstracted view of the jester's life in his second-act patter song there is the parallel with his own situation: "Though your wife ran away with a soldier that day . . ." His sorrow is all the more pathetic since he must by profession continue to be a humorist. That all his samples of humor fall particularly flat only adds to the sadness of his plight.

The controversy that has surrounded *Yeomen* from the first year of its production lies in whether or not Point dies in the end. Since Gilbert wrote "falls insensible" most critics assume that he meant it, and that it is an unauthorized perversion of his idea for Point to die. Yet the latter interpretation is the one that is usually played, and it seems to work effectively enough in the theatre. Perhaps this is a case in which Gilbert's conscious intentions are irrelevant, for the heavy atmosphere of death that is suggested by the Tower, by Dame Carruthers' song, and by the Funeral March is brought to an admirable climax in the death of a character who is given no further reason to live. The expected happy ending is defeated by a character who might easily have remained of minor interest, and the casual way in which Elsie and Fairfax have been brought together is allowed to have tragic consequences.

## CHARACTER SKETCHES

### Sir Richard Cholmondeley

Sir Richard, being the Lieutenant of the Tower, is a man of commanding authority. He is also concerned about propriety ("I have daughters"), and this is probably what blunts his sense of humor and makes him such a hard taskmaster for poor Jack Point. His sympathy for Colonel Fairfax, however, softens his character somewhat. Vocally he is a baritone of medium range. His surname is pronounced "Chumley."

### Colonel Fairfax

The Colonel is distinguished much more for charm than for depth of character. Life means little to him, and he is quite willing to part with it if necessary, but given the opportunity to escape he has no qualms about causing widespread confusion and breaking the heart of his chief benefactor. A dashing and easygoing manner are required in the acting.

The singing allows opportunities for sensitivity not suggested anywhere in the dialogue. The two solos as well as much of the work in the finale require real subtlety of shading, though they do not make unusual demands on the tenor range.

### Sergeant Meryll

The Sergeant is full of romantic memories of his own glorious past and assumes the same kind of glory in all others who wear uniforms. He is the paragon of the ideal soldier: staunch, loyal, true, and brainless. He should be played with bravado that is all the more vociferous because it is aging.

The singing does not offer the performer much opportunity to distinguish himself, but it is important and rather difficult and requires a heavy and bright bass-baritone.

### Leonard Meryll

Sergeant Meryll's son, Leonard, has most of his characteristics, though they are not so fully developed. He should be personable, dashing, and capable of singing a rather difficult tenor part in his one trio.

### Jack Point

This is the comic baritone role that brings out the Shakespearean ambitions of comedians. Because of his unrequited passion for Elsie, Point can be given pathetic as well as humorous qualities. Martyn Green developed the pathos and prepared for the death at the end by giving him the symptoms of a victim of malnutrition and heart disease. This was accomplished partly by whitening the makeup from the beginning and by gradually increasing its whiteness throughout the second act. A few anemic coughs also added to the effect.

Point is sincere in his attempts to be a humorist, but they generally fall flat with his audience. He is not easily discouraged, however, and is perhaps better qualified as a salesman of his abilities than as a jester. At any rate he has no illusions about his job, as his second-act patter song makes clear. It reminds one of Harry Truman's remark, "If you can't stand the heat, stay out of the kitchen," and is an excellent example of the way the professional man acclimatizes himself to the drawbacks of his profession. Although the song is generally applicable, however, one feels it also has special reference to the details of Point's own experiences, and it thus makes him seem something of a hero.

Above all, Point must be lovable. It is difficult for us to understand why Elsie should turn from him to the dashing but rather insensitive Fairfax when he is appealing in so many ways. The tragedy is in part hers, as we feel he would have made her an excellent husband. He is evidently too timid, however, to discuss his feelings with her openly, and perhaps that is why she rejects him. His lovableness is to be found not only in his personality, but also his voice, which is light and wistful and contains a great deal of warmth. His words are important in the songs, and they are projected as much by his personableness as by his good diction.

The role contains many opportunities for good dancing, and indeed in a sense Point dances his way through the entire opera, as every gesture communicates something of his emotional state in a way that is in sharp contrast to the military stiffness of the Yeomen.

## Wilfred Shadbolt

Although this role is usually given to the actor who plays Pooh-Bah, and is consequently likely to be played as a grotesque old man, Wilfred describes himself as young, sees himself logically as a suitor for Phoebe's hand, and undertakes to study for a second profession. He is Head Jailer and Assistant Tormentor and does his work conscientiously and with a certain lugubrious satisfaction, though he claims not to like his job. Indeed, he goes about it with a comedian's, rather than a sadist's spirit, and he has much in common with the Mikado, who finds torture in boiling oil to be humorous. In both cases we are in the presence of that kind of fantasized punishment that never finds fruition in reality: You can do all you like to your enemies in your imagination provided they never become conscious of what you are doing to them. Wilfred is a personification of the fantasies of timid people who would love to imagine their enemies tormented, so long as they don't *really* suffer.

Although it is easy to see why Phoebe rejects Wilfred, inasmuch as he hasn't the slightest smidgeon of *savoir-faire*, we suspect that he wouldn't be an altogether bad husband, and might in fact play the role much better than Colonel Fairfax.

Wilfred is in a certain sense a foil to Point. His situation is a parody of Point's more serious one, and he provides the low comedy parallel of the latter's high comedy. Consequently he should be somewhat exaggerated in his mannerisms, makeup, and posture.

The role requires a baritone voice, not particularly deep, but dark in timbre and attractive to listen to, as some of the melodies given to him are quite beautiful.

## The Headsman

His head is covered with a mask, but he wears a body-fitting black costume, and he should be big and muscular. He stands on stage motionless for about fifteen minutes, and is therefore really a part of the scenery.

## First Yeoman

This part should be given to that member of the chorus who has the best tenor voice. He has to sing two couplets in the finale of Act One, and that is all.

## Second Yeoman

This character takes over a song and part of the dialogue originally allotted to Sergeant Meryll, and the demands on his voice are therefore similar to those made on Meryll's. His opening solo is worthy of a fine rendition, and if a suitable performer cannot be found there is no serious reason that the major part of this role cannot be returned to Meryll and the role itself reduced to the couplets that follow the First Yeoman's and are to be sung in a low baritone voice.

## First and Second Citizens

These are rowdies who make passes at Elsie and threaten Point. They should be given to chorus members who are good actors and can appear reasonably threatening. Their lines must be paced rapidly so that they add to the general confusion of the scene in which they appear.

## Elsie Maynard

Singing is the most important feature of this role. Quite a range of dramatic and lyric abilities is required, from the folksy quality of the opening duet to the cadenza that concludes her aria. To a large extent the quality of the singing will determine the quality of the character, as there is little in Elsie's lines that can lead an audience to sympathize with her, but the music raises her suffering to tragic heights, even though it is only temporary.

Elsie is in some ways the most vixenish of Gilbert's heroines because she willingly participates in Fairfax' tormenting of Point, even though she knows how much he loves her. She may be excused to some extent since she is much in love with Fairfax and, being engaged in the process of winning his love, has little time to concern herself with Point.

At the end of the opera Elsie was given the following words:

It's the song of a merrymaid, peerly
 proud
Who loved her lord, and who laughed
 aloud
At the moan of the merryman, moping
 mum. . . .

These were changed in 1897 to:

It's the song of a merrymaid, nestling
 near,
Who loved her lord—but who dropped
 a tear
At the moan of the merryman, moping
 mum. . . .

This change is not observed in the Schirmer vocal score, but it should be made if Point is to die in the end. Failing to make the change causes Elsie to seem much more hardhearted than she really is and gives an unpleasant flavor to the finale.

### Phoebe Meryll

In some ways this role is the female counterpart to Point. She, also, combines comedy and pathos, though her comedy is not so great nor her pathos so profound. She is responsible for setting the tone of the production, since she opens the opera all by herself. Much of the time she is in danger of seeming to be merely irritable, since she is so busy objecting to Wilfred's attentions, but a competent actress should be able to let Phoebe's basic charm shine through even those moments.

The part is written for a mezzo or contralto and will probably have to be transposed in some places if it is given to a soprano. Although Phoebe has some beautiful music, particularly her opening solo, it is not unusually demanding. Thus the acting is as important as the singing, and some small sacrifice can be made on the musical side of things in order to obtain an actress who can project an attractive personality.

### Dame Carruthers

This grand old lady derives her dignity from her association with the tower, which she to a certain extent personifies. Her opening solo should not be allowed to become crude in any respect, though there will be some tendency to crudity in her character if the closing duet is included in the production. She has a sense of humor and varies from the frighteningly stern to the jolly and robust old dame. The voice required is a heavy contralto with a pure, almost trumpetlike tone to echo the Tower motif in the orchestra.

### Kate

No solo singing is required in this part, but she must be musical, as she has some important ensemble work. In auditioning for her, look for musicianship and ability to blend rather than beauty of tone. Little is required in the way of acting, as her only function seems to be to echo her aunt. It is effective to caricature her as a girl whose voice sounds considerably younger than she looks.

### NOTES ON STAGING

Perhaps the best preparation for staging *Yeomen* is to listen carefully to the Overture several times and imagine ways in which the qualities Sullivan has suggested in his music can be represented visually. The director should work closely with the set and lighting designers so that a unity of effect will be achieved, since a large part of the success of the production will depend on its visual qualities. Bear in mind that a realistic setting will call for more realism in the acting, and an abstract setting will allow for greater abstraction and caricature, perhaps giving more prominence to such characters as Dame Carruthers and Wilfred than would otherwise be the case.

For the opening scene the D'Oyly Carte Opera Company for a while used an inset representing Phoebe's room in the Tower. Wilfred appeared looking through the window. This presented problems. For one, it greatly restricted Wilfred's movement. Secondly, the delay caused by the need to change scenes interrupted the flow of the action rather drastically.

A possible variation of the above procedure is to play the opening scene in front of the curtain, so that the scenery makes its full impact with the entrance of the Yeomen. It is also possible to have a painted backdrop that can be lifted as Wilfred exits. Either solution will solve the two problems mentioned above.

During her opening solo Phoebe is spinning. The music suggests the action of the spinning wheel as well as certain moments when the spinning stops and Phoebe gives way to reflection. Wilfred's entrance abruptly changes the mood, and care must be taken that the two

*Fisher Morgan as Wilfred Shadbolt in* The Yeomen of the Guard: *"I didn't become head-jailer because I like head-jailing."* (D'Oyly Carte production)

actors do not merely shout at each other. Although they are arguing, there are sympathetic qualities in each of them that must be suggested from the beginning. If Wilfred, taken aback by Phoebe's initial outburst, sits mournfully and protests her accusation rather sadly, making his allusion to sorcery almost with reluctance, he will not seem quite so overbearing later. Sympathy for Phoebe can be established through her obvious love for Fairfax, which is played as love and not merely as anger at Wilfred. Later, Wilfred's confession of his jealousy should seem sadly introspective rather than overtly aggressive. He is reduced almost to tears, and this gives Phoebe the upper hand so that she is almost calmly sarcastic on her exit line, which should be good for a laugh. Wilfred's anger then builds gradually to a boiling fury and carries him offstage at a run.

The entrance of the crowd is most effectively played if the crowd appears to be gathering rather than all coming together from some other place. The people in the crowd are sightseers who know that the Yeomen are about to appear, and they come on in groups of two or three, laughing and talking together and then discovering the Yeomen in the distance. The irregularity of the crowd will contrast with the military appearance of the Yeomen, who march in with the stylish elaborateness characteristic of the pageantry of the British. Once they are in place there is little action other than an occasional repositioning of the Yeomen and continued animation among the citizens. Furthermore, the crowd should not exit all together in a line at the end of the song, but should drift off gradually, as it drifted on. This effect can be intensified if the actions of the crowd relate to those of the leading characters. For example, if a unit set is used, a few women could enter right at the end of Wilfred's soliloquy, so that as he rushes off at the end of it he bumps into one of them and must shamefacedly apologize and perhaps pick up the contents of an overturned market basket. Then, at the end of the chorus Dame Carruthers might drift on along with Kate and engage in conversation for a few moments with some of the women before the music stops. As her dialogue begins, Kate might continue talking with this same group and only later join her aunt. This would help to establish her familiarity with the sight of the Yeomen. Phoebe could then make her entrance somewhere in the midst of these activities, and appear at first to be part of the crowd. If she is among those talking to Kate, she could suddenly break off the conversation when Colonel Fairfax is mentioned and come over to join the conversation between Carruthers and the Second Yeoman.

There is little action apart from a few gestures in Dame Carruthers' solo. The song is about the Tower, and the emphasis is on the words. Movement here will only distract from the idea of the Tower's timeless endurance. Fairly pictorial gestures, however, are appropriate from both Carruthers and the chorus.

In the dialogue between Phoebe and her father the main object should be to distinguish between the two characters—Meryll with his brusque heroic manner that tosses off "cutting his way through fifty foes who would have hanged him" as if it were a daily occurrence, and Phoebe with the petty concerns of a little girl just growing up and her love for a man whom she knows merely as being handsome and brave. It is clear that Meryll wants to save Fairfax as much to gratify the girlish whims of his daughter as to satisfy a concern for justice.

With Leonard's entrance the pacing, which has previously been rapid, increases even more. Leonard is ready for action, and Meryll supplies it much as if he were in the habit of clearing up difficult situations at a moment's notice. (One suspects that he has seen some action in the Secret Service.) Leonard is obviously close to his father, but in the habit of fighting with his sister. Her affection for him is newborn, based on the hope that he brings her. He should take no notice of her until the line before the song, which is said not angrily, but halfway in jest, and should be really funny.

The trio requires regroupings of the characters in a way that reflects the development of musical ideas in it. At the beginning of it Meryll struts to the back of the stage to look off and make sure that no one has been listening to the preceding conversation. Phoebe puts her hand to her forehead and moves forward. The three characters thus will be apart on the opening ensemble. Leonard then moves to the side of the stage opposite Phoebe for his solo, and on the following ensemble the others move in toward him to suggest that they are all working together in their daring deed. Meryll then takes a step forward and gestures to the audience, putting himself in front of the other two, who are one on each side of him. When his next solo moment comes, he crosses the stage as if thinking, and turns back facing the others on "Unworthy thought!" All remain stationary until "We may succeed," when they move to-

*Ann Drummond-Grant as Dame Carruthers in* The Yeomen of the Guard: *"I was born in the old keep, and I've grown grey in it, and, please God, I shall die and be buried in it; and there's not a stone in its walls that is not as dear to me as my own right hand."*
(D'Oyly Carte production)

*Colonel Fairfax in* The Yeomen of the Guard: *"Take my word for it, it is easier to die well than to live well—for, in sooth, I have tried both."* (D'Oyly Carte production)

ward one another at the center. On the first "farewell" Leonard shakes hands with his father; on the second, with his sister. During the closing bars Leonard embraces his father and then his sister. Phoebe turns aside weeping, but Meryll follows his son halfway and waves to him as he exits.

If entrances are made from the front, the entrance of Fairfax would be a good place to begin this practice. It is more natural for Phoebe to see him coming down the aisle than from offstage. Also, bringing him down the aisle allows for the use of more Yeomen accompanying him, plus others who may move out from the sides of the stage to greet him as he goes.

The Lieutenant (pronounced "Leftenant") enters on the opposite side from Fairfax, and the two greet each other warmly, neither seeing the two Merylls, who are upstage from them. The Lieutenant's "Halt!" is directed to Fairfax' guards, not the Colonel himself. Fairfax' manner suggests that in spirit he is anything but a prisoner; and though those who surround him all appear sad, he is as happy as he can be. When he discovers Meryll, he has almost the manner of a host welcoming a guest to a party.

Fairfax' ballad will gain in interest if he uses it to relate to the other people onstage. He devotes an opening phrase or two to get Meryll looking cheerful, and then turns to the Lieutenant, who is sadly shaking his head. Having cheered him up, he turns his attention to one of the guards. The final object of his attentions is Phoebe, who has so far bravely kept back her tears. His remarks directed to her, however, cause her to break down, and she has to be led away by her father. This momentarily perplexes Fairfax, but he shrugs it off and turns to address the Lieutenant. Throughout he has related to people not merely by addressing them, but by actually grasping them by the arm or patting them on the back. In this same manner he leads the Lieutenant into complicity in his plan to outwit Sir Clarence.

When Fairfax makes the offer of an hundred crowns, he pulls a purse from his doublet and presses it in the Lieutenant's hand. This gives the Lieutenant's next line a hesitancy it would not otherwise have, as he is holding the money, and Fairfax has moved away. Although his conscience pricks him, he already sees no way out of the request. When he has made up his mind to grant it, he attaches the money to his belt. Just before he exits he again notices the money, grasps it in his hand, and laughs cheerfully before making his last remark.

The entrance of Point and Elsie precedes a crowd who this time originate all from the same source. Quickly they surround the stage and then attempt to trap the surefooted couple. Both Point and Elsie athletically elude several attempts to seize them, but finally Elsie is caught by a surly fellow whom Point bops on the head with his folly-stick, causing him to let go of her. At this the other villagers laugh and retreat a little, just in time for Point's speech, which is given with concealed terror. As he is giving it, another surly fellow, much bigger than the first, grabs Elsie, and as a challenge to Point holds one hand up over his head. Point responds by clapping the fellow on the shoulder and taking him aside as if he were talking to him confidentially. He walks him across the stage in this manner, and the citizen altogether forgets Elsie in his interest in what Point is saying. Point uses the citizen's hands to represent the characters of *pro* and *con*, and the latter becomes so intrigued with this that he skips off to a friend and several times reënacts Point's manipulation of his hands until the friend, disgusted, takes both the man's hands in his own and stops his mouth with them.

When Point mentions the various dances, he claps his hands after each one as a command to Elsie to give a little suggestion of each.

The duet is managed by having the singing member of the couple stand aside while the nonsinging member pantomimes the action of the song.

The following dialogue is simple enough, except that when the Lieutenant says that Fairfax is to die "on this very spot," he points to the ground at the place where Point is standing, and Point, seeing this gesture, leaps to the side in terror. When the Lieutenant mentions the hundred crowns the second time, he holds up the purse he has been given. Point examines it carefully, though the Lieutenant does not relinquish it. After a little he makes up his mind and walks to the corner of the stage, leaving the Lieutenant and Elsie in the center.

The Lieutenant's opening stanza causes conflicting emotions in Elsie, and though he is singing, the spotlight is on her reactions. Her reactions seem to go beyond the mere need for the money, as she argues a little too strongly that that is the only reason she is considering the proposal. Perhaps she already has an inkling of what will follow. At least the idea of matrimony to someone once rich and powerful has a singular effect upon her feelings.

Point, observing from his corner, senses momentarily that Elsie's reaction bodes no good for him, but he puts the idea out of his mind and attempts to convince himself and Elsie that the money is the only consideration as he sings his stanza. The reference to a "well-earned grave" is accompanied by a glance at her from which she turns away.

The effect of the words "Temptation, oh, temptation," quite powerful words in view of the situation, is different on each of the characters. The Lieutenant stands aside and smiles smugly, his mission accomplished. Point dances about in the center of the stage, basing his dance on gestures suggesting confusion and making up one's mind. Elsie looks out at the audience, trying to control and even conceal the passion that is growing within her.

When the singing is over, Wilfred enters, and at the Lieutenant's instructions, blindfolds Elsie and leads her off into the Tower. Point watches this action rather soulfully, and apparently has second thoughts about it, since just as Elsie is disappearing he starts to rush after her, but is stopped by the extended arm of the Lieutenant.

Point's speech preceding his song is punctuated by gestures and leaps about the stage, appropriate to each of the qualities and jests he mentions. He is not merely cataloguing his accomplishments, he is representing them in the hope of employment. These antics are carried over into the song, which should be carefully choreographed with the movements suggested by the musical accompaniment.

During the following dialogue the Lieutenant's humorless reactions to Point's jests cause the latter to keep trying all the harder. The scene depends for its humor on the Lieutenant's carefully understated distaste for the jokes he is hearing. He should not be overbearing nor too obviously revolted. He should be merely calmly disinterested in Point's approach to life.

Elsie's solo requires little movement but a great deal of acting. The musical accompaniment suggests a passion that transcends the words, and this passion should be responded to fully by an Elsie who is already in love—with her situation.

The scene between Phoebe and Wilfred raises some aesthetic problems. Phoebe's wooing of Wilfred can easily be turned into low comedy that is wrong for Phoebe's character, and the temptation is the greater because it is so right for Wilfred's character. The situation should be played sincerely for what it is, Phoebe merely providing the elusive bait, Wilfred the one who is going after it. The song is usually staged by having Wilfred and Phoebe sit together in one place throughout. Wilfred's antics and facial expressions if carried to extremes, may create laughter that drowns out the music. The number can also be staged by having Phoebe move away from Wilfred from one bench to the other, engaging several different kinds of flirtation. It is possible to do it this way so that the effect is amusing without being excessively funny, so that the words of the song will not be lost.

Wilfred's next speech climaxes as his earlier soliloquy did, only this time it is paroxysms of joy rather than jealousy that move him, and the effect is much funnier. The humor is increased if Wilfred suggests with his own movement the different kinds of wooing he observed, provided he does not belabor this process.

The opening section of the finale involves much moving about of the Yeomen into different formations. This is the primary source of variety in the spectacle, and there are numerous musical interludes on which to do it. Sergeant Meryll's simulation of bravado over his son's accomplishments can be funny if it is rendered with sufficient gusto, and Fairfax' gradual acclimatization to his new role occasionally threatens to reveal the situation even to the unobservant Yeomen. His aside, "Truly I was to be pitied," for example, is sung to Meryll, who appears worried lest it be overheard. Meryll's worries are further increased when Phoebe appears on the scene, and he keeps trying to inform Fairfax who she is, but with no luck, as Fairfax is far more responsive to her beauty than to Meryll's gesticulations. Ironically it is Wilfred who informs him that Phoebe is his sister, and who supervises the lovemaking between them with evident delight. For his part of the trio Wilfred takes Fairfax aside and instructs him on the proper care of his sister. Phoebe grabs him back, however, and walks across the stage with him, getting as far away from Wilfred as possible in time for Fairfax' stanza. Thus the kisses are reacted to by Wilfred at some distance, and his reactions can, as a consequence, be all the better projected.

At the conclusion of the trio the lights dim, and the characters fall into formation for the

*Joyce Wright as Phoebe, Peter Pratt as Jack Point, Muriel Harding as Elsie, and Leonard Osborn as Col. Fairfax in* The Yeomen of the Guard. *Fairfax: "Tush, man, thou knowest not how to woo."* (D'Oyly Carte production)

Funeral March. The block is brought into place upstage by two assistants to the Headsman. The latter then appears carrying a huge axe. Just before the chorus begins to sing, he drops the axe and buries its head in the block with a tremendous thud.

There is no motion during the Funeral March except when Elsie comes forward to sing her solo. With the entrance of Fairfax and the two Yeomen the lights suddenly come up a little, though not to full daylight. From that point until the end of the singing, the action is confined to the principals, who take their places near the center of the stage at the obvious

moments. Although Elsie's solo is marked "aside to Point," it is more effective to make it a distraught remark to the world as Elsie moves across the front of the stage. (In the excitement, we are to sense, nobody in the crowd is listening to Elsie.) Point enters upstage center just in time to hear her remark and comes down to her on his line. The scene concludes with a general exodus, leaving only Elsie fainting in Fairfax' arms and the Headsman in place onstage.

If entrances and exits are made from the front of the stage, it is effective to have the crowd move down into the auditorium during the last ensemble while the Yeomen remain on the stage. They can then turn and face the Yeomen and sing toward them, giving much more illusion of interplay between the various parts of the chorus.

Act Two opens on a moonlit scene. The Yeomen are lined up on both sides of the stage and the ladies at the back. As they sing, the ladies use their arms to make long, graceful gestures suggestive of the words. Dame Carruthers enters, followed by Kate, moving between the ladies and the Yeomen from the upstage corner, and coming downstage as she sings. While the chorus of women echo her words, Dame Carruthers moves to a downstage corner and seats herself on a bench. On their music the men move forward and line up across the front of the stage, using appropriate gestures as they sing. The ladies then break through their line, and the number ends with an ensemble sung by ladies and men in two alternating lines across the front of the stage.

Jack Point enters and sits, reading from a large antique volume. Although he is somewhat scornful of what he reads, Point nevertheless values it, since it is his only source of professional instruction. Upon Wilfred's entrance he lays the book beside him on the bench. His condemnation of Wilfred is motivated not only by his anger that Fairfax is free, but also by his need to pick on someone just as he feels himself to be picked on by the Lieutenant.

Point's song, like his earlier one, should be accompanied by dancing appropriate to a jester. In this case, however, the dancing need not accompany the words, which are adequately illustrated by gestures. The dancing may be confined to the interludes.

Point promises to teach Wilfred how to be a jester if Wilfred will pretend that he has shot Fairfax. As he is making this bargain, he shows Wilfred the book of his source materials. Wilfred tries to grab it, but Point withholds it and replaces it on the bench. At the beginning of the duet he breaks into a dance, which Wilfred tries to imitate. As they begin to sing they join hands and shake hands as they dance. Each then takes a pose for his solo. During the duet that ends the stanza they do an awkward bounce, crossing over their legs, followed by a pirouette to end the phrase. In this Point is clearly the leader, and Wilfred is watching him closely. At the end of the song they link arms and dance off, picking up the book as they go.

The encore is a repeat of the last verse in the same manner. They enter and put the book down on the bench. As they exit at the end of the encore, they again pick up the book. Wilfred stops and points offstage in the opposite direction, and while Point is looking away he grabs the book and runs off.

Fairfax' monologue and song should have both seriousness and elegance. He has little or none of the passion that characterizes Elsie, and is more inclined to see his situation as a philosophical dilemma. His reference to fetters might be accompanied by holding the arms up close together, as if they were bound.

The following dialogue is dominated entirely by Dame Carruthers, who subtly manipulates the emotions and reactions of the other characters. She half suspects the truth, and she is having a delightful time making the others uncomfortable. Their reactions to her remarks should be handled so that real tension develops in this scene. Most of the time Meryll stands near the exit, just waiting for a chance to slip off. Fairfax is with him, and Kate balances the stage by remaining on the other side. As Carruthers says her last line, she crosses toward Meryll, who winces and delivers his aside with his back toward her and then turns and smiles just in time for the music, which is accompanied by a minuet turn by both couples. The actual singing of the quartet involves no action whatever.

The dialogue between Elsie and Fairfax is perhaps the funniest in the opera. Its humor stems entirely from the fact that Elsie does not know who Fairfax really is. The humor will be conveyed best if all Elsie's reactions are completely sincere and Fairfax' just a little overdone so that it is clear he is play-acting the situation.

When the shot is heard, Elsie and Fairfax together run upstage as Meryll enters and stops Fairfax with his question. The chorus then make their entrance, the Yeomen marching in formation, but the women rushing from all directions as they did on their first entrance. The Lieutenant enters upstage center, and Point and Wilfred from a downstage corner. They take the center of the stage for their duet, which is acted with exaggerated gestures to help make the story more convincing to the chorus. The chorus pick up the gestures that the two singers have used as they sing the refrain. The question of whether stone or lead is the better image is settled between Point and Wilfred during the final chorus refrain. Point pulls out a coin, which he flips. When the refrain is concluded, he looks at Wilfred, who cries out, "Stone." Point then examines the coin, which proves to be his choice, and smugly replies, "Lead." On the final chorus, Wilfred is carried off on the shoulders of four men.

The lights come up for the scene that follows. Poor Elsie has her emotions cruelly played upon by the other three characters, and it will be important in the scene to avoid allowing the cruelty to become excessive. This will best be accomplished by focusing on the humor of Point's remarks.

Point elicits the following trio from the other characters through a gesture to Fairfax, asking him to elaborate on his final statement. The two women seat Point at Fairfax' feet as the latter begins to sing. Phoebe runs to Fairfax when he sings "the heart of a queen," but Fairfax on the repeat of these words gestures to Elsie, who joins the group in time for a dance performed by the three of them hand in hand on the ensemble.

Point remains on the floor during the second stanza, and Elsie sings to him. When she gets to the word "touch," she reaches down and touches him, and he grasps her hand and kisses it lovingly. On her second "ought to be treated as such," Elsie goes to Fairfax, who is then joined by Phoebe for a repeat of the ensemble dance.

Phoebe takes Point by both hands and lifts him up. She then wheedles him into a corner of the stage, much as she has earlier wheedled Wilfred. Point begins to warm to her advances, and she repays him with a box on the ear on the appropriate words. As the dance begins, Point attempts to join in, not, however, holding hands as the other three do, and doing a somewhat awkward imitation of their step. Eleven measures after letter D in the Schirmer score, Elsie takes Point aside and seats him on the bench while the others watch, meanwhile shaking her finger at him instructively. By the sixteenth measure Fairfax is standing just upstage of Point, and Phoebe on the other side of him. Point picks this up by wagging his finger at his folly-stick. On the final trill, Phoebe wags his rabbit ears, one with each hand, while Fairfax puts his arm around Elsie.

On the encore this business is repeated, except that Point interposes his folly-stick when Phoebe attempts to box him on the ear. If there is a second encore, Phoebe surprises Point by hitting him on the other ear. This time Point leaps up from the bench on the final measure and attempts to kiss both Elsie and Phoebe, while shaking the bells of his folly-stick in time to the music.

In the following dialogue, Point listens to Fairfax woo Elsie with his back to the couple, nodding and commenting on the words that Fairfax uses. It is Phoebe who observes the way that Fairfax is treating Elsie. Not until the end does Point also realize this, and suddenly the mood of the piece becomes tragic. The lights should dim somewhat at the beginning of the quartet to tie in with a more somber mood.

Elsie and Fairfax sing their duet downstage left. Phoebe moves downstage right for her solo, and Point sinks sadly on the bench for his, directing some of the words to his folly-stick. There is no movement during the ensembles, except for meaningful glances on certain words, which help to clarify how the characters feel about one another.

As Fairfax exits with Elsie, Point attempts to follow. Fairfax stops him with a gesture that Elsie does not even see. Fairfax then puts his arm around Elsie and guides her off, with Point following pleadingly behind. Phoebe weeps during the music, but then turns, and with a gesture prevents applause, so that the music flows right into the dialogue. Her speech here is not rushed and hysterical, but thoughtful and self-reprimanding. She is carefully reviewing all that has happened and blaming herself accordingly.

Wilfred enters, and Phoebe pours out on him all her disappointment in an avalanche of emotion. Suddenly she realizes she has revealed everything, and sinks distracted on the bench. When Wilfred reveals his secret, she leaps up suddenly and confronts him with it. When Leonard enters, Wilfred is thrown for a loss and he threatens to do him violence. But Leonard turns out to be bigger and stronger than Wilfred, and when threatened turns around coolly, causing Wilfred to squeal at Phoebe with helplessness. Leonard is silently involved in the ensuing exchange, becoming more and more puzzled, until with a shrug he walks off.

Meryll enters to discover Phoebe and Wilfred together. Phoebe explains the situation by offering Wilfred her hand, which he takes and kisses passionately. Her *"Is* it?" is offered so coldly, that Wilfred stops kissing and looks at her quizzically. Phoebe then crosses in front of him, and Wilfred after a moment's thought dismisses her coldness from his mind, and rushes after her to enjoy another kiss.

When this business is paralleled between Meryll and Carruthers, the latter does not show any such hesitation. In reply to Meryll's "*Is* it?" she immediately nods vigorously and possessively.

The following duet has for some years been absent from D'Oyly Carte performances on the grounds that it interrupts the tragic mood that has been building toward the finale. There have also been objections to the quality of both words and music in this piece. Nevertheless, it is a number that can be very appealing to audiences, and it is possible to avoid the feeling that it spoils the mood of the finale simply by making it the end of Act Two, Scene One. After a short break the finale can commence in an entirely new spirit. Making this break also makes it more logical for Elsie to be fully outfitted as a bride after having been wooed and won only a few moments before.

If the duet is retained it is important that it not be allowed to become vulgar. Meryll retains his dignity through it, and Carruthers, though going overboard a bit in the matter of flirtation, does not violate the character she has established earlier. Carruthers begins by skipping around the Sergeant, taking him by one hand and leading him to a downstage corner. On "Joy and jollity," he begins to steal away, a fact that she notices only when the phrase is repeated, at which she rushes to retrieve him. During his solo, Meryll paces back and forth across the stage, his hands behind his back, hitting the open palm of one hand with the clenched fist of the other. He comes to a standstill as her solo begins, and she takes a flower from her hair and pins it in his lapel. Meryll then, on his solo, paces the stage as before, this time waving his hands in the air as if tearing his hair. During the ensemble Carruthers does a delicate little dance on one side of the stage while Meryll, on the other side, paces back and forth exactly as he did on his first solo. During the closing bars they dance together toward the exit. Carruthers then turns to embrace Meryll, but he steps neatly out of the way, and she misses him and goes flying offstage. He then steals toward the opposite side of the stage, but breaks into a run as he sees her coming, and runs off, hotly pursued.

The women enter, dressed as bridesmaids, strewing flowers behind them as they come. About halfway through their chorus they have reached their final positions. At this point the Yeomen enter from both sides at the back, filling in the area behind the women. The ladies turn, welcoming with gestures Dame Carruthers

and Phoebe, who walk slowly in, followed by Elsie. These three reach their position at the front of the stage just in time for the trio, during which there is no stage action. On the chorus that concludes the trio, Wilfred and Meryll enter and join their prospective mates.

At the sound of the trumpet the chorus part at the back of the stage, and the Lieutenant enters upstage center, the three soloists having moved to one side. The Lieutenant moves down as he sings, so that he confronts Elsie. His announcement is greeted by disturbed conversation among the chorus and by desperate fleeing across the stage from Elsie. The three male soloists cross the stage following Elsie and try to comfort her. She breaks away from them and runs back to the two women, who only warn her of the reality of the situation. She then moves to the center of the stage and buries her face in her hands, weeping convulsively. All the soloists have their arms outstretched to her, offering comfort or warning, and the chorus by this time are all focusing their attention on her.

At the trumpet call the crowd again part. Fairfax appears upstage center, dressed in a wedding garment and accompanied by several gentlemen similarly dressed. The chorus shrink from them and crowd to the sides of the stage, so that the gentlemen, who remain standing (as individuals, not as a group) in the up center area, appear particularly foreboding. Fairfax crosses down and stands in front of Elsie, who is still weeping and so does not see him. On the chorus, Elsie raises her face from her hands and stares dully out toward the audience for a moment before kneeling. On "Thy husband he!" all onstage point their arms toward Elsie. Elsie's entire aria is sung kneeling with no movement from anyone else onstage. It may be effective to have all the lights out except for a spot on her.

When Fairfax and Elsie are united, they move to one side of the stage, leaving the center for Point. If auditorium entrances are used, he should walk up the aisle, singing his opening recitative as he comes. Otherwise, he appears up center. The crowd, which has filled in the center of the stage during the jollifications, respectfully moves aside to allow him to pass. Point's solo is sung with relatively little movement except a few pathetic gestures. It is during Elsie's solo that he has his opportunity. Gradually during the opera he has developed a closer relationship with his folly-stick as he has realized that Elsie does not love him. The skillful actor can handle this business most effectively by introducing it occasionally during the first act at times when the final tragedy is being prepared for. For example, he can consult the stick just before he says, "For my part, I consent." Again, when he rushes after Elsie but is stopped by the Lieutenant, he can turn sadly to the folly-stick. Now, at the end, he engages in a dance that becomes increasingly hysterical, and in which he seems to be sharing the secrets of his heart with the folly-stick. The dance reaches a climax during the final chorus, right at the end of which he is suddenly stricken, breaks into hysterical laughter, and collapses. The chorus then move in around him, arms outstretched toward him, and form a final tableau as the curtain falls. The tradition, established by Henry Lytton, of kissing a lock of Elsie's hair just before Point falls, may or may not be used. It is a question of whether the actor wishes to remind the audience at the last that Elsie has broken Point's heart, or prefers to play a picture of abstract loneliness and retreat into the self, the folly-stick representing the alter ego. At any rate, these final moments provide the finest acting opportunity in the entire series of operas. This is also the time when the actor tells the audience exactly how Point has reacted to the entire action. He should therefore consider several alternative ways of playing the scene and think through all the implications of each. The director, also, will have to decide in reference to the playing of this scene just how central he wishes to make the role of Point, and consequently how much he is going to emphasize the sentimental side of the opera.

One thing is certain. The ending must not be played comically. There is a story, which is probably apocryphal, that George Grossmith, not feeling up to the more tragic side of his role, lifted his feet in the air and wagged them just before the final curtain. Such an approach is certainly out of character with this finale and should be avoided.

## SCENERY AND COSTUMES

We have already commented to some extent on the scenery for *Yeomen*. There is no need for more than a single set, though the 1897 revival used two, portraying two views of the Tower. One simple and effective solution to the set problem is to use a slide projection of a photograph of Tower Green. This is entirely in line with Gilbert's purposes, as he imagined an entirely realistic setting and apparently achieved one that the opening-night reviewers found virtually indistinguishable from the real Tower.

If the set is painted and not very good artistry is available, it would be just as well not to try to reproduce the Tower accurately, but rather to use the more abstract type of set now in use by D'Oyly Carte.

There should be at least one and preferably two places to sit down on the stage. These may be benches or stumps, or one of each. The use of two benches makes possible a more elaborate kind of stage business in Phoebe's wooing of Wilfred than would be possible with one, or with just a stump.

The costumes for the Yeomen, as has been mentioned, should probably be rented. The others are relatively easy to make. The crowd should be dressed as typical early English villagers, and if the costumer is imaginative, a lot of variety is possible here. In a budget production long skirts and blouses may prove adequate. In the final scene the ladies may dress as bridesmaids.

Of the women, Phoebe, Carruthers, and Kate will be dressed rather elegantly, as they are ladies of some social standing. Elsie is a peasant in the first act, but she wears clothing that is decorated suitable to a traveling entertainer. She must have a bridal gown for the final scene.

Of the men, Jack Point presents the only problem, as he must be convincingly a jester. Furthermore, it is customary to give him two costumes, the one for the first act being rather shabby, whereas the one for the second act reflects his greater prosperity. An amusing touch is to redo the folly-stick in the same way. Wilfred is dressed in dark brown, with a doublet, knee breeches, and long socks. He also has a long-haired wig. Leonard is dressed as a stylish Elizabethan gentleman. Fairfax' prisoner's garb can be similar to the costuming used for the male villagers, though an added cape may appear more dashing. An ambitious production might model him after Sir Walter Raleigh. Meryll and the Lieutenant wear Yeoman costumes, though these may be made more elaborate with capes, feathers in their hats, and the like.

The costumer will be significantly aided in this case by color photographs and drawings of period costumes. The uniforms worn by the actual Tower Warders are black with orange trim. The Beefeater uniform, however, is more colorful, and is always used in productions of the opera.

# Chapter XV

# THE GONDOLIERS, OR THE KING OF BARATARIA

## PRODUCTION NOTES

*The Gondoliers* is thoroughly delightful in a good performance, but it can easily become tedious if performed with less than professional polish. Anyone who intends to produce it should carefully investigate the demands it makes on his resources for providing spectacle, both in the scenery and the staging, as well as finding performers who are skilled musicians.

The opera should be visually beautiful throughout. It invokes a world that, though human, like that of *The Yeomen of the Guard,* is untainted by any hint of the tragic, or even the somber. Not only the scenery and costumes, but also the staging, should be managed with unusual opulence. Because of the unending tunefulness but comparative lack of variety in the music, a poorly staged production can become monotonous. Furthermore, the words and situations often fail to suggest the cleverness of stage action that is indigenous to the other works. Thus details in the handling of the chorus or large groups of characters become more important than they otherwise would.

Furthermore, the opera makes heavy demands on the musicianship of both principals and chorus. Although the vocal ranges required are not unsually great, the complexity of the music combined with its length makes this an opera that must have an unusually long rehearsal period. It should also be noted that though the opera is tuneful to listen to, it is not tuneful for the men's chorus to sing. Much of the time they are providing accompaniment to the women's voices that is intricate but not very interesting in itself.

## CRITICAL DISCUSSION

*The Gondoliers* is the sunniest of all the Gilbert and Sullivan operas. Little cynicism is found in the libretto, the satire is attenuated, and the characters are not caricatures. In an important sense, however, its social criticism is by implication rather than direct statement. Barataria, being a fictional kingdom, is subject to none of the laws of reality (not even a satirical reality). It is possible, under the ideal circumstances that this consideration permits, to gratify by hypothesis all wishes an enterprising imagination can conceive for a government. We have, therefore, two kings who are rather ruled by their subjects than rule them. The implication might seem to be that if all were given equal voice in the government an ideal society might be forthcoming.

Not so in Gilbert's account book. Barataria is ideal only from an egalitarian point of view. The hierarchical values upon which so wise a person as the Grand Inquisitor has been raised dictate that "When every one is somebodee,/ Then no one's anybody!" After all it is man's desire to be superior to his fellow man that casts a blight upon even this ideal kingdom, and it is with a sigh of relief that we learn that the aristocratic drummer boy, Luiz, who prior to his elevation to the throne has always known his proper place, will rule Barataria.

Barataria was the name of the island ruled by Sancho Panza in *Don Quixote*. The name of the island is derived from a Spanish word meaning "trick," and indeed his governorship turns out to be an enormous practical joke played upon Sancho, who begins his rule by demonstrating true wisdom. Perhaps it is the hypothetical impossibility of the Philosopher King, paralleling for the moment the absurdity of the chivalrous knight that is demonstrated by Sancho's brief exercise in government. Surely Gilbert's Barataria provides some of the same atmosphere, since, though the subjects of Marco and Giuseppe are more polite and cooperative (albeit no less aware of their rights and privileges) than those of Sancho, they are just as much in control of their benevolent monarchs. But Gilbert's kingdom has not the same kind of mixture of hope and despair as Cervantes'. It is pure in its cheerful beauty, and thus pure in its implication that true government is and ever will be the opposite of what is portrayed in this topsy-turvy kingdom. We thus have satire by opposition rather than caricature.

It is significant that in Gilbert's world (as we have already observed in reference to *The Mikado*), though there is occasional sadism and violence, no one ever really gets hurt. Here the background of political upheaval that is briefly sketched is accompanied by all the bloodshed usually associated with such upheavals, but it all occurs in such a cheerful atmosphere and is so tangentially referred to that it seems not to have occurred at all. We are in the tradition of Dean Swift, with his Modest Proposal, and Bernard Shaw, with his occasional suggestions of massacre of those who hold the wrong sorts of views—it is easy for the urbane Englishman to indulge in hypothetical bloodshed because he is so thoroughly insulated from the actuality. That is the veneer that was Victorian civilization's greatest achievement, a veneer that is nowhere better dramatized than in *Heart of Darkness* in the contrast between the world of Kurtz in darkest Africa and that of his widow in fashionable English society. It is the latter that romanticizes the former out of all recognition. *The Gondoliers* is the zenith of the British tendency to romanticize human nature into its most idealized opposite. It is a creation of a sophisticated, sentimental, and unself-critical society at its peak, a creation the irony of which we are reminded of in Gilbert's occasional cynicism, but that is almost buried in the general atmosphere and Sullivan's lascivious music. (For example, notice the cautionary sidelight in the lines, "When the breezes are a-blowing/The ship will be going,/When they don't we shall all stand still!"—lines one would have to read the libretto to catch.)

Whereas *The Yeomen of the Guard* managed to blend comedy and sentiment, *The Gondoliers* keeps these elements largely separate. Indeed, there are two different sets of characters: Marco and Giuseppe and their wives, who are sentimental, and the Duke of Plaza-Toro, family, and suite, who are comic. These two groups are bridged by the Grand Inquisitor, who is macabre, and easily the best character in the opera. To him are given the most quotable lines, including the opera's theme. And indeed it is perhaps this character alone who provides the kind of disturbing insight that raises *The Gondoliers* above the level of its imitations.

Since Gilbert's words were not of quite such ingenious variety as he had earlier distinguished himself by writing, Sullivan became more experimental in his rhythms and harmonies (a kind of experimentation that was to continue through the next two collaborations). Every now and then he takes something fairly commonplace of Gilbert's and makes it unforgettable. Such touches include Marco and Giuseppe's duet in which they alternate in the middle of lines and even words, and the contrapuntal masterpiece, "In a contemplative fashion." Elsewhere Gilbert gave Sullivan the opportunity to carry Victorian sentiment to its pinnacle, as in "Take a pair of sparkling eyes," one of the hit songs of its day.

To sum up, *The Gondoliers,* aside from a few notable and detachable songs, makes its effect much more as a totality of sunny freedom from reality than it does by way of moments that are individually brilliant. In that sense it is the antithesis of *Ruddigore,* that most disunified work, which nevertheless has several scenes that far outshine anything in *The Gondoliers*. Perhaps the latter is the best way to meet Gilbert and Sullivan for the first time, as its appeal is immediate, though it tends to fade somewhat with increasing familiarity.

### CHARACTER SKETCHES

*The Duke of Plaza-Toro*

The Duke is among the most delightful of the "Grossmith" roles, though Grossmith had left the D'Oyly Carte company before *The Gondoliers* and never played it. Here is a little man who exaggerates his dignity to compensate for his size, a prototype of the braggart warrior, carried to the extreme at which he can present his own cowardice as evidence of excellence (a step or so beyond Falstaff in the evolution of this type). He dominates any situation in which he finds himself, even those involving the extremely domineering Grand Inquisitor (though he has to try hard to hold his own with the latter). It is only his wife who can upstage him, an ability she achieved, as she explains, after severe marital struggle.

Vocally the role makes the most moderate demands, but the voice should have a great deal of character, and indeed the role diminishes in importance if the Duke is heard singing too musically. This is because his entrance breaks the continuity of an extremely long and beautiful musical opening that threatens never to develop much character.

The Duke should also be a good dancer, as his gavotte scene is the comic climax of the opera. Martyn Green played this scene so well as to suggest he might have had a career in the ballet.

### Luiz

The drummer boy who turns out to be King must have a dashing, youthful appearance and an agreeable high-baritone voice. His love scene with Casilda, which is virtually all that is required of him, can be quite funny if it is played with intense sincerity, but will otherwise be tedious in the extreme. Great acting ability is not required, but polished sophistication is. He should also be adept at playing his drum.

### Don Alhambra del Bolero

This macabre and funereal gentleman delivers every word as if it were a quiet, but, to him, delicious, decree of Fate. His demeanor and calculated movements give the impression that he is from another world than are the other characters. He is the repository of information that they do not have, and consequently seems to be the manipulative agent behind the plot.

In his remote and punitive nature he bears some resemblance to the Mikado. Both are a little like cats in their general behavior. But whereas the Mikado seems to be a cat at times stalking and at other times toying with his prey, the Inquisitor is a cat preening himself quietly before the fire.

He is the most intelligent of the characters, and should always appear so. He seems to be looking down upon them, aware of their gaucheries, which only amuse him internally unless they affect the welfare of the state.

His voice should be heavy and dark in the bass-baritone range, and should have a great deal of character, since in his two solos the interplay between words and music is unusually important.

### Marco Palmieri

Marco is a Republican, both in principle and in manner. He believes in the dignity and nobility of the common people, and is thus something of a burlesque of that branch of socialism that is influenced by Rousseau. He is strong, handsome, and rustic. His rusticity does not, however, prevent him from having a natural feeling for chivalry, and he is the more romantic, less humorously inclined of the two brothers. He should have a strong and beautiful tenor voice.

### Giuseppe Palmieri

Giuseppe is similar to Marco in his behavior, but he is a little more earthy and less genteel in his behavior. Vocally he must have a pleasing high-baritone voice and be enough of a musician to handle the somewhat difficult ensemble work. He should also have good diction, as his "Rising early in the morning" is one of the more demanding of the patter songs.

### Antonio

This role, which is often given to the understudy of the Duke, requires the ability to dance well and make the short solo sparkle at a rapid tempo. Aside from his one song he is little more than a chorus member.

### Francesco and Giorgio

Tenor and bass members of the chorus will do for these parts. They have brief sung and spoken passages and must exude the same jollity that characterizes the Gondoliers as a group. Any attempt to make them individual should be avoided, as that would be merely distracting.

### Annibale

An excellent comic acting role, though a short one. Annibale is given some good lines in the beginning of Act Two in which he exerts the upper hand over Marco and Giuseppe. He is a junior descendant of the Judge and the Lord Chancellor. He should not only be commanding, but also something of a snob. Rightly handled, this part can give a delicious flavor to the opening of the second act.

### The Duchess of Plaza-Toro

This is one of the more rewarding of the contralto roles. The Duchess, for all that she is domineering over her husband to the point of being military, is in her way an attractive and dignified woman. Although she never plays as central a role in the action as does her husband, one feels that she is the motivating force behind all that he does, and that without her he would have accomplished little.

She needs a contralto voice richer and more attractive in sound than Katisha's, and should have excellent diction in order to make the most of her patter song in the second act.

### Casilda

Although there is little for her to do in the second act, Casilda makes a profound impression in the first act, in which she appears to be the romantic lead. Her dignity and coldness are quite in contrast to the unassuming warmth of Tessa and Gianetta. Her two duets require a first-rate soprano, as do her interesting ensemble numbers. She has the opportunity to make an impression beyond the length of her role because she is so frequently onstage with the Duke and Duchess, and can derive interest from them.

### Gianetta

A leading soprano part of considerable length, though not of unusual difficulty vocally. She is the female counterpart of Marco, being the more staid and romantic of the two girls. Her songs require an ability to make sentiment attractive, particularly because they are rather long, not terribly exciting, and occur at times when the action tends to drag. Thus a warm personality will help her to project her role perhaps better than an outstanding singing voice.

### Tessa

Lower in range and generally more appealing than Gianetta, Tessa has the lovelier melodies of the two and the opportunity for more humor. Otherwise her part is in every way comparable to that of Gianetta, with whom she always appears on the stage.

### Fiametta

This character should be chosen entirely for her singing ability, as her opening solo will determine to some extent how the audience responds to the musical values of the opera. She should have an attractive soprano voice.

### Vittoria, Giulia

These are minor mezzo-soprano parts, which again should be chosen primarily on the basis of singing ability, though sunny personalities will help establish the sunny quality of the first few moments of the opera. They, together with Fiametta, carry the burden of supplying the female charm until Tessa and Gianetta begin to sing.

### Inez

Inez is the *dea ex machina* of the opera, having a single recitative just before the end. It is not very long, but it is dramatic enough so that a fine actress can make a memorable impression in the role. Care should be taken that Inez does not become too exaggerated in any particular direction, but she should have some of the mystique of the Grand Inquisitor, since she is of his world.

### Chorus of Contadine

The Contadine are attractive girls who observe the action rather than participate in it, except perhaps when they make their entrance in the second act. They should thus add brightness to the stage without striving for too much in the way of character.

### Chorus of Gondoliers

The Gondoliers share the fate of the Contadine in the first act. But their second-act opening is an opportunity for a great deal of individual characterization as they sit about the stage engaged in various activities. They are all individualists, and the more they characterize themselves during the second act the better.

### Notes on Staging

Much of the staging for *The Gondoliers* requires beauty of effect rather than cleverness. It would be well for the director to work closely with a choreographer, particularly during the opening musical section in which so many types of dancing must occur. The typical operetta chorus lined up in semicircles would be more deadly than usual here. A recent D'Oyly Carte production attempted to use naturalistic staging of the chorus, so that there was relatively little formal movement, but the characters milled about and talked to one another in the style of *verismo* opera. This also proved dull, since the style of the music does not suggest such staging and seems to contradict it. There is no way of avoiding the intricate movement of groups into varying patterns in order to create a constantly diverting stage picture.

In the opening chorus all the Contadine are not only tying up bouquets of roses, they are also apostrophizing them. Although this must not be taken too literally, numerous appropriate gestures can involve the roses in the action almost as characters. The words are, of course, a parody of such poems as "Go, Lovely Rose," and the actions should suggest the parody.

During Fiametta's solo the chorus should respond to the words, indicating their passion for the two Gondoliers of whom she sings.

Toward the end of the repeat of the chorus the Gondoliers begin to enter, not all together, but in small groups. By the time the men's solos occur, the Gondoliers have mingled with the women so that each has a partner, though these partnerships do not as yet indicate much closeness, since the girls do not consider themselves available. As each of the solo lines is sung, the choristers of the appropriate sex indicate the same idea in pantomime to their partners. This action fills the stage.

On the line, "Till then, enjoy your *dolce far niente,*" the girls move to the sides of the stage as if to exit. Antonio takes the center and stops the movement with a commanding voice. The men, meanwhile, have turned to follow the girls, but then turn back, so that the center of the stage has been cleared for Antonio's dance. This will be most effective if Antonio does most of the dancing and about six chorus members situated downstage do the rest, while the others merely use appropriate gestures. This will make precision possible in the dancing, and will also prevent the stage from appearing too crowded for the dance.

A gondola pulls in at the back of the stage and Marco and Giuseppe enter from it, up center. As they come down they exchange greetings with the girls in the exaggerated manner of Italian opera. They have mandolins slung across their backs with which they accompany themselves during their duet. This number can be enlivened further if several of the Contadine dance to it, not all at once, but individually as the words happen to strike their fancy. When the duet is finished, the mandolins are passed offstage.

When the two Gondoliers announce their intention to choose their brides, the Contadine engage in various subtle and not-so-subtle means of being noticed. This action comes to a close when it is announced that Fate will make the selection.

The action of binding the eyes and the blindman's buff that follows are obvious, but will be more interesting if the game has a certain amount of suspense and several of the girls nearly get caught.

The final number of this section should be relatively static, but accompanied by peripheral dance steps in the background as the solos are sung. The exit should be danced, and this danced exit may well be the most intricate choreography so far, as it involves all the characters and must have just the right vitality and precision.

The entrance of the Duke and his family is one of those that may be made down the central aisle, and the entire opening song can be sung as the gondola is making its way to the stage. If the entrance is from the back, the first stanza may be sung before the characters disembark. The song is accompanied on the drum by Luiz, who beats the notes immediately following the solo line. The ensemble patter section is more effective and likely to be better sung if all the characters are completely motionless while singing it than if they attempt some sort of dance.

Luiz' business with his drum is quite amusing during the dialogue. After he steps forward on "Your Grace, I am here," he beats on it loudly. He does so again after he kneels. Again, when he exits, he executes a complicated roll on the drum, comes to attention, about-faces twice, and marches off, beating the drum in time to his march. The attempt is to make himself appear as much as possible like an entire army.

When the Duke says, "Consider his extreme youth," he bundles up his cape in order to suggest a baby that is being rocked to sleep. He then personifies the Wesleyan Methodist by taking the "ears" of his wig between his teeth in order to suggest a long gray beard.

*Philip Potter as Luiz, Jennifer Toye as Casilda, John Reed as the Duke of Plaza-Toro, and Gillian Knight as the Duchess of Plaza-Toro in* The Gondoliers: *"That celebrated, cultivated, underrated nobleman."*          (*D'Oyly Carte production*)

Luiz reënters and has his best moment with the drum when he accompanies with a long and fancy drum roll the kneeling of the Duke and Duchess before Casilda. While he is doing it, the Duke snaps his fingers to remind him also to kneel, which Luiz does without interrupting his drum roll.

The Duke's song should be executed with great military bravado. The other characters can take part in this. For example, on "He led his regiment from behind," the four of them are lined up in marching order, the Duke in the rear. In this manner the action of the entire song may be pantomimed.

The duet for Luiz and Casilda is staged as a conventional love duet. In the following dialogue Casilda has the opportunity to play two characters—the loving sweetheart and the aloof superior. Whenever they refer to the time, they check their wristwatches. In the duet following the dialogue there should be less

movement than in the previous duet, as the music is less active. The director should think, however, in terms of sculptured poses that will create a memorable stage picture.

The Duke and Duchess reënter with the Grand Inquisitor. Casilda immediately moves downstage, her back to them. Luiz retires upstage. On "Jimp, isn't she?" the Duke digs the Inquisitor in the ribs. He, in return, slaps the Duke on the chest, bruising his fingers on his breastplate. The Inquisitor makes what he thinks is a clever lewd remark on, "I could have wished . . ." and moves to slap the Duke on the chest again, but remembers just in time and uses the handle of his cane instead. On his last speech before the song, the Inquisitor takes snuff from a snuffbox in a manner carefully timed with the details of the lines.

The following song should begin with a stately dance. The Inquisitor uses appropriate gestures when he sings, and has a particularly

*Sydney Granville as Don Alhambra in* The Gondoliers: *"In the entire annals of our history there is absolutely no circumstance so entirely free from all manner of doubt of any kind whatever!"*
(D'Oyly Carte production)

elaborate set of them for the refrain, the last few of which are echoed by the other characters as they sing.

When, in the following dialogue, the Inquisitor refers to Luiz' accomplishments on the drum, the latter obliges with a cadenza, to which the Inquisitor reacts with polite but offended dignity. Luiz is shushed by the Duke and Duchess. Luiz' naive "How did he know that?" seems like an attempt to establish his own innocence of decorum. The Inquisitor crosses to Luiz and addresses him directly. Luiz smiles and is about to reply with another cadenza, when the Inquisitor puts out his hand indicating his desire for silence.

The quintet is staged mostly without action, but during the fast part the characters join hands and skip around in an adaptation of the grand right and left, their legs lifted very high. At the end of the song, two of the Inquisitor's emissaries enter and take Luiz off in the gondola. They are dressed mysteriously in dark cloaks. The others exit into the palace.

The entrance of the chorus is quite informal. They come from all directions, join one another in conversation, and wave to the principals as they enter. While they are singing they group themselves sitting or standing so that as Tessa sings her song she can walk among them, sharing her happiness with various groups of friends. Giuseppe sits on the side and watches her happily, but does not participate in the action, except as she exchanges an occasional glance with him. Marco and Gianetta respond more specifically to the meaning of her words. During the last chorus those who are sitting stand, so that they can go to greet Tessa. This is to prepare for their exit on the Inquisitor's entrance.

This exit is a difficult one to manage, as it is not to be taken during the music that ends the song, which should be a tableau. Certainly the chorus should not straggle off in one or two lines either. A few who are upstage should notice Don Alhambra immediately upon his entrance and make a hasty, though apparently nonchalant, retreat. Others, meanwhile, are reacting to the first few lines of dialogue, some of which are addressed partly to them. These people, seeing the others leave, wave good-bye and leave in their turn, so that the stage is clear of chorus by Don Alhambra's first line.

The dialogue should be paced rapidly and lightly, as it depends for its effect on the contrast between the eager young people and the businesslike Inquisitor. There is little stage business beyond the usual blocking. On Giuseppe's line, "Like this?" the two Gondoliers strike for the first time the pose they will assume whenever their royalty is referred to. This consists of arms around each other's shoulders and outside legs raised with the knees bent, the foot vertical and the toe touching the ground next to the other foot. The bent knees are pointed out to the sides. This position is assumed with a little jump.

For Gianetta's song Marco and Tessa retire upstage together, where they sit engrossed in each other. The Don stands at the center, and Marco listens at one side. The first time she sings the refrain, Tessa lays her hand gently on the Inquisitor's arm. Then, having concluded the stanza, she turns to Marco, who embraces her. The second time she sings the refrain, Tessa moves to put her hand on the Don's arm, and he raises his hand to enclasp hers. She, however, places her hand on her own heart.

Following the Don's recitative, the two couples put their arms round each other's waists and skip toward the front of the stage on the "Viva!" section. The introduction to the song is a lively dance that involves spinning the girls around. As Gianetta begins to sing on one side of the stage, Marco and Giuseppe kneel, one on each side of Tessa, as she pantomimes the words that are being sung. During each chorus the dance that was used on the introduction is developed a little further. On Marco's stanza, Marco and Gianetta stand together center, while the others assume the attitudes of horses, standing in front of them. The four together suggest the business of driving about in a carriage for the first eight measures. Then Marco pretends to assist Gianetta down from her carriage, while she shows off her shoes and dress and moves toward an imaginary table. When Tessa sings, Marco and Giuseppe alternately bow to Gianetta as she walks past them and pantomimes the business of the words. When Giuseppe sings, each of the two men pantomimes the words with his wife as partner.

The chorus enter in couples and stand in groups while Marco and Giuseppe reply to their questions after assuming their "linking" pose. As each sings he faces out, but as he ends he turns his head toward the other. Then as they sing about appointing officials to the court, they move among the men's chorus and make their appointments, the men who are selected responding in appropriate ways and then getting together in groups to discuss their new appointments.

On the chorus repetition of the song there should be a general dance. At the appropriate moments the newly appointed officials may step forward and bow. At "Then hail! O King," the men wave their caps in the air and the women wave handkerchiefs. Marco and Giuseppe stand up center again in their "link-ing" pose. If possible, they are on a platform, so that the two women can stand below and facing them. On their recitative they end by extending their arms toward their wives. Gianetta responds by leading Marco downstage, while Tessa remains upstage with Giuseppe.

The song should be handled seriously, and the focus should be on the soloists. Martyn Green suggests dimming down the general lighting and spotlighting each of the couples in their turn. This means that no movement is necessary. Gianetta simply turns, having completed her stanza, and looks up toward Tessa as she begins to sing. On the concluding quartet, Tessa and Giuseppe come slowly down to the front of the stage, so that all four singers are together.

The focus now shifts to the large ship that is making its entrance at the back. The chorus should gesture upstage toward it, the four principals running up to examine it. If the Duke and Duchess have made their entry down the central aisle in a gondola, this gondola may now be converted into a sailboat by putting up a mast and raising a sail on it. The four principals can then sail back down the aisle on the concluding chorus.

The men run up to the boat and pull on ropes to pull it into its final position. During this section most of the chorus will be on the sides of the stage and comparatively motionless, but a few people around the boat will engage in a great deal of activity. By the time Marco sings again he has boarded the ship along with the other principals, and all are ready to make their exit on the final chorus.

This last scene will be more effective if the lights are not brought up all the way after the quartet, and the final few minutes are used to depict a sunset, so that the characters are in silhouette by the final tableau.

The second-act opening provides an opportunity for all members of the men's chorus to characterize themselves as individuals. The scene is most effective if Gilbert's directions are followed exactly.

When they begin to sing, Marco and Giuseppe march downstage, still polishing their crowns and scepters. After the held "and" they both breathe on their scepters before giving them a final rubdown. During the chorus repeat, Marco and Giuseppe, having finished their polishing, crown each other, attend to each other's robes, and take their final position holding out their scepters.

After Marco's first remark there is talking among the chorus, who pay no attention to him. He repeats his remark quite loudly in order to shout them down. There is some indignation in their reply, and Marco feels a little nervous at having lost the sympathy of his audience.

When Annibale speaks, he comes forward dressed in the costume of a lawyer, complete with wig. He carries a lawbook in his hand and looks very solemn. Giorgio stands next to him, dressed as his assistant. On his final line he turns to consult Giorgio.

Giuseppe's song may be sung quite successfully with the chorus all remaining in their places and listening to him. There need be no movement when they sing the refrain, all the movement of the song coming from Giuseppe. It is also possible, however, to do the song as a full production number with members of the chorus acting out the various characters referred to in the song. This can be a real show-stopper if it is handled well, but if it is not carefully rehearsed it will merely look cluttered. The effect is partly achieved by having the characters come forward, partly by having Giuseppe travel about to various groups. At the end of the song when the kings retire to their beds, each of them may be picked up and held in a reclining posture by a line of chorus members.

During the following dialogue Giuseppe picks up a mandolin and later takes a seat at one side of the stage so that he can accompany Marco while he sings his song. This song needs nothing more than the conventional staging for such a song.

On the introduction to the next number all of the girls enter from a single entrance and line up across the front of the stage. The men rush on from different entrances and embrace their girl friends before the singing begins. On the entrance of Tessa and Gianetta, the chorus part to leave the center of the stage free for the reunion of the principals. The following duet will carry itself without more than the obvious staging.

"Dance a cachucha" is the most complicated number in the show and should be handled by an experienced choreographer familiar with

The Gondoliers: *Finale, Act I.*     (*D'Oyly Carte production*)

Spanish dancing. Although it is possible to have the entire company engage in the dance, it is usually considered more satisfactory to bring on about eight dancers while the chorus merely provide the singing. This allows for greater intricacy and more spectacular effects than can be achieved by a large chorus, few of whom are likely to be trained dancers.

During the dialogue the high spirits of the two kings are only gradually dampened by the funereal presence of the Inquisitor. When he says "Yes—gout," the Inquisitor raises a finger in a lecturing manner and then points it down toward his foot. During his long speech the Inquisitor becomes impassioned. He crosses downstage, his back to the two kings and hastily takes snuff. In response to "a Lord High Cook?" he gives a huge sneeze.

The Inquisitor's song should take into account the fact that he is lecturing the two kings and should be delivered with all the explanatory gestures associated with a professorial manner. All three should dance during this song, but Marco and Giuseppe have the most dancing to do, as they must move about in reaction to what is being said and must have an intricate dance when they sing the refrain.

Don Alhambra now addresses the two kings on the particulars of the situation. When he mentions the beautiful daughter, Casilda, they both wander off, causing him to have to raise his voice to call them back. As he continues to talk to them, they continue to wander off until, from time to time, the tone of his voice is carefully modulated to attract their attention back to him. When, for example, he says,

"I congratulate that one," he extends his hand, but finding no one nearby he shouts "(whichever it is)" in a military manner, causing the two of them to run back to him, at which point he withdraws his extended hand and smiles coldly.

When the wives run forward they immediately become rather vixenish with their husbands for being already married until the Inquisitor frightens them out of it. Then there is a little concern for the old woman in the torture chamber until the Don reassures them that she has all the illustrated papers, and everyone breathes a sigh of relief.

"In a contemplative fashion" involves the four standing rigidly in a straight line holding postures suggestive of thinking. Whenever one or more has a solo line in counterpoint he or she takes a step forward and adopts a distracted manner quite in contrast to the calm in the background. They exit slowly in rhythm to the music, still holding their thinking poses.

Martyn Green suggests a blackout before the entrance of the Duke and Duchess, followed by a gradual fading up of the lights. It is desirable but by no means necessary to have a second men's chorus here dressed in elegant costumes appropriate to the Duke's newly purchased magnificence. If a pit chorus is used, a small handful of retainers may be all that are brought on the stage, and these may be extras. If the same chorus as appeared in the opening are used, the Duke should nevertheless have two retainers of his own in costumes not previously seen.

The Duke and Duchess, being much better dressed than they were in the first act, are also somewhat more inclined to swagger. This means that they may enter several measures before they begin to sing and haughtily bask in the attention that they are getting. Casilda enters a little later and comes downstage between them on the appropriate words, looking very beautiful and curtseying a great deal.

When the Duke commands that his presence be announced, the attendants go through some of the same gyrations that Luiz used in Act One, making their exit an elaborate and humorous spectacle.

The Duchess' song is by way of instruction to Casilda, and so should be kept rather simple in the staging. During the second stanza, the Duchess takes the Duke's arm and smiles at him beginning, "Was the only thing required . . ." From that point on the two of them act out the sense of the words.

The duet for the Duke and Duchess requires merely that the main soloist remain in the center of the stage while the other slowly moves in a large semicircle around behind, taking a pose for each of the rejoinders. On the short section during which they sing together, the Duchess should place her arm on the Duke's extended one, and they should do a dignified dance across the front of the stage, facing the audience. At the end, on the word "Duke," the Duke bows, and the Duchess curtseys when her title is mentioned.

When the Duke addresses the gentlemen whom his daughter married, he does so in a grandiose manner, looking straight forward with his arm extended, so that he does not see Marco and Giuseppe wandering off and chuckling audibly as they examine the scenery, until he says, "There is some little doubt . . ." At the Duchess' "Sir!" the Duke cries out, fortissimo, "*If* possible!" When the Duke refers to ringing the Visitors' bell, he pantomimes the action of doing so. On Giuseppe's line about taking off anything else, the Duke becomes concerned about the propriety of such a remark in the presence of ladies. When Giuseppe refers to giving Casilda as many salutes as she likes, he throws her a kiss.

The final speech in the scene has several interpolations, and should read as follows:

DUKE. There must be a good deal of this sort of thing. (*Bows with elaborate ceremony.* MARCO *and* GIUSEPPE *imitate the action. The Duke watches them approvingly.*) And a little of this sort of thing —(*Peers at the Kings through a make-believe spyglass*) Ah ha. Saw you in the park. Any time you're passing.
MARCO. (*As he and* GIUSEPPE *imitate the action*) Ah ha. Saw you in the park.
GIUSEPPE. Any time you're passing— pass!
DUKE. And possibly just a *Soupçon*—
GIUSEPPE. A *what* song?
DUKE. *Soupçon*—French word—of this sort of thing! (*Blowing several kisses at a lady in the audience*)—Ah—I see you, you little heart-killer!
MARCO *and* GIUSEPPE. (*Imitating action*) Ah—I see you, you little heart-killer!
DUKE. (*Blowing still more kisses.*) And so on.

For the gavotte song much of the business is obvious or indicated in the text. While

Marco and Giuseppe sing during the first stanza, the Duke dances meditatively around them. During the second stanza, the Duke, who has been doing the gavotte with them, gradually elaborates on the dance. In the first encore the elaboration is extended. In the second, ballet is introduced. Finally, the Duke is exhausted and shows it. As he runs up the steps to the throne he stumbles and nearly falls.

When Gianetta and Tessa enter during the following dialogue, they go to their husbands, who put their arms around them. During the quintet the two men are at first interspersed with the three women. When they sing alone, however, they move together to one side of the stage, following which the women move to the other side. Beginning at measure 21 the men and women are facing one another somewhat defiantly. At "O moralists all," they keep their bodies facing opposite sides of the stage, but turn their heads toward the audience. They walk forward lifting each leg high, toe pointed, bringing it to the floor, and then drawing it back a little. The hand toward the audience holds a handkerchief that flutters up and down in time to the music. On the second "O moralists all," they are again interspersed and they now face the audience gesturing like orators. Casilda is in the center. On the section beginning, "Moralists all," the pulled back step used a moment before is reintroduced, this time with one foot only (in place) and with the hand performing the same action. On the held "call" the arms are extended widely. On the concluding "ye" the two men gesture toward Casilda, who gestures toward one of them only, while the other ladies gesture toward the men. On "or you" the men gesture to their wives, Casilda gestures toward the other man, and the wives gesture toward the empty air next to them and make faces expressing disappointment. On the concluding music they all move back so that they will be out of the way of the characters who are entering.

The entire company now enter, Don Alhambra center and the other principals distributed around him at a little distance, those lowest in rank being farthest away. Inez is politely led in by the Inquisitor and stands in the center of the stage looking dignified and inscrutable, not responding to the questions addressed to her. The grouping of the characters behind her is such that Luiz can enter unnoticed while she is singing and be ready to ascend the throne in full costume the moment she steps aside to indicate him. The moment he is at the throne Casilda rushes to his arms and they embrace. There is almost no further stage action except for the kneeling when Luiz crowns Casilda and the dance at the end, which should be performed by the full company if possible, and otherwise by a group of trained dancers who take the stage on "Once more *gondolieri*." Inez quietly exits as soon as Casilda has been crowned.

SCENERY AND COSTUMES

There should be as much opulence and brightness as possible in both sets. In the scenery the style of Canaletto would be a good influence. The first act should have both a practical gondola and xebec (three-masted ship). The background represents a scene on the canal with boats and Venetian architecture in the distance. The buildings onstage include the entrance to the Inquisitor's palace. The second act can be more fanciful, the Baratarian royal palace being an architectural spectacle with plenty of ornate nude and allegorical figures on the walls. At the center back is the throne, which has several steps in front of it. There are entranceways on each side of the throne as well as in the usual places at the sides.

All of the noble characters wear eighteenth-century wigs. This in fact includes everyone except the Contadine, since the men are courtiers in the second act. The Duke and Duchess and Casilda are dressed in shabby finery in the first act, gloriously refurbished in the second act. Don Alhambra wears a black Spanish hat, a black cape, a long black ministerial coat with a clergyman's collar, black trousers, and black shoes with buckles. He has white lace at the ends of his sleeves and he carries a long walking stick. The gondoliers wear stocking caps, short colorful jackets, knee pants, long stockings, and sandals. Their necks and forearms are bare. In the second act they look more like extremely elegant footmen than like kings, and most of the courtiers are dressed with greater dignity than they are. Luiz wears a drummer's uniform in the first act and a king's robes and crown (much more elegant than anything Marco and Giuseppe have) in the second act.

The girls are dressed as Italian peasants in the first act. They have bodices, long dresses, perhaps with aprons, and flowers in their hair.

In the second act they are dressed more elegantly, since they have been traveling in style, and should look like fashionable ladies of the eighteenth century.

It should be noted that although it is possible to stage *The Gondoliers* inexpensively, the opulence of the music continually suggests an opulent visual effect. Cutting corners on scenery or costumes for *The Gondoliers* tends to make the theatrical experience seem much more incomplete than is the case with any of the other operas.

# Chapter XVI

# UTOPIA, LTD., OR THE FLOWERS
# OF PROGRESS

## PRODUCTION NOTES

Two things stand out about *Utopia, Ltd.:* its elaborateness of spectacle and its unusually large cast. In this opera, spectacle is one of the chief sources of satire, as it is the formality and pageantry of British high society that is lampooned. If Gilbert's original intentions could be followed exactly today, much of the point would be lost, as the specifics of the pageantry would, in many cases, have been forgotten. Even in its own day the point was blunted by the fact that many people found the lampoons offensive. Therefore, although spectacle is necessary, it may be scaled down somewhat and may explore high comedy, which has universal appeal, rather than the specific parody that characterized the first production.

As to the large cast, it differs from that of *The Gondoliers* in that almost all of the minor characters are cleverly conceived, so that the opera is filled with amusing and distinctive vignettes. This means that merely singing the songs or declaiming the lines is not enough in a minor character: He must be a distinct personality who will be remembered long after his specific contribution to the action is forgotten.

*Utopia, Ltd.,* because it is infrequently performed, and because of its unusual settings, provides an opportunity for unusually imaginative production. A company that wishes to escape from the constant decisions about whether or not to perform an opera traditionally will enjoy *Utopia,* because there is so little tradition connected with it. Of course, there are a few standard British items requiring particular costumes, such as the First Life Guards, but much of the opera can be designed and staged in whatever way whimsy may suggest.

*Utopia,* like *Patience,* is an opera that can easily become tedious if the production does not sparkle. Neither lyrics nor music are unusually distinguished; they must be made to seem so. Furthermore, the opera gets off to a rather slow start.

When it is indifferently presented, it is invariably regarded as a demonstration of the tiredness of Gilbert and Sullivan at the end of their collaboration. The original production, though it was one of the most spectacular and highly anticipated events ever seen on the British stage, proved not very satisfying either, perhaps because it was overelaborate. When, however, *Utopia* is given a sprightly production with more emphasis on the acting than on the spectacle, it is usually very successful. In 1956 the American Savoyards presented it in New York, working in a church basement with piano and organ accompaniment, and the production received rave notices, including special attention from Brooks Atkinson in *The New York Times.* It is too bad that the opera has not found its way into the D'Oyly Carte repertoire, as it cannot be regarded as inferior to all the operas that are better known. It is certainly better than *The Sorcerer,* and may be compared favorably with *Patience* and *Ruddigore.*

## CRITICAL DISCUSSION

In *Utopia,* Gilbert undertook a more ambitious project than he had essayed since *The Mikado.* The latter comments on human institutions in the abstract, the former satirizes British society. It does not lampoon a specific institution, such as the House of Peers, but concerns itself with every level of society from the monarchy to the workhouse. Liberal and conservative impulses exist side by side, with Lady Sophy representing that view of life that finds total satisfaction in the preservation of correct forms, protocol *par excellence,* and Princess Zara exemplifying the social reformer who would transform an entire nation at one fell swoop.

We have not only individual impulses, but also the structure of government itself represented in this opera. Scaphio and Phantis are a primitive version of the Mafia. The Flowers of Progress are a Presidential Commission making a study and offering proposals to be transformed into legislation. Nekaya and Kalyba are students transforming the educational system. Mr. Goldbury is the corporate system already announcing its intention of taking full advantage of special privileges awarded it by the government.

We have here all the ingredients for a satirical *tour de force* of supreme excellence, but Gilbert was not fully enough committed to his materials and sometimes fails to follow through on his ideas. If we examine his treatment of Lady Sophy (probably the finest of his contralto roles because she manages to be a comic character without ever becoming unattractive), we shall have an idea of what he might have done with other elements of the plot if he had handled them as well.

Lady Sophy begins by dictating the proper conduct of young ladies in her excellent Valse Song. (Did Leonard Bernstein borrow this tune for his "I Feel Pretty"?) The essence of Victorian courtship is suggested by this song with its cultivated snobbery in the young ladies, its demand that the stranger who seeks their affections have proper references, and its unexpected denouement—the ladies do not quarrel over the gentlemen, they are too genteel and bloodless for that; they toss. This is love without passion, alliance determined by the superficial demands of society, affection stimulated by the girls' physical charms.

As we shall see, Lady Sophy is guilty of the typical hypocrisy of educators in proposing this series of actions. She herself is motivated by far deeper concerns. She has an Ideal that she has carried in her heart for many years, and it is thanks to that Ideal that she has so far remained a spinster.

Having achieved mastery over the characters of his daughters, Lady Sophy attempts to achieve similar mastery over the King. He is the victim of sniping attacks by yellow journalists. (She does not yet know that the King has been forced to write these attacks himself.) It does not matter to her what the King's character really is, it matters what people say. Why does the King not slay those who attack him? She is unmoved by his humanitarian concern for the journalist's need to make a living; nothing less than a King who is known by all to be spotless will satisfy her. Until he has achieved a good reputation, he is in her eyes guilty of shady conduct, and her respectability will have none of him.

Lest we come to see Lady Sophy as too cold and cruel (respectability totally without heart), when we next meet her, we are treated to her spiritual autobiography. She treats of her search for a spotless king to satisfy the dreams she first conceived as a child of fifteen. We learn that Lady Sophy is a true child of her age, spiritually imprisoned by Victorian propriety. There is only one solution to her problems—she must find her spotless king. Fortunately, she does, since Paramount has been forced against his will to libel his own character, a course rendered unnecessary by the reform of Utopia and the consequent destruction of the power of Scaphio and Phantis. She and her lover sing a happy duet and perform a graceful dance.

Lady Sophy's role in the plot has been perfectly conceived and executed. In her, character and action are one, and both are expertly satirical as they strike at the essence of the Victorian attitude toward love.

Far less successful are the roles of Scaphio and Phantis. They conceive a hopeless passion for Princess Zara upon which neither can act until one or the other has been killed in a duel. Until then Fitzbattleaxe, her real lover, is to keep the lady in trust for the two rivals. This is funny, but hardly relevant to anything else the opera is trying to accomplish. Gilbert's interest in duels (explored more fully in *The Grand Duke*) is derived from literature and is irrelevant to the facts of social life in his day. Furthermore, though they have dedicated a whole scene and a delightful quartet, to their rivalry, Scaphio and Phantis find nothing further to say about it, and it is simply dropped. Their true function in the opera is to serve as the unscrupulous powers behind a puppet king. There is ample room for satire in this idea, but it is not very well developed, despite the fact that it is the subject of three entire scenes.

Another example of disunity in plot structure is the role played by Mr. Goldbury. In a brilliant song he explains the concept of limited liability. One would expect that his chief function in the plot would be to demonstrate the role played in a society by finance, but instead he later devotes himself to teaching the repressed Princesses how to make love. His song about the English girl is another brilliant lyric, but entirely out of line with his character as established in the first act.

It is this weakening of plot structure that prevents *Utopia* from being a first-rate libretto in the manner of, say, *Iolanthe.* Had he handled all his characters as well as he handled Lady Sophy, Gilbert might well have surpassed *Iolanthe,* which is more limited in the scope of its satire. As it is, *Utopia* degenerates into little more than a series of vignettes, much in the manner of *The Sorcerer,* though far more powerful in their implications than those of the latter.

Sullivan provided *Utopia* with some outstanding, as well as some mediocre music, but he did so in a manner that tended to emphasize rather than disguise Gilbert's weaknesses. Had he handled the Act One finale with the same ingenuity in moving from one episode to the next as he used in *Trial by Jury,* we would not perhaps have the feeling that we are being treated to a catalogue of British virtues and nothing more. Had he explored more subtleties of characterization in the music for Scaphio and Phantis, he might have given them greater artistic importance. In the first-act chorus music he makes the same mistake he made in *Patience:* The idyllic music becomes boring and the military music is not sustained enough properly to offset it. Furthermore, we do not have the advantages of the delicious counterpoint that adorns the first act of *Patience.*

Nevertheless Sullivan is, in this score, exploring rhythmic and harmonic possibilities not used in earlier works. The orchestration is more subtle and uses more instruments than in any of the previous operas. There are a number of delightful effects that do not survive in the vocal score, such as the rapid violin accompaniment to the duet for Nekaya and Kalyba, a way of suggesting their youth and vitality that humorously contradicts their words. The harmonies of "Words of love too loudly spoken" suggest that in spite of himself Sullivan was influenced by the serious Wagner. The harmonies of the trio for Scaphio, Phantis, and Tarara, and the instrumental comments on the action, together provide an example of Sullivan being musically funny without reference to the words. The rhythm change in the chorus repeat

of "Make way for the Wise Men" avoids the simple repetition so common in the earlier operas and points the way to a number of similar devices in *The Grand Duke.*

Then there are the songs that are simply good songs because the music perfectly fits the words, and the combination of the two is delightful. These include primarily the King's song, "Society has quite forsaken," the Valse Song for Lady Sophy, and the two songs for Goldbury. Lady Sophy's "When but a maid" would be excellent if it were not a little too short. A number of other songs in crucial places fall just short of excellence both in words and music and are therefore dependent upon a good performance.

In one major way Sullivan has fallen short in this score. Most of the more successful operas have a pervasive atmosphere that is difficult to define through musical examples, but that makes it possible to sense that a number belongs, say, to *The Mikado* or *The Yeomen of the Guard.* The former has an oriental flavor, the latter seems always to be overshadowed by the presence of the Tower. This atmosphere is achieved despite the fact that many of the songs in a given score are likely to be examples of traditional English forms. Such an atmosphere is distinctly lacking from *Utopia,* despite all Gilbert's efforts to provide for it. Had Sullivan investigated Polynesian music in the same way he had earlier become acquainted with that of Japan, he might have given the opera a flavor that would have redeemed all of its weaknesses. It may be primarily for this reason that *Ruddigore,* which has such a musical atmosphere, but is weaker than *Utopia* in every other respect, has achieved a popularity that may forever elude the latter opera.

## CHARACTER SKETCHES

### King Paramount the First

Rutland Barrington created this role, but in 1920 when Rupert D'Oyly Carte contemplated a revival, he told Ivan Menzies (a predecessor of Martyn Green) that he intended he should play it. When excerpts from the opera were finally recorded under the direction of Bridget D'Oyly Carte, the role was assigned to Donald Adams, normally identified with the Richard Temple roles (Dick Deadeye, The Pirate King, and The Mikado). There is thus a certain amount of "official" latitude in the general interpretation of the role. The musical writing suggests a rather heavy baritone voice with emphasis on melody as well as diction.

Paramount is onstage far longer than most of Gilbert's characters, but he is given less comic individuality. He is a weak king, manipulated by the Wise Men, and to a lesser extent by his subjects, whose primary joy in life is in the cleverness with which he ghost-writes attacks upon his own character. When Utopia is reformed along English lines he feels rather uncomfortable with all the ceremony, though relieved to be free of the tyranny of the Wise Men. These qualities are handled repetitiously enough so that the King easily becomes tedious if he does not enrich the part from his own imagination. In the first act the Milquetoastian quality only suggested in the dialogue can be explored with humorous effect. In the second act the King may become a bull in a china shop, surrounded by stiff formality over which he happily trips at every turn.

Yet he cannot be entirely meek and unassuming, as he must revel in his triumph over the Wise Men in Act Two. Also, there should be a Wagnerian grandeur in the recitative with which he announces to Lady Sophy that he wrote the paragraphs she finds so objectionable. Finally, he must be a good dancer capable of mocking Scaphio and Phantis in his trio with them, comically suggesting the various stages of life in his first-act song, and gracefully joining Lady Sophy in his dance with her.

### Scaphio and Phantis

These two roles together suggest the Grossmith style of performance. They are broadly comic, they abound in patter songs, and they heavily emphasize dancing ability. Although they constantly threaten the King with explosion, they are not really villains; they are simply government officials performing their functions with the usual percentage of corruption. Utopia being a South Pacific island, this means that their attitude toward life is more relaxed than would be found in a civilized society, and they can gloat like children over their power, express their antagonisms toward each other, the King, and the Flowers of Progress rather more openly than is customary in more advanced circles; and they can fall head over heels in love with Princess Zara in a thoroughly adolescent manner.

Little vocal excellence is required in the singing, but there should be a great deal of personality in each. As the two characters are almost exactly alike in the way they are written, there is danger that they will be confused with each other by the audience. It therefore helps if there are obvious physical differences between them; for example, if one is quite large and the other rather small.

### Tarara

Although he is a minor character, Tarara has much in common with Ko-Ko in *The Mikado*. He is a meek little man who fears the duties of his office, which he is not likely to be called upon to perform. He was originally played by Walter Passmore, who went on to distinguish himself as one of the finest of Grossmith's successors, and this is one indication that the part should not be entrusted to a second-rate actor. It is his responsibility to set the tone of the production, as he is the dominant character in the first scene. He must also contrast adequately with the characters of Scaphio and Phantis in his scene with them. (The effect should be something like the combination of Ko-Ko, Pooh-Bah, and Pish-Tush in *The Mikado*.) He is the dominant figure in their trio together, a musical number that requires little in the way of good singing, but is harmonically quite difficult.

### Calynx

This character has only a few spoken lines and nothing to sing, but he should be clearly characterized as a stuffy public official who suffers from excessive idolatry of the British. It is he who announces the satirical point of the whole opera, and who consequently will be to some extent responsible for the manner in which the audience responds to the satire.

### Princess Zara

Vocally one of the least demanding of the soprano leads in the operas, Zara must nonetheless be a commanding stage personality, as she dominates the action through most of the Act One finale and must somehow tie together its various episodes. Furthermore, it is she who delivers the denouement pronouncement at the end of the opera, and who is therefore largely responsible for its final effect. She is a character who is likely to have more appeal to modern audiences than she did when the opera was first presented, because she is a thoroughly liberated woman. Indeed, she is one of Gilbert's few characters who might have been created by Shaw, which perhaps partly accounts for Shaw's preference for this opera. Furthermore, her liberation is not the object of satire, as in the case of Princess Ida, but is genuinely attractive. She manipulates all of the Flowers of Progress, including her lover, Fitzbattleaxe, who greatly admires her intelligence and recognizes her superiority as he executes the reforms that she has designed. Only Scaphio and Phantis insist on seeing her as nothing more than a love object, and they are bitterly rewarded for their male chauvinism.

For all her dominance as a character, Zara does not have a great deal to do musically. She sings no solo, though she has three good duets. She has some of the opera's best music to sing ("Words of love" and the music with which she introduces the First Life Guards are both gems) and some of its most pedestrian. (There is little inspiration in the writing for her in either of the finales.) The role was originally played by the only American to create a character in the operas, Nancy McIntosh. Her American accent, contrasting with the British accents of the Utopians, may have been an attempt at topsy-turvy casting, but the Flowers of Progress were all as British-sounding as the Utopians. In a modern production it might be interesting to develop consistently contrasting accents for these two groups of characters.

### Princesses Nekaya and Kalyba

Like Scaphio and Phantis, these two characters are very similar in the writing, but, unlike the Wise Men, they should remain similar in characterization. Their education has made them exactly alike, so they react identically to all situations. Their first-act duet is a precursor of the singing commercial: It is an advertisement for English etiquette. They are absolutely shameless in their pride about their modesty, a pride that has been bred into them by Lady Sophy and epitomizes the essential paradox of Good Manners.

When they are introduced to the joys of liberation by Dramaleigh and Goldbury, their joy is completely childlike. They are immediately transformed from stuffy insufferability to charming innocence. This transformation is one of Gilbert's best jokes, and the scene, if properly handled, is one of the finest in the operas.

### Lady Sophy

We have already discussed this character to some extent in our critical comment. She is a paragon of etiquette, the essence of Victorian manners, and as such, extremely stiff. She is never, however, unpleasant, for all her commercialism about Propriety. In the second act it is revealed that she has a heart, and nothing could be more delightful than her long-delayed union with her "spotless king."

The role is rewarding vocally, as all of her music is both attractive in itself and helps to define her character. She should be played by an actress with a reasonably good voice and an excellent sense of style and dignity of manner. Vocally she is a contralto, but the voice need not be as heavy in sound as many of the contraltos in the operas. It should have enough lightness and flexibility to give real bounce to the Valse Song.

### Salata

A member of the chorus with two spoken lines. She is a radical, in favor of reforming Utopia along British lines, and she has a great deal of enthusiasm for everything English. Her excitement draws mixed reactions from the other maidens, some of whom are conservative.

### Melene

She has one line, which contrasts completely with Salata's. She is a conservative. She likes Utopia as it is and expresses lazy contempt for change.

### Phylla

She has only a solo in the opening chorus. A light and extremely beautiful soprano voice is required. It should have enough power to sustain the high A at the end of the solo above a chorus entrance.

### Lord Dramaleigh

This Lord Chamberlain is extremely elegant in manner, as well he might be, since it is he who engineers the Drawing-Room Scene in Act Two. He is deservedly proud of his success in achieving a first-class social event. In combination with Mr. Goldbury he teaches the two younger princesses how modern English girls *really* behave. He has a tenor or high-baritone voice a little lighter than Goldbury's, as he carries the tenor line in the quartet. If, however, casting would work out better by making Dramaleigh a low baritone, the two characters can merely switch vocal lines in the quartet.

More is required in the way of style than acting ability. In appearance he should be tall and handsome and rather sexy.

### Captain Fitzbattleaxe

Theoretically the romantic tenor lead, Fitzbattleaxe is however most effective if acted rather stiffly, like the Duke in *Patience*. He is Captain of the First Life Guards, and never quite loses his military stiffness. His protestations of love at the opening of Act Two concentrate far more on his own nervousness and difficulties of digestion than on the lady in question, and he is actually called upon to burlesque romantic tenors in the concluding cadenza of the song. Later, when he refers to his passionate enthusiasm, Zara in effect tells him to lower his voice. Clearly she likes having a lover not too skilled in the art of love. She likes telling everyone what to do, and that includes telling her lover how to make love.

If Fitzbattleaxe actually has a high "C" at his disposal, there is nothing wrong with using it, but if he doesn't, he may substitute a strangulated falsetto for the required note, which is what Gilbert seems to have had in mind.

In addition to having a good military command of the situation, Fitzbattleaxe seems to have a slight dose of the legal mind, as exemplified in his advice to Scaphio and Phantis. There he becomes first cousin to the Lord Chancellor in *Iolanthe*. All in all, the best clue to portraying his character is perhaps to be found in his name.

### Captain Sir Edward Corcoran, K.C.B.

This character has stepped right out of *Pinafore,* and he should have the same dashing appearance and beautiful baritone voice he had in that opera, though the vocal line lies a little lower.

### Sir Bailey Barre, Q.C.M.P.

A tenor with a small part in the Act One finale. He is a solicitor who is skilled at maneuvering the truth in favor of his clients. He should have a slightly subhuman aura about him, suggesting that he will do anything if he is properly paid for it. He is the only Flower of Progress who specifically identifies himself with corruption.

### Mr. Blushington

This delightfully obtuse baritone concerns himself with sanitation and such matters. He is a typical civil servant, doing what is required without imagination or concern for people. If he seems to live in his own little world of paper work and rubber stamps, all the better.

### Mr. Goldbury

This character is unlike any other in the entire series of operas. He comes closest to the light baritone typified by Pish-Tush in *The Mikado,* but he has a personal charm and sexiness that make him seem more a part of modern musical comedy than of Gilbert and Sullivan. The kind of projection associated with Fred Astaire or Noel Coward would be effective in this part. Although he initially presents himself as a financier, there is a sleight-of-hand character about his dealings that make them seem more theatrical than businesslike. Soft-shoe dancing and the twirling of a furled umbrella should accompany his first song. The second song about the English girl takes us right out of the Victorian age into a world in which "prudery knows no haven." The girl of whom he sings is an athlete, a child of nature, whose emotions are genuine, and whose soul is her own. As he sings, the effect is almost hypnotic. No such character as this English girl ever existed, but she is not of the world of topsy-turvydom either. She is more like a character in *Oklahoma!* or *Brigadoon.* It is with this song that Gilbert shows his awareness of the changing style of musical theatre, and gives us a hint of what he might have written had he lived thirty years later. Sullivan catches the mood very well, and the effect of the song is a clue to the portrayal of the character.

### Utopian Citizens

The chorus in this opera play less of a part in the action than in almost any other opera in the series. They simply observe and comment on what is happening. The one time when they emerge as a distinct entity is in the chorus, "Upon our sea-girt land," just before the finale of Act Two. In the finale of Act One the problem of handling the chorus is similar to that in *The Mikado:* The director must use great ingenuity to keep them from becoming mere automatons. At other times they take on a slightly more distinct character, as in their reactions to the King when he first appears.

The best place to make the chorus emerge as an interesting collection of characters is in the Drawing-Room Scene. Here a variety of subtle and differentiated reactions to a developing series of pantomimed situations is possible. It is easier to make the chorus interesting in Act Two because they have been enlivened by their participation in the Anglicizing of Utopia. In Act One they are almost a part of the scenery, and the problem is to make them picturesque.

### The First Life Guards

This group appears for a single effective scene. It is made up of five of the six actors who play the Flowers of Progress, in different costumes; and since all have solo voices, they can sound like a whole chorus. Of course, if the company is a large one, there is no reason they cannot be expanded to a group of twenty or so.

Since they represent the first intrusion on the scene of the British, it is important that they contrast in appearance with the Utopians. The pantomimed business during which they stand at attention and the maidens gather admiringly around them is most effective if they stand rigidly at attention and ignore everything that the girls do.

### NOTES ON STAGING

The opening chorus is a little like that of *Patience* in its effect. The maidens are grouped in various poses that appear artistically beautiful as the curtain rises. They should create a tableau until they begin to sing. During this time the lights should gradually come up, so that the scene takes on a variety of colors as though the sun were rising. As they sing, the maidens move their arms in a manner suggestive of the luxury to which they are accustomed, but having a somewhat balletic style. Most of the movement comes from Phylla, who crosses the stage as she sings, using abstract gestures suggestive of the natural images in the words.

The almost liquid quality of the music and the movement is shattered by the entrance of Calynx, whose stiffness in announcing the good news is suggestive of the British style that will soon be imposed on the Utopians. As the maidens do not react with the excitement he hopes for, he keeps getting louder and more enthusiastic, trying to provoke a reaction.

Tarara bursts on the scene, making things even more tense. It is immediately obvious that his full name should be "Tarara-Boom-De-Ay." His words, based on Polynesian, mean something like, "Idiot, I run around screaming but can't make much noise, since I am hoarse. Crossly I drag myself into the open and go spinning around sweating." The horrified reaction of the ladies to these remarks indicates that they are consistently off-color.

Tarara pulls out a "cracker," which Calynx pulls. No one gives the slightest reaction to the noise it makes except Tarara, who jumps into the air screaming with terror.

At the beginning of the music, the ladies scramble off the floor and run to the sides of the stage as two lines of guards enter bearing large fans made of palm leaves. The dignity of the chorus contrasts with the roguish appearance of the Wise Men, who appear somewhat bent over and swallowed up in their cloaks. They enter nodding to the chorus, acknowledging their greeting, and alternately patting one another on the back and shaking hands. Their entrance is something between a dignified walk and a sly dance step. When they begin to sing they echo one another with their gestures just as they do with their words. Real dancing begins only as they sing in unison, and becomes less restrained during the musical interlude.

In the following dialogue there must be a combination of romantic overemphasis and decayed gentility. We must believe that Scaphio is in love, but we must also see the ridiculousness of his passion without any awareness on his part that it is ridiculous.

At the beginning of the duet Scaphio claps Phantis on the back and moves with him from center to down right slowly as he sings. On Phantis' rejoinder he turns and slaps Scaphio on the back. They exchange slaps until they sing in unison, at which point the intended slaps are halted in the air and changed to a handshake. Scaphio now sits on a stump and watches while Phantis dances wildly about the stage (the more ridiculously the better). When they again sing together, Scaphio attempts to imitate Phantis' dance. Phantis then drags Scaphio to the center of the stage and pantomimes the actions of his verse. On "then woe betide" he pulls out a firecracker and holds it under Scaphio's nose. Scaphio does the same, and the action is repeated until the unison section, at which point they both dance around in circles, holding their firecrackers above their heads. Phantis now sits on the stump and watches Scaphio's dance and then imitates it at the end.

The maidens now enter, dancing and scattering rose petals about the stage. The men do not enter until letter C (Chappell score). They march in stiffly, again carrying their fans. One line of men enters on the first two measures, and then the girls dance into a new position for two measures while these men wave their fans. A second line enters on the following two measures, and again the girls dance. Then the men move into their final position, and when all have assumed deferential attitudes, the King enters. During the first half of each stanza of his song the chorus appear deferential and the King imposing. During the second half the chorus relax and assume attitudes of laughter and buffoonery, while the King exchanges his imposing attitude for one of meekness. During the chorus refrain they engage in attitudes of enjoyment, flirting with one another, fixing one another's hair, and generally carrying on happily. In the recitative this attitude is dropped as soon as the King mentions Great Britain. At that moment, all assume attitudes of adulation.

To introduce his daughters, the King moves to upstage center. The two girls come in together dressed in proper English costume and carrying fans, behind which they hide their blushes. They move slowly toward the front of the stage, their fans working in association with the violin obbligato. During their song they simply stand center stage looking sedate and occasionally using *very* conservative gestures.

Lady Sophy is then led on by the King. Although he shows obvious admiration for her, she in no way compromises her dignity by responding. She carries a lecturer's pointer and uses it during her song. The entire action of the song is acted out by the young ladies, with Calynx playing the role of their suitor. At the end of the song Nekaya wins the toss and shyly takes the hand of Calynx. Lady Sophy skillfully intervenes and dismisses Calynx from the action. She then leads the two girls off by a downstage entrance. The maidens recapitulate their opening dance to the accompaniment of palm-waving by the men.

In his dialogue with Scaphio and Phantis the King is constantly breaking into unrestrained laughter (in which they join) at the cleverness of his jibes against himself. His song is a combination of dancing by all three during the interludes and choruses and his own descriptive gestures during the stanzas.

His following soliloquy finds the King confused about his feelings. On the one hand he admires the cleverness of the *Palace Peeper*. On the other hand he senses the moral difficulties of his situation. His love for Lady Sophy and his sense of her reaction to his predicament leaves him feeling very sorry for himself indeed.

Lady Sophy's entrance inspires in him mingled delight and awe at her presence and a mincing sense of his own humiliation. She is dramatic and powerful in her Respectability, rising at certain moments to true passion. He is, by contrast, silly and helpless.

On the first two measures of the introduction to the duet, the King moves toward Lady Sophy beseechingly. On the next two she moves scornfully away from him as his face falls and he turns sadly away. His grief at this rejection is not sufficient to crush his delight (which he shares with the audience) in his "poetical phrase." To dramatize his sadness, however, he uses melodramatic gestures. When she sings, Lady Sophy condescendingly turns toward him to congratulate him on his "poetical phrase," a congratulation toward which he eagerly leaps, only to be again rejected as she crosses in front of him menacingly brandishing the *Palace Peeper*. She again faces him on "Come, crush me this contemptible worm," and gestures suggesting triumph and torture of one's victim. Her pride in her "forcible term" is addressed to him, and his expression compliments her on it. Her gestures subsequently become more melodramatic as she warms to her thoughts of vengeance. She holds a threatening pose while he sings, not even responding to his praise of her words. One begins to feel that she has confused the King with the writer as during their interchange beginning at letter B (Chappell score) she stalks him and backs him away, towering over him in stature and manner. They reverse their direction as they sing together, she walking haughtily toward the exit, he beseechingly behind her. These attitudes are developed in pantomime during the three-measure interlude, and even further during the closing bars as the two exit, the King following Lady Sophy.

The entrance of the First Life Guards must be spectacular. A great deal depends on the way they look and move. The effect must be

*Lady Sophy, Nekaya, and Kalyba in* Utopia, Ltd.: *"English girls of well-bred notions shun all unrehearsed emotions. English girls of highest class practise them before the glass."*       *(Lyric Theatre production)*

the kind of pageantry traditionally associated with Britain, in which exact similarity of appearance and movement is the primary impression. The arms of the First Life Guards swing in a metronomelike manner, and their knees are raised high. The beginning and end of each movement is exaggerated in order to increase the impression of exactness. Whenever the Guards turn, they snap their whole bodies into position in a single motion.

At the beginning of Number 7 the chorus enter from the sides, making an arrangement attractive enough to suggest that they are trying to impress the British by appearing at their best, but yet informal enough to suggest the comparative laxness of the Utopian society.

The four troopers and Captain Fitzbattleaxe, who leads them, make their entrance at the end of the fourth measure, and from that point until the girls begin to sing, the focus is entirely on their marching in intricate formations parodying the ceremony of the changing of the guard, and ending with the troopers spaced rather widely across the front of the stage. At letter B (Chappell score), Zara enters, and is immediately joined by some of the girls, who keep a respectful distance as she moves toward the front, displaying her British sophistication, all the more exaggerated for having been newly acquired. Yet her manner is not stiff, but conforms to the gentle quality of the music that accompanies her, so that the sharp contrast of the troopers' interpolations will be visual as well as musical.

When they sing (letter D), the troopers present arms and stand at attention until "On the royal yacht," when they begin to mark time with appropriate illustrative gestures. Four measures before letter E, they begin to march into a new formation in which they will stand at ease while Zara sings her next stanza. The above business is repeated for the second stanza.

By letter G the troopers are in guard position in the four quarters of the stage, Fitzbattleaxe in the center, and the girls gather admiringly round them. Zara stands by Fitzbattleaxe. At letter H she begins to mark time and uses her hands to imitate a trumpet. This action is echoed by Fitzbattleaxe, and then by all the troopers. At the 12/8 section, the troopers again march into new formations, continuing their marching in elaborate display until the end of the number.

The King enters from a downstage side, followed by his two other daughters and Lady Sophy. As he crosses to Zara to embrace her, the troopers present arms. While Zara is embracing her two sisters, the King is looking with great admiration at the troopers, who characteristically give no reaction. After Fitzbattleaxe has silenced the musical outburst, the troopers once again take positions in the four quarters of the stage, where they are examined even more enthusiastically by the ladies. This proves highly shocking to Lady Sophy, and she blindfolds the two younger princesses, using specially monogrammed blindfolds, and prepares to lead them off.

Little movement is needed for Number 8, the primary effect being that of the stage picture. At the second 12/8 section the troopers should march into a formation straight across the front of the stage, and should be in place in 3½ measures. On "Tantantara," they make gestures imitating trumpets. They also mark time all the way to the end of the number. The orchestral score has a musical tag not present in the vocal score, and this is needed to provide exit music for the troopers. This tag is based on measures 15–22 of the accompaniment, with the ending changed to provide a cadence. Note also that the score is incorrectly marked for both this and the previous number. Nekaya and Kalyba are indicated as singing when they are actually offstage.

In the following dialogue scene it is necessary that Scaphio be as exaggerated in his passion

as possible. Probably no other love scene is quite like this one, with its ridiculous contrast between two characters who are in every other way so much alike, and the wilder Scaphio's passion, the drier Phantis can appear by contrast. Phantis' almost sinister dryness is entirely different from Fitzbattleaxe's stiffness. The latter must not be played as the conventional handsome tenor in love with the soprano, but rather as a trooper who never forgets his role as protector of the lady. We are to believe that he cites an actual piece of legislation, rather than that he is cleverly concocting a plan on the spur of the moment.

At the beginning of the quartet Fitzbattleaxe puts his arm around Zara and walks with her across the front of the stage while Scaphio and Phantis interestedly supervise this action, one on each side of the couple, and one walking backward. Once they have assured themselves that Fitzbattleaxe is properly in control of the lady, the two Wise Men come face to face and begin shaking their fists at each other and otherwise suggesting conflict. During the ensemble, we have a couple on each side of the stage, one loving and one warring. Then Scaphio leads Fitzbattleaxe across the stage, singing to him confidentially. The same action is reversed by Phantis, returning Fitzbattleaxe to the arms of Zara. Then Scaphio and Phantis meet nose to nose in the middle of the stage and alternately back each other across the stage until the sustained notes at the end. During the concluding music each of the Wise Men shakes hands with Fitzbattleaxe before exiting.

The two lovers rush into each other's arms, center. They remain center stage until "When sages try to part," at which point they move toward the bench. Zara sits on the bench a measure or two before letter A. Fitzbattleaxe then crosses the stage away from her, as if thinking and then turns to her on "Now please infer." He kneels before her on "what would you do?" She assumes a thoughtful pose and then rises and draws him to his feet by "In such a case." The rest of the number is conventionally staged as they walk slowly across toward the exit.

The scene between the King and Zara is a problem because it is so similar to the King's previous scene with Lady Sophy. The key to making it work lies in characterization. Whereas Lady Sophy has been overbearing in her reprimands, Zara is sophisticated almost to the point of being casual. It is her taste, rather than her moral sense, that is offended by the *Palace Peeper*. The King, who was pleadingly in search of approval with Lady Sophy, is trying in the presence of his daughter to preserve what little dignity he has left under these embarrassing circumstances. He is stuffy, reserved, and defensive. Moreover, the scene ends on a note of affirmation when the King, having broken down and admitted that he is controlled, is suddenly offered a way out of his difficulty. The last two speeches should climax in a spirit of joy that is picked up and enhanced by the music that follows.

The chorus enter at a summons from Calynx, who claps his hands at one downstage exit, then crosses the stage and performs the same operation at the other. The chorus enter, filling the sides and back of the stage, and the King introduces his daughter, who curtseys dramatically, after which he retires to a downstage corner. Scaphio, Phantis, and Tarara, who have entered with the chorus, have watched the King from a position upstage enough so that he does not see them. As they sing their line, they move stealthily downstage and then exit. This they do while the King is moving away from them, so that he does not see them at all. The effect is to suggest trouble brewing for the King without his knowing it. Zara takes the center of the stage for her solo, then moves downstage to confer with her father while the chorus reply to her solo. Scaphio, Phantis, and Tarara move in again from the wings just long enough for their brief comment.

The entrance of the Flowers of Progress, which occurs at letter C, is quite different from that of the First Life Guards (who were played by the same characters in different costumes). Each of these men immediately emerges as an individual, and should assume some characteristic gesture from the beginning. Yet they are perfectly in step and individually appear very snappy and proper. Watched by the King and Zara they march across the front of the stage and then circle back so that they end in a diagonal in front of the chorus on the side opposite the King. Fitzbattleaxe, who is in charge, leads them in. They come to a halt facing front on the last note of the march and bow deeply during the trumpet call.

As Zara begins to sing she moves back to the center of the stage, where she marks time, military fashion. On " 'Tis then," she gestures toward Fitzbattleaxe, who steps forward and bows. On her next line he snaps to attention and remains so until the chorus have finished

singing. Then he faces right and marches back into line.

At letter E, Calynx enters with a table on which are several law books. This is placed down center, so that when Sir Bailey Barre comes forward he can thumb through the books for a moment before bowing to the chorus. When he is finished, Calynx takes the table away.

Lord Dramaleigh attempts to create the impression of being extraordinarily upper crust. He looks snootily at his nails, polishes his monocle, and otherwise appears to be superior enough to make a whole nation's moral judgments for it. On the chorus echo of his words, he bows to Zara, who curtseys back, then crosses the stage, turns, and kisses her hand very elegantly.

Mr. Blushington, by contrast, appears rather silly. He grins broadly, obviously pleased at the attention he is receiving. When he performs the same business as did Lord Dramaleigh, the effect is ludicrous.

Mr. Goldbury is the epitome of the smooth operator. He is suave, debonair, and sexy. He carries a furled umbrella, which he uses to punctuate his remarks, holding it in various positions, causing his entire figure to take on a variety of stances. He also makes important use of his gloves, which he pulls on in a debonair manner. At the end, while the chorus is singing, he crosses back to his place grinning and twirling the umbrella.

Captain Corcoran is military in style without resembling Fitzbattleaxe. His main property is a spyglass with which he surveys the horizon as he is being introduced. During his song he uses pictorial gestures much more freely than Fitzbattleaxe would. A hornpipe during the chorus from *Pinafore* might be effective.

During the chorus, "All hail," * the Flowers of Progress move into a new position near the downstage side of the stage, opposite their previous position. Meanwhile, the chorus regroup themselves so that they are all in diagonals on the side where the Flowers were previously. In front of the chorus group are, in order beginning up center, Fitzbattleaxe, Zara, the King, and Lady Sophy. (It may prove desirable to omit Lady Sophy from the finale, since her presence in it is dramatically super-

---

* At the top of page 76 in the Chappell score, one measure after letter R, the altos should sing a B-flat instead of a C.

fluous. If this is done, her part in the quartet can be sung by Phylla.)

Calynx has brought on a bench and placed it so that two of the Flowers can sit on it while the other three group themselves behind. The effect is of a family portrait. Once they are in place they remain absolutely motionless while the chorus sing to them. The singing of the quartet is accompanied by descriptive gestures so designed as to provide a kind of choreography of hands and arms.

At the beginning of the *allegro moderato,* Scaphio, Phantis, and Tarara enter in order that they may overhear the specific proposals of the Flowers of Progress, who march to the center of the stage while Calynx takes away the bench. Each of the Flowers now steps forward in turn and makes his proposal, accompanying it with a characteristic gesture. Fitzbattleaxe salutes, Dramaleigh holds up his monocle, Corcoran pantomimes shoveling coal and pulling on rope, Sir Bailey puts on a pair of glasses, and so on.

The turning point in events has now come. The King doesn't know what a Company Limited is, but he has a feeling that it will give him power against Scaphio and Phantis. As they sing their aside, the King turns and notices them. At the conclusion of their singing he moves toward them with a new confidence, almost menacingly, and they shrink offstage. The Flowers of Progress now move back to the side of the stage opposite the King, while Mr. Goldbury executes a soft-shoe dance appropriate to the introduction to his song.

This song depends on gestures, personality, and some dancing to put it across. Once again the umbrella is important as a property. For example, Goldbury spins it around by the handle on the line, "Make the money-spinner spin!" A more elaborate staging of this number is possible if a group of gentlemen from the City are brought on to pantomime the action of the song while it is sung.

The King comes forward to comment and finally to accept the idea of a Company Limited. Scaphio, Phantis, and Tarara sneak up behind him threateningly, but he merely snaps his fingers at them and moves away toward the center. On "Ulahlica!" the chorus move, hands up, waving palm leaves, into a double line behind the principals. At about this time Lady Sophy enters, bringing with her Nekaya and Kalyba. The Flowers of Progress are now on one side of the King, the governess and three princesses on the other side, and the three

Wise Men cowering behind them. The final chorus requires a rapid dance that can be executed largely in place and is easily performed by the entire company. It is important that the dance should reflect and exaggerate the rhythm of this music and should have great precision. These final moments of the finale will have a disproportionate effect on the audience's total impression of the first act, and they must be projected with gusto and a feeling of ease and certainty. A wise choreographer will rehearse this section thoroughly. It is a good place to begin rehearsing the chorus staging, as the dance step may take several weeks for some members of the chorus to assimilate.

Act Two opens with Gilbert's revenge on tenors. Zara is seated looking adoringly up at Fitzbattleaxe, who is feeling very nervous about his voice. The traditional gestures of love balladry are used, but they are slightly exaggerated and from time to time mixed with other, more nervous gestures that suggest the singer's true state of mind. Zara accepts all with uncompromised idolatry.

In the following dialogue the opening tones are quiet and affectionate, but the scene quickly takes on the robust enthusiasm of two revolutionaries gloating over their success. The duet should be staged in the traditional manner described on page 257.

The scene that follows is potentially the best in the opera. Unfortunately it was spoiled in the original production by Gilbert's unwise parallel between the Court of St. James's and that of St. James's Hall, at which the Christy Minstrels performed in blackface. The original staging would be even more distasteful and quite meaningless today. The following staging was introduced in the American Savoyards production, and though it is simple it is exactly right for the music and delightfully humorous.

Seven chairs are brought forward. Bamboo chairs are effective for this because they suggest the South Pacific. All seven characters sit in a line across the front of the stage, the King in the center. They are all wearing white gloves. The arms are held parallel to the legs and the hands are bent at the wrists so the tips of the fingers just touch the knees. At the rate of two beats to the measure, the hands and feet crisscross simultaneously and then return back to the original position. The right foot is in front when the right hand goes above the left hand, and vice versa. This action takes the first eight measures of the introduction. During the rest of the accompaniment, the Flowers hold their hands parallel to the floor, palms down, above the knees. The knees are raised to touch the hands twice each measure. The King does not do this, but uses gestures appropriate to his song. When the chorus is sung, the Flowers lean forward, moving their heads from left to right, hands on hips, snapping back into their previous position immediately after the last note. (The left-to-right motion is reversed each time a chorus is sung.) On "In short," the Flowers lean forward without the head motion. On the second two "completely's," they lean forward a little more for each one. On "It really is surprising," the hands are held straight down on the left side (the back is straight) and then brought up over the head and straight down on the right side, making a big arc. This takes four measures. The action is then reversed for the remaining four measures. As the hands move in the arc motion, the fingers flutter in time to the music. The first three times this action is performed, the music is sung more quietly each time. The fourth time it is sung very loudly.

The King performs the introductory actions perfectly with the others, but flounders completely on the arc at the end. He tries to figure out how to do it, is taken by surprise, and a little scared. It is only the fourth time that he finally gets it perfectly and is the best and most energetic of the lot.

For its effect this number must be rehearsed until it can be performed with absolute precision. All six Flowers should look exactly alike with every gesture. The basic movements can be learned easily in twenty minutes, but the number will have to be rehearsed for two or three hours if it is to be flawless.

The success of the entrance of the Royal Household depends largely on the costumier. The Utopians are now dressed for various positions about the court in English ceremonial costumes, and they enter one by one or in groups of two or three and take their positions about the throne room. The director must find interesting patterns of movement and groupings about the stage. Although the entrance is formal and requires the greatest dignity, the Utopians are new to it and so may be expected to have characteristic idiosyncrasies. This playing of the individual against the formal structure of the occasion can be quite humorous provided the formal structure is clear and the idiosyncrasies are kept rather subtle.

In the next number the ladies enter, and the King embraces each of them. The possibilities for humorous pantomime here are good because the King can gradually warm to his task from the tentative kiss of a hand to the final passionate embrace, bending the lady almost to the floor. Lady Sophy's reactions to this pantomime increase its possibilities. Further humor is added by the announcements of the names, all of which are ridiculous Utopian nonsense names, except for the last—the name of some *femme fatale* currently in the news. It is a nice touch, too, if the names are each announced several times as the cards are passed down the line, and the clarity of pronunciation increases in the process, so that the audience really catches the name only the last time. At the end of the number the King steps forward into position downstage center.

For "Eagle high," the entire company move forward, forming a straight line across the front of the stage and stand motionless as if performing an oratorio. The concluding orchestral section is used for an exit that has the same formality as did the entrance.

Scaphio and Phantis have been concealed behind the throne. On the opening chord of Number 18 one head sticks out and is quickly retracted on the second chord. Then Scaphio works his way stealthily out. When the musical pattern is repeated, Phantis repeats the action from the other side of the throne. They then pace back and forth rapidly, facing their heads toward the audience while actually singing and looking straight ahead when they are not singing. At letter D, when they sing in unison, they face the audience and dance together, hitting each other on the back and shaking their fists. They freeze in midgesture as the King enters suddenly at the end of the number.

Scaphio begins the next trio by taking the King by the elbow and leading him across the stage. Phantis then leads him in the other direction. The King shakes him off and repulses Phantis, standing in the center of the stage while the two look extremely shocked at his defiance. He then begins his dance while the other two watch him in attitudes of contemplation. Later Scaphio and Phantis contribute their dance, which is in contrast to the King's, the latter being light and happy, using frolicking gestures and gliding steps, the former being heavy and tight with a liberal shaking of fists.

The trio, "With wily brain," almost stages itself. Using their robes and wigs for concealment, the characters move about the stage in postures suggestive of plotting. Much of the action consists of one character calling the other two over to where he stands in order to whisper to them, and of their pantomimed reactions to his idea. These reactions are rather explicitly suggested by the musical accompaniment. It is possible, as the American Savoyards did, to use gestures to tell the audience what the plot is. Explosions, decapitation, and the like can be suggested quite easily with the hands. It may be better, however, to leave everything to the imagination, as Gilbert seems to have intended.

When the characters reprimand one another, they can shake their fingers at one another, and when they congratulate one another, they can shake hands and pat one another on the back. When they sing together in unison, a dance step should be used, but it should be in keeping with the generally subversive quality of the rest of the action.

The above staging ideas seem simple and obvious, and the imaginative director may be tempted to work out something more elaborate. The danger is that he may create a routine that draws attention to itself at the expense of the song and of the characterizations. The rather clumsy quality always associated with Scaphio and Phantis contrasts with the elegance of the British imports. In the next chapter it is suggested that this number may be interpolated in *The Grand Duke.* If it is used there it lends itself to quite different, more elaborate and grandiose treatment because of the characters who sing it.

The one place in which the director's imagination should augment the number considerably is in the business at the very end when some sort of pantomime should be used symbolizing the new relationship the three characters have developed.

The mood changes abruptly, and this should be reflected in a change in the lighting. Mr. Goldbury and Lord Dramaleigh, both the ultimate in suave sophistication, enjoy their memories of the drawing room. But what is really on their minds is the beauty of the King's younger daughters, which they intend to cultivate. The stiffness of the princesses is in sharp contrast with the worldly wise, almost risqué quality of their new mentors. They stand together facing the audience and respond in identical ways to everything that happens. On "Oh, don't! You mustn't," they run over and sit down on the bench. Goldbury then sidles up behind them and leans over to whisper the

words "full play" in both their ears in highly suggestive tones.

Goldbury's song can be effectively staged using all four characters. The idea is that the young ladies act out many of the suggestions made in the song, just as they did in the first act with Lady Sophy's song. Now, however, each has a partner in one of the men. On the introduction, Nekaya rises and goes to Dramaleigh while Kalyba remains seated, listening to Goldbury, whose foot is up on the bench. Together Dramaleigh and Kalyba perform actions suggested by the words until the references to cricket. At this, Goldbury moves toward the middle, Kalyba stands up and pretends to be the bowler (equivalent to a pitcher in baseball) and Nekaya the batsman. At letter B, Nekaya runs over to the bench and both sit down, while Goldbury dances into a new position on the refrain.

At the beginning of the second stanza the two girls stand and alternately pantomime the actions as Goldbury sings and Dramaleigh looks on. On "She'll waltz away like a teetotum," the two men waltz with the two girls into positions on opposite sides of the stage. The girls then play tennis, and at the appropriate moment each man pulls a comb out of his girl's hair, and the hair falls down about her shoulders. On the refrain the partners again waltz together.

For the third stanza the lights come down, the men fade into the darkness, and spotlights pick up the girls. Goldbury sings very softly. There is little motion now, but each girl in pantomime goes through a change of character, finding herself to be a serious and independent young lady. At letter E, the lights come up again, the girls rush eagerly to join their partners, the waltz is done with less inhibition this time, and the number ends with each couple in an embrace.

In the quartet it is necessary to play the opening statements not as questions but as realizations. The girls have just found a new freedom and they are enjoying its implications. On "Whatever you are," Goldbury leads Kalyba from her position at center to the downstage corner. At letter F, Dramaleigh mirrors this action with Nekaya. They are now in position to do a dance that takes them across the stage. Standing shoulder to shoulder they join hands. The two couples move toward one another. They are on slightly different planes so that one can pass in front of the other. On the

*Lord Dramaleigh, Mr. Goldbury, Nekaya, and Kalyba in* Utopia, Ltd., *Act II. Nekaya:*
*"And please don't look at us like that; it unsettles us."* (*Lyric Theatre production*)

interludes the couples face one another and do a fox trot or some similar step.

For the second stanza the two girls take positions downstage at opposite sides, the men fading back. On "No, no!" the men step forward, and the four are spaced evenly across the front of the stage, hands held as in a prayer for "It needn't be a hymn one." The rest of the number is done as in the first stanza, except that the couples dance off at the end.

Lady Sophy's recitative is melodramatic, her song whimsically sentimental. There must be continuity between the two, but the contrast is striking, since Lady Sophy finds herself reliving the past. The total effect of the song reminds one of Helen Hokinson's cartoons that used to appear in the *New Yorker,* and a careful study of some of these cartoons might help as much as anything to suggest the manner in which the song should be performed. It is a combination of dignity and fantasy—ludicrous, perhaps, but never unbelievable.

The King is a new man as he enters now. His record having been cleared, his fear of Lady Sophy is gone, and though she towers over him he is not the shrinking, simpering character he was in the first act. For this recitative the sort of arm-waving declamation often associated with grand opera is appropriate. This is the most hammed-up section of the opera except for Scaphio's discovery of his love for Zara. It should be noted that a line has been omitted from the vocal score. It was intended that after Lady Sophy's "I *couldn't* think why you did not boil the author on the spot!" the King should speak the line, "But *I* know why I did not boil the author on the spot!" On their unison "Boil him on the spot!" the two rush into each other's arms and embrace.

In the duet that follows we have passed the moment of melodramatic reunion and enjoy the fond happiness of love during the twilight years. As Lady Sophy sings, the King dances about the stage in a manner suggestive of the joys of new-found love. His dance is blissful but restrained and never becomes ridiculous. Then Lady Sophy dances while he sings. These two dances should not be the same: Each of the characters has a unique way of expressing the situation. For the second ending it is effective to have the two characters face each other holding upstage hands, stepping together and back, raising their hands as they step together. At "have vanished," they face the audience, standing side by side with arms joined and dance slowly toward the front of the stage.

Their graceful dance should suggest the formality of the eighteenth century and be in sharp contrast to the tarantella that follows. Gilbert's direction reads, "The King and Lady Sophy dance gracefully. While this is going on Lord Dramaleigh enters unobserved with Nekaya and Mr. Goldbury with Kalyba. Then enter Zara and Capt. Fitzbattleaxe. The two girls direct Zara's attention to the King and Lady Sophy, who are still dancing affectionately together. At this point the King kisses Lady Sophy, which causes the Princesses to make an exclamation. The King and Lady Sophy are at first much confused at being detected, but eventually throw off all reserve, and the four couples break into a wild Tarantella, and at the end exeunt severally."

The chorus, "Upon our sea-girt land," is one of the most violent eruptions in the entire series of operas. It lends itself very well to the movement of masses of people rapidly in a variety of patterns. One pattern that is easily achieved and quite effective is to form two concentric circles of people walking rapidly in opposite directions. Lines at sharp angles to one another are also effective.

The entrance of the King requires a fanfare similar to those in *Princess Ida,* Act Three, and *The Mikado,* Act Two. Unfortunately no such fanfare exists either in the vocal score or the orchestration, and it is necessary to compose one for the occasion.

The long speech for Scaphio is greatly improved if it is divided into a series of short speeches for Scaphio and Phantis, who rush about the stage waving their arms and trying to top each other's expressions of indignity. The chorus should sing its response to Zara's speech, and the appropriate music may be extracted from the Act One finale, p. 70 in the Chappell score.

No special staging is needed for the finale. The King takes his place on the throne with Fitzbattleaxe and Zara next to him and the other Flowers and Princesses grouped about them. The chorus is lined up so as to form an attractive final tableau.

## SCENERY AND COSTUMES

*Utopia, Ltd.* provides an opportunity for unusually imaginative scenery, particularly in the first act. The Utopian palm grove should be luxuriantly South Pacific, perhaps including an oriental palace or temple and an idol or two in addition to the varied foliage and view of the sea. Indeed, the designer may make the setting almost a compendium of impressions of highly developed tropical civilizations.

Act Two provides an opportunity to mix British pomposity with tropical relaxation. The mix might be anything from an imitation of the throne room at Buckingham Palace to an exotic courtroom with just a few British touches superficially added.

For the Utopian costumes one might draw inspiration from South American or South Sea cultures such as the Aztec. The contrast between fantasy in Utopian costumes and historical precision in the British can be very funny, but a company not so inclined need not be too exact about the latter. The satire of a modern revival must draw its effect from the universal problem of one culture attempting to impose its civilization on another rather than from the specifics of Victorian protocol. Appropriate military costumes for Fitzbattleaxe and Captain Corcoran should probably be used, and they are easily obtained. The other Flowers may wear top hats and tails. In the second act Lady Sophy and the three princesses may be dressed in anything elegant suggesting the Gay Nineties. In the first act Lady Sophy and her charges were in the original production given costumes cleverly mixing British propriety with tropical luxury. Also in that production Scaphio and Phantis were bald and wore robes with hieroglyphic-like designs on them.

Gilbert's instructions are that Paramount should appear in the second act dressed in a Field Marshal's uniform. His typical fondness for dressing his characters in military uniforms has little dramatic point, and there is no particular reason to conform to the demand other than a reference to it in the dialogue, which can easily be changed. In any event, Paramount will add more to the splendor of things if he is given robes more usually associated with royalty. Scaphio and Phantis should have judge's wigs in the second act. Bright red robes for them, rather than the usual black, help to establish their lack of sympathy for the British reforms.

# Chapter XVII

# THE GRAND DUKE,
# OR THE STATUTORY DUEL

## PRODUCTION NOTES

"In justice to Sullivan's memory as well as Gilbert's, it is to be hoped that *The Grand Duke* will never be heard again," wrote Thomas F. Dunhill in 1928, and the music critic Paul Hume summed up his impressions of a concert performance of the opera in 1965 with, "Gilbert and Sullivan should have stopped sooner." These reactions to the book and music of *The Grand Duke* when it has not been given the advantage of a fully staged production suggest the kind of challenge the producer must face if he is to make the opera appeal to audiences. Nevertheless highly successful productions are possible, and the initial critical response to the work was by no means entirely gloomy. Typical is the reaction of *Theatre* magazine, which wrote, "That the new Savoy opera is a great success there can be no possible doubt. It may have faults; it may be inferior to more than one of its predecessors; but the fact remains that *The Grand Duke* is from first to last a delightful entertainment." When the opera was revived in 1937 by the Blue Hill Troupe it proved one of that organization's most successful productions, playing for three nights to standing room only.

In 1962 a revised version of the opera made by this writer in collaboration with Roger Golde was presented for four performances at the Trinity Theatre in Washington, D.C. Peter S. Diggins greeted the production with a review in *The Washington Post* that is worth quoting at some length. Under the headline, "Hurrah for Gilbert und Sullivan," he wrote:

The town of Titipu, the quarterdeck of H.M.S. Pinafore and the rocky Cornwall seacoast are familiar to every Savoyard, but only a few know the delights of the Grand Duchy of Pfennig Halbpfennig. . . .

The work was the product of the embittered years of the librettist and composer, but time and again they show the wonderful turn of phrase and melodious musical flow that give their works a lasting place.

The Lyric Theatre spent many harried pre-production months trying to track down a full orchestral score of the work and met with success only near the time of rehearsal.

But the difficulties were worth surmounting for the work is a delight . . .

Throughout the work are echoes of their earlier and more successful collaborations, but Pfennig Halbpfennig retains a flavor all its own. The patter song, the rousing chorus, the plaintive ballad are all there. And so are typical Gilbert and Sullivan characters . . .

One happy patron asked, "Why isn't this performed more often?"

That this was not an isolated opinion is reflected in the fact that Milton Berliner in *The Washington Daily News* more or less echoed the above sentiments, saying that the show "moves along quite zippily."

This writer's impression upon seeing an excellent production by the American Savoyards in New York in 1961 was distinctly contrary to the last quoted remark. Produced full-length in the published version and seen for the first time, *The Grand Duke* distinctly does not "move along quite zippily," but drags mercilessly. The fault is mainly Gilbert's, though Sullivan must take some of the blame. The first act is filled with lapses of taste and style that become cumulatively offensive. The Act One finale is intolerably long and overdevelops several ideas that should have been discarded in the first place. The second act is artistically better, and the music generally delightful, but the effect of hearing too many pretty tunes becomes after a while like eating too much candy, and the entrance of the Herald, one of the finest moments in the show, loses effectiveness by having been preceded by too many tunes a little bit like it.

The point of all the above remarks is that a producer of *The Grand Duke* must begin with a basic decision: Will he perform the work as originally written, or in a revised version? If he chooses the former, as most producers do, he should expect an audience of die-hard Gilbert and Sullivan fans and not hope to please the general public. On the other hand, *The Grand Duke* contains enough good material so that it may be made to seem to the uninitiated almost as good as *The Mikado* if it is carefully revised. For that reason complete details on the Lyric Theatre version of *The Grand Duke* together with an explanation of how it was arrived at are to be found at the end of this chapter.

Several other concerns must be addressed by a producer of *The Grand Duke*. Once again a large and talented cast is required. The role of Julia Jellicoe is unusually demanding, requiring a first-rate actress and dramatic soprano who can manage a convincing German accent. Even more demanding is the role of Ludwig, the principal comedian. Rutland Barrington, who created the part, said of it, "The veriest glutton for work might have been satisfied with my part in this opera, about the longest and most hard-working I have ever undertaken, and yet one in which I failed to find too many chances of scoring." The fact is that Ludwig is onstage nearly all the time, that he is not a very funny character, and that he must have a good resonant voice and be capable of delivering patter songs. Since the part is not in itself funny, the actor will have to rely on his own personality to make it funny, and on his ability to do so depends much of the success of the evening.

None of the other roles is unusually demanding, and a company weak in tenor leads will be happy to learn that only Ernest Dummkopf is a tenor, and his role is no more difficult than that of the Duke in *Patience*.

No other opera in the series makes as much use of the chorus as does *The Grand Duke,*

though, unfortunately, there is little opportunity for the chorus to become interesting in itself and there is no number designed to show it off musically. The rhythmical patterns in the music are unusually subtle and varied and lots of fun for a good chorus to sing. This may explain why most people who have been in this opera have greatly enjoyed the experience.

As with *The Gondoliers,* elaborate sets and costumes are essential, and great ingenuity is required in the staging.

After the above cautions have been taken to heart it should be observed that *The Grand Duke* is by far the most interesting of all the operas to stage. In Gilbert's other libretti the subtlety of the satire greatly limits the range of what the director can do. Too much imagination may produce effects that simply compete with the words and music for the audience's attention. The weakening of the satirical subtlety in *The Grand Duke* gives the director a responsibility and an opportunity to enhance the libretto through drawing on his own imagination. If he does so effectively enough, he can turn an esoteric curiosity into a popular hit. This may explain why, although until recently revivals of *The Grand Duke* were extremely few and far between, within the last ten years there has been a rash of productions, many of which have been very good and very much admired. For the experienced company who is getting a little tired of tradition, *The Grand Duke* may be the ideal choice.

CRITICAL DISCUSSION

*The Grand Duke* suffers by comparison with other Gilbert and Sullivan operas not so much because of its inferiority as because its merits are of a different nature and tend not to be seen if one looks at it with too many preconceptions. It is a sad irony that Gilbert and Sullivan were so often accused of repeating themselves, and yet when they genuinely struck out into new territory the results went unappreciated.

Part of the problem, of course, is that the libretto was not given the kind of polish lavished upon its predecessors. Gilbert's taste for bad puns and humor that does not quite make its point was generally purged from his libretti for Sullivan, though it is liberally represented in his lesser works. Perhaps advancing age had dulled his sensitivity. In any event, one feels that additional care with the libretto might have avoided many of the problems that the work meets in production.

But *The Grand Duke* represents new territory for both Gilbert and Sullivan. Its plot is pure farce that rises at times to comedy but almost never to the satire that had previously been Gilbert's trademark. As farce it has a kind of significance better appreciated by devotees of the theatre of the absurd than by those schooled in the tradition of comedy of manners. Indeed, *The Grand Duke* explores some of the same thematic material later developed by Eugene Ionesco; in it, role-playing is carried to extremes that altogether break the bonds of rationality. Topsy-turvydom depends for its effect on the assumption of a rational world in which, for humorous effect, relationships that are conventionally understood in one light are reversed in order to be viewed in some other light. The basis of seeing the world as philosophically absurd is a perception that there is no meaningful rational order: no right way for things to be. The statutory duel is based on the absurd assumption that it is possible for one person to be exchanged for another so that, without losing his former personality, he in effect becomes that other person. Philosophically this is equivalent to saying that there are no absolutes of personality. In the twentieth century, confronted as we are by the specter of dehumanization through political, bureaucratic, and technocratic giantism, the absurd assumption of the statutory duel begins to take on a frightening reality. Today we are far better able to see the significance of this opera than its original audience could have been.

Using a company of actors as his basic set of characters, Gilbert explores the implications of the metaphor, "All the world's a stage," by confusing the actor with the dictator. Just as Hamlet used the drama to unmask the corrupting influences in Denmark, so Dummkopf's troupe uses its theatrical activities to overthrow the evil tyranny of Grand Duke Rudolph. But the metaphor is carried a step further. Once the actors have won the duel, the Grand Duchy is remodeled along theatrical lines, and everything takes place as if it were part of a drama. Art replaces life, and a kind of reality is established that has its own gratuitous rationality. The existentialist, realizing that the world has no meaning except the one he gives it, is prefigured in this plot. The world indeed acquires a meaning: it is absurd, but in an absurd world, one meaning is as good as another.

We are beyond the realm of political satire,

probing instead the very roots of the political animal, calling into question the validity of political organization, and then reaffirming that validity on the grounds that it will do just as well as anything else. Gilbert, whether consciously or not, has perhaps come closer here to touching the pulse of human existence than in any of his other works. The concept seems to have been important in his thinking, as he had already explored it in *Thespis;* but in that work he used the situation as an excuse for whimsical ironies rather than as a means of examining the essence of role-playing in human experience. Role-playing had continued to intrigue him in his fascination with the lozenge plot that Sullivan so often rejected, and that finally reached fruition in *The Mountebanks.* The lozenge was a crutch, however, a magical device by which a person's role became his real essence. In *The Grand Duke* we are asked to assume that roles can be changed without supernatural assistance. The quiet acceptance by all the characters of a law that imposes upon them a ridiculous set of conditions is totally human because it reflects the passivity with which most of us accept the assumptions of our culture and allow it to determine our roles for us.

Farce, then, rather than satire, was the form; but a farce based not so much on the wackiness of people as on the wackiness of systems and institutions. We have the association of conspirators with its secret sign—the eating of a sausage roll. Here the dehumanizing effect is symbolized by the difficulty of digesting the sausage roll once one has eaten it. Yet this device, which some critics have objected to, is not at all farfetched, since many groups signify their membership partly by the foods they eat. From the ancient Jewish dietary laws to modern soul food, eating particular things has been an important way of showing togetherness. We have the Grand Duke with his miserliness, which transcends his personal life and is imposed upon the whole Grand Duchy. Thus, for example, all love scenes must take place in the public square in order to increase the income from telescopes rented by the Grand Duke. This kind of governmental invasion of personal life may have been merely a farfetched joke in Gilbert's day, but it has since become a gruesome reality, and we are reminded not only of actual forms of computerized spying, but also of such less-obvious things as building codes designed to benefit special-interest groups. We have the legalized death of individuals without reference to their actual death, an innovation motivated by humanitarian considerations. Today, again for humanitarian reasons, we consign supposedly insane people to mental institutions, depriving them of all their legal rights, and making them, in a certain sense, legally dead. Increasingly we have become aware that some of these people are quite capable of living normal lives in society. In general, the operation of the law, with its tremendous emphasis on the importance of technicalities, such as that the Princess of Monte Carlo must appear in person to claim her husband, and, again, the fact that the ace is lowest, has a farcical effect. In present-day society the wholesale use of legal technicalities to carry on large-scale legalized crime has the same farcical quality, grim though it is.

Gilbert's characters are all puppets (with a few possible exceptions, such as Iolanthe and Jack Point), but nowhere is their puppet nature so much a part of the overall scheme of things as in *The Grand Duke*. This is because human concerns interact with the world of Pfennig Halbpfennig, and are negated by it. Ludwig's gradual accumulation of four wives argues that marriage is a purely legal arrangement. Ernest, striking fear into the heart of Julia because he is a "technical bogey," finds his attempts at lovemaking frustrated by his new identity.

Gilbert has even carried his examination of systems into the realm of language. Giving Julia, the English maiden, a German accent is not merely an instance of topsy-turvydom, it suggests that languages are interchangeable as if there were no cultural differences, a point of view that seems to be held by our State Department. And there is the one jibe (unique in the series) at the system of rhyming:

> When exigence of rhyme compels,
> Orthography forgoes her spells,
> And "ghost" is written "ghoest."

This kind of force-fitting belongs in *The Grand Duke*, as it does not belong in any of the other operas, because it is so reminiscent of the way systems force-fit human beings to serve non-human purposes.

To a certain extent Sullivan has responded to the change in Gilbert's technique. He too is experimenting, and one hears in the music much more rhythmical variety than usual. Indeed, this is the one opera in which he sometimes seems to abandon his regard for the words and let the music play its own kind of games. Often he does this by arranging the words in odd patterns that deprive them of anything but musical value, as when the basses sing, "Her bouquet is simply, simply frightful, frightful, simply frightful, frightful." Then there is the repetition of words until they lose their original meaning, as in the repeated "What's the matter?'s" in the Act One finale. Again words may be broken into syllables without reference to their original pronunciation, as in "be-eautiful" in the Herald's song. This treatment of words is something of a transition between the setting of a lyric or a hymn, which is where Sullivan found the art, and the kind of wild experimentation with words separated from meaning that has so often been found in the music and drama of the twentieth century.

Sullivan also responded to the locale of the opera by providing music sometimes reminiscent of Strauss and Lehar and other Continental composers who were coming into vogue, and who represent a transition between light opera and musical comedy. If one examines the scores of Edward German, Sullivan's successor at the Savoy, one finds an increasing tendency to do the kind of rhythmical experimentation that typifies *The Grand Duke*, as well as to move further in the direction of musical comedy.

That is not to say that the music sounds unlike Sullivan, as there are many songs that have the Gilbert and Sullivan trademarks and might have appeared anywhere in the series. "As o'er our penny roll we sing" sounds as traditional as Sullivan ever got—until you get to the dance at the end of it, which has a Continental flavor. But it is followed by the strange-sounding "When you find you're a broken-down critter" with its impressionistic musical setting that is on the verge of being nonmelodic.

To sum up, it is clear that *The Grand Duke* is far from being a masterpiece. Many of its experiments have not been carried far enough so that they really work. At times it has a strange hybrid quality that is rather disturbing. Certainly it contains many lapses, more in the words than the music. To some extent it may be convicted of being naïve in terms of the overall kind of design that makes, say, *The Pirates of Penzance* so effective. But it is not a work that should be forgotten. It can be made appealing in the theatre, and it is extremely interesting to work on in production.

Probably no one who succeeds in making this opera work in the theatre will end up feeling that it was not worth the effort lavished upon it.

## CHARACTER SKETCHES

### Rudolph

Rudolph is a miser and as such has something in common with Molière's famous character, except that he is much more affable about his miserliness. It is almost a duty with him; he bears the cross of his compulsion with amiability and a certain objectivity. Unfortunately, however, his penuriousness has affected his health, giving him a gaunt and sickly air. He is the patter man of the opera, although no fast singing is required of him. He may, in fact, best be compared with King Gama in *Princess Ida,* whose attractive repulsiveness is of much the same quality. Vocally, the role makes demands on the ability to project with equal volume through a fairly wide range. The intervals in the opening song are more demanding than those usually found in patter roles. There is need, too, for more than usual acting ability. The opening monologue can be very funny if done properly, but imagination is needed to keep it from becoming repetitious. It is in the song, "When you find you're a broken-down critter," that the greatest skill is needed. On paper this song doesn't look like much, but in the theatre it can be extremely exciting if the actor lives the part and reacts appropriately to the orchestral interjections. For a gifted actor this is an attractive role whose greatest drawback is that it is confined almost entirely to the first act.

### Ernest Dummkopf

Ernest is the tenor lead, and though he has certain romantic pretensions, he is largely a comic character. His love for Julia is cruelly spurned, and it is easy to see why, as he has little of the flair for the dramatic that she has. His attention is largely taken up with the difficulties of managing a theatrical troupe, particularly one that is simultaneously involved in a conspiracy. He is small-minded and irritable, and it is easy to see why the company prefer the rather bumbling administration of Ludwig, as he has real imagination and a sense of humor. Vocally, the part requires an attractive tenor voice and good musicianship. All of

Ernest's singing is ensemble work, except for his opening solo. Much of the ensemble is musically rather difficult. A certain amount of acting ability is certainly desirable, but the role is quite easy to portray. Although the second act scene between Ernest and Julia is the funniest dialogue in the show, Ernest is so much the straight man that it will be just as funny if he is not a gifted comedian.

### Ludwig

Ludwig is the leading comedian both of the theatrical troupe and of the opera. Like many comedians he tends to be unfunny offstage and he must shine in his role not as a result of what he does but rather of what is done to him. He is silly and unassuming and blunders his way into some ridiculous situations. On the other hand, he is better able to think on his feet than any of the other characters, and it is to that fact that his sudden rise to success must be attributed.

Ludwig is a star role in the sense that it must be brought to life by a star performer and cannot otherwise be successful. If Ludwig is boring (and he easily can be), the entire production will be. A good Ludwig, on the other hand, can largely make up for other failings in the production.

Vocally he must have a strong voice that projects well and is capable of complicated and rapid patter. He must also be enough of a musician to respond to the rather unusual rhythms he is given from time to time. The voice, however, need not be beautiful nor extend beyond the normal baritone range.

One thing in favor of the role is that its best moments come near the end of the performance. As the wives begin to accumulate, Ludwig becomes funnier, and so does the opera.

### Dr. Tannhaüser, a Notary

Like Rudolph, this character does almost all of his work in Act One. He is the light-baritone member of the company, vocally similar to Pish-Tush in *The Mikado.* He has something in common with that character, as his role is largely explanatory. He is more of a prime mover in the plot, however, than Pish-Tush. Early in the opera he lurks about in the background, offering explanations when needed. When Lisa says to him, "What are you grinning at, you greedy old man?" she gives an important clue to his character. He is smug and somewhat mysterious. Inasmuch as the law has an almost godlike quality in this opera, the role of the Notary takes on some of the qualities of a high priest.

### The Prince of Monte Carlo

The quality of this character depends to a large extent on whether or not his Roulette Song is included. If it is, he should have a really fine baritone voice and a great deal of facility in French. If not, much less is demanded of him vocally beyond excellent breath control and a pleasant baritone voice.

He is the opera's *deus ex machina,* coming in at the last moment (even later than the Mikado does) to hopelessly complicate things. Furthermore, his entrance is practically unanticipated.

He should have a foppish eighteenth-century style that humorously contrasts with the artlessness of his hired nobles. Behind his elegance lurks eccentricity, and a tendency to expect and admire eccentricity in others. He has all the *savoir-faire* that Ludwig lacks, which makes extremely funny Ludwig's attempts to take him by surprise.

### Viscount Mentone

A low comedian of the most dissolute sort. He has been hired to dress up as a noble, but it is obvious that the Prince's limited ability to pay has forced him to scrape the bottom of the sociological barrel. Mentone has only one line, unless the first-night libretto is used.

### Ben Hashbaz

A Jewish costumier complete with accent and appropriate mannerisms, hired to produce nobles at bargain prices. Although he has only a few lines, Hashbaz, because he comes in near the end of the opera, has an unusual opportunity to make a strong impression.

### Herald

Although this part is small, consisting almost entirely of a single solo, it is one of the most delightful roles in the entire series of operas. The music given the Herald is some of the best in the opera. Furthermore, if he is creatively portrayed he can be the most memorable character in the production. We shall have more to say about this in the section on staging. An attractive baritone voice with subtle character

is needed for this role, which is anything but a glorified chorus part.

### The Princess of Monte Carlo

A rather vixenish character, who is probably the prime mover behind her father's escape. She has a sharp enough tongue to make her a match for Ludwig's other three wives, two of whom are rather gifted in that department themselves. She hasn't much to sing, but a strong voice and a lot of breath control are needed; and she has to hold her own in a large ensemble in which she is the only woman.

### The Baroness von Krakenfeldt

The "large fat contralto with a voice like a foghorn," as Anna Russell describes her, is archetypally represented by this role. Like Rudolph, she is a miser, but unlike him she has a real love of gaiety and ceremony. In the first act she is little more than an adjunct to her betrothed. In the second she blossoms out and fills the stage with a great deal of excitement and gaiety. Her champagne aria is one of the weaker numbers in the show and can easily be cut, but a really glowing Baroness may make it worth including. She should also be a good comic dancer, as her dance with Rudolph in the first act is one of the highlights of the performance.

### Julia Jellicoe

Julia is a dramatic soprano with extremely melodramatic acting ability and a German accent. Vocally the role is not as difficult as Princess Ida, though it is probably more difficult than any of the other roles in the series, with the possible exception of Mabel in *The Pirates of Penzance.* Unlike Ludwig, this part is relatively easy for a performer with the necessary capabilities because little inventiveness is needed beyond the obvious demands of the role. Julia has much rewarding music to perform, and her emotions run the gamut.

### Lisa

Lisa is a soubrette who has little more to do than look charming, but she must sing elegantly, as she has some of the most beautiful numbers in the opera. This role has much in common with Iolanthe and Phoebe in *The Yeomen of the Guard* except that it lies in the soprano rather than the mezzo-soprano range. Lisa's emotions are the most serious in the opera, and we should be moved close to tears by her loss of her lover.

## Olga, Gretchen, Bertha, Elsa, Martha

There is little to distinguish between these parts, since they simply verbalize the chorus point of view in the dialogue. Since they are almost without individual characterization, there is no reason the roles have to be sung by the same people who are given the spoken lines, and one can safely distinguish between chorus members with good singing voices and those with acting ability in assigning these parts. One of the prettiest moments in the finale of Act One is the little song, "My Lord Grand Duke, farewell," which is quoted heavily in the Overture. Three of these characters participate in the singing of it, though only the libretto, not the vocal score, assigns names to them. If that section is included, voices that match Lisa's should be used. If they are not to be found, there is no real reason the entire section cannot be given to Lisa.

## Chamberlains

Six men from the chorus who accompany Rudolph in his first entrance. They have the opportunity for some effective comedy using their faces and their gestures to good advantage.

## Nobles

Six men (perhaps the same six as above) who accompany the Prince of Monte Carlo and are the dregs of society, dressed up in fine costumes (a delicious parody of the nouveau riche). As the song indicates, "their language is lamentable," and "their nails are not presentable."

## Chorus

Perhaps because they are actors, these are the most caustic of Gilbert's choruses. The restraint that is so often appropriate in chorus staging is not as necessary here, and a certain amount of vixenish behavior from the women is effective. If your chorus is made up of ham actors, there will be moments when they can be given free rein.

Notes on Staging

Before you begin work on *The Grand Duke*, reread *Alice in Wonderland*. Like *Princess Ida*, this opera has outgrown any need for realism in the staging, and all sorts of possibilities can be explored. It may be that Lewis Carroll's characters will suggest ways of designing and staging the show that could not and should not occur to a director of *Iolanthe*. The card-game motif suggests, for example, that some of the characters might be costumed as members of a deck of cards. This is most immediately obvious with the Herald, whose intrusion into the action is a bit like an unexpected trump. But one need not be confined to the cards. The Notary might be a sort of Mad Hatter. The Baroness is a little like the Red Queen.

If that approach does not appeal to you, you might consider doing the opera in modern dress, as if the whole thing were happening in Washington, D.C., or in Buckingham Palace, during the twentieth century. Rudolph might appear in a gray flannel suit, Ludwig as a hippie. The Continental flavor might be better preserved, however, if the characters were costumed after the manner of the film, *The Mouse that Roared*.

If your orientation is more traditional, the opera is quite colorful if done according to Gilbert's design, as the change from German costumes in the first act to Greek in the second is both colorful and amusing. We shall in our staging comments assume that you have decided to take the latter approach.

Gilbert's directions call for the placement of a well up L. C. This equipment is never used, however, and on a small stage it might be very much in the way. Several small tables are essential, however, as the company is discovered eating a wedding breakfast. Variety is added if some of the chorus are brought on after the curtain rises, sopranos gathering upstage center, altos at the downstage corners, all talking together, the men later insinuating their way into these groups. When the soloists begin to sing, the chorus should be gathered entirely around the tables. Beginning at "Here they come," the men form a bridge with their hands and the ladies move under it, emerging into diagonal lines opening out downstage of the parallel lines of the men. Ludwig and Lisa are the last to pass through this bridge, and thus they make their entrance. The action is confined to movement between the soloists until the chorus again begins to sing. ("If he ever

*Lisa and Ludwig in* The Grand Duke: *Sausage roll song.*   (*Lyric Theatre production*)

acts unkindly.") By this time the men have interspersed with the women and are standing slightly behind them. They dance in place a step based on the waltz, but they do not face one another, as this would take the attention away from the soloists, who do waltz about the stage.

Little movement is needed during Ludwig's next song, but the chorus must all have sausage rolls, which they eat immediately following their first response and react to subsequently through the rest of the song. The number ends with every member of the chorus holding up a second sausage roll and then throwing it at the audience.

As Ludwig describes the Athenian wedding procession, it is effective to have the chorus spontaneously break into "Eloia!" at the appropriate moment. The necessary music is on pages 101–102 of the Chappell score, taking the last three measures of the first page and the first two of the second.

As Ernest sings his song, he can point to actual members of the company who act out the people he is referring to. On the second refrain of the song, several members of the company crouch in front of Ernest as if they were horses, and he pretends to brandish a whip over them. When the chorus begin to sing, they prance about the stage to his consternation and finally raise him up on their backs.

In Ernest's monologue before Julia's entrance, it is funny if when he says, "Am I happy?" he seems to be asking for information. In the scene with Julia an interesting effect can be achieved if the two characters assume various positions of lovemaking while they talk. For example, as Julia says, "you'll be mean enough to hold me to the terms of my agreement," she presses her body against Ernest and has her lips almost up to his in a tantalizing position. Then, just as he is about to kiss her, she breaks away suddenly on the line, "Oh, that's so like a man!" Again, when Ernest speaks of "long and repeated scenes of rapture," etc., he acts out those scenes by kneeling before her, kissing her arm, and so on. This means that when Ernest asks for a demonstration, the lechery in his voice can be very funny indeed. It also means that Julia's ballad can be turned into a parody of the overdone love scene, which continues right up to the duet. As they begin the duet, the two characters snap out of their passionate embrace, face the audience, and sing completely deadpan to the end of the number, using mock operatic gestures. They then throw in one last kiss and exit in opposite directions, Ernest looking lecherously blissful, Julia bored and disgusted.

There is a slight problem with the wording of the following chorus. Evidently Gilbert originally intended some of these words to be sung by Ludwig and then decided to have the chorus sing them without making the necessary changes. Properly amended, the chorus would read:

For goodness sakes! what shall we do? Why,
    what a dreadful situation!
It's all your fault, you booby you—you lump
    of indiscrimination!
We surely don't known where to go—it's put
    us into such a tetter—
But this at all events we know—the sooner we
    are off, the better!

An alternative possibility is to return to the original, perhaps more dramatic plan, and have Ludwig sing the line assigned in the score to the girls, having the entire chorus sing in unison the line assigned to the men. If the arrangement in the score is retained, it is effective to have the men enter in a straight diagonal line pursuing Ludwig, while the girls enter at a 45° angle to the men and in a less rigid line. The lines overlap enough so that Ernest appears to be breaking through the crowd as he enters up center.

Ludwig's song is based on his pantomime of the actions he describes, while the chorus use appropriate gestures in response. On the last choral response it is necessary for Ernest to protect Ludwig from the raging crowd as they march around the stage shaking their fists at him. Finally they rush off in great confusion.

In the following dialogue, several lines should be cut because though intended to be funny they only succeed in lowering the tone of the proceedings. For example, Ludwig's line about baboons and the business about not eating sausage rolls if you are not a conspirator.

As the Notary sings his song, Ludwig and Ernest pantomime the action while the two girls look on, occasionally entering the action, as when the two men draw cards and the girls look at them and react. The Notary may wish to use a law book, which can be conveniently on one of the tables, as a source of the specifics about the law.

Again in the following dialogue there are some obvious cuts, such as Ludwig's "*I might be the survivor,*" and the business about the blade, the blood, the ball, and the bang.

The quintet is easily staged. Group the characters about one of the tables, three sitting and two standing behind, in the manner of old English madrigal singers. The following number is also not difficult, as the action of drawing and shuffling the cards is a major part of it and the rest consists of an appropriate dance step. It might be a cute idea to have all but the Notary pick up giant playing cards at some point. (They can be concealed on the tops of the tables.) As they hold the cards in front of them, the Notary can skip in and out among them, elaborately shuffling a pack of cards as he goes.

The entrance of the Chamberlains should be visually humorous. They are dressed in rags, but every attempt has been made to make their rags look as elegant as possible. As they enter they look extremely sour. They move downstage and then turn to cross the stage. As each man turns the corner he faces his head toward the audience and suddenly pastes on his face a wide, toothy, and humorless grin. Then as he turns the second corner he again becomes sour. The Chamberlains end up in a diagonal line on one side, preparatory to the business that follows. They all look expectantly offstage on one side, and the Grand Duke enters at the last possible moment on the other. As Gilbert says, "He is meanly and miserably dressed in old and patched clothes, but blazes with a profusion of orders and decorations. He is very weak and ill, from low living." No special stage effects are needed during his solo, as the words are sufficient. On the music following "my snuffbox," however, the snuffbox is passed down the line of Chamberlains until it reaches the end, where the Grand Duke takes it just in time for a sneeze before his last remark. The passing of the box down the line should be solemn, almost angry, but performed with a ceremonial flourish that is pleasing to the Grand Duke's desire to make an impression. The same sort of business is performed with the handkerchief, although this time there can be a greater flourish, as the handkerchief can be twirled by each man in turn. Rudolph, as the handkerchief is passed down the line, is working up to a gigantic sneeze.

During the following monologue there is ample opportunity for the Chamberlains to make an impression. After "Pass that on," the Chamberlains whisper down the line as indicated, until the last Chamberlain performs an extremely elaborate salute that manages to continue even after Rudolph assumes that it is finished. As each of the Chamberlains is named in the dialogue he steps forward and acknowledges in his own unique way his acceptance of the responsibility. It would perhaps be well for the director to allow the Chamberlains to evolve this business themselves.

The exit of the Chamberlains is provided with music that is a recap of the entrance music up to the point that they begin to sing. It might be well to have them exit singly, each of them grinning at the audience in his own way as he goes. This business can be so handled that it brings spontaneous applause.

The only problem with the following dialogue sequence is its length. It is well-enough written so that it should play effectively unless the performers are weak, in which case it could be reduced to about half its original length.

The staging for the duet and dance will be most effective if Rudolph happens to be quite small and the Baroness rather large. At the beginning the Baroness is center and Rudolph observing her on the left. At "Upon a scale extensive," Rudolph stands behind the Baroness, his hands on her waist. He should be completely hidden. For his first line he sticks his head out from behind her on the right side. On her line she chucks him under the chin. Next his head appears on the left side. When they sing together, Rudolph steps out beside her and they use the step used by Ko-Ko in "As someday it may happen," as described on page 140. They move toward the right on the first phrase and back to the left on the second. Bending the knees on each step and moving the arms in and out will add to the effect. On "And pays for such expensive tricks," Rudolph searches in his pocket for a coin, which he holds up under the Baroness' nose (not looking at her) on the next phrase. She then takes the coin. They both look amazed. He takes the coin back. Again they both look amazed. On "Sometimes as much as two-and-six" (duet), he holds the coin up on the other side. The

Baroness speaks didactically to Rudolph on her next two phrases, and then searches in her purse for a coin, which she holds up under his nose (not looking at him) on "A better man by half-a-crown." The business of taking the coin and looking amazed is then repeated in reverse. When they sing together again, each holds a coin up on the opposite side as they look at each other approvingly. During this they should be several steps upstage. Beginning at letter C, they face the audience and embrace cheek to cheek, their downstage hands clasped and held straight forward as far as they will go. They move forward toward the audience, bent slightly at the waist and leaning into the step, using decisive steps that are almost stamping. They take four steps on the syllables, "let," "mod," "mer-," and "ry." This pattern is repeated on the next phrase. Beginning "For to laugh," they stand next to each other, their arms out to the side for four measures. The cheek-to-cheek stance is then repeated moving backwards. On "For to laugh" the second time, Rudolph stands in front of the Baroness, her hands on his waist. They do a rapid run to the side for the first measure of the interlude, she twirls in place on the second, and they end the interlude with a clap. At the beginning of the second verse, Rudolph stands to the right of the Baroness. At the mention of water he runs down right, showing signs of disgust. The Baroness searches in her purse and pulls out a bankroll on "This pleasing fact." When they sing together, Rudolph also has a bankroll, and they both look down at their money and count it, snapping their heads suddenly up on the slurred end of the phrase. This is done twice. On "Two-shilling gloves," Rudolph turns to the Baroness, offering money. On her response she pantomimes a readiness to sell gloves. On the four-note interlude she bats her eyelashes. Again Rudolph offers the money; but just as she is about to take it on the last note of the second interlude, he snatches it back. On the next duet phrase they put their money away. The Baroness kneels on "Cheap shoes," while Rudolph stands behind her. At the end of the phrase he pirouettes around to her left, as if to look at the shoes and ties. At the end of the next phrase he pirouettes to the right, where he pretends to listen to the ticking of a watch. On "Which he's *not!*" he taps her on the shoulder and she rises. He then bows to her, and she kisses his hand as he grins at the audience. At the 6/8 section their previous dance routine is repeated.

At the 2/4 section, p. 61 (Chappell score), their dance begins. Although this is not technically a tango, it can be effectively staged as one. We shall refer to measures by number, beginning at the 2/4. The two start near upstage center and move toward down right. They hold each other cheek to cheek in the manner previously described. On the first two measures the outside foot is extended forward and then back, once for each. On measures three and four, three steps are taken, beginning with the outside foot. The routine is repeated on measures five through eight, except that the dancers are bent more at the waist. Again, during measures nine through twelve they repeat the routine, bent even more, this time moving across the front of the stage toward the left. On measures thirteen through sixteen, Rudolph assumes the pose of a Spanish dancer and claps his hands in rhythm above his left shoulder while the Baroness dances around him, lifting her skirts with her hands so that they do not obstruct her feet. On seventeen the Baroness, using dainty steps, runs to the right, where she stands, her arms extended on both sides. Rudolph, on eighteen, runs to the right in the same manner. On nineteen she, standing behind him, grabs his hands, and he tilts his head back and smiles at her. On twenty-one, the Baroness does a pirouette to the right. On twenty-two he does one also, but it gets a little out of control, so that on twenty-four she catches him at the waist to keep him from falling, to his grateful surprise. Rudolph now stands in front of the Baroness as they extend their left arms, hands clasped and their necks turned to the left. On measure twenty-five they take one step out to the left. On twenty-six, the step is retracted. On the next two measures they take three side steps. On measures twenty-nine through thirty-two (beginning), this business is repeated in reverse. On thirty-two and thirty-three, the Baroness bends Rudolph backwards. On the next two measures he bends her back. On the last two chords he bows to her and kisses her hand.

The next section is most melodramatic. Rudolph's behavior during the song should dramatize his low condition, using facial expressions, posture, and pantomime. The song is a show-stopper if Rudolph really convinces the audience that he feels very ill indeed. It should be pointed out that although this song has been compared to the Nightmare Song in *Iolanthe,* it actually has little in common with it. It is unique among Gilbert's lyrics in that it encourages empathy and takes the audience on a bizarre trip of physiological experiences. Therefore, more than is usually the case in Gilbert and Sullivan, the actor should attempt to live through the experiences himself, drawing perhaps on the Stanislavsky method of acting. No specific directions about gestures can create the necessary effect.

The main problem with the dialogue between Rudoph and Ludwig is that the actors should avoid imitating each other's styles, a fault that the dialogue encourages, as Gilbert's writing for the two characters is stylistically similar. The joke is that Rudolph is the sly, little, calculating character, Ludwig the big, bumbling idiot. But the two characters operate in the reverse of what one would expect. Thus, each must be careful to preserve his basic character, though the action seems to deny it.

At the beginning of the finale there is a disagreement between the libretto and the vocal score as to the assignment of lines to characters. The libretto division is more dramatic, and as the libretto (even the first-night libretto, in which this division is also made) postdates the score, it probably represents Gilbert's later thinking on the subject. As Rudolph goes to one side of the stage to call the people, Ludwig moves over to the table and carefully puts a card up his sleeve. Then, while Ludwig is singing, Rudolph puts a card up his sleeve. The chorus creep in looking terrified, and one member of the chorus serves as a second for each of the combatants. They stand on opposite sides of the stage, conferring with their seconds, while the chorus sing. On their recitative the two meet center stage and talk to each other "aside." The next chorus is directed to the audience: The chorus lean forward and seem to whisper, shielding their mouths with their hands. During this, Rudolph and Ludwig move away from each other in big semicircles toward the back and meet again upstage center. Ludwig snaps his finger under Rudolph's nose precisely at letter B. As they are threatening each other, the necessary action is obvious, except that beginning with "Take that," each alternately slaps the other in the face with a glove. On the chorus interruption, the two men return to their seconds. On "Awful are the words they use!," the chorus stick their fingers in their ears. On the second ending, the two men are seated at tables on opposite sides of the stage looking glum, and being urged to action by their seconds.

At letter D, the Notary enters, just in time

to see the two men rise and slowly turn toward each other. They cross toward each other, each rolling up a sleeve, preparatory to violence, but the Notary interposes himself between them and from an open book instructs the chorus about the statutory duel. Upon request, the Notary produces a pack of cards. Each man in turn draws a card, hands it to his second without looking at it, and pulls from his sleeve the card previously hidden there. Seeing that he has lost, Rudolph faints into the arms of his second, who draws him to the side of the stage, while Ludwig is hoisted onto the shoulders of two chorus men, who carry him about while he is cheered by everyone. Rudolph revives for his solo line, but then immediately collapses again. As the farewell chorus is sung to him, several girls crowd around with smelling salts and other attempts to revive him, but he remains in his collapsed condition. Finally one of them puts a flower in his hand, which is over his chest, and he smiles sweetly at the compliments he is receiving.

At the bottom of page 76, on the next to last measure, the chorus laughs, and this is not indicated in the score. The laughs revive Rudolph, who shakes his fist at them. They grow sweet again, and he looks confused. Then they laugh again, which helps him make up his mind what to think of them. His fury mounts until it finally carries him off the stage. The chorus breaks into hysterical mocking laughter as he exits.

Ludwig parades proudly around the stage while the chorus hail him. Meanwhile, the Notary, who missed out on the wedding breakfast, is helping himself at one of the tables and paying no attention to what is going on. He has on a bib, and as he turns to speak to Ludwig he rises and offers him a drumstick, from which Ludwig takes a bite before he replies. The Notary then returns to his seat and eats his way through Ludwig's song. This song is put across through gestures by Ludwig and the chorus.

When Ludwig discusses giving out the appointments, he crosses toward the Notary, who suggests that they join each other in a glass of wine. Ludwig and the Notary drink the wine and converse during Julia's big scene, taking no interest in it until later.

Julia breaks suddenly through the crowd upstage center, pushing everyone aside in the most dramatic fashion. Her attempt to get Ludwig's attention through sheer dramatic projection fails, and she soon turns her attention to Lisa, who stands on the opposite side of the stage. Gradually she gets Lisa so upset that the latter rushes to Ludwig, trying to draw his attention to what Julia is doing. He thinks she wants wine and offers her some. Only when she rejects it does he turn and notice Julia and comment on what she is doing. Julia's dramatic excesses are so drawn out and boring to him, however, that he returns to the wine, and has just taken a huge mouthful when he hears her say that the part of the Grand Duke's wife is hers. Julia now takes Ludwig and leads him to the center of the stage, where she begins making love to him, to Lisa's horror and Ludwig's confusion. When he finally responds, she slaps him. Lisa, as she protests, begins to make love to Ludwig too, so that the two women are pawing over him from opposite sides. When she sings, Julia moves around between Ludwig and Lisa and draws Ludwig downstage away from Lisa, becoming gradually more passionate until the "you bet's," by which time she is embracing him and running her fingers through his hair. Lisa, meanwhile, rushes to the Notary to consult him. At first he offers her wine, but then he gets the idea and looks through his law book. On "The lady's right," he moves downstage center. Julia is holding Ludwig in an embrace, and Ludwig is gesturing to the Notary to show him the law book so that he can read the relevant passage. It is finally held up so he can read it over her shoulder.

Lisa moves up center, and stands on the platform at the back. Everyone faces her, so that most backs are to the audience. The lights go down and a spotlight is on her. During her aria, no one moves. At the end of her aria, she exits, and so does the Notary.

Ludwig and Julia are now the only principals onstage. Appropriate to the "jolly jinks" number is a folk dance, preferably one involving the waving of hats in the air. While the chorus is singing, Ludwig and Julia join hands and skip around in a circle. Then they engage in a game of alternately clapping their own hands and each other's.

When Ludwig sings about the court costume, he gestures, and the Grecian robes are brought on. While the chorus sing "Yes, let's upraise," Ludwig and Julia put on these robes as cloaks. At letter W, Ludwig and Julia cross around in front of the chorus, facing them, in gestures of triumph, and then meet center. Julia kneels and Ludwig crowns her with vine leaves. Then Ludwig kneels and Julia crowns him. After this, a large couch is brought in. Ludwig reclines on it in sybaritic delight. Julia stands behind the couch and dangles a bunch of grapes over Ludwig's open mouth as the curtain falls.

Gilbert's directions for the Act Two opening read as follows: "Enter a procession of members of the theatrical company (now dressed in the costumes of *Troilus and Cressida*), carrying garlands, playing on pipes, citharae, and cymbals, and heralding the return of Ludwig and Julia from the marriage ceremony, which has just taken place." As usual, Gilbert is fond of putting musical instruments into the hands of his people, but little seems to be accomplished by using them here, and we recommend the following opening instead.

As the curtain rises, the men and women each form two diagonal lines from the front to the back of the stage, the men on the inside, the women on the outside. The men carry bowls in their hands, held to about chest height. The women have wine bottles on their heads. The men step forward, one step per measure, bobbing down as they step, except when they sing "Eloia!" On this they raise their bowls up in the air. On "Opoponax!" the women move to the sides, in between the men. On "Eloia!" they raise their bottles up off their heads. On "Wreaths of bay," the men and women move forward together. On "Fill the bowl," the women fill the men's bowls. On "And to revelry," the men drink from their bowls. From then on everyone moves forward on the sustained phrases, or to the side on "Opoponax!"

Ludwig's patter song needs appropriate gestures but nothing more, as the words will be difficult enough to catch without anything to distract from them. On the reference to umbrellas in the third stanza, two of the company go offstage and get umbrellas, which they pass out to the entire chorus. Thus when the chorus sings "Eloia!" again, the same business as before is used except that now it is the umbrellas that bob up and down.

Ludwig is now left alone with his two wives. The couch that was brought on in the first act is placed in such a position that he can recline on it luxuriously. Julia stands downstage of him, and he sits on the couch looking at her possessively. Lisa's song begins with Lisa crossing to Julia, but gradually she works her way back to Ludwig and demonstrates on him some of the things she sings about. Ludwig's silly smiles during this number add greatly to the comedy. For variety it may be well for Lisa to bring him downstage during the second verse.

In the dialogue Ludwig should be as dramatic as possible in suggesting the appropriate behavior of his new wife. This is to provide a foil for Julia's coming monologue.

The duet is easy to stage. A cross or two from Ludwig are all that are needed from him. During the monologue he fades into the background, and the scene is entirely hers. (Rutland Barrington said that he was dragged about the stage during this number, but involving him in the action must have been pointless and distracting. In any event he did not seem to like the idea.)

A Julia who is good enough to play the role is good enough to stage this monologue herself, stalking her prey about the stage and responding in pantomime fully enough so that we can actually see the other characters. It should be noted that the first two lines of Julia's monologue are missing from the vocal score and must be supplied from the libretto. Her hysterical laughter should be like Mad Margaret's in *Ruddigore* (see page 159).

The chorus rushes in helter-skelter, preceding the Baroness. For some reason, the Baroness' miserliness is not emphasized when she is not in the presence of Rudolph, and it is appropriate, therefore, for her to be dressed in a large and fancy wedding dress. If her dress fills the stage enough, there is no need for any action following her entrance beyond her confrontation with Ludwig and her presentation of her card (a better idea than Gilbert's pocket-handkerchief).

After a brief passage of dialogue, the chorus again sing. The music that they sing is put together in the following way: "For any disappointment" through "unexpectedly" is sung in unison to the music beginning at letter D, p. 120 (Chappell score). "Tol the riddle lol!" begins at the last measure of the second bar on p. 121 and continues to the end of the page.

In the dialogue matters must be handled so that the Baroness is the strongest of the characters without compromising Julia's melodramatic talents. Her "set the merry joybells ringing" begins a crescendo of trumpetlike declamations that rises to a height at the end of her next speech and is nearly deafening.

At the beginning of each of the four phrases of the Baroness' next solo, two men kneel side by side near the front of the stage, facing left, so that at the end there are four pairs of men across the front. Their costumes are so made that they have streamers hanging from the shoulders. When the chorus begin to sing, each man takes hold of the streamers of the man in front of him so that they look like reins. On "So summon the charioteers," all the men leap up and prance forward, looking like horses and charioteers at the same time. They make a big circle about the stage and become the beginning of a chorus line arranged in the same way with the streamers, so that the entire chorus make one big circle about the stage and then prance off on the dance music.

By letter K, Julia is alone onstage, and the lights come down, leaving a follow spot on her. She goes mournfully to the couch and looks down at it, making it a symbol of what she has lost. On "So ends my dream," she comes downstage, but returns to the couch again on "the Ducal throne." At letter M, she crosses down right, where she remains until letter N. Here she takes a dagger from her bodice and walks slowly across the stage holding it up as if about to stab herself. On the next phrase she averts her face. On "No," she moves the dagger away, so that it no longer threatens her. On "living," she raises her left fist in a gesture of defiance. At letter Q (*sic,* should be O), she again moves toward the left, and on the following phrase she again gazes at the dagger, though it is not this time in a threatening position. On "No," she looks away from the dagger and out at the audience. Six measures after letter P, she sinks to her knees despondently. On the last measure of p. 126, she drops her head sadly to her chest. On the next measure she raises her head suddenly with hope, and two measures later leaps to her feet. After the second "No, no," she runs to the back of the stage. This permits her to cross down center, arms extended forward, on the long trill. On "I bow me," she curtseys, and again on "God save you," and "Your servant" the first time. On the second "God save you," and also on the second "Your servant," she blows a kiss from her hand. At letter U, she runs down left, and then curtseys and blows kisses several more times, as seems appropriate.

The duet involves the use of appropriate gestures until the *tempo di valse,* when Julia begins to skip around Ernest in a circle, interrupting the skipping sometimes to curtsey to him on appropriate words. Ernest, on the other hand, holds his position in about the center of the stage, except for an occasional pass at her, which she eludes.

At this point it is possible to interpolate a scene involving the trio, "With wily brain," from *Utopia, Ltd.* (See pages 230 and 278–284.) This is sung by Ernest, Rudolph, and the Notary. The staging should be quite different from that suggested on pages 209–210, as these three characters are much more suave and sophisticated.

On the first downbeat, Ernest takes a position facing right. On the next, Rudolph gets behind him, placing his upstage hand on Ernest's upstage shoulder. On the third measure, the Notary repeats the above. On the last note of the introduction, all heads face the audience. The upstage toe reaches forward on "wi-" and the step is completed on "brain." The same for two more steps. "Plot we'll plan" goes step, step, about-face. The bodies turn, but the heads remain facing the audience. This pattern is now repeated in the other direction. On "That's understood," they face the audience, arms folded. Rudolph's fist goes straight out in front of him on "striking." Ernest tops it on "iron's," and the Notary both of them on "hot." Again they fold their arms. Ernest's hand goes to his chin in a thinking pose on "now," Rudolph's on "like," and the Notary's on "de-." At the *allegro con brio,* the outside two skip to the corners of the stage, and Rudolph beckons them back. After their rejection of the idea, they again skip to the sides, and now the same business is performed, first in one corner of the stage and then the other.

That kind of precision work should dominate the staging of this number if it is used here. The characters should never become awkward or rough-and-tumble in their actions, but should preserve their dignity. Their dance steps should be relatively formal, having something in common with the theatre dancing associated with Fred Astaire.

The chorus enter happily, all carrying champagne glasses, which are filled by two or three elegantly dressed waiters. The Baroness and Ludwig come in in a jolly mood, carrying glasses. Ludwig's is filled and he immediately drains it, whereupon it is filled again. He then sprawls himself on the couch to listen to the Baroness' song. During her song, the focus of the chorus is always on her, but they are broken up into little groups and keep sipping from their glasses and nodding to one another, discussing among themselves the import of what she is saying.

At the trumpet blast, Ludwig leaps from his seat and gazes off into the audience, trying to see who is coming. The entire chorus follow suit, and at the end of No. 22 they are crowded across the front of the stage, peering off into the audience in search of someone who is presumably coming from that direction. There is a pause in the music and nothing happens. Then the Herald walks across the platform at the back and stands up center. Seeing everyone peering into the distance, he does so too. Then someone discovers him, and all the chorus fall back laughing into diagonals that allow them to view him comfortably. At that point the music for his number begins.

The Herald should be so costumed and characterized that the moment he walks onstage he introduces a note of wild fantasy. One way to do this is to costume him like one of the characters in a deck of cards and have him walk holding his body in an odd angular position.

He delivers his opening statement from up center, but comes down as the chorus begin to sing. From that point on, he renders a modern dance interpretation of the number, exploring abstract angularities in a way that reflects the interesting and odd patterns of the music. The chorus need not move at all—the number belongs to the Herald, and he should make enough of it to justify his receiving star billing in the show.

Some of the Herald's style of movement might be adopted by Ludwig for his recitative, No. 24. The music following the recitative is given over to the Herald's elaborate exit (again a modern dance interpretation). Ludwig's words to music (found in the libretto only) begin at the *piu vivace*.* Following this it is possible to interpolate the chorus adapted from *Haddon Hall,* "Now step lightly." (See pages 230 and 284–290.) The idea is to get the entire chorus up on the platform behind the curtain. They get into positions suggesting stealth. Then one person from one side of the stage skips over to meet a person from the other side, and together they move up onto the platform. Doing it this way takes the entire extent of the chorus, and means that most of the voices are always facing the audience.

The march is heard, and the Herald enters. The nobles march in just far enough to be onstage. The Herald takes each in turn and arranges him in a proper position on the stage. The contrast between the Herald's elegant

movements and the slovenliness of the nobles can be very amusing. When all are in place, the Prince and Princess enter, followed by the Costumier, who inspects the nobles, making minor adjustments in their apparel. The Prince, being rather foppish, makes a good deal of use of his handkerchief, and this reaches a climax during the cadenza at the end, when the handkerchief in his hand does a dance all its own.

Most of the business in the dialogue is clear enough. The highlight of the scene is when the nobles assume positions suggestive of various moods. It may be a good idea to elaborate this scene with verbal comments in the manner used by the Duke in *The Gondoliers* (see page 194.)

At the strike of the gong the curtain is pulled, and the entire chorus engage in a reckless dance in which the Prince and his followers eventually join. This is unlike all other Gilbert and Sullivan dances, because it is meant to evoke general mayhem. A good choreographer schooled in modern dance can have no end of fun with this scene, in which all sorts of individual vignettes are desirable.

The Roulette Song was evidently cut sometime after the first night, as the revised libretto does not contain it. If it is used, the following lines from the first-night libretto must be interpolated:

PRINCE. I mean I've paid my debts! And how d'you think I did it? Through the medium of Roulette!
ALL. Roulette?
LUDWIG. Now you're getting obscure again. The lucid interval has expired.
PRINCE. I'll explain. It's an invention of my own—the simplest thing in the world—and what is most remarkable, it comes just in time to supply a distinct and long-felt want! I'll tell you all about it.
(*Nobles bring forward a double Roulette table, which they unfold.*)

Gilbert's directions indicate that at the beginning of the section in French the chorus crowd around and stake gold on the board. During the chorus refrain, the Princess and Costumier rake in all the stakes. In the second verse all stake again, and this time the Prince rakes in all the stakes. He also gets them at the end of the third verse, after which the nobles fold up the table and take it away.

An alternative staging would be to have the

---

* If the preceding recitative is not used, the following words for Ludwig may be inserted prior to those printed in the libretto: "We are not acquainted with either his Highness or his residence; but, as he guesses, this is indeed the shop for cut-and-dried formality. Let him appear. He'll find that we're remarkable for that." These words plus those given in the libretto fill out the *piu vivace* section exactly.

Prince sing the song while a modern dance interpretation of Roulette is presented.

At the end of the following dialogue, the chorus get in position to dance off, and are in the middle of a particularly wild moment when they freeze as the three *dei ex machina* suddenly appear up center and descend from the platform.

If Rudolph's song is used, it should be noted that the second verse was omitted in the first-night libretto. Rudolph should take over the stage during this song, examining various aspects of what has been going on and reprimanding not just Ludwig, but everyone present.

It is nearly impossible to make much sense out of the last dialogue scene, which is a shambles of dramatic writing. The first-night version is actually a slight improvement because it is a little better paced, the various adjustments not taking place quite so fast. Here it is, beginning at the point where it deviates from the final version.

JULIA. My objection falls to the ground. (*Resignedly.*) Very well. But will you promise to give me some strong scenes of justifiable jealousy?

ERNEST. Justifiable jealousy! My love, I couldn't do it!

JULIA. Then I won't play.

ERNEST. Well, well, I'll do my best! (*They retire up together.*)

LUDWIG. And am I to understand that, all this time, I've been a dead man without knowing it?

BARONESS. And that I married a dead man without knowing it?

PRINCESS. And that I was on the point of marrying a dead man without knowing it? (*To* RUDOLPH, *who revives.*) Oh, my love, what a narrow escape I've had!

RUDOLPH. Oh—you are the Princess of Monte Carlo, and you've turned up just in time! Well, you're an attractive little girl, you know, but you're as poor as a rat!

PRINCE. Pardon me—there you mistake. Accept her dowry—with a father's blessing! (*Gives him a small Roulette board, then flirts with* BARONESS.)

RUDOLPH. Why, what do you call this?

PRINCESS. It's my little Wheel of Fortune. I'll tell you all about it. (*They retire up, conversing.*)

LISA. That's all very well, but what is to become of *me*? (*To* LUDWIG.) If you're a dead man—(*Clock strikes three.*)

LUDWIG. But I'm not. Time's up—the Act has expired—I've come to life—the parson's still in attendance, and we'll all be married directly.

ALL. Hurrah!

At the beginning of the finale the chorus are all a little back so that the principals have some room. As the singing begins, Rudolph kneels to the Princess, who embraces him enthusiastically. He rises on the sixth measure from the beginning of the number. On measure seven, the Prince kneels to the Baroness. She blushingly waves to him. He rises and takes her hand on the ninth measure. On measure twelve, Ludwig and Ernest kneel to their ladies. On measure fourteen, Lisa and Julia assume thinking poses. On measure sixteen, they meet and confer. They cross back on measure eighteen, and the two men rise on measure twenty-two, after a short lecture.

At this point the men make a bridge under which the women pass, followed by the four couples, so that the last one comes through just as the singing ends. The men then join the women on the final chords.

SCENERY AND COSTUMES

The action takes place in Germany about 1750, suggesting first-act costumes that the young Mozart might have known. The second act is costumed in Grecian robes, except for Ernest, the Notary, and Rudolph, who retain their first-act costumes, the Baroness, who is in a much fancier dress that fits the design of the fancy ball, and the retinue of the Prince. Ludwig compromises his Grecian costume by wearing a Louis XIV wig, a coat of mail, and leg pieces. The characters from Monte Carlo are dressed foppishly, and the men wear long wigs.

In the first act it is necessary to have several tables for the wedding breakfast, and the suggestion of a public square in the background. In the second act there is an elaborate Grand Ducal hall with a platform at the back in front of which curtains can be drawn, so that the entire chorus can be concealed without leaving the stage.

REVISING *The Grand Duke*

Because *The Grand Duke* is excessively long, of uneven quality, and poorly structured, I prepared, in collaboration with Roger Golde, a revised version for the Lyric Theatre Company production in 1962. This version attempted to solve a number of problems, and in these remarks I shall try to make clear what changes we made and why.

Two major structural flaws in the opera are immediately noticeable. One is that three of its most interesting characters virtually disappear in the second act. This, combined with the lack of the usual comic trio, which is almost always to be found about halfway through the second act of a Gilbert and Sullivan opera, suggested the use of the trio, "With wily brain," from *Utopia, Ltd.*\* Inasmuch as the three characters in question have in common the need to overthrow a despot and subsequently succeed in doing so, the interpolation seems felicitous. We found it desirable also to substitute the words *"coup d'état"* for "private plot." If this kind of transplant seems offensive to the tradition-oriented, they should bear in mind that Gilbert and Sullivan themselves set a precedent for the practice in *The Pirates of Penzance.* Unfortunately, in the present case, it was necessary to invent some dialogue to introduce the trio. The dialogue composed for the occasion follows, and permission is hereby granted to use it without application to the author:

RUDOLPH. If there's anything more distressing to an unusually sensitive digestion than a conspiracy, it's a wedding procession. What a devil of a lot they're bound to have spent on that. Why it's enough to bring *anyone* back to life. (*Seeing* ERNEST.) Hallo! Aren't you defunct?

ERNEST. Oh yes, I suppose I am. But it's not much good, you know. I feel terribly alive. My existence has become unendurable. My fiancée won't have me. She insists I'm too insubstantial for her.

RUDOLPH. Dear me. And mine seems to be making *me* less substantial by the moment. It's a devil of a thing, being defunct. But at least we shall be alive in a few hours.

ERNEST. Not at all. Haven't you heard? The act has been revived. We shan't be free to resume our responsibilities and marry whom we like until 1996. Can you wait?

RUDOLPH. No. No, I don't think I can wait. Why, I shan't have a pfennig left!

ERNEST. Nor I. There's only one thing to be done—defy the law and come to life again.

---
\* See pages 278–284.

RUDOLPH. Defy the law? Why I don't think my constitution could stand it.

(*Enter* NOTARY.)

NOTARY. When gentlemen are suffering the injustice of the law the customary thing is to retain an attorney.

RUDOLPH. For a fee?

NOTARY. A fee is always germane to the issue.

RUDOLPH. (*To* ERNEST.) You'll pay the the fee, of course.

ERNEST. I'll do anything if I can only come to life and marry Julia.

RUDOLPH. The fee will be paid.

NOTARY. Very good. (*Gestures to them to gather round him.*) Why break the law? Why not simply get around it?

ERNEST. What do you mean?

NOTARY. It's quite customary. Everybody does it. Nobody could afford to pay taxes otherwise.

RUDOLPH. Dear me. I wish I'd known. Think of what I've squandered not knowing that.

NOTARY. What is required for the occasion is a loophole.

BOTH. A loophole?

NOTARY. Something in the law not understood by the *hoi polloi*, which may perhaps give the two of you an advantage over the uninitiated.

RUDOLPH. It sounds very shady. Are you sure it's all right?

NOTARY. It's always done.

RUDOLPH. Well, if it's always done—Very good, I consent.

NOTARY. Together we must evolve a *coup d'état*. Something to make the blood boil. But subtle. With just the right touch of intellectual drollery.

RUDOLPH. But all perfectly legal?

NOTARY. Oh yes—perfectly legal.

Our next concern was that the chorus has no moment of glory similar to "Hail, Poetry" in *Pirates,* the madrigal in *Ruddigore,* or "Eagle high" in *Utopia.* To provide them with such a spotlight, a quartet from *Haddon Hall,* a Sullivan opera unlikely to be revived despite some fine music, was introduced with a few word changes. This quartet with its revised text is reprinted on pages 284–290.

Examining the dialogue, I found a number of lapses of taste and made several judicious cuts here and there. My main concern, however, was the extremely unsatisfactory dialogue that concludes the opera. Just after seeing the American Savoyards production of 1961, I had composed a new ending that I felt extended the improbability, absurdity, and complexity of the opera while avoiding the vulgarity of the original. I was also concerned to keep Rudolph and the Baroness together, as they seemed such an appropriate couple that separating them was quite a jarring note. My revised ending follows:

LUDWIG. Not a bit of it! I've revived the law for another century!

RUDOLPH. You didn't revive it! You couldn't revive it! You—you are an impostor, sir—a tuppenny rogue, sir! You—you never were, and in all human probability never will be—Grand Duke of Pfennig Anything!

ALL. What!!!

RUDOLPH. Never—never—never! (*Aside*) Oh, my internal economy!

LUDWIG. That's absurd, you know. I fought the Grand Duke. He drew a King, and I drew an Ace. He perished in inconceivable agonies on the spot. Now, as that's settled, we'll go on with the wedding.

NOTARY. I'm afraid there's been a little mistake. Actuated by a sense of responsibility toward the National Exchequer, I have consulted the Act that regulates Statutory Duels (which at this moment is on the point of expiration), and I find it is expressly laid down that the Ace shall count invariably as lowest!

ALL. As lowest!

NOTARY. Furthermore, extensive research into the history of the Grand Duchy of Pfennig Halbpfennig has revealed the interesting fact that it is in reality *two* independent Grand Duchies, whose dividing line runs inconveniently enough through the center of the public square. The monarchs of these two Grand Duchies are hereditary enemies. One hundred years ago, the monarch of one of them illegally abdicated in his youth in order to become the manager of a theatrical company, thereby creating the erroneous impression of having forfeited his own Grand Duchy to the other. The gentleman of whom I speak is the great grandsire of the man who stands before you now as Ernest Dummkopf. By a series of legal technicalities far beyond the grasp of the ordinary layman, it is he who was betrothed in infancy to the Princess of Monte Carlo, not the Grand Duke Rudolph.

LUDWIG. Dear me—how dreadfully careless of everyone.

ERNEST. Well, Rudolph, it seems we are at war.

RUDOLPH. Oh, it's too much. I shall expire of nervous indigestion.

ERNEST. Then why not bury the hatchet and rule jointly?

RUDOLPH. That would be capital, provided neither of us spends too much.

ERNEST. Oh, I'm afraid that's quite impossible. I'm a frightful spendthrift. One must always have a grand spectacle, you know.

RUDOLPH. Then I don't know what's to be done.

PRINCE. Allow me as an old Machiavellian to offer a suggestion. Simply appoint me as your Chancellor of the Exchequer. I shan't be returning home—too many former creditors about. Whatever this gentleman spends (on grand spectacles and the like) of this gentleman's fortune can always be replenished by operating under government auspices a corrupt house of gambling.

ERNEST. That does sound like a perfect suggestion all round. Except that it deprives me of my Julia.

PRINCESS. Oh, you needn't bother about *that*. I can quite assure you, my love, that you'll find *me* ever so much more attractive.

ERNEST. Are you quite sure?

PRINCESS. I am certain of it, and I have a widespread reputation for never being wrong.

ERNEST. Then it's a bargain. I love refined self-assurance.

JULIA. Ah, then I am, after all, to be left without either a husband or a part.

PRINCE. My dear, I'm quite certain that I can offer you a part, to say nothing of a husband into the bargain. It's rather a dramatic role, actually. As the corrupt power behind the two thrones of Pfennig Halbpfennig, I shall be in need of a jealous and fiery-tempered little bride to impede my reasoning powers and political judgment.

JULIA. Then I *shall* have the leading role after all—the brains behind the brains behind the brains that rule the Grand Duchy. And much admired for my splendid character.

RUDOLPH. Then I suppose we may all be married and live happily and cheaply ever after. How say you, my love?

BARONESS. It sounds delightfully economical.

Having now extended the length of the opera by about fifteen minutes, we attempted to remove as nearly as we could forty-five minutes from the total, as the New York production had seemed half an hour too long. (Even when our production was mounted and proved highly successful, some people said they found its length excessive by about twenty minutes.) Examining the first act we found one entire song that could go. Delightful in some ways as "Were I a king" is, it does not contribute to the advancement of the plot. Furthermore, the awkwardness of some of its lines is quite noticeable, and it helps establish the impression quite early that Gilbert's humor in this opera is too often forced. Next we took out the second verse of "Strange the views." We also took out the second verse of the following quintet, except that the Notary's and Ludwig's solo words for that verse were attached to the corresponding but different music of the third verse. This replaced a line of the Notary's that suggests a plot device never developed, although it is a thin echo of an also undeveloped situation in *Utopia, Ltd.*

Our remaining cuts in the first act were confined to the finale, which was considerably reduced in length. Some of the music we took out is quite beautiful, but the cumulative effect of its beauty produces a cloying effect that interferes with the enjoyment of the second act. We attempted to make the finale produce a greater impression of variety, even though this meant leaving in some undistinguished things and taking out some rather good ones. We cut from the last two and a half measures on p. 74 up to the last note on p. 77. This made Rudolph's exit occur earlier—right at the beginning of the cut. We then omitted Ludwig's song beginning on p. 79. Some objection was raised to making this cut on the grounds that the audience would not be informed of Ludwig's intention of reviving the law. Since the audience can't follow the plot anyway without an explanation in the program (as is often observed by reviewers), this objection seems rather unimportant. Furthermore, Ludwig mentions the fact several times in the second act, so that any possible confusion will be cleared up. In any event, the song seems in performance like just another not very good patter song.

A great deal of repetitiveness from Julia was eliminated by cutting from most of the last measure on p. 82 to the second measure on p. 86, interpolating a measure of rest. Although this eliminates some interesting writing by Sullivan, it eliminates nothing that has dramatic value. Again, the last two and a half measures on p. 87 were removed, and from there to the third measure on p. 90. This took out a charming but dramatically uninteresting duet for Julia and Lisa, and was our last cut from the finale.

In Act Two we took out the second verse of the patter song, "At the outset I may mention." The Baroness' champagne aria was removed because of its inferior music and its failure to forward the action. All of No. 22 except its introduction was omitted, the introduction serving to provide entrance music for the Herald. No. 24 was cut, up to the *piu vivace*. The Roulette Song was reluctantly omitted, even though it is one of the best numbers in the show, on the grounds that it represents a slowing down of the action at a time when the plot should be working itself out as quickly as possible. The same can be said with even greater emphasis of the song for Rudolph (No. 28a).

It may be that even more substantial cuts should be made in order to make the opera really palatable on first exposure. One must be philosophical about the process of cutting. In the case of a proven masterpiece it is inexcusable. But when one is attempting to ressurrect a work that most writers agree has passed mercifully into oblivion, it is necessary to be somewhat heartless. If you find that you are forced to take out a great many things you would like to leave in, then arrange for a second intermission, after which you can perform those numbers for the benefit of anyone who would like to stay and hear them. This is simply a way of having one's cake and eating it too. Another way out is to do what the Lyric Theatre Company did—perform the work in a cut version and record it absolutely complete. A recording, unlike a performance, has the virtue that one can lift up the phonograph needle whenever one chooses and do one's own cutting.

# Chapter XVIII

# OTHER OPERAS

A company that has been producing Gilbert and Sullivan for many years may decide upon occasion to get a little into uncharted territory. A number of other works more or less in the same vein are worth considering. If you would like to look into some of them, Mark Lubbock's *Complete Book of Light Opera* (see Bibliography) is a good place to start. Both Gilbert and Sullivan wrote a number of works with other collaborators, and those collaborators in turn produced some delightful works. It would be interesting, for example, to see a production of *Dorothy,* which ran a year longer than *The Mikado,* and at about the same time. Its composer, Alfred Cellier, proved himself amply talented in his score for *The Mountebanks* with Gilbert. In recent years the English have begun to rediscover some of the works of Edward German, Sullivan's successor at the Savoy, and the composer who completed the latter's last unfinished work. Recordings of *Merrie England* and *Tom Jones* have proved the music and orchestration of those works to be first rate, although their words are quite inferior.

In this chapter we shall give brief attention to four works that are likely to be rather frequently revived: *Engaged, Cox and Box, Ages Ago,* and *The Mountebanks.*

*Engaged* is amply explained in the following review by Howard Klein, which appeared in *The New York Times* on April 24, 1965:

The Village Light Opera Group, Ltd., an amateur company founded in 1935 and dedicated to the operas of Gilbert and Sullivan, gave the United States premiere last night of a possible addition to the canon, "Engaged! or Cheviot's Choice."

The performance, at the Fashion Institute of Technology Theater, follows the premiere at the Bristol Opera School in Britain by three years. And while there was much to admire, enjoy and be amused at in the three-act comedy, it is too soon to pass final judgment.

It is authentic in that the dialogue is all Gilbert, from the play "Engaged"—which had no music in 1877 and was unsuccessful. And the music is almost all by Sullivan. It was stitched together by two Savoyard specialists, George Rowell and Kenneth Mobbs, after the copyright on Gilbert's work expired in 1961.

Mr. Rowell has done well with the zany plot. Cheviot, the amorous hero, falls in love merely by looking at a pretty face. He proposes to three women, and the complications develop.

Add a tippling uncle, a Svengali, a blustering major, a bevy of Scottish lassies and you have the ingredients. They have been well stirred in the treatment. The topical banter still retains its point, a source of continuing delight with Gilbert's books, and in all it seems a workable show.

Most of the music is Sullivan's, and the overture "di ballo" introduces the work. Arias and ensembles have been culled from the lesser-known operas "The Grand Duke," "The Sorcerer," "Utopia Limited," and there is one of the two surviving numbers of the lost opera, "Thespis." Other sources have been Sullivan scores with other librettists, such as "Haddon Hall," "The Chieftain," "The Rose of Persia" and "The Sapphire Necklace."

And Mr. Mobbs has contributed music that is a fair stylistic copy of Sullivan.

The canon of 14 operas contains 10 sure-fire masterpieces of undeniable charm and lightness. What "Engaged!" lacks is the economy of the originals. Its 22 numbers overload the three acts, pleasing though they are. And in the opening solos and duets from "Haddon Hall," which Sullivan wrote to Sidney Grundy's words, the music's specific gravity is heavier than it should be . . .

*Cox and Box* predates Sullivan's collaborations with Gilbert and is musically very fresh and lively. Its libretto by F. C. Burnand, is simply Maddison Morton's most popular farce, *Box and Cox* with songs and a Mrs. Bouncer transformed into Sergeant Bouncer. Morton's play was in turn derived from a French farce, so the work had several chances to prove itself in the theatre.

The situation is that Sergeant Bouncer has let one of his rooms by day to one character and by night to the other, as the two lodgers are so employed that they never occupy the room at the same time. As luck would have it, one of them gets the day off, and so they meet. In the end all is well because it turns out that they are long-lost brothers.

There are three characters and no chorus. Box is a tenor, and all three singers must be rather accomplished musicians. The work exists in two forms. One, published by Boosey and Hawks, represents the current D'Oyly Carte acting version, and is available. The other, published by Oliver Ditson, is recently out of print, is the original version, and is about twice as long. Anyone ambitious enough to produce the work might wish to work out a compromise between the two.

A work that will appeal to anyone who has produced *Cox and Box* and is looking for rather similar material is *Ages Ago*. The following article by Raymond Ericson, which appeared in *The New York Times* on April 25, 1971, should provide the necessary information:

Remember Strephon in Gilbert and Sullivan's "Iolanthe"? Half-fairy and half-mortal, he could only squeeze halfway through a keyhole. Remember Frederick in the same pair's "The Pirates of Penzance"? Because he was born on Feb. 29, he was going to be apprenticed to the pirates till he was 84 —his 21st birthday. Or think of "Ruddi-gore," in which portraits step down from their frames to converse and sing.

Similar notions turn up in one of Gilbert's earliest librettos, written not in collaboration with Sullivan but with a composer named Frederic Clay. The work in question is "Ages Ago," which had its first performance on Nov. 22, 1869, at Thomas German Reed's Gallery of Illustration in London. (A "gallery" where "gatherings" could watch "illustrations" was one way the more proper Victorians could get to the theater and keep their consciences clear.) With its premiere, "Ages Ago" was joining for a double bill an already very successful entertainment called "Cox and Box." This was the work of Sullivan and a writer named Francis Burnand. The conjunction of the two pieces also brought about the meeting of Gilbert and Sullivan, although their collaboration was not to begin for several more years.

As Frederick S. Roffman writes, "Ages Ago" is now only a footnote in theatrical history books, but this one stimulated Roffman to gather together a group of young performers and record the little musical. The two-disk album is available by mail from him, 280 Riverside Drive, New York, N.Y. 10025. The price, including postage in this country, is $7.98, plus sales tax for New York residents.

As a relatively small musical piece for the theatre. "Ages Ago" has scarcely any plot. It has the kind of situation Walter Kerr was describing with approval in *The Times* recently, one that is loose enough to develop at any point a comic sequence or a good song. It is the amusing central scene of the operetta that makes it very agreeable to listen to today.

The story is about a castle that has been uninhabited for 500 years. It had belonged to one Sir Roger de Bohun, who sold it to a "fiend" for money to support his dissolute life. When he died without heir, on July, 1369, it accordingly would not come into anyone's possession for another 100 years. Title to the castle was acquired by Lady Maud de Bohun in 1469. She died in 1490, also without heir, and the castle remained empty again until 1569. The title owner this time was Sir Cecil Blount. The sequence continued with Lord Carnaby Poppytop in 1669 and Dame Cherry Maybud in 1769.

The operetta opens in 1869, with Sir Ebenezer Tare, an alderman and tallow chandler recently moved into the castle without a by-your-leave. He has a niece, Rosa, in love with Columbus Hebblethwaite, a young visitor. Also residing with them is Mrs. MacMotherly, a housekeeper, who makes dire predictions about Tare, including the loss of the castle. It turns out that Hebblethwaite will come into the title, it being the right year, and everyone will settle down together happily in the castle.

If you can't understand the plot, forget it. For some unexplained reason, the portraits of Lady Maud, Sir Cecil, Lord Carnaby and Dame Cherry adorn the walls of the castle. They were painted respectively by Leonardo da Vinci, Michelangelo, Sir Godfrey Kneller and Sir Joshua Reynolds. There is also on the wall a "wretched daub" of one Brown, Tare's "maternal grandfather."

At night, the portraits come out of their frames and meet each other. This is where Gilbert has his fun, fooling around in his elegant and straight-faced way with the complications of the people's ages as they are in the portraits and their value in their painted state. The people are related, so that a grandson can sing "my grandmama is 17," and "grandmama" can flirt with a man a century younger with propriety.

One man threatens to send the portrait of another to the National Gallery to hang among sham Rubenses, where he will be ignored and never bought. "But I'm genuine!" is the retort. "I'll have you restored," he is told, so that no one will recognize the artist. Brown, whose portrait is the "wretched daub," is asked to descend from his frame. "I can't come down," he says, "because I'm only a half-length."

It is a genially funny scene in the best Gilbert style. The songs and ensembles that run through the operetta are pleasant rather than striking. The ensembles, at least, are written with the skill that came by heritage and experience to most well-trained English composers. There is a "good night" quartet in the style of the one from Flotow's "Martha," and it is quite charming. Gilbert's lyrics are not as accomplished as they were to become, but those of "I Live, I Breathe," sung by Lady Maud when she first descends from her picture, manipulate the words amusingly.

Gilbert and Clay went on to other collaborations besides "Ages Ago." One of them, "Princess Toto" (1876), was extraordinarily popular in its day, both in England and America. Today, Clay's only claim to fame is a song, "I'll Sing Thee Songs of Araby," which was the delight of parlor musicales well into the 20th century.

The recorded performance is only fair, but it will do under the circumstances. The dialogue comes off with more style than the music. The men sing well enough, but only Nell Evans among the women—she is Dame Cherry—handles her numbers smoothly. At the end of the recording she sings "I'll Sing Thee Songs of Araby."

The accompaniment is played on instruments for which it was originally written—piano, harmonium and harp. Unfortunately, the harmonium used here is electronic, and it really grates on the ear, besides occasionally obscuring the sung text.

*The Mountebanks* was the lozenge plot that Sullivan so often rejected, and that Cellier finally composed. It was written during the period of estrangement between Gilbert and Sullivan, and Cellier died two weeks before it opened, so that the final touches were not put on the music, and no overture was composed. Nevertheless, the score is outstanding and will appeal to some people who find Sullivan's music a bit thin. (One of its numbers, deleted from the second edition, is reproduced on pages 291–293.)

Bernard Shaw reviewed the original production, and some of his remarks are worth quoting:

Need I say more in justification of The Mountebanks . . . than that it made me laugh heartily several times. The brigands whose motto is "Heroism without Risk"; the alchemist who pays his bills with halfpence, accompanied by a written undertaking to transmute them into gold as soon as he discovers the philosopher's stone; the girl who thinks herself plain and her lover handsome, but has to confess to him that she finds herself in a hopeless minority on both subjects; the unsuccessful Hamlet who so dreads to be ever laughed at by the public that he has turned clown; the mountebank who, pretending that he has swallowed poison and is in the agonies of stomach-ache, is forced to swallow an elixir which has the magic property of turning all pretences into realities; the transformation by this same elixir of the brigands into monks, the clown and columbine into automatic clockwork figures, the village belle into an old hag, the heroine into a lunatic, and the rustic hero into an old duke:—if all these went for no more than one laugh apiece, the opera would come out ahead of many of its rivals in point of fun. With them, however, the merit of the piece stops: every line that goes a step further is a line to the bad.

*     *     *

Cellier's strength never lay in the working up of finales; but this one flickers and goes out so suddenly that one can almost hear ghostly muffled drums in the orchestra. The rest of the score is what might have been expected from the composer—that is, better than the occasion required it to be; and in this very superfluity of musical conscience one recognizes his want of the tact which has saved Sir Arthur Sullivan from ever wasting musical sentiment on Mr. Gilbert. Musicians will not think the worse of Cellier for this. There are many points, such as the graceful formalism of the little overture,[1] with its

orthodox "working out," and the many tender elaborations in the accompaniments, all done from sheer love of music, which will shield Cellier more effectually than his new dignity of *de mortuis* from that reproach of musical unscrupulousness which qualifies every musician's appreciation of the Sullivanesque *savoir-faire*.[2]

It must be confessed that *The Mountebanks,* even when substantially cut, does not hold an audience very well. Its music is not as appealing on first hearing as it is after repeated hearings, and it lacks the sparkle of Gilbert's other libretti. It is nevertheless worth considering for production because it is so rewarding to work on. Its opportunities for the chorus are as good as those in any of the G&S works, and a great deal of fun to sing. The men will have enormous fun playing brigands who become monks.

The opera was produced recently by the Chamber Opera Players of New York and the Lyric Theatre Company of Washington. It was the considered opinion of most members of both groups that the opera had been one of the most rewarding they had ever worked on.

---

[1] Transplanted for the occasion by the conductor, Ivan Caryll, from Cellier's Suite Symphonique, composed twenty years earlier.—Ed.

[2] Eric Bentley, ed., *Shaw on Music*. New York, Anchor Books, 1955, pp. 209, 211–212.

Chapter XIX

# FORMING A COMPANY

Let us suppose that you, the reader, have decided to form a company for the presentation of a Gilbert and Sullivan opera. You have had no previous experience in production, or perhaps in theatre or music of any kind, but you have a strong desire to mount a particular favorite of yours for the benefit of an audience. How will you begin?

The first thing to do is think in terms of schedules. Before you have asked a single other person to join with you in this venture you will need to have formed some idea of what you are going to do when. If you are planning to rehearse about three nights a week, you should allow about two months between the first rehearsal and the opening performance. Schedule yourself, then, a two-month period of time not more than a month or so from the time you intend to take the first step toward forming your company.

Your next step is to determine where you might hold your rehearsals and performances. The best company in the world would fall apart immediately if there were no place to rehearse, so don't try to sign anyone up for your venture until you have determined where it might take place. For rehearsals, look for a community center, a church basement, or a school. Many churches have space that they would be glad to have used by the community for such a project as yours, and you might be able to obtain the space at no cost. Most likely you will have to pay a few dollars a month to hire a janitor to clean up after you and lock up after you are finished. A performance hall will provide more of a challenge, but if you are willing to keep things on a modest scale at first, you can probably find a church or community center with a small stage that can be used at very little expense. A large, well-equipped stage will probably cost you $200 or $300 a performance, and you might be unwise to commit yourself to that on your first production.

After you have lined up the facilities that you will need, you must find a musical director and a stage director. Anyone who has directed a church choir or any kind of group singing that involves teaching people to sing in harmony and being aware when they are doing so incorrectly should be capable of handling the musical part of musical direction. But there is another factor to consider. Some musicians are rather temperamental and impatient when things are not done exactly right. If you have a volunteer chorus of well-meaning but untalented people and a musical director who thinks of himself as another Toscanini, you are going to lose either your chorus or your musical director, or both. A pleasant manner in handling people is as important in keeping an amateur company together as is the relevant artistic talent.

There are no special qualifications for the stage director. Whereas a musical director must have enough experience to follow the score, a stage director need have had no previous experience. Furthermore, his temperament is not nearly so important, since once a chorus have made the investment of time to learn the music, they will take a good deal of punishment while being told what to do on the stage. Furthermore, if the music falls apart, the performance is a disaster, whereas if the staging falls apart it is merely undramatic. And if the staging director is not good, the leading performers may very well compensate for his inadequacies.

These remarks are not intended to encourage

a lack of desire for quality, but rather to indicate that the absolute minimum requirements are not as high as one might think. Naturally you will want the best musical and stage directors you can find.

Sometimes the music and staging are done by the same person, but this is not often desirable, as the person who performs in this manner is likely to slight one in favor of the other, few persons being equally well trained in both music and drama. It is even possible that a single person could direct the music and staging and appear onstage as one of the performers. This presupposes that the chorus have been well-enough trained so as not to need direction during the performance, a difficult task that, nevertheless, has on occasion been effectively achieved.

If the performance is to be a large one with orchestra, the musical director may be divisible into two, one of whom prepares the chorus, the other preparing the orchestra and conducting the dress rehearsals and performances. There may also be an assistant to each of these directors, making a possible total of four.

The stage director may become five or more people. One does the dialogue, another stages the chorus, another stages the ensemble numbers, another provides the choreography, and a fifth comes in during the last few rehearsals and polishes up the production, tying together the ideas of the other four. An unusual degree of compatibility would be necessary in such a situation, but it has been done on occasion and worked very well.

You will probably, however, begin with only one of each. Your first task is to sit down with the two of them and work out a rehearsal schedule and performance dates. This you will have to refer to when you set out to find other people for your company, so that you can make sure they will be available when you need them.

You now have an important decision to make. Do you wish to limit the group that will perform on the stage in any way? Is the production to be produced by a club of some sort that is already in existence? Do you wish to have only people of a certain age group in your company? In other words, the range of possible performers is something that you must decide. If you would like to have anyone in your company who wishes to join it, you have created for yourself the possibility of a most excellent production.

If you have never produced a show before, there is one way you will not be able to succeed in getting a cast, and that is by announcing tryouts and then sitting back and waiting. You are going to have to go out and get people. Keep in mind at this stage that the greatest single factor in determining the quality of your production will be the quality of your leading performers. The better the performers you can get, the more successful you are likely to be.

You will find that people of talent who are willing to take part in an amateur production will be attracted to a particular production if they know that others whose talents they respect will be in it also. The trick is to get one outstanding performer into your company with the offer of a juicy part. You can then attract other performers of similar abilities. As your potential cast grows, you will find it easier to get other people that you need. This means of course that you are guilty of precasting, to which some of your company will strenuously object. Remember, however, that open tryouts are a luxury that only an established company can afford, and that precasting is indulged in by all professional companies as well as many amateur ones. It becomes unwise only if you limit the group that may perform your production; for example, if it is a school production. In that case there is no need to precast, and the roles should go to those who try out most effectively.

While you are lining up your leading performers, you also need to be getting together a chorus. It helps if you are a member of some existing organization, many of whose members are possible members of your chorus. You can persuade your friends among those people to form a nucleus, which will grow as they bring their friends.

Up to the time of your first rehearsal, don't worry too much about anything except getting the performers committed. If you are wise, you will have spent a year or two previous to your own production visiting performances in your community so that you have in mind lots of people you can persuade to be in your production. Save programs and, when you are ready, call the people whose talents you respect. If you have found a contralto you think would make a good Katisha, call her and ask her to join your company. If she can't do so, ask her to recommend someone who is as good as she is. She'll be flattered and want to help you. You'll probably end up with two or three names, each of whom might be good for two or three more. Don't hesitate to ask her also who might make a good Ko-Ko. The big secret, you'll find, in getting your production going, is to get other people to do as much of the thinking and legwork for you as possible. Your job is to coordinate their efforts.

Once rehearsals are under way it's time to start thinking about other things. You'll want people working on costumes and scenery, and others working on publicity. There will be other kinds of problems, too, personality problems that can't be foreseen, that you will have to handle. Somebody that you are committed to may turn out to be incompetent and you'll have to get rid of him. Someone else may throw a wild party for the entire company after rehearsal one night, a party that is raided by the police and that forces you to think about some kind of social regulations for your group, particularly if minors are involved. Someone else on whom you are dependent will be unexpectedly called out of town and will have to be replaced. One of the most exciting features of your job is going to be in the amount of ingenuity called for in solving unanticipated problems.

One special problem is likely to be in providing piano accompaniment at rehearsals. If you are extremely lucky you will find someone able to play the music and willing to attend all the rehearsals. More likely, you will have to find several accompanists and double-check to see that each rehearsal is covered. You should have your musical director audition each accompanist to be sure that he can play the music well enough, as much of it is quite difficult.

As time goes on, and the momentum toward approaching performances grows, you will probably find that new people show up from time to time and are helpful in performing the various tasks that are needed. Cultivate these people and discover what they can do. They will prove valuable to you, particularly if you plan to go on to more productions.

A word or two now about your own personality. People will tend to want to work with you if you are pleasant and not too autocratic. There will be times when you wish things were done differently, but you will have to be careful how you bring about changes. Surreptitiously repainting a set will cost you your set designer, as reblocking a scene will cost you your stage director. The art of making suggestions for improvement under the guise of compliments is something you will need to cultivate. If you are having trouble in this area, read Dale Carnegie's *How to Win Friends and Influence People*. At the same time that you are not autocratic, you will need to be decisive. People want their questions answered, they don't want to be told, "I'll tell you in a week or so." It is better to make a firm decision that turns out to be wrong than to create the impression that you don't know what you are doing.

Another kind of problem you will have to deal with is money. It will cost something to put on your production, probably more than you anticipate. Hopefully you will get most or all of this back by selling tickets, and of course many of the tickets can be sold in advance. You will save some money by asking the performers to pay for their own scores. You might even ask them to pay the expense of their costumes. And some groups charge a membership fee large enough to pay the cost of production.

It may be that you will be able to persuade someone to underwrite your production. This will be easier if you legally organize your company as a nonprofit corporation, which means that all contributions made to it are tax-deductible. If a lawyer is willing to contribute his services, you may be able to have this done for about $40. Otherwise it might cost as much as $200.

Another way out of money problems is to deal with other organizations that act as sponsors. The simplest way is to get some group to agree to pay all your expenses in exchange for all your profits. This is fine if the profits are not too great, or if a great deal of money isn't lost. If the production is a great hit, and the sponsoring organization makes a disproportionate amount of money for their efforts, the members of your company will be bitter about the results. If you lose a lot of money, your sponsor will not be interested next time.

A more equitable plan might be to sell your production for a flat fee that will cover your expenses and leave a little to start the next production. The group that has bought it then tries to sell the tickets and make as much money as possible.

In general your group will work better if money problems are not always hanging over them, and so will you. If you can get yourself a financial manager who can responsibly solve the money problems in consultation with you, you will be better able to devote your attention to the artistic problems.

This chapter is necessarily brief because there is no way to anticipate all the various problems that will befall you. The only way to learn to be a producer is to produce. If you have a clear picture in mind of what you would like to achieve and can form realistic plans on paper for achieving it, you should have a rewarding experience. It will take a great deal of your time and energy, however, and like a mother with a young child you will have to be available whenever you are needed. As a matter of fact, your company will be your child.

At this point I should like to reminisce about some of the crises that occurred during various productions by the Lyric Theatre Company. The same things will not happen to you, but if you know what happened to me, you will have a better idea what sort of thing to expect.

Just before a production of *Iolanthe*, the stage crew were setting up the lights. In the auditorium we had rented, the lighting equipment was rather old. About four hours before the performance, a whole bank of lights suddenly fell onto the stage. Had these fallen during the performance, they might easily have killed several of the performers.

A production of *The Sorcerer* was threatened with being closed the morning of the first performance because some of the stage crew had got water paint on a piano bench belonging to a temperamental but powerful member of the organization from which the hall was rented. It was necessary for several members of the production staff to spend two or three hours consoling him in order that we might perform that night.

The conductor of a production of *Princess Ida* happened to be a member of the musicians' union. Forty-eight hours before the show opened he was told that if he conducted the orchestra, made up of nonunion people, he would lose his union status, on which he depended for his income. This was Lyric's second production of *Princess Ida*. The conductor of the first production, Michael Greenebaum, was then living in Chicago. A long-distance call persuaded him to fly to Washington and conduct the first performance after exactly twenty minutes of rehearsal with the orchestra.

A hall that was rented for a production of *Ruddigore* was not ordinarily used for public performances. The commotion involved in getting the company in and out of dress rehearsals was such that a man who lived in that neighborhood attempted to get an injunction against the performances. The father of a member of the company was a highly paid lawyer, and he spent an entire day fighting the injunction, thereby donating several hundred dollars' worth of legal services to the company.

The man who had been cast in the role of Paramount in *Utopia, Ltd.* proved unable to perform his role well enough to make possible a successful production, and it was necessary to fire him. His wife was doing an excellent job with the role of Zara, but she understandably resigned her role. Six days before the performance it was necessary to recast four of the roles, filling the leading parts by moving people up through the ranks of the cast.

It became necessary to change from one opera to another after the designer had completed plans for all the sets and costumes and gone off to Saudi Arabia, planning to return two or three days before opening night to put the finishing touches on everything. It was impossible to reach him by phone and necessary to airmail him a copy of the new opera and to work from the directions that he airmailed back. Work on the second-act setting was begun the morning of the opening performance.

Music for *The Grand Duke* was shipped from England during a dockyard strike. As the strike was likely to continue for months, it was necessary to do something before it ended. A manager of the shipping company promised to look for the music in a pile of packages two miles long. Strangely enough he found it. It was then necessary for a former member of our company, now a New York district attorney, to ride through the picket lines in a police car in order to get the music.

You can see that being a light-opera producer can make you feel at times as if you were James Bond. If you don't enjoy the thought of trying to deal with apparently insoluble crises, you'd better keep your productions on a small scale. If you do, you're in for lots of thrills and chills.

# Chapter XX

# THE PRODUCTION STAFF

In this chapter we shall consider some of the specific duties of each member of the production staff. We are assuming a company that is completely self-contained. If the opera is being produced in a school or some other separately existing organization, it is possible that some of those duties will be simplified or eliminated.

## THE PRODUCER

Considered in the previous chapter to some extent, the producer's duties include coordinating the entire production and otherwise doing anything he can't find someone else to do. This may mean that he finds himself building the set at the last moment or ordering flowers for the leading lady, but the wise producer will delegate as many responsibilities as he possibly can. As a gardener uses seeds, a producer uses people. He creates the production largely through the people he selects rather than through telling them specifically what to do. The good producer will respect the integrity of his artists and give them free rein in developing their ideas.

## THE CONDUCTOR

As overall musical director, he is responsible for the total musical effect of the production. He must secure the music and the orchestra parts, check them to see that they are adequate for his purposes, plan the rehearsal schedule for leads, chorus, and orchestra as separate entities, and work carefully with the director to make sure that staging and musical values do not conflict. He should be in charge of the final rehearsals and make the final decision when there is a disagreement between people,

unless the producer has reserved the right to final authority.

## THE STAGE DIRECTOR

He is responsible for the total dramatic effect of the production, but in most cases must defer to the conductor if there is a disagreement. Seldom, however, will the interests of these two be in conflict, especially if they are sensitive to each other's work.

The stage director confers with the designer so that sets and costumes will conform to the needs of the staging. He should have the power to reject design ideas that do not support the effects he is trying to achieve.

He is responsible for the quality of any of the staging he delegates, such as the choreography, and he should make clear to any of his subordinates just how much he reserves the right to re-do what they have done.

He should be aware that there are at least three kinds of directing that he must do: dialogue, ensemble numbers, and chorus staging. These require different sorts of talent and must be handled differently in rehearsal. That is why he may prefer to delegate some of the staging to others.

## THE DESIGNER

There actually may be two designers, one for sets and one for costumes. If there are, they should work out the color schemes together and keep in constant touch as their work progresses. Not only must the designer produce guidelines on paper that will help others execute his ideas, he must be constantly available to see that those ideas are being carried out properly. He may or may not actually do any of the painting of the set or making of the costumes. He should also confer with the technical and lighting directors to see that they agree with and are able to support his ideas.

### THE TECHNICAL DIRECTOR

He must oversee the building of the sets, translating the designer's ideas into accurate blueprints and then building or supervising the building of platforms, flats, and other constructed materials. He may or may not be the same as the lighting director.

### THE LIGHTING DIRECTOR

He designs the lighting. This involves hanging, aiming, and gelling the lights and working out a detailed lighting plot to guide the changes that take place during performance. He must hold special lighting rehearsals before the dress rehearsal, training his crew so that during the performance they will know exactly what to do. It should be possible for him to solve his problems without ever actually interrupting a rehearsal at which performers are present.

### THE COSTUMER

Working from the designs provided for him, the costumer supervises the making of the costumes, buys the materials, and makes the necessary measurements. It is hepful for him to have a standard form that must be filled out for each performer, giving all the necessary measurements. If the costumes are rented, he acts as liaison between the company and the rental agency.

### THE PUBLICITY DIRECTOR

His job is to see that people know about the production. He is responsible to the business manager, both in terms of how much he can spend and of how well he is doing in assuring the production a large audience. He should concentrate his efforts primarily on trying to get newspaper coverage. This means contacting the newspapers repeatedly, beginning at least a month in advance of production time. He should get to know people on the theatre page, the society page, and at the city desk. He should find as many varied angles as possible for presenting the story of the production. A major source of publicity can be getting interviews with various members of the cast and production staff, which will appear in the society columns. He should be able to get some human-interest stories from the city desk. The theatre page will carry more than one story on the production if it receives a variety of story angles through press releases. It should be possible to get one large city newspaper to do ten or fifteen stories on various aspects of the production if the publicity director handles his work imaginatively.

He should make sure that the production is listed in publications that carry calendars of events around town. Many of these publications are only peripherally related to the theatre.

He should get public service announcements (which are available free) from the local radio stations, particularly those that specialize in classical music. He should arrange interviews with radio personalities for members of the production staff. It may even be possible to get some television interviews.

He should see to it that posters are distributed in public places, particularly food stores, where they will be seen by large numbers of people. A well-designed poster can draw a large crowd, a poorly designed one may actually keep people away.

Finally, he should see that tickets are easily available from as many sources as possible.

### THE STAGE MANAGER

It is his job to manage the backstage elements of the production during dress rehearsals and performances. He makes certain that people are ready in time for their entrances, keeps the backstage area properly cleared, indicates when the performers are ready to begin the act, checks the stage before the curtain rises each time to make certain that everything is in place, and particularly that the floor is clear so that nothing will cause dancers to slip or stumble. He is also on the lookout for any emergency, and in the event of one, the entire company must obey his orders. Emergencies include such things as illness or accident among the cast, the outbreak of fire backstage, or something falling from the fly gallery. For this reason it is well to impress the cast with the fact that the stage manager must be obeyed instantly and without thought on their part. This can be and has been a matter of life and death.

## THE PROPERTY MAN

This may seem like an unimportant job, but an imaginative property man can add a great deal to the success of a production. The properties used will either look as if they had been scraped together at the last minute or will make an impression because of their elegance. The property man should consult with the director about any properties that may be added as a result of his interpretation of the text. (For example, during the Nightmare Song in *Iolanthe* the Lord Chancellor might enter carrying a pillow and bed sheets.) He might even suggest additional possible properties. He should be aware that much of his work can occur at the last moment if, for example, during a dress rehearsal the director suddenly decides that all members of the chorus should have pink handkerchiefs.

## ORCHESTRA MANAGER

This can be a very demanding and somewhat thankless job. It is his responsibility to see that all the necessary parts are covered by competent players. This may mean holding auditions, if he is not experienced in playing in a variety of amateur orchestras so that he knows the quality of available people. He should be prepared for two major headaches: String players of adequate ability will be difficult to find, and orchestra players are somewhat prone to change their plans at the last minute and be unable to show up for a performance, unless they are paid. On the positive side, he will find that most amateur players are eager to participate whenever there is an opportunity, and he will not have to do much arm-twisting.

## BUSINESS MANAGER

It is his responsibility to see that the company does not get too far into debt. The business manager for a theatrical company cannot think the way a business manager for a more stable organization does. In the heat of production it is seldom possible to anticipate exactly what may be needed, and installing a system of advance purchase orders can make artistic people extremely frustrated. The business manager should attempt to determine a reasonable budget for each important member of the staff and make the necessary money easily and promptly available within that budget. He should also be realistic about the fact that some budgets will be exceeded.

It is his duty to retain a cool head in the heat of production crisis. Certain kinds of discipline must be imposed on the company. It is reasonable to ask that receipts are always presented for items purchased, and that permission for purchasing must be granted by some few responsible people so that duplicate or unnecessary purchases are not made. It is also his duty to warn the company when they are in danger of really overspending. A business manager who keeps books well but does not assert himself at the right time can cause financial disaster. Just how far this can go is demonstrated by the example of one amateur company that went out of business when more than $200,000 in debt. Criminal proceedings are likely to result from such misjudgment.

## CHOREOGRAPHER

The choreographer is assigned by the stage director specific numbers involving dance. It is not the choreographer's responsibility to understand the opera as a whole. (Many choreographers are strangely obtuse when it comes to understanding dramatic action.) He should, however, understand the general style of the staging and know what is needed to make a particular number conform to that style. Breaches of style may mean that a number has to be redone by someone else.

## ASSISTANT CONDUCTOR

In the event that the conductor does not have time to prepare the entire production musically, he may wish to have the chorus and even some of the leads prepared by someone else. The assistant conductor should know what kind of tempi will be used in the performance and how much interpretive latitude he has, so that the chorus will not be confused by last-minute changes of interpretation.

## DIALOGUE DIRECTOR

This task may be effectively handled by someone with experience in directing plays who does not feel comfortable staging musical numbers. He should consult with the director about interpretations of character, and he should make sure that he understands where the characters must be placed at the end of a dialogue scene in order to begin the following musical number. Otherwise he should have a free hand so long as he conforms to the general style of the production.

## MASTER DIRECTOR

When the production is essentially finished and almost at the dress-rehearsal stage, particularly if it has been worked on by several staging directors, it can be effective to bring in a new director who has not previously worked on it to put on the finishing touches. The master director does not introduce new material or change what the other directors have done, but rather makes sure that the characters respond with sufficient vitality, that their posture is good, that they do not look at the floor, that they do look at the person who is singing, and so on. New life can be infused into a show by bringing in such a person when everyone is feeling a little tired and discouraged.

## MAKEUP SUPERVISOR

Too many operetta productions handle their makeup at the last minute with the result that everyone looks about the same, that the makeup does not go well with the lighting, and that it lacks subtlety. A person who carefully studies all the characters and determines in advance what makeup will be needed, and then carefully trains a makeup crew to apply it artistically, can add to the polish of the production. It is important for him to consult with the director and the lighting designer. He should also study photographs to determine what a good professional makeup job looks like. The makeup should be used enough in advance so that it can be changed to fit the lighting. This means purchasing it in sufficient quantity and variety about a week before the first dress rehearsal.

## PROGRAM DESIGNER

A production is enhanced by a good program. The audience will want to know the plot, for example. Other write-ups should include a critical comment on the opera, written by the staging or musical director, a biography of each of the principals, and a history of the company. It might be a good idea, also, to include a glossary of words used in the text whose meaning might be unclear to the audience. Some programs also contain a list of musical numbers.

The program designer may wish to organize a campaign to sell advertising in the program. This can pay for the expense of an elaborate program, perhaps add a little toward the expenses of the production, and help to make the community a little more aware of the fact that the production will take place.

## PHOTOGRAPHER

Having a photographer on the staff from the beginning of the rehearsal period can help enormously with publicity. If a few costumes are ready well in advance, some publicity photographs can be taken, which, if they are good, will be welcomed by the newspapers. Care should be taken that the same photographs are not given to different newspapers, but there is no reason a given newspaper should not receive a new set of photographs every three days or so. The more material they get, the more they are likely to use. Furthermore, if your photographs are good enough, the newspaper may be tempted to send its own photographer to capture some visually interesting material.

Photographs need not always be posed. Human-interest shots taken at rehearsals can also have publicity value.

Another job of the photographer is to document the production. Many members of the company may wish to order photographs later, and orders can be taken during the performances. Good photographs on view in the lobby add a tone of professionalism to the occasion.

The photographer who is a real hobbyist might enjoy making a film strip of the production, which can later be shown while a tape recording of one of the performances is played back. A few weeks after the production has closed, the cast may greatly enjoy a reunion that brings back memories of the performance in this manner.

## RECORDING DIRECTOR

There is an increasing tendency for amateur companies to want to record their productions, particularly in the case of unusual works that are not available in commercial recordings. It is relatively easy and inexpensive to have records pressed by a commercial company. Too often these records are made with a microphone placed near the footlights during a performance, and give little idea of the actual quality of the performance. If you are planning to make recordings, decide to do so several weeks in advance of the opening and make appropriate arrangements. The cast will not mind recording sessions if they are well planned. Indeed, they serve as an excellent way to review the music once the staging has been completed, and may be scheduled as musical rehearsals.

The recording director should plan the recording schedule, provide the equipment, edit the tape, and negotiate with the pressing company. He should have some experience in recording large-scale productions and should know that separate miking is necessary for chorus, leads, and orchestra. Trying to do the production with one or two microphones is not worth the investment of time in making the recording. He should be experienced in getting the proper balance between voices and orchestra. Nearly all recording engineers place the voices either too close to the microphone or too far away from it, so if a subsantial investment is to be made, the prospective recording director should show samples of his work of a similar nature.

If the group plans simply to document the performance, two takes of each number will be sufficient. This will take about three times the length of an actual performance. If a more polished recording is desired, a great deal more time will be needed. Such a recording should not be attempted unless the recording is done by experienced professionals or the group has recorded many times before.

## COMPANY PSYCHOLOGIST

Artistic temperaments are such that there are bound to be two or three production crises of a psychological nature. Everyone will be much better off if there is someone in the company to whom they can turn to resolve these crises. This person is likely to emerge unofficially and become a kind of peacemaker. He will probably not have any training in the field of human relations, but he will have an intuitive ability to deal with people effectively. Look for him in your company, and learn to trust him. He may turn out to be very important to the overall success of the venture.

## REHEARSAL MANAGER

When several directors are working, the development of a rehearsal schedule becomes quite complex. This complexity is augmented when some crucial person suddenly becomes unavailable. It is the responsibility of the rehearsal manager to coordinate all the schedules and to receive notice if someone will be unable to attend rehearsals. He should also see to it that rehearsals start on time, and should check up on whether a particular rehearsal accomplished what it was supposed to. Most rehearsal schedules need to be revised two or three times before the production.

It is fairly common among amateur companies to be saying at the dress rehearsal, "If only we had two or three more weeks . . ." The absurdity of this remark should be clear through hindsight. If the rehearsal manager can turn hindsight into foresight, the production will be at dress rehearsal exactly what it should be. A good rule is to figure out the maximum number of rehearsals that could possibly be needed and then schedule a third again as many. Nothing makes people feel better than the canceling of a rehearsal that is not needed. The converse is also true.

## TICKET MANAGER

The selling of tickets can be a major undertaking, particularly if a real attempt is made to sell them in advance. An enterprising and enthusiastic ticket manager who shows up at rehearsals, gives pep talks on selling tickets, and then makes them available to sell is worth his weight in gold. He must also supervise the sales at performances, keep track of the money, go to the bank and get change to use at performances, and give out complimentary tickets to critics and other people who have benefited or might benefit the production. If seats are reserved, of course, his job becomes much more complex, as he must know at any given time what seats have and have not been sold. He must be particularly careful not to sell more seats than the house contains. An overexuberant ticket manager may have to face a good deal of embarrassment.

## PROMPTER

No matter how well rehearsed the company may be, an actor may sometimes draw a blank. It is therefore necessary to have somebody with his eyes on the book at all times. Unfortunately, too many prompters get stage fright at the crucial moment and whisper the needed line over and over while the actor continues to fumble. A good rule is that if the audience can hear it, the actor can, and the audience would far rather hear the prompter than wait in embarrassment while an actor fumbles. During rehearsals an actor should always ask for a line before being prompted, but during a performance he cannot be expected to. The prompter should be present at all rehearsals after the actors have stopped using their scripts.

# Chapter XXI

# CASTING

There is no completely fair and successful method of casting. This is because there is no way of anticipating how a given performer will respond to rehearsals. Some people have a gift for shining at auditions but do not develop afterwards. Others do poorly at auditions because of nervousness or lack of imagination, but develop well during rehearsals and really shine during the performance. The best way to judge how a given performer will develop is to have worked with him before. Even so, special problems may arise that cannot be anticipated, resulting from the performer's personal difficulties, or from lack of affinity for a particular role.

We have earlier observed that it is difficult to avoid some form of precasting. It is important, however, to create as fair a situation as possible and to give each member of the company a chance at any role that interests him. This means holding tryouts in such a manner that everyone who wishes to audition has ample opportunity to be heard. It is also a good idea to give people an idea of what will be looked for in the audition. The hopeful performer who has already learned some of the part he is trying out for is obviously in a better position to do well than someone who is totally unprepared. The ready availability of recordings makes it relatively easy to familiarize oneself with a given role, and this might be encouraged.

In general it is a good idea to hold private auditions, with as few spectators as possible. During the audition an informal, relaxed atmosphere should be maintained to put the performer at ease so that he can do his best. He should be given some help and encouragement, and perhaps a little preliminary coach-

ing, but he should not be told his limitations. A great deal of ego is at stake in any audition, and the discomfort of the performer should be respected and not intensified.

For the leading roles, several factors should be tested. The performer should first sing a song that shows off his solo voice. The director should then determine whether he has vocal abilities not demonstrated by the song he has chosen that might be relevant to the casting of a particular role. It would be well also for the director to give him a little coaching, to determine how malleable he is to direction. If the role is unusually demanding, the director may wish to determine the range of the performer, and possibly also his ability to read music.

Once the musical part of the audition has been completed, a dramatic audition should follow. The director should hear the performer read several roles to determine his range and flexibility. He should indicate how he wants each role interpreted, in order to see how the performer responds to direction. The performer should be given an opportunity to read through the dialogue in order to get the gist of it, because some people do not read well at sight.

The director should then test the dramatic movement of the performer by giving him some actions to perform, such as running across the stage toward something and then running away from something, or turning in several ways. Care should be taken to connect these actions in the performer's mind with character, or he may merely do them mechanically, without realizing what they are supposed to test.

In many cases the directors will decide quite early in the audition that they cannot use a particular candidate in the cast. The temptation is to cut short the audition at that point. If possible this temptation should be avoided; people who are not cast should be made to feel that they have been given every possible opportunity.

When the preliminary auditions have been completed, there may be some question as to which of two or three persons should be given a particular part. In this case call-backs are advisable, and the candidates in question may be made to read in competition with one another.

It is a poor idea to leave the casting unsettled for too long after auditions. The longer hopes are encouraged before they are dashed, the more bitter the performer may become. Arrive at a tentative cast as soon as possible after auditions, and make sure that everyone who tried out knows about the decision. It may be necessary to call candidates on the telephone to inform them of the casting. In that case, be sure to call those who have not been cast.

When the cast list is posted, it should be emphasized that it is tentative. Rarely is it necessary to make a change, but if changes are made there will be far less resentment if it has been clear from the beginning that the possibility was anticipated.

Chorus auditions may or may not be held, depending on the size of the company and the number that can be used onstage. Many groups like to give everyone who is interested the opportunity to sing in the chorus. If chorus auditions are held, they should be different from solo auditions. Here, the ability to sing on pitch and to read music are the criteria. It is a good idea to have the performer sing one of the parts in a hymn while the entire hymn is played on the piano. His range should be tested, and the conductor should try to find out how loudly he can sing with encouragement. Most chorus people seem to have very small voices at tryouts because they have never sung out except in a large group. With a little encouragement, however, you can usually get the chorister to show what volume he has.

Chorus auditions should also include a little stage movement in order to avoid casting people who are too clumsy. But the tryout need not be rigorous. Teach the chorister a simple dance step, or simply have him run across the room. Chances are that if he can sing well enough to suit your purposes, he can also move well enough.

One pitfall to avoid is to complete the list of principals and then find that someone who tried out did not really want the part. For that reason

it is a good idea to have a questionnaire filled out by each person before his audition. The questionnaire clearly indicates the time of rehearsals and performances and asks the performer to commit himself to those times. It also asks him to indicate whether he will accept a major lead, a minor lead, or a place in the chorus. It may ask him, also, in what other ways he would like to help with the production, and it may ask him to list his previous experience in the theatre and music. When the performer comes into the auditioning room, he brings his questionnaire with him, and the directors use it to take notes on the audition. The questionnaire is then kept in a confidential file and is available only to the directors and the producer.

Auditions are confidential and they involve a certain kind of trust. No director should ever discuss outside of a confidential situation what happened in an audition. There is nothing crueler than to allow a person to audition for you and later make fun of his performance. No one who is aware of your doing such a thing will ever want to audition for you again.

Casting involves the appointment of understudies as well as principals. Understudies involve a special problem. It is unfair to expect a person to learn a role well enough to perform it without benefit of rehearsal and without ever performing it. If a full set of understudies is used, they should be adequately rehearsed and given some opportunity to perform. Some companies solve the problem by having two completely separate casts who perform alternately. This means that every part is always covered.

If the understudy is clearly not good enough to perform the role and represents only insurance against a dire emergency, it may be that he will appreciate the opportunity to receive some coaching and occasionally perform the role at rehearsals when the principal performer is absent. In such a situation, he should understand exactly where he stands and what is expected of him. In the event of emergency, he will probably need a great deal of last-minute coaching, and this should be provided.

If there are no understudies, and an emergency arises, it is sometimes possible to recruit someone from another similar company, or to hire a professional. In a reasonably large city it is unlikely that a situation will occur in which a production must be closed because no one can be found to replace an ailing performer. Professional actors can sometimes learn a part well enough to walk through it script in hand on a few hours' notice, and will gladly do so for compensation. As emergencies of this sort are few and far between, a company need not be overly concerned about providing a complete set of understudies.

There is a great deal of controversy about whether one should try to direct a show and also perform in it. Many people feel that it is unwise to do so, and yet from Aeschylus to Sir Laurence Olivier many star actors have directed themselves in leading roles. It sometimes happens among amateurs that a director really cannot find anyone who can perform a crucial role as well as he himself can perform it. If this is the case, he should use a stand-in at some of the rehearsals, so that he can get a proper perspective on the performance; and he should have an assistant to take notes for him whenever he is onstage. If he is an excellent performer, his doubling of capacities will not offend anyone, although he will have to make the adjustment of seeing himself sometimes as a director and sometimes as a fellow actor.

From the finest professional company to the rankest amateur, politics is never completely lacking from the business of casting. Inevitably there is some resentment and disappointment when the cast list is posted, and politics may be suspected when none existed. Nevertheless, it is difficult not to cast one's best friend when a complete stranger proves slightly better in the audition, and it is difficult not to reward a long-term faithful member of the company with a small role that an outsider might have done a little better. Such considerations are not always negative, particularly if the end result is not the most important consideration. Then there is a legitimate question of differences of taste. A director may see a role quite differently from the person auditioning, and may cast a performer who seems on some counts to be inferior because he really likes his performance better. Everyone involved will be happier if such differences of opinion are buried and forgotten as soon as possible. Performers who attempt to undermine morale because they did not get the part they wanted hurt everyone in the company, but themselves most of all.

The achievement of an effective cast will be easiest if the directors are thoroughly familiar with the opera and know exactly what effects they want before they hold auditions. Attempting to learn the basics of the show while rehearsing it is a policy that can lead to disastrous mistakes of artistic judgment.

In general, try to create an atmosphere in your company that makes people feel it is possible to work one's way up from the chorus to leading roles. You will do this best if you are constantly looking for and encouraging developing talent. After all, one of the most important functions an amateur opera company serves is to make its members feel that they are capable of achieving more than they originally suspected they could.

# Chapter XXII

# REHEARSALS

The following things must be achieved during the rehearsal period:

1. The chorus must learn their music.
2. The principals must learn their music.
3. The dialogue must be staged.
4. Ensemble numbers must be staged.
5. Choreography must be worked out.
6. The chorus action must be staged.
7. Each act must be run through several times by the entire company.
8. The orchestra must be rehearsed alone.
9. The orchestra must be rehearsed with soloists.
10. The orchestra must be rehearsed with the entire company.
11. The chorus performance must be reviewed to eliminate sloppiness that may have slipped in during staging rehearsals.
12. The company must work onstage with scenery, costumes, and lighting.
13. There must be two completely uninterrupted dress rehearsals.
14. There must be warm-ups before each performance.

We shall now discuss each of the above in turn.

1. Early chorus rehearsals can be difficult if some members of the chorus do not read music well. The conductor may have to teach some parts note by note, and may have to hold sectional rehearsals from time to time. It is important that the notes be taught right at first and that the chorus not be allowed to sing through music before it has been learned correctly. A passage learned wrong will take at least twice as long to get right.

After the first two or three rehearsals, some time should be devoted at each rehearsal to something learned earlier, so that there is continual review. It may be wise to spend the first five or ten minutes of a rehearsal going over familiar music to get the chorus warmed up and to allow for a few stragglers. After that, the early part of the rehearsal should be devoted to learning new things, while the chorus is still fresh, and the latter part to review so that their spirits will rise toward the end of the rehearsal when normally they would be getting tired, and so that they will leave the rehearsal with a sense of accomplishment. If they think they are doing well, and are having fun doing it, the chorus will learn the music much faster. A conductor with a positive, encouraging approach will get much better results than one who is overcritical. Critical conductors are legendary, but they achieve their results with professionals, who do not need encouragement the way amateurs do.

Early in the rehearsal period, the conductor will get a sense of what his chorus can do and how much music can be learned at each session. He can then draw up a schedule that allows him to complete the necessary work without encroaching on time needed by the stage director. He should take into account that although getting the notes right is necessary in early rehearsals, it is a waste of time to be too much of a perfectionist about the interpretation until after the music has been memorized. The important thing is to get some pieces memorized as soon as possible so that staging can begin. About halfway through the second week the evening can be divided between music and staging rehearsals. If the opera has several choruses sung by men and women apart from one another, it is possible to stage the men while the women learn music and vice versa, so that both directors can work the entire rehearsal.

2. In dealing with principals the conductor faces a different set of problems. Experienced performers will learn their music almost entirely themselves and will not need to go through rote-learning sessions with the conductor. If the principals are very young, however, the conductor may have to teach them their parts almost note by note.

Once the music has been learned, it is the conductor's job to teach them his interpretation of it. It is also his job to correct the mistakes they may make by reading the music inaccurately. Many performers learn their parts by listening to recordings, and many of the songs have been recorded inaccurately. A painstaking examination of the score without reference to recordings should help the conductor discover such mistakes and correct them, as Sullivan's rhythms are usually a little better than those substituted for them by Martyn Green or some other famous interpreter. Such careful examination of the actual notes and rhythms may turn up some real surprises for those already familiar with the operas through recordings. The conductor will receive valuable assistance in his study of the score if he reads *How to Sing Both Gilbert and Sullivan* by William Cox Ife. (See Bibliography p. 296.)

Once or twice through each of the solos should be enough for the conductor to get what he wants. He will have to spend more time on the ensemble numbers, particularly in blending the solo voices. It is all too seldom that one hears a well-blended Gilbert and Sullivan madrigal, because the performers are too busy projecting their own personalities. The conductor will have to work hard to overcome this tendency, and he may need several hours of work on a single ensemble.

All of this work should be done with the performers alone, and not in the presence of the chorus. By the time the performers rehearse with the chorus, they should be well practiced and in need of very little correction. This will protect their egos and also avoid a waste of chorus rehearsal time.

3. It is wise to schedule two rehearsals, a week or two apart, for each dialogue scene, and each of these rehearsals should take an hour or two. In all probability the performers will be reading their parts for the first time at each of these rehearsals, because they will have been concentrating on learning the music. Let them read through the scene two or three times

and see what they can do with it. Then begin intensive work, developing characterizations through discussion of motivations and through helping the actor find the right kind of vocal and physical style. Gradually introduce appropriate stage business, wherever possible letting the actor discover and develop it for himself. The scene should be fully enough developed during the first rehearsal so that it can be polished during the second. At that time pacing will be important. The tendency of actors to pause before speaking a line should be corrected, so that dead spaces do not slow the dialogue. This is also the time to work on projection, and on giving the dialogue the sort of elegance that transcends natural speech.

After a few dialogue rehearsals, you may find that some of your performers, cast primarily because of their fine singing voices, need special coaching in acting, and you should schedule sessions with them in which actor training is the point rather than rehearsal of anything in particular.

4. Before the director attempts the staging of an ensemble number, he should have carefully worked it out in advance. Improvisation in this area wastes everyone's time. Gilbert used little wooden figures and moved them about on a model stage. However you do it, you should have done it thoroughly enough so that you are always able to remember what comes next as you present it to your actors. Markings in your score will help to refresh your memory, but they will be necessarily cryptic. Recordings are extremely helpful to the director in working out staging. He can play the record and try out each of his ideas to make sure that it fits the music. Of course, if he has memorized the score he can do the job much more easily and quickly; thus it is helpful to listen to each number several times before even attempting to stage it.

No matter how well your actors are doing a number at the end of the first rehearsal, they will have forgotten much of it the second time. Get used to teaching everything twice, and allow time for this process. The number of rehearsals you need of a particular ensemble will depend on the dexterity of your cast; you should find out about that early enough so that you can schedule all the rehearsals you will need.

5. Choreography involves actual dancing and should be used in only a small percentage of the ensemble numbers. Probably the principals will be learning to dance for the first

time, so the steps should be kept simple. Otherwise the problems of teaching choreography to principals are the same as those outlined in section 4, above.

Chorus choreography is another matter. Don't try to teach more than two or three steps at a given rehearsal, and allow extra time for drilling on them. In a large chorus there will inevitably be two or three people who have great trouble getting the dance steps and who tend to throw everyone else off. Allow enough rehearsal time so that the slowest member of the chorus is completely confident of what he is doing. Only then will your chorus look really good. You cannot possibly do too much drilling.

6. Chorus staging is difficult primarily because of the number of people involved. Chorus members have a tendency to want to relax and talk when not actually doing something, and this is just as true of professionals as amateurs. Consequently the stage director has to be something of a performer himself in order to hold their attention. In general an hour of rehearsal time should be allotted to a given number, with the possibility of an additional hour or two for difficult numbers. Even though the staging is quite simple, precision requires drill, and drill takes time.

One problem that a director should consider in presenting material to a chorus is whether or not to reverse actions so that they can mirror him. This is not much of a problem with gestures, but it becomes important with intricate footwork. The simplest solution may be to turn around, so that you are facing the same direction as they are.

Although rigid discipline is necessary at times, relax the rehearsal now and then so that people do not get overtired. Tell a few jokes and clown a little, then regain control and proceed. Do not attempt to work more than an hour without a break. Allow people to relax as much as possible when they are not actually working.

7. Few things are so painful and disappointing as the first run-through of an act. Your entire company will seem to you to be hopeless idiots who forget the most obvious things. Furthermore, you will find that you have not yet done several things in the act, and so there will be some holes in the run-through. Try to get through it that first time with as few stops as possible, in order to give the cast a sense of how everything fits together. The second run-through will be infinitely better, but each

run-through will reveal things that need additional rehearsal, and each will provide opportunities to correct minor faults. Often you can do this without actually stopping the rehearsal by pointing in the direction a person should move or physically moving him yourself. As a person comes offstage you can take him aside and remind him of something he forgot to do. Remember that the less often you stop the run-throughs, the sooner the production will begin to take shape, all other things being equal. There is no point, of course, in wading through a scene that is a hopeless mess. Skip it and schedule an immediate separate rehearsal for it.

8. The purpose of the first orchestra rehearsal is to read through the parts and discover any trouble spots. Some of these will be passages the orchestra members cannot play. Others, unfortunately, will be inaccuracies in the parts, which must be corrected. The conductor should be alert to these, as they are quite common in most sets of parts. If cuts are to be made, they should be given to the orchestra at this time. In general, the conductor will be finding out what his orchestra can do, considering simplifications where necessary, and working himself up to a desperate plea to the orchestra manager to recruit some more string players. He might have to settle for a tuba to play the double bass part.

9. Orchestra rehearsals with soloists allow the conductor to hear the finished effect of some of the music and to discover, without wasting too many people's time, how to establish a good relationship between orchestra and singers. He will have to adapt his beat so that he differentiates between what he is telling the singers and what he is telling the orchestra, and these rehearsals with soloists provide him an opportunity for working out matters of this kind.

10. Probably two complete evenings should be spent working with the entire company on music alone, one evening for each act. The orchestra still will not sound perfect, but a lot of the conductor's energy will go into coordinating the collective forces, rather than correcting individuals. The chorus may have difficulty following him while he is conducting the orchestra; they will have to adjust to the fact that he is farther away from them. Everyone will experience occasional problems in finding his note somewhere in the orchestra. It may be necessary to teach one performer to listen only to the cello, which is playing the same notes he

is singing during a quartet. All of these matters should be worked out without the distraction of staging.

11. There may be as much as two weeks when the chorus works on staging without actually looking at the music. There should be a musical rehearsal or two to correct the errors that inevitably creep in during this period. This is also the time when the conductor can put the final touches on his interpretation of the chorus music. A sudden *accelerando* or an added *firmata* should be carefully drilled at this time so that it will remain fresh in everyone's mind in the stress of performance.

12. The first rehearsal onstage may be terrifying. The company, in adjusting to the newness of their surroundings, will temporarily forget many of the things they have learned. Then there are the interruptions of the stage crew, who are likely to be behind in their schedule for getting the scenery up. Everyone may have to sit around and wait for an hour or two before the stage is even ready. If the theatre has a pit, the company may have trouble hearing the orchestra. These and other factors may contribute to a general impression of chaos at this first stage rehearsal, but the chaos will clear up sooner than might seem possible as the problems are corrected.

This is the time to make sure that the performance can be heard. Many of the principals may turn out not to be projecting well enough. The orchestra will probably be too loud, and blankets may have to be hung in front of it to dampen the sound. The conductor must be warned, too, that the brass in particular will have to be held back. It may turn out that amplification is necessary, and this may have to be brought into an auditorium that does not have it. The difficulties inherent in correcting this problem are augmented by the fact that it is almost impossible to keep the house quiet with people milling around talking and working on scenery, lighting, and costumes. Furthermore the acoustics are different when the house is empty and when it has an audience. In short, there may not be as serious a problem with projection as you might think, but if you can't hear the words above the accompaniment you must do something about the orchestra.

The rehearsals that precede the dress rehearsals are also the time for the stage director to do a lot of polishing. He should concentrate on several points: Make sure that the chorus members maintain good posture and stay in character at all times. Make sure that people get out of the habit of looking down at the floor, particularly when they are dancing or going down steps. Make sure that when a soloist is singing, all eyes are on him. Make sure that people have the appropriate expressions on their faces and respond to the action with vivacity. A good stage director will do a lot of shouting at the chorus, and will run up on the stage from time to time to correct a chorister when he is unaware that he is distracting from the total effect. He must emphasize over and over again that a single person scratching his nose at the wrong time can ruin the effect of a chorus of thirty carefully drilled people. The more polished the performance, the easier it is to spoil it.

Matters other than these should be handled through taking notes, which can be given to the company at the end of the rehearsal.

Meanwhile, the costuming designer is checking on the appropriateness of all costumes to the stage picture and making sure that they do not create staging problems because they are difficult to wear. The lighting designer is re-aiming lights that do not properly enhance the effect of the staging. The technical director is rebuilding portions of the scenery that cannot handle the stress to which they are subjected, and is instructing people about sight lines and how to walk up and down the rickety stairs backstage. The makeup artist is trying out his makeup on a few people to see how it goes with the lights. The ticket manager is concentrating heavily on trying to make sure that every member of the company sells his quota of tickets. And the producer is clearing up all sorts of unanticipated problems having to do with the use of the hall and other last-minute adjustments.

13. It is a crucial moment in the performance. A leading character is about to make an exciting entrance after a quick costume change. The leading character does not appear, and the performance grinds to a halt. Why? During the dress rehearsal the conductor and the stage director insisted on stopping to make corrections. No one knew exactly how long the performance would run. The actor in question thought he had more time to make his change. He is understandably as angry at the directors as they are at him.

The dress rehearsal, preferably the last two rehearsals, should be conducted under performance conditions. The company needs the chance to get the feel of the show. Except for a few shouted exhortations that do not stop the rehearsal, corrections should be made at the end of the rehearsal, not while it is in progress. Anything that goes wrong should be handled exactly as it would be in the performance. It is even a good idea to have a small audience present, so that the performers can get used to applause and other responses.

Members of the chorus will insist that they want to watch as much of the rehearsal as possible, and this is all right, provided they are responsible for making their entrances on time. However, they should go out the stage door and come in at the back of the house, so that there is no running back and forth through the exits that lead up to the stage. If anyone misses an entrance as a result of watching the show, the privilege of watching should be withdrawn from everyone. This will help to impress people with the seriousness of missing entrances.

It is well if the final dress rehearsal is a little overdone. If everyone works a bit too hard, then concentration during the performance can be on holding back slightly, which means that the performance is more controlled and polished, and at the same time a little more relaxed.

Sometimes a show is so well rehearsed that it is in danger of becoming mechanical by performance time. An antidote to this is to have some of the performers clown during the rehearsal, adding or changing lines, and getting out of their systems all the "in" jokes they would like to pull. If such behavior occurs during a rehearsal, the director should point out that it belongs there and not in the performance. He should point out that ad libs, although they are often funny, may be the wrong kind of humor, and may spoil an effect that many people have worked a long time to produce.

14. Everyone needs to warm up before each performance. The principals should do this themselves, vocalizing in the dressing rooms. About fifteen minutes before curtain time the conductor should call the company together and run them through a series of vocal exercises. Following that it is well to give a pep talk that sends everyone off feeling positive about the performance.

The pep talk before the second performance should include a warning about the second-night letdown, which occurs as a result of people having heard too many things about how good they were. A few brief criticisms of the opening performance are possible, but usually it is enough merely to mention the problem so that people will be thinking about it. Should there have been reviews in the papers that were negative about some aspect of the performance, the director or the conductor can joke about these in order to release the tension they have caused in the company. This is a way of saying, "We're all in this together and we think we're doing a great job," which is the spirit in which a performance should begin. Another thing to do after the warm up session is to read the telegrams and letters of congratulation the company have received from friends. Everything possible to create a relaxed and happy tone should be done at this time. Stage fright will take care of the need for discipline.

Lastly, during the performance something will go wrong, and the problem is to keep it from looking wrong insofar as possible. Leads should be trained not to lose their stage presence when they forget lines. If someone makes an entrance at the wrong time, the conductor will have to signal the orchestra to add or cut measures, and he should have thought through how he is going to do this. Part of the scenery may fall, but the actors onstage should let the backstage crew worry about this and go on as if nothing had happened. If a character does not make it onstage, the people who are there should attempt to add his lines to their part. If there is a major emergency, such as a bomb going off or a fire breaking out, either the stage manager or the conductor will signal the interruption of the performance, and the actors should continue until they receive such a signal. For one thing a gradual interruption of the performance will help to keep the audience from getting panicky.*

All in all, the attitude of everyone should be that the show must go on, and that it is possible to keep it going on if everyone is aware of his responsibilities.

Let us conclude these remarks on rehearsals by appending a sample rehearsal schedule used during part of a production of *Utopia, Ltd.*

| Wednesday, July 24 | 7:30 *Girls' chorus*—stage No. 1, 4 (first part), and 7 (first part) |

**MEN NEED NOT COME TONIGHT**

---

* During the performance of an oratorio in the Washington Cathedral a bomb went off. The performing soloist did not even bat an eyelash and the performance continued uninterrupted, as no damage had been done.

|                        | 7:30 | *King and Lady Sophy—music (duets)* |
|                        | 9:00 | *King, Fitz., Goldbury, Blushington, Sir B. Barre, Corcoran, Dramaleigh—music, No. 14* |
| Thursday, July 25      | 7:30 | *Chorus—stage No. 7 and 8* |
|                        | 7:30 | *Zara, Fitz., King, Nekaya, Kalyba Sophy, First Life Guards—dialogue between No. 7 and 8* |
|                        | 9:00 | *All above—full staging of No. 7 and 8* |
| Saturday, July 27      | 2:00 | *Chorus—run-through of all staging* |
| Sunday, July 28        | 2:00 | *Full company—run-through of Act I* |
|                        | 8:00 | *Full company—run-through of Act II* |
| Monday, July 29        | 7:30 | *Chorus—music review* |
| Tuesday, July 30       | 7:00 | *Full company—complete run-through* |
| Wednesday, July 31     | 7:00 | *Full company—complete run-through* |
| Thursday, August 1     | 7:00 | *Full company—complete run-through with piano* |
|                        | 7:30 | *Orchestra* |
| Friday, August 2       | 7:00 | *Full company—complete run-through* |
| Saturday, August 3     | 6:30 | *Full company—makeup and dress at performance hall. (Schedule included here directions on how to get there.)* |

|                        | 7:00 | *Full company—onstage for 1st dress rehearsal* |
|                        | 7:30 | *Orchestra—at performance hall.* |
| Sunday, August 4       | 6:30 | *Full company—makeup and dress at performance hall* |
|                        | 7:00 | *Full company—onstage for 2nd dress rehearsal (technical stops; no orchestra)* |
| Monday, August 5       | 6:30 | *Full company—makeup and dress at performance hall* |
|                        | 7:00 | *Full company—onstage for 3rd dress rehearsal* |
|                        | 7:30 | *Orchestra—at performance hall* |
| Tuesday, August 6      | 7:30 | *Characters as assigned—polish as necessary at rehearsal hall* |
|                        | 7:30 | *Orchestra—at rehearsal hall* |
| Wednesday, August 7    | 6:30 | *Full company—makeup and dress at performance hall* |
|                        | 7:00 | *Full company and orchestra—final dress rehearsal* |

TELEPHONE NUMBERS:

Musical director
Stage director
Producer
Orchestra manager
Stage manager
Costume and set designer
Set construction

# Chapter XXIII

# STAGING PROBLEMS

A number of problems that a staging director must face are more or less unique to the production of Gilbert and Sullivan opera.

The first of these concerns the overall design of the production. Most of the operas are artfully arranged so that the sequence of numbers allows for just the right kind of variety of mood. Some of these numbers require elaborate staging, others should be simple. In general, beginning directors tend to be overconscientious and want to put in more than the work really needs. Cleverness can be inexhaustible, but too much cleverness can actually be tiring for an audience to watch. It should also be remembered that songs that are important dramatically and musically need not be elaborately staged. Too much action may draw attention away from the words and music. Before he begins to rehearse the opera, the director should decide which numbers need what kind of staging. Let us begin to build up a pattern.

The number that will be remembered the longest from a staging point of view is probably the comic duet or trio that comes between the middle and the end of the second act. "Here's a how-de-do" in *The Mikado* and the Bell Trio in *Pinafore* are typical examples. Some of these numbers involve elaborate comic dancing, and when they are done professionally are encored five or six times. The director should decide where this number lies in the opera and how he is going to handle it. If it is to be the high point of the show, nothing else must be allowed to overshadow it. The question "where it lies" may seem a bit odd until we consider that sometimes there is a choice. In *The Yeomen of the Guard,* for example, the number in question could be either the duet "Hereupon we're both agreed,"

which is near the beginning of the second act, or the duet "Rapture, rapture," which is near the end. The total effect of the production will be different, depending on which of these numbers is given the most emphasis. If the second one is, the almost tragic mood that has been slowly building through the act is, for better or for worse, interrupted. If the first one is emphasized, then it may be a good idea to cut the second and move right into the finale.

Another example is *The Pirates of Penzance.* The comic trio would seem to be "A paradox," but it may be that primary humorous emphasis should fall instead upon the Major-General's dance during the "Gentle breezes" song.

After the comic number has been selected and tentatively designed, the director should think about the kinds of spectacle he wants. In almost every opera there is an opportunity to indulge in the British love of pageantry by the use of costumes, props, and special effects. The entrance of Sir Joseph in *Pinafore* is one example, the entrance of the court in *Utopia, Ltd.* another. A different sort of spectacle is the fight scene in *Princess Ida.* For the spectacular scene to have full effect, the director should think visually. What kinds of costumes will be provided? Can extra characters be used? Can musical instruments be used onstage? Should the entrance be made through the audience? What is needed to make sure that exactly the right effect is produced so that the spectacle is really stunning and not just an ambitious try?

Next the director should examine the three or four other ensemble numbers that require dancing and try to make sure that these are not going to be repetitive in effect. A different sort of dance should be worked out for each, so that there is always something new, and the impression is not created that the company met a last-minute obligation to get these numbers staged any way they could.

Having gone this far, the director might think about what sort of really unusual new approach might be possible to make his production more than a carbon copy of other productions of the same opera. The approach may be a matter of overall design, or it may simply involve doing one number in an unusual new way. Let us give one example of how this can be done.

A production of *Iolanthe* at Sandy Spring Friends School achieved an improbable first: a well-sung Nightmare Song in which the Lord Chancellor did his best to attract the attention of the audience without anyone ever once looking at him. It sounds like a catastrophe, but it was actually one of the most delightful and imaginative pieces of staging one might hope to see.

After the recitative was completed, there entered "The Great Victorian Dream Machine." This was a group of about fifteen dancers in leotards, except for one dressed to resemble the Lord Chancellor (in red pajamas). There followed a modern dance interpretation of the song that did not attempt to stick exactly to the words, but rather to create in dance the same kind of bizarre sequence of images that occur in the words. One by one the dancers came to life by representing simple mechanical actions until the stage was filled with such actions all going at once. Then they all rushed together and held a blanket that was used to bounce the character representing the Chancellor almost into the ceiling. Subsequently other actions were performed. The Chancellor walked across a series of bent backs when crossing the Channel. The bicycling was represented by people on their backs with their legs peddling in the air. It is, of course, impossible even to suggest the effect of this dance in words, but one can point out that a creative choreographer was able to produce a surprising new effect that universally delighted the audience and somehow fitted into a generally traditional production style.

Having surveyed those aspects of the production that will make a strong impression and bear the stamp of the director clearly, it remains to determine how the numbers that are more routine from a staging point of view will be handled. Many of these are solos, and depend on the personality and projection of the performer, not on staging ingenuity. In fact, a good sense of rhythm and timing among all the performers will greatly enhance everything that is done. Let us now examine how such a number should typically be handled.

Divide the song into four to seven sections. Each of these will be sung from a slightly different area of the stage. Movement into a new stage area should accompany a slight change of idea or mood in the song. Add to the song a few descriptive gestures, if they are appropriate (that is, if concrete images are used in the song). Otherwise, the gestures should be emotive. The problem will be to keep the gestures from being repetitive, and it might be well to have the singer do some excerises that explore a variety of possible gestures and then work out the details for himself. For most solos more detail than that would be simply distracting.

Only a slightly greater degree of complexity is necessary in staging a love duet. Sometimes choreographers introduce ballet dancing along with the singing, but such touches suggest a lack of faith in the entertainment value of the words and music themselves. Having the lovers walk across the stage arm in arm, stand together, move apart a little, gracefully switch positions, and use their arms in gesturing with some imagination should be sufficient. Having one sit on a bench or kneel to the other may help to create more interesting images. Little more is needed.

Let us now consider the staging of the chorus. There are two main problems: where to put people, and what to have them do once they are in place. A certain amount of ingenuity will be needed in order to avoid the inevitable semicircle. The director should break the chorus down into groups and move those groups about the stage in interesting patterns. He may wish to work out a series of staging diagrams, and even to reproduce those diagrams for use by the chorus. A sample of what such diagrams might look like appears on p. 258.

Once people know where they are supposed to go, it is necessary to determine what they will do there. This involves three basic considerations: general posture, hand and arm work, and footwork. Posture is useful in communicating emotions. Heads hung down suggest sadness. Chins held back suggest snobbery. As a director you should have five to ten basic postures that you can give your chorus from time to time to represent various attitudes.

Footwork involves the way of standing, as well as any dance steps that are used. In general, equal weight should be on both feet so that

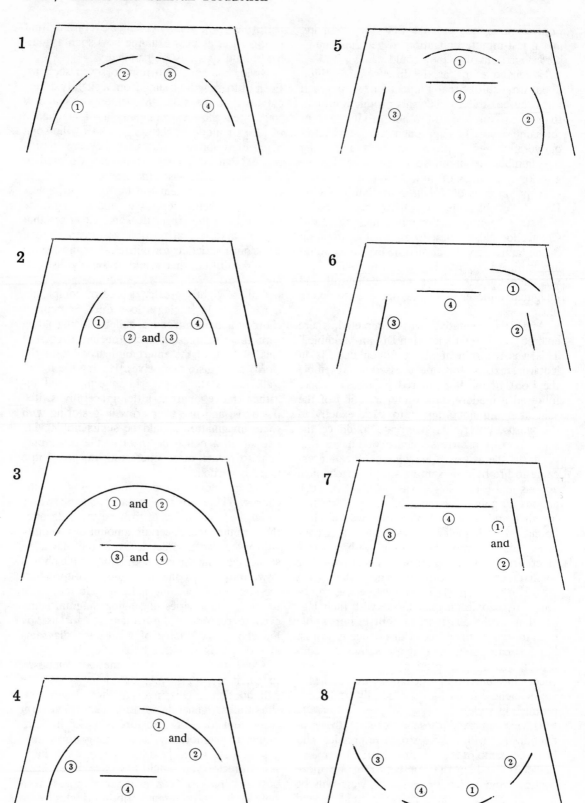

*(The numbers refer to groups of choristers. The lines indicate their positions on the stage.)*

posture is balanced. Amateurs always have to be nagged about this: They love to stand in sloppy ways that spoil the effect. Merely making sure that everyone stands in a balanced position does wonders for the stage picture.

Dance steps should be simple and precise. If the entire chorus can't do it, simplify it. An ingenious dance step that is poorly executed spoils the effect. A simple one well done looks professional.

Work with the hands and arms should involve a great many pictorial gestures. Many choruses, particularly patter choruses, are vastly improved if the company rattles off a series of gestures, one at the beginning of each measure. The shaking of the index finger, the rippling of all ten fingers, an action suggesting lifting, one suggesting cutting, and so on—those are the kinds of gestures that can be used. As a director you should work them out in advance. If you have trouble with this sort of thing, develop for yourself a repertory of twenty-five pictorial gestures and then invent and memorize symbols for them that you can write down. This may take you a total of eight hours, but you will have developed a tool that you will forever afterward find useful in chorus staging.

The chorus staging must be taught mechanically and drilled until it is done perfectly every time. Only then does the director worry about motivation. He tells the chorus how they feel about what is going on so that they can infuse life into their reactions. Telling them the motivations too early in the game tends to make the staging less precise, and also destroys the possibility of increased spontaneity in the last few rehearsals.

After you have done all the detail in the chorus staging you will find that there are many times when the chorus are merely watching the action. You should give them a stance for those times, though it need not necessarily be uniform for the entire chorus. A good one for men is one arm at the side and the other arm held across the front of the body just above the waist. Girls may use "hands typical," which is one palm placed in the other, palms parallel to the floor, hands at the base of the rib cage.

Let us consider problems with the principals.

First is the dialogue. Gilbert's lines are not intended to sound like natural speech. In fact, they are closer to operatic recitative than they are to the dialogue in a modern play. This means that a special kind of sound must be cultivated in the speaking voice, a little more resonant and highly articulated than seems natural. Inflections should be greatly exaggerated. If your actors are not experienced in this kind of acting, they will resist your efforts to make them speak in a way that seems unnatural to them. It is necessary to keep working with them until they can speak in a style appropriate to the text and feel natural and comfortable doing so. One way to help them make the transition is to have them sing the lines, making up the tune as they go along.

In the musical numbers there will be less difficulty getting the performers to act appropriately. If their singing voices project well, it will seem natural to them to project in other ways as well. Gestures should be big and decisive, posture should be excellent unless characterization calls for the contrary, and the habit of looking at the floor should be broken.

Finally, the director should consider how the staging may be most effectively lighted. Realistic effects are unnecessary. Instead, the lighting should enhance the mood, dimming or brightening, sometimes gradually and sometimes suddenly. Effective use of lighting might be the only staging some numbers require.

If you have done your work effectively, you will find that during the dress rehearsals the staging begins to take on a kind of elegance and "glow" that is thoroughly enchanting to watch. Be careful and critical. Don't mistake your own creative involvement with the production for polish. Try to see it as if you were seeing it for the first time, and to find out what you need to do in order to erase the rough spots and make the total effect one of continuous elegance. Always remember that probably no other works in the literature of the theatre depend as much for their true effect on subtly articulated polish of style than the "golden fourteen" operas of Gilbert and Sullivan.

# Chapter XXIV

# HOW TO GET WHAT YOU NEED

If you have never before done any kind of production, you should obtain a copy of *Play Production* by Henning Nelms, which is in the College Outline Series and is available in most drugstores. This book presents briefly and clearly the problems that arise in most theatrical productions. For more detailed instruction in most of the areas covered by that book, you should consult other books in the *Theatre Student* series.

The first purchasing or renting you will probably have to do will be the musical scores, which must be available before the first rehearsal. These will have to be ordered from a music store, and it will take two weeks or more to obtain them, so you should plan ahead. Most of the Gilbert and Sullivan operas are published by G. Schirmer, and are available in complete vocal scores (for use by directors and principals), and chorus parts, which are far less expensive. If you are planning to do one of the lesser-known operas, the scores may have to be obtained from England, and this could mean a delay of several months. For the relevant publishers, see the Bibliography.

It is cheaper to rent scores than to buy them. It may be that some other organization in your area has performed the opera you are planning to produce and would be willing to supply you with what you need. If not, you should be able to rent them from Tracy Music Company, 37 Newbury Street, Boston, Massachusetts 02116. Another possibility is the Tams-Witmark Music Library, 757 Third Avenue, New York, N.Y. 10017.

If you wish to rent orchestral scores, you will find that several publishers have them available, but that quality varies to an extreme degree. Also, as only one copy of a set of parts is usually available from a company, you should reserve them as far in advance as possible. The American representative for the D'Oyly Carte Opera Company is Tams-Witmark (see above), and they have the original Sullivan orchestrations for thirteen Gilbert and Sullivan operas, plus Cellier's orchestration of *The Mountebanks.* Tracy Music (see above) has the original orchestration of *Utopia, Ltd.* minus three instrumental parts, but including an introduction not found in the D'Oyly Carte parts. This version also contains a thoroughly unacceptable overture made by someone other than Sullivan.

Tracy also has orchestrations for eleven other Gilbert and Sullivan operas, but these were made in America for high-school productions and are of only average quality. G. Schirmer offers a set of orchestrations for small orchestra. Many other publishers offer sets made at various times by American arrangers. Should you wish to use two or three instruments along with the piano, you can probably make your own arrangement by marking for each instrument the notes in the piano accompaniment to be played by that instrument. Listening to a recording should help you do this.

It should be noted that at present there are no full scores of Gilbert and Sullivan operas widely available. Conductors are accustomed to working from cued vocal scores. A complete set of full scores has been compiled by John Landis, and it is to be hoped that these will be available soon. When published they will set a new standard, as even the D'Oyly Carte orchestrations are filled with minor inaccuracies, which Landis has corrected.

It should also be noted that if you order

scores by a publisher other than Schirmer you may have to order libretti too, as many of these scores do not contain the dialogue. Be sure to check that point with your music store. Should you need libretti, it may be cheaper to get them by ordering a paperback anthology of the operas.

Another major problem is the obtaining of costumes. Several costume companies will rent you a complete set of costumes for any of the standard Gilbert and Sullivan productions. As these vary widely in quality, it would be best to see the costumes before you commit yourself. Most of the larger New York companies, as well as Brooks-Van Horn in Philadelphia, have excellent quality. For names and addresses, see the ads in theatre magazines. Tracy Music (see above) has costumes for most of the operas, some of which are excellent.

If you decide to make costumes, you should immediately become aware of the vast difference in price between textiles. Costumes do not have to be as rugged or as high quality as clothing, so you should look for cheap materials. You should also consider how much you can do with crepe paper, particularly if the costumes are stylized. A clever designer can make for less than $1.00 a wig that is far more interesting than an authentic wig costing over $100. Still, if you are doing *Trial by Jury,* you will probably wish to rent a few authentic wigs even if you make all the rest of your costumes. They can usually be rented for about $5.00 apiece.

In addition to shopping for inexpensive textiles and other materials, you should visit the thrift shops, Good Will Industries, and other places where secondhand clothing is available at very low prices. There you may find a beautiful formal dress for $1.00 or so, and you can remake it to be just right for your leading lady.

Some costumes can be supplied by members of the cast themselves. Try to plan around standard clothing that everyone has, which can be adapted in a nonpermanent fashion for the duration of your performances. Arrow shirts with collars turned up and Ascot ties look very Victorian, for example.

Scenery may well be your largest expense. Consider the possibility of borrowing flats and other items from another company. If you have to build flats, you will keep your expenses down by shopping around for lumber that has been exposed to the weather, and by using unbleached muslin (available in department stores) rather than canvas. For a cyclorama you may be able to use a large roll of paper, which your art supply store can order for you.

Lights can usually be rented from a commercial stage-lighting company if they are not available on your stage. Once again, however, you will probably save money if you can borrow or rent at a lower fee from a school or theatre group in your area.

Tickets and programs are cheaper mimeographed than printed. Probably someone in your company has easy access to a mimeograph machine and can do this job for you at the cost of buying the materials.

Should you decide to go into the recording business, you may be able to find a tape recorder enthusiast in your community who will record your show at a relatively low cost. Tape editing is easily learned, and you should do it yourself rather than go to the expense of hiring a professional. Once you have the tape in final form, if you wish to make pressings, you can have this done by a commercial pressing company. The cost of doing so can be made up by selling about fifty copies of the recording to members of your company at about the same price they pay for commercial recordings. A good pressing company is Raleigh Records, Inc., Room 1225, 250 West 57th Street, New York, N.Y. 10019. When ordering records, you should be aware that no company guarantees to supply the exact number that you order, that some of the records may be damaged, and that the cost of making additional discs is very small, provided they are all made at the same time. Therefore you will be wise to order at least 20 percent more copies than you expect to need.

In general you will find that if you plan ahead and let enough people know what you are trying to do you can get many of the things you will need at a small fraction of what they would otherwise cost you. Expenses mount up when last-minute purchases are made on the basis of too little research. You will probably be amazed at how much the people in your community are willing to help you get what you need if you give them enough notice and arouse their enthusiasm about your production.

The following pages contain musical numbers that have either been dropped from the various operas or may be added to them. They are included here because of the great difficulty of obtaining them from other sources, and because some producers may wish to include them in their productions.

The following is one of two extant numbers from *Thespis,* the other being "Climbing over rocky mountain," which was later used in *The Pirates of Penzance,* and may be found there. This song is sung by Sparkeion in the second act.

# LITTLE MAID OF ARCADEE.

Words by W. S. GILBERT.

Music by ARTHUR S. SULLIVAN.

To her lit-tle home she crept, There she sat her down and wept;

Maid-en wept as maid-ens will, Grew so thin and pale and ill,

Till an-oth-er came to woo, Then a-gain the ros-es grew.

Hap-py lit-tle maid-en she, Hap-py maid of Ar-ca-

The following is the Act Two opening chorus that was used in the original version of *The Sorcerer*.

Happy are we in our lov-ing fri-vol-i-ty, Happy and jol-ly as peo-ple of qual-i-ty;

Love is the source of all joy to human-i-ty, Money, position and

Tho' we're been hither -to deaf, dumb, and blind to it, Pleasant enough when you've made up your mind to it.

Pleasant enough,    ver - y  say we,    Pleasant enough,  say  we . . . .

The following number appeared in the original vocal score of *The Mountebanks,* but was deleted from the second and currently available edition. It is of interest because of its similarity to "When you find you're a broken-down critter" in *The Grand Duke*. It is sung by Pietro, and follows the second-act trio, "Where gentlemen are eaten up with jealousy."

# O BLISS! O RAPTURE!

### Recitative.

soothe and com-fort your de -clin-ing days. No, don't do that. Yes, in -deed, I'd ra - ther.

To-mor-row morn our vows shall all be plight-ed, Three lov-ing pairs on the same day u ni - ted.

The following scene was included in the original version of *Iolanthe*. The lyric for Mountararat was not sung but recited, and proved a highly effective moment in the production. The scene follows Phyllis' monologue after "Oh foolish fay."

MOUNTARARAT. Phyllis! My own! (*Embracing her.*)

PHYLLIS. Don't! How dare you? But perhaps you are one of the noblemen I'm engaged to?

MOUNTARARAT. I am one of them.

PHYLLIS. Oh! But how came you to have a peerage?

MOUNTARARAT. It's a prize for being born first.

PHYLLIS. Oh, I see—a kind of Derby cup.

MOUNTARARAT. Not at all. I'm of a very old and distinguished family.

PHYLLIS. And you're proud of your race? Of course you are; you won it. But why are people made peers?

MOUNTARARAT. The principle is not easy to explain. I'll give you an example.

De Belville was regarded as the Crichton of his age;
His tragedies were reckoned much too thoughtful for the stage;
His poems held a noble rank, although it's very true
That, being very proper, they were read by very few;
He was a famous painter, too, and shone upon the line,
And even Mr. Ruskin came and worshipped at his shrine;

But, alas! the school he followed was hero-
ically high,
The kind of art men rave about, but very
seldom buy;
    And ev'rybody said,
      "How can he be repaid—
This very great, this very good, this very
gifted man?"
But nobody could hit upon a practicable
plan.

He was a great inventor, and discovered, all
alone,
A plan for making everybody's fortune but
his own;
For in business an inventor's little better than
a fool,
And my highly-gifted friend was no excep-
tion to the rule.
His poems—people read 'em in the sixpenny
Reviews;
His pictures—they engraved 'em in the *Illus-
trated News;*
His inventions—they perhaps might have en-
riched him by degrees,
But all his little income went in Patent-Office
fees.
    So everybody said
    "How *can* he be repaid—
This *very* great, this *very* good, this *very*
learned man?"
But nobody could hit upon a practicable
plan.

At last the point was given up in absolute
despair,
When a distant cousin died, and he became
a millionaire,
With a county seat in Parliament, a moor or
two of grouse,
And a taste for making inconvenient speeches
in the House.
Then Government conferred on him the
highest of rewards:
They took him from the Commons and they
put him in the Lords.
And who so fit to sit in it—deny it if you
can—
As this very great, this very good, and very
gifted man?
    Though I'm more than half afraid
    That it sometimes may be said
That we never should have revelled in this
source of proper pride,
However great his merits, if his cousin hadn't
died.

(*Enter,* LORD TOLLOLLER.)

TOLLOLLER. Phyllis! My darling. (*Embraces her.*)
PHYLLIS. Here's the other! Well, have you
settled which it's to be? . . .

The following song for Strephon immediately
follows the trio, "If you go in" in *Iolanthe.* No
dialogue changes are necessary if it is used.

RECITATIVE & SONG—(Strephon.)

ve - ri - ty I wield a pow'r sub - lime, And one that I can turn to migh - ty us - es! What

joy to car - ry, in the 've - ry teeth of Min - is - try, Cross-Bench, and Op - po - si - tion, Some

ra - ther ur - gent mea - sures— quite be - neath The ken of pa - triot and po - li - ti - cian!

Fold your flap - ping wings, Soar - ing Le - gis - la - ture! Stoop to lit - tle things—Stoop to Hu - man

Na - ture! Ne - ver need to roam, Mem - bers pa - tri - o - tic,

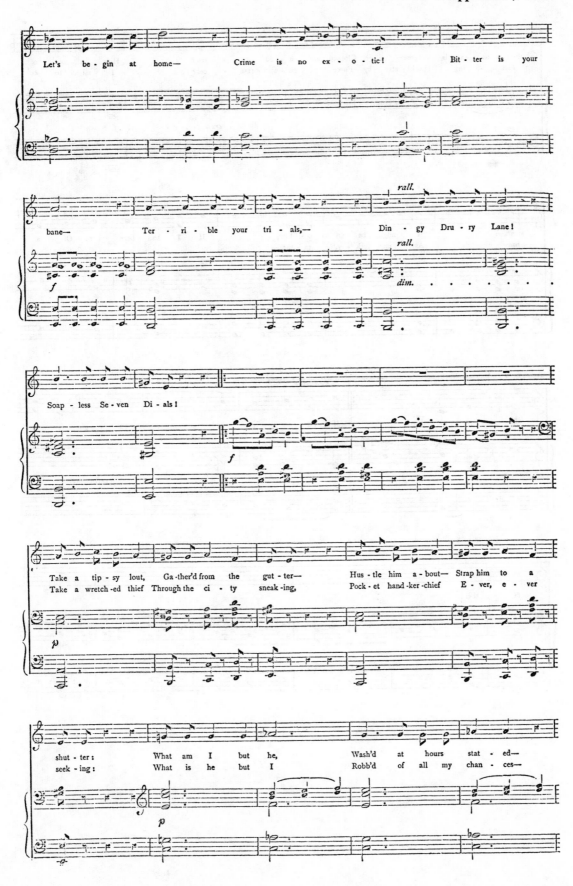

Fed on fi-la-gree— Clothed and e-du-ca-ted? He's a mark of
Pick-ing pock-ets by Force of cir-cum-stan-ces? I might be as

scorn,— I might be an-o-ther, If I had been born Of a
bad— As un-luck-y, ra-ther— As un-luck-y,

tip sy mo-ther! If I'd on-ly had . . . Fa-gin for a

fa ther!

In the original version of "So please you, sir" in *The Mikado,* Pish-Tush was included, and the number was a quintet. Preserving the original form provides a stronger bass part and more interesting harmony. In addition, Pish-Tush sang the words, "That youth at us should have his fling is hard on us, is hard on us."

These words are now given to Pooh-Bah. The voice part given below was originally sung by Pooh-Bah, while Pish-Tush sang the lower notes now given to Pooh-Bah. It seems wise at the present time to reverse the original procedure, since Pooh-Bah usually has the heavier and deeper voice of the two.

The Mikado - No. 8 - Pish-Tush's Part

The following trio from *Utopia, Ltd.* may be used in *The Grand Duke.* (See pages 229–230.) If it is so used, it should be sung by Ernest, the Notary, and Rudolph. It may be desirable to substitute the words "coup d'état" for "private plot."

The following number is adapted from *Haddon Hall* by Sydney Grundy and Arthur Sullivan. It may be sung by the chorus in *The Grand Duke,* if placed between Nos. 24 and 25. For further information, see page 230.

19,348.

19,348.

19,343

19.348.

The following recitative immediately precedes the finale to Act Two in the original version of *Pinafore*. It follows Sir Joseph's line, "It does to a considerable extent, but it does not level them as much as that," and replaces the rest of the dialogue.

pint of warm oil in your throat, And a pound of tin-tacks in your chest; When you've
spiders crawl o - ver your spine, And your mus-cles have all got the mumps; When you're

got a bee-hive in your head, And a sew-ing ma-chine in each ear; And you
bad with the creeps and the crawls, And the shiv-ers, and shudders, and shakes And the

feel that you've eat-en your bed, And you've got a bad head-ache down here; When your
pat-tern that cov-ers the walls Is a - live with black-beetles and snakes; When you

lips are like un-der-done paste, And you're high-ly gamboge in the gill; And your
doubt if your head is your own, And you jump when an o-pen door slams, And you've

mouth has a cop - per - y taste,      As   if you'd just bit - ten   a   pill;      And wher -
got   to  a state which is known      To the  med - i - cal world as "jim - jams,"—      If such

- ev - er you tread, From a    yawn-ing a - byss  You re - coil   with   a   yell,—    You are
symptoms you find  In    your   bo - dy  or head, They're not ea - sy   to   quell,      You may

bet - ter  in  bed, For   de - pend up - on this, You  are  not at all, not at all  well.
make up your mind That you're bet - ter  in  bed, For you're not at all, not at all      well.

A NOTE ON LIBRETTI, SCORES,
AND RECORDINGS

There are many editions of the libretti, but the most useful, because of its wide and consistent availability, is the Modern Library edition, which contains all fourteen operas. It is entitled, *The Complete Plays of Gilbert and Sullivan.* An edition published in 1932 by Random House adds the *Bab Ballads, His Excellency, The Palace of Truth,* and *The Montebanks.* The bulk of Gilbert's plays, including all the operas, was published in four volumes by Scribners, under the title of *Original Plays.* Other editions usually omit *Thespis,* and sometimes other operas as well. The best edition of *Bab Ballads* is edited by James Ellis and published (1970) by the Belknap Press of Harvard University Press, Cambridge, Mass.

All of the vocal scores with dialogue are published by G. Schirmer, except for *The Sorcerer, Princess Ida, Utopia, Ltd.,* and *The Grand Duke. The Sorcerer* is published in England without dialogue by J. B. Cramer. The others, also without dialogue, can be had from Chappell. Chappell also publishes *The Mountebanks, Ivanhoe,* and *Haddon Hall. Cox and Box* is available in a condensed version from Boosey and Hawks. Other operas by Gilbert and Sullivan working with other collaborators are out of print and must be found in libraries or secondhand music stores.

Anyone interested in studying the development of performance style should investigate the many recordings that have been made over the years. Information about the very earliest of these is to be found in an article, "Early Gilbert and Sullivan Recordings," by John Freestone in *The Savoyard,* January, 1969. Complete D'Oyly Carte recordings fall approximately into four series, the first including nine operas, and made acoustically between 1918 and 1925. The first electrical series included ten operas complete, two versions of *The Mikado,* and condensed versions of four operas, and was made between 1927 and 1936. The first

LP series was made between 1949 and 1955. Most of this series is now available on the Richmond label. The current series on the London label began in 1958, and includes two complete versions of *The Pirates of Penzance,* the second with dialogue, and two of *H.M.S. Pinafore,* as well as the first recording of *Cox and Box* and excerpts from *Utopia, Ltd.*

During the 1960's a series of recordings was released on the Angel label with the Glyndebourne Festival Chorus and conducted by Sir Malcolm Sargent. Top-ranking opera singers were used, and the attempt was made to emphasize the musical values of Sullivan's score. Unfortunately, some of the singers did not have the appropriate sense of style, and Sargent paced many of the songs too slowly. Nevertheless, these recordings helped to set new standards of attention to musical detail.

Also worthy of mention is the *Reader's Digest* set of excerpts from six of the operas. These were made with the Royal Philharmonic Orchestra under the direction of James Walker, and they included leading British singers, several of whom were members of the D'Oyly Carte Opera Company. Although the performances vary in quality, some of them are stylistically and musically excellent, particularly those of Donald Adams.

Numerous other recordings have come and gone outside the auspices of D'Oyly Carte. Widely circulated at present is one of *The Pirates of Penzance,* which features Martyn Green. Unfortunately he is the only member of the cast whose performance rises above the routine. If you are planning to use a recording as a guide or to set the standards for your performance, you should probably stick to those mentioned above, unless you are doing *Utopia, Ltd.* or *The Grand Duke.* Complete recordings of a nonprofessional nature have been made of these operas, but their availability has always been sporadic. Tapes of the Lyric Theatre versions are available from Byron G. Hathaway, Jr., 49 Merbrook Lane, Merion, Pennsylvania 19066.

BOOKS RELEVANT TO GILBERT
AND SULLIVAN

Allen, Reginald, *The First Night Gilbert and Sullivan,* The Heritage Press, New York, 1958. Originally published with facsimiles of the first-night programs, this book is now hard to find and should be republished. It contains all the libretti as performed on the first nights, together with descriptions of those performances, quotations from the reviews, and discussions of textual changes since then.

Baily, Leslie, *The Gilbert and Sullivan Book* (revised edition), Coward-McCann, New York, 1957. The best and most widely used history of the operas. Profusely illustrated with contemporary and current drawings and photographs.

• Barrington, Rutland, *Rutland Barrington,* Grant Richards, London, 1908. The creator of Pooh-Bah and similar roles writes entertainingly of his experiences with the members of the original Savoy company.

Bassuk, Albert O., *How to Present the Gilbert and Sullivan Operas,* Bass, New York, 1934. An extremely brief statement, consisting mainly of plot summaries.

• Boas, Guy, *The Gilbertian World and the World of Today,* English Spring, London, 1948.

• Bond, Jessie, *The Life and Reminiscences of Jessie Bond, the Old Savoyard,* Lane, London, 1930. One of the longest-term members of the original company recalls her experiences in the original presentation of the operas.

Bradstock, Lillian, *Pooh-Bah and the Rest of Gilbert and Sullivan, A Story Version,* Figurehead, London, 1933.

Bristow, Mary R., *Gilbert and Sullivan Bibliography,* published by the author at 615 Hickory Avenue, Bel Air, Maryland, 21014.

Browne, Edith. *William Schwenck Gilbert,* Lane, New York, 1907. Written while Gilbert was still alive, this has the advantage of immediacy, but is not as accurate as some more modern versions.

Cellier, François and Bridgeman, Cunningham, *Gilbert, Sullivan and D'Oyly Carte,* Pitman, London, 1914. The conductor of the original productions began a book of reminiscences of the D'Oyly Carte Company. It was completed after his death by a librettist associated with that company. This book is one of the best source materials on the original productions. Republished, 1970.

Compton, J. *Scenes and Songs from the Savoy Operas,* MacMillan, London, 1930.

• Cox-Ife, William, *Training the Gilbert and Sullivan Chorus,* Chappell, London, 1956. The late chorus master of the D'Oyly Carte Opera Company offers a series of specific musical pointers that should be studied by the musical director of any of the operas.

• ———, *How to Sing Both Gilbert and Sullivan,* Chappell, London, 1959. This book covers the solo numbers, relating words and music, and showing how to conduct so that both musical and dramatic values are preserved.

———, *The Elements of Conducting,* John Day, New York, 1964. Frequent, though not exclusive, examples from the operas to make general points about conducting.

Dark, Sidney, *William Schwenck Gilbert, His Life and Letters,* Methuen, London, 1923. A serious and lengthy biography.

Darlington, W. A., *The World of Gilbert and Sullivan,* Crowell, New York, 1950. A biography with critical assessments.

Dunhill, Thomas F., *Sullivan's Comic Operas. A Critical Appreciation,* Arnold, London, 1928. A good critical analysis, with emphasis on the music. The operas are examined in chronological order.

Dunn, George E., *A Gilbert and Sullivan Dictionary,* Allen and Unwin, London, 1936. All unusual words and phrases in the libretti are defined, and various additional information is provided, all in alphabetical order.

• Ferguson, William C., Jr., *A History of the Savoy Company,* Savoy Company, Philadelphia, 1950. A history with photographs of one of America's oldest and most distinguished nonprofessional Gilbert and Sullivan companies.

Findon, B. W., *Sir Arthur Sullivan, His Life and Music,* Nisbet, London, 1904. A brief and early biography, containing a complete list of the composer's works.

Fitzgerald, Percy, *The Operas of Gilbert and Sullivan,* Lippincott, Philadelphia, 1894.

Fitz-Gerald, Shafto, *The Story of the Savoy Opera,* Appleton, New York, 1925. A history specifically limited to productions, giving all the casts, and including everything produced at the Savoy under the management of Richard D'Oyly Carte.

*Fortune,* February, 1937, "Gilbert and Sullivan." A detailed article on the occasion of the American tour of the D'Oyly Carte Company. Beautifully illustrated.

George, Charles, *Iolanthe, Pinafore, The Pirates of Penzance,* Bakers' Plays, Boston, 1940. Half-hour versions of these operas, published separately.

*The Gilbert and Sullivan Journal.* Published in January, May, and September by Miss N. M. Clark, 37 Frankland Close, Croxley Green, WD3 3AR, Herts, England, for the Gilbert and Sullivan Society.

Godwin, A. H., *Gilbert and Sullivan, a Critical Appreciation*, Dent, London, 1926; Kennikat, Port Washington, New York, 1968. A zealous, if somewhat sentimental analysis, containing such subjects as "Latin and Logic," "Sullivan the Humorist," and "Thoughts about Jack Point."

Goldberg, Isaac, *The Story of Gilbert and Sullivan,* Simon and Schuster, New York, 1928. One of the best biographies, containing some information not to be found in any earlier publications.

Goldovsky, Boris, *Bringing Opera to Life,* Appleton, New York, 1968. The only book of its kind, this may be valuable to the serious stage director, though the problems of staging grand opera are somewhat different. It is a serious book that sets higher standards than are met by most opera companies.

Green, Martyn, *Here's a How-De-Do, My Life in Gilbert and Sullivan,* Norton, New York, 1952. Informal reminiscences shed some light on the production practices earlier in the century.

————, *Martyn Green's Treasury of Gilbert and Sullivan,* Simon and Schuster, New York, 1961. "The complete librettos of eleven operettas accompanied by Martyn Green's comments on their history and how to stage and perform them. The words and music of more than 100 favorite songs." Delightfully illustrated by Lucille Corcos.

Grossmith, George, *A Society Clown,* Arrow-Smith, London, 1888. Reminiscences of the original patter man.

Halton, F. J., *The Gilbert and Sullivan Operas, a Concordance,* Bass, New York, 1935. Taking each of the operas in turn, Halton elucidates obscure references in the order in which they occur. Illustrated.

Hewitt, Tony, *The School Gilbert and Sullivan,* Albyn, Edinburgh, 1949.

Hudson, Derek, and David, Cecil, *The Savoy Operas,* Oxford, London, 1962.

Hughes, Gervase, *Composers of Operetta,* St. Martin's, New York, 1961. A comprehensive treatment of French, Continental, and British operetta. The chapter on Sullivan is more useful to the beginner than Hughes's other book, because it treats the operas in sequence. It is interesting to learn about the work of Sullivan's contemporaries in the same field.

————, *The Music of Arthur Sullivan,* St. Martin's, New York, 1960. Technical discussion of such topics as rhythm and word-setting, harmony, counterpoint, orchestration, etc. The most scholarly work on the subject.

*The Jack Point Press.* Published semi-annually by John Craig Toy, 2423 Portland Ave., Apt #206, Minneapolis, Minn., 55404. Jam packed with unusual articles, old and new, and information about current productions all over the world.

Jacobs, Arthur, *Gilbert and Sullivan,* Parrish, London, 1951. A brief but surprisingly scholarly little book, well illustrated.

Johnson, Albert, *We Give You Gilbert and Sullivan,* Baker's Plays, Boston. A comedy with music from the operas, based on the lives of the collaborators. One act, 1¼ hours long.

Jones, John Bush (ed.), *W. S. Gilbert: A Century of Scholarship and Commentary,* New York University Press, New York, 1970. Articles by Max Beerbohm, Edith Hamilton, Walter Sichel, Jane Stedman, and others, including Gilbert himself. Particularly interesting is "The Genesis of *Patience*."

————, "Gilbert and Sullivan's Serious Satire: More Fact Than Fancy," *Western Humanities Review,* 21(1967), pp. 211–224.

Kupferberg, Herbert, "They Shall Have Music;

Five Operas Better Than They Seemed," *The Atlantic,* April, 1966.

Lambton, Gervase, *Gilbertian Characters and a Discourse on William Schwenck Gilbert's Philosophy,* Allen, London, 1931.

Lavine, Sigmund A., *Wandering Minstrels We —The Story of Gilbert and Sullivan,* Dodd, Mead, New York, 1954. A biography designed for young readers.

Lawrence, Arthur, *Sir Arthur Sullivan, Life Story, Letters, and Reminiscences,* Stone, Chicago, 1900. Based on a series of interviews with the composer, and containing facsimile letters and manuscripts as well as a complete list of Sullivan's works.

Lubbock, Mark, *The Complete Book of Light Opera,* Appleton, New York, 1962. A collection of plot summaries that is very comprehensive. Includes many of the operas contemporaneous with Gilbert and Sullivan.

Lytton, Henry A., *The Secrets of a Savoyard,* Jarrolds, London, 1922. Possibly the greatest of all Savoyards, Lytton was a prominent member of the D'Oyly Carte Company from the original *Princess Ida* until 1934. He sang almost all the baritone roles in the operas. His reminiscences, therefore, shed considerable light on performance practices.

————, *A Wandering Minstrel,* London, Jarrolds, 1933. Revised version of the above.

Mander, Raymond, and Mitchenson, Joe, *A Picture History of Gilbert and Sullivan,* Vista, London, 1962. The best collection of photographs and drawings.

Moore, F. L. (ed.), *Crowell's Handbook of Gilbert and Sullivan,* Crowell, New York, 1962. Although intended to be a reference book, this is little more than a history and a collection of plot summaries.

*The Palace Peeper,* monthly mimeographed publication of the Gilbert and Sullivan Society of New York, c/o Mrs. Vivian Denison, 137 Riverside Drive, Apt 1E, New York, N.Y. 10024.

Pearson, Hesketh, *Gilbert, His Life and Strife,* Harper, New York, 1958. Extensive use of Gilbert's private letters sheds light on many of his attitudes and actions.

————, *Gilbert and Sullivan,* Hamilton, London, 1935. Although not always completely accurate, this book is highly entertaining and is probably the most popular of the biographies.

Poladian, Sirvart, *Sir Arthur Sullivan: An Index to the Texts of his Vocal Works,* Information Service, Detroit. Apparently complete, this book is of limited usefulness, since it gives no publishers or other sources or locations of the works listed.

Purdy, Claire Lee, *Gilbert and Sullivan, Masters of Mirth and Melody,* Messner, New York, 1947. Another popular biography.

Quiller-Couch, Sir Arthur, *Q Anthology,* Macmillan, New York, 1949. Contains a "Lecture on W. S. Gilbert," which argues, among other things, that these operas are the most satisfactory solution to the aesthetic problem of music drama. (Also contained in Jones, *q.v.*)

Rees, Terence, *Thespis, A Gilbert and Sullivan Enigma,* Dillon's University Bookshop, London 1964. A scholarly discussion of the first production, with a text of the libretto edited to bring it into conformity with the actual performances as much as is now possible.

Rickett, Edmund and Hoogland, B., *Let's Do Some Gilbert and Sullivan, a Practical Production Handbook,* Coward-McCann, New York, 1940. Production notes and character sketches comprise the bulk of the first part of the book, though the second part contains some useful general principles of production and a detailed analysis of two sample dialogue scenes. There are some unfortunate errors and a number of misleading generalizations.

Rollins, Cyril and Witts, R. John, *The D'Oyly Carte Opera Company in Gilbert and Sullivan Operas—a Record of Productions 1875–1961,* Michael Joseph, London, 1962. Complete cast lists for all productions and recordings. The collection of photographs is among the best available.

Rowell, George, and Mobbs, Kenneth, *Engaged! or Cheviot's Choice,* Chappell, London, 1963. Vocal score of the new fifteenth Gilbert and Sullivan opera (*See* Chapter XVIII.)

*The Savoyard.* Published in January, May, and September by the D'Oyly Carte Opera Trust Limited, 1 Savoy Hill, London, W. C.2.

Searle, Townly, *Sir William Schwenck Gilbert, a Topsy-Turvy Adventure,* Alexander-Ouseley, London, 1931. Consists almost entirely of a long and detailed bibliography.

Shaw, Bernard, *Shaw on Music,* Anchor Books, New York, 1955. Contains interesting reviews of the original productions of *Utopia, Ltd.* and *The Mountebanks.*

*The Sphere,* "The Gilbert and Sullivan Operas Illustrated—Season 1939." A special edition issued by the English magazine. If you can find it, you'll find it rewarding, as it's lavishly illustrated with photographs.

Stedman, J. W. (ed.), *Gilbert before Sullivan,* University of Chicago Press, Chicago, 1967. A collection of Gilbert's early plays.

Stevens, David, *All at Sea,* Birchard, Boston, 1921. Dialogue designed to string together a lot of favorite songs from the various operas by the device of bringing all the characters together on board the *Pinafore.* There are nineteen characters who have solo singing parts.

Sullivan, Herbert, and Flower, Newman, *Sir Arthur Sullivan, His Life, Letters and Diaries,* Cassell, London, 1927. One of the early standard biographies. It's extensive, and contains facsimiles and a complete list of the composer's works.

Walbrook, Henry, *Gilbert and Sullivan Opera, a History and a Comment,* White, London, 1922.

Walmisley, Guy H. and Walmisley, Claude A., *Tit-Willow; or Notes and Jottings on the Gilbert and Sullivan Operas.* Background information on textual references. Published by the authors, 14 Westgate Terrace, Redcliffe Square, London, S.W. 10.

Waters, Alma Shelley, *The Melody Maker, The Life of Sir Arthur Sullivan,* Dutton, New York, 1959. A biography for children.

Wells, Walter J., *Souvenir of Sir Arthur Sullivan, A Brief Sketch of His Life and Works,* Newnes, London, 1901. A brief biography, containing facsimiles, interesting pictures, and a complete list of works. Also included is the text of a song deleted from *The Gondoliers.*

Willeby, Charles, *Masters of English Music,* Osgood, London, 1893. The chapter on Sullivan contains some interesting analyses of his serious music, particularly *The Golden Legend.*

Williamson, Audrey, *Gilbert and Sullivan Opera, a New Assessment,* Macmillan, New York, 1953. Attempts to treat the words and music on equal terms. Contains many interesting insights and some valuable comments on performance practice, despite a rather chaotic writing style.

Wilson, Edmund, *Classics and Commercials,* Farrar, Straus, New York, 1950. The essay, "Gilbert without Sullivan," contains some unusual praise of Gilbert as a dramatist, as well as some unusual condemnation of him as a lyricist, together with a plea for the revival of *Utopia, Ltd.*

Wood, Roger, *A D'Oyly Carte Album,* Pitman, New York, 1954. A generous collection of photographs of productions during the early 1950's.

Wymer, Norman, *Gilbert and Sullivan,* Dutton, New York, 1963. A biography for the general reader, almost novelistic in style.

Wyndham, Henry Saxe, *Arthur Seymour Sullivan,* Kegan Paul, London, 1926. A biography, containing many interesting letters and discussions of Sullivan's method of composition.

Zavon, Peter, *Titipu Town Crier,* periodical available from 28 Gayhead Street, #2, Jamaica Plain, Massachusetts 02130.